The Geologist's Wife

Ophelia Finsen

The Yorkshire Saga

Hob Hurst's House
Hob Hurst's Daughter
Hob Hurst's Legacy
Lost Children
The Geologist's Wife

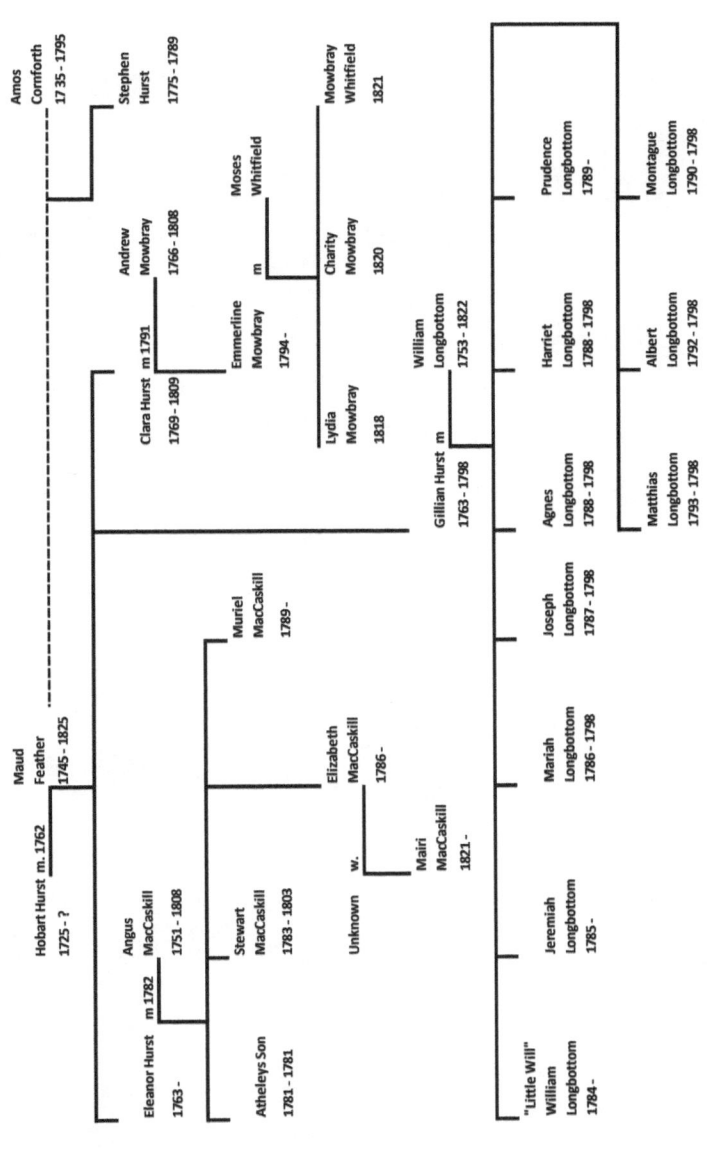

Amos
Comforth
1735 - 1795

Stephen
Hurst
1775 - 1789

Maud
Feather
1745 - 1825

Hobart Hurst m. 1762
1725 - ?

Mowbray
Whitfield
1821

Andrew
Mowbray
1766 - 1808

Moses
Whitfield
m

Charity
Mowbray
1820

Clara Hurst m 1791
1769 - 1809

Emmerline
Mowbray
1794 -

Lydia
Mowbray
1818

William
Longbottom
1753 - 1822

Prudence
Longbottom
1789 -

Harriet
Longbottom
1788 - 1798

Montague
Longbottom
1790 - 1798

Albert
Longbottom
1792 - 1798

Gillian Hurst m
1763 - 1798

Agnes
Longbottom
1788 - 1798

Matthias
Longbottom
1793 - 1798

Muriel
MacCaskill
1789 -

Joseph
Longbottom
1787 - 1798

Elizabeth
MacCaskill
1786 -

Angus
MacCaskill
1751 - 1808

Stewart
MacCaskill
1783 - 1803

Unknown   w.

Mairi
MacCaskill
1821 -

Mariah
Longbottom
1786 - 1798

Eleanor Hurst   m 1782
1763 -

Atheleys Son
1781 - 1781

Jeremiah
Longbottom
1785 -

"Little Will"
William
Longbottom
1784 -

5

1838 May
Lincolnshire

In her last moments Mairi MacCaskill gazed mute and forlorn at the roses. I am only seventeen, she thought, and this is the end of Mairi MacCaskill. This is not what I had hoped for in life.

She had always explicitly trusted her mother; blindly assumed that her dear mamma had her best interests at heart. Not just that, but everything she did was for the best.

The reverend met her eyes and faltered momentarily before pronouncing the end of Mairi MacCaskill. He didn't look convinced that this was such a good idea either. The retching merely assured their opinion. The man of God darted nimbly backwards in time as the foul stink of vomit splurged forth and the groom collapsed to his knees on the tiled church floor. Did this sort of thing happen frequently, Mairi wondered, for the reverend had seemed ready for it. She regarded the splattered vomit on the skirts of her wedding dress and was glad she'd only first seen the dress this morning. She had no sentimental attachment to it.

Mairi Gaskin, nee MacCaskill, met the eyes of her new father-in-law as he clung to his son's arm and tried to keep him from falling face-first into the pool of vomit at Mairi's feet. She tightened her double handed grip around her roses, to make it clear she wasn't about to help, even if the wretch was now her husband. She had come across varying degrees of drunkenness and intoxication at mother's parties over the years – parties she was not even supposed to know had happened – but this was diabolical. The man reeked of gin. Had they bathed him in it before attending? She could usually find some sense in all of her mother's schemes, but this defied logic. How was marrying this man providing security?

She twisted around to find her mother in the church. It wasn't hard, for the guests were very few. Her mother had hung a smile on her face. She peered out of her furs and scarves despite the May warmth, and nodded to Mairi as if to say 'yes, this will be a blessing to you'. She had refused to explain anything to her daughter. In fact the morning had started as a farce, with the sulking maid shaking her awake and telling her to put on this stupid dress. Mairi had done so, and stared at herself in the mirror as the maid dressed her hair, thinking it was a strange choice, for it looked like a wedding gown. Then they were in the carriage and her mother was thrusting roses at her and telling her that she must trust her mother and she must go through with it this morning. Time was of the essence and she needed to know that Mairi was going to be safe.

They could not have been more different than that morning. Mairi was youth and innocence, dressed in white, blonde hair in long waves, trusting and inexperienced. Faced with her mother, known for her dark hair and ravishing beauty but of late so wrapped up in cloths and silks that it was almost hard to catch sight of her face. Even her much-prized wasp waist was lost to the layers these days.

Her mother told her that they were going to a church and Mairi was to be married.

Married? But she did not even have a suitor, let alone an engagement. This had to be some joke...

No joke. She must agree to the arrangement. They had to take advantage of this marvellous opportunity. It had unexpectedly fallen at Elizabeth's (her mother) feet a couple of weeks ago. No, she had not heard of the man, but Elizabeth knew the family and knew that this would provide a good future for Mairi. She would be safe, cared for and Elizabeth would not need to worry on this front.

Mairi had laughed. Her mother had never married, and positively delighted in the fact. She hadn't even stayed with the one man, but had been a courtesan moving ever upwards through aristocracy, first in England and then on the continent. What nonsense to say now that a simple wife was the best thing to be. Elizabeth had clutched her daughter's hands with her own. She did not want her daughter to end up like her.

Very well, Mairi had shrugged. She would marry, but there was no rush. She could look for a man, someone with good taste and common interests. Her prospects would be hampered because of Elizabeth's lifestyle and reputation but...

There wasn't time, Elizabeth had spoken earnestly. I do not have the time to wait and you do not have the luxury of taking your pick from respectable society. We must take this chance for there will not be another.

"Well, who is he?"

"You will find out soon enough."

And so it was that she did not know her future husband's name until the reverend spoke it at the ceremony. Mairi had wondered earlier what the groom had been told when they had persuaded him to take part, but having seen how drunk he was, thought perhaps her mother was paying for this, paying for his debts to get him to agree. But then was tying her to a drunken debtor a good way to secure her future?

In the marriage stakes she didn't suppose the daughter of a courtesan had a lot to hope for, especially when no aristocrat would acknowledge her as his bastard, but even she had had some small hopes for what a wedding might be like. An unknown groom vomiting down her dress was not her girlhood dream.

And who was this dishevelled creature? Even swaying on his knees, held up by his father, she could tell he was tall, and rather broadly built. His hair was coming loose from his ribbon. She had a good view of the top of his head. He had copper brown hair and a good head of it. The reverend had called him Stephen Gaskin, and beyond that she knew nothing. Apparently the banns had already been read out on their behalf – it was suspect that Mairi had not even needed to know about this – and they were in a church and being noted in the register. A frighteningly quick ceremony, cut to the essentials on account of the groom's ill health, and then with words and signatures Mairi was involved in a legal contract that she would be unable to get herself out of. She was no longer part of her mother's household. With horror, it struck her that she no longer had a home, rather a somewhere as unknown as the man before her.

The stink of vomit rose like unearthly vapours and was starting to make her feel nauseous. She had not breakfasted that morning.

With the ceremony complete, the two mothers came rushing up to the front. The groom's mother flapped about her son and husband in an ineffectual manner, barely able to look at Mairi, in fact speaking as though the girl did not exist, and occasionally glancing at Elizabeth but unable to engage with the woman other than to glare at her.

Another man, another stranger, came to Mr Gaskin the elder's aid, and with a man at each arm, they pulled Stephen Gaskin to his feet. His head lolled downwards, his eyes virtually closed but Mairi caught sight of blood shot eyes and dark shadows underneath. He looked like an adult and a wretch, that was to say, older than her, perhaps thirty or so. Nothing boyish lingered about the face.

The father-in-law looked sadly at Mairi, guessing at an innocent, then to Elizabeth. "I know there are traditions and ways of things being done, but perhaps in the circumstances..." he broke off as his son went to collapse again. "Perhaps it would be better if your daughter returned to your apartments for today?"

Elizabeth pursed her lips. "My maid is packing her things as we speak. A married woman is not to be abandoned."

Mairi was going to be sick. She wasn't going home today? Her mother wanted to send her away with this man now? A wedding night? Oh no, she wanted to cry. She was a contradiction to many, for as a courtesan's daughter she knew exactly what went on between men and women, yet she herself was untouched. Elizabeth had never thought it wise to keep a blossoming woman in the dark about the facts of nature, and had explained the necessary to Mairi. The awareness had stood her in good stead, knowing when to defend herself or slip out of situations, where those child-like and respectable yet utterly clueless daughters of the marriage market didn't understand what was ahead. Some assumed because of her mother she was not pure, but the fact was that Elizabeth had been very certain of keeping Mairi out of the way of all that, despite receiving a number of ridiculous cash offers for Mairi's first night. As if her girl was cattle to be traded, the very idea!

"And she won't be abandoned. *We* are respectable people."

Elizabeth's eyes flashed at the inference that she was not.

"But I think it would be better if Stephen had time to sober up. My son does not usually drink to this degree..." This produced a snort from the other man, and a comment that Stephen had certainly needed some help with his drink. "I would like the chance to appraise him of the situation..."

"Very well," Elizabeth nodded. "We will arrive at his home at noon tomorrow." They would be prompt and early in the morning, she said to herself, with no chance for fleeing the marriage. In fact, she would hire a boy to keep an eye on the address. "Mairi, come along. We need to get you out of that dress."

Mairi, now according to tradition, the respectable woman of the two, followed her mother. She glanced one last time at her new husband and she realised from what had been said, that this marriage would be even more of a shock to him than it had been to her. He didn't know yet. And potentially he wasn't a drunkard. He didn't drink. Had they purposefully made him drunk so that he would marry her? Sober he would have refused? Just what exactly had her mother gotten her into?

Elizabeth MacCaskill fussed over the scarf around her neck, tugging at it so that she felt confident her jawbone was covered. She turned away from the shop front on Low Petergate and watched as a well-dressed woman went about her shopping errands, with children and nanny in tow. The mother would be at least twenty years Elizabeth's junior, and yet Elizabeth was the statuesque beauty, certainly better in figure. Even in her fifties, she had not seen a waist in York that could compete with her own.

On turning she caught sight of her tempered reflection in the shop window. The bonnet covered her hair, which was not the lustrous black it had been of her youth, now beset with long white strands. She knew from close examination in her looking glass that there were fine wrinkles around her eyes and mouth, cutting across her forehead and marking time like rings in a tree. Regardless of the natural passage of time, she was mostly in much better condition than a lot of women her age. Indeed the very fact she was still alive spoke volumes.

The side of her hand nudged against the swelling and she winced. It was relatively new and unfortunately quite visible with this trend of lower necklines she so liked. At least the ample sleeves covered over the first swellings without her needing to be self conscious, but they had not yet shrunk down, and as they multiplied and travelled up her body, Elizabeth had grown increasingly aghast at the thought of anyone seeing her. She needed to get away from the cities where everyone knew her. It was a horror when acquaintances came charging up to her in the street to greet her, unconsciously sensing when she was feeling indelicate. So for the second time she informed her daughter that they would be leaving Belgium and returning to England, and this time it had happened.

The first time she had announced rather pompously that she was returning to her countrymen had been in reaction to a lover's tiff.

The ladies had tittered and he had merely tilted his chin a little higher so that he might stare down his nose at her. A Viennese count, what could one expect, she huffed to herself, and went to sort her correspondence. A letter from her sister told her about the cases of cholera breaking out in the country. In York, where Elizabeth had decided to resettle, cholera had not yet fallen, but Muriel was sure it was only a matter of time. And indeed the following year, in 1832, cholera had broken out. By then Elizabeth was popular and in love again and had no intention of returning to that island and leaving the culture of the continent. She'd danced through the years.

Now she was in her fifties and lovers were harder to come by. Worse was this affliction that plagued her. Ashamed by her appearance, she wrapped up and decided she needed seclusion for a time, away from the mocking eyes of younger women and society beauties. And so the wardrobes and finery had been packed, the furnishings and china boxed up, arrangements made with banks to see a large part of her wealth transferred to England. Apartments in York, hers purchased decades ago by a grateful sponsor, had given notice to the tenants, so that Elizabeth, her daughter, her ladies maid and staff could move in.

"Why, as I live and breathe, Elizabeth MacCaskill!"

The exclamation boomed down the busy street, vibrating off the stone paving, the timbered and stone walls, bounding back and forth between the storeys of the tightly packed buildings. Elizabeth shrunk into her scarves and bonnet, feeling a sickness in the pit of her stomach. It had been a long time since she had left York. Surely no one would see her and immediately recognise her. If nothing else she ought to be so out of context...

She winced as a hand gripped her arm through the flounces of the sleeve, knocking one of the swellings. Turning she was met with the expectant gaze of one, accompanied by the bemused smiles of another woman. The younger of the two was a fashionably dressed young lady, clearly someone of financial means, and yet lacking in certainty about herself. As if walking out with a sweetheart, she had her arm linked with her companion, a curious woman dressed in black. It was a black of choice and not of mourning. Her dress was dignified and seemed to shun

13

unnecessary flounces and trimmings. Matched with her odd hat, she cut a very strange character, and yet there was a bold forwardness about her body posture that suggested she really didn't care what other people thought. At least in public. In private our minds can be consumed by paranoia, even the bravest of us.

Elizabeth looked from one woman to the other, certain she did not know them, and ready to deny her own name, when a memory of a brief affair of over ten years past lurched up. An oddity in that it had been of no financial or societal gain, and it had been so short and kept secret from her circles, that she must have repressed it herself until this moment. A memory of lounging in bed and watching her lover making notes burst out. Notes for a diary, she was told, but no she was not to read it. Elizabeth had flounced back into bed. "Well, for heaven's sake, make sure you don't mention me. I've worked hard to have full control over my life and my person."

Anne had put down her fountain pen. "You wish me to pretend this did not happen?"

"As far as your diary is concerned."

"It is only I who will read it."

"You say this now, but once documented, one does not know what will happen in the future."

Elizabeth returned to the present moment. "Anne Lister," she spoke, now aware of the women in black, only still confused as to the simpering thing that accompanied her. Another ten years had passed by. Why, Anne Lister must be in her forties now. A little older, a little more refined and sculpted somehow in that way women shifting from youth to middle age were want to do if they had not succumbed to corpulence.

"It is very good to see you again," Anne beamed.

"Indeed," Elizabeth spoke uncertainly, aware that passers by were glancing at the group. She had not come to York for attention. For the first time in her life she felt a need for solitude and seclusion. Anonymity. She looked to the younger woman.

"May I present Miss Anne Walker," Anne introduced her companion.

"Two Annes."

"Indeed," Anne the elder nodded. "We're in York shopping in advance of our trip. We're heading to Belgium in a couple of months."

"Oh," Elizabeth looked blank, but felt sick. She did not wish to be reminded of that country so soon after departure.

"I heard you were on the continent," Anne continued.

"You did?"

"I have come across your sister from time to time, Mrs Must..."

"Oh yes."

"She mentioned Belgium in fact. Perhaps you could..."

"You must excuse me, ladies," Elizabeth interrupted. "I am already late for a prior engagement, and if I start on travels, I'm sure I will never stop talking."

"I understand. Travel is such..."

"I must be going now," she cut Anne Lister short for the second time, wishing she would take the hint.

"Perhaps we can see you whilst we are in town, speak of Belgium?" Anne called to Elizabeth's retreating figure.

"Perhaps," Elizabeth returned as she hurried away.

Of course, they had no idea where Elizabeth was staying or how to contact her, Anne reflected. Perhaps Elizabeth had been embarrassed when she recalled their former connection, although given Elizabeth's means of supporting herself, Anne found it hard to believe their little dalliance to do even so much as raise an eyebrow in her list of romantic conquests. She did not worry too much on the matter, for with Anne Walker on her arm and a trip in the final stages of planning, she was exuberantly happy.

Raindrops chased one another down the pane of glass. The unexpected rain shower had only just started. If it continued for any length, they would expect Mairi back earlier than planned. She had been known to work through light showers, but no one could persevere with sketching through a deluge.

"How long have you been back in the country?"

"Barely a month if that. York not even a week yet." Elizabeth turned away from the window. "I wanted a little quiet, not to be noticed..."

"You?"

She ignored the barb. "And already, wrapped up as I am, I have been accosted on the street. I have been away from here for so long. Why are people immediately recognising me?"

Muriel, Elizabeth's younger sister, lowered her eyes to Elizabeth's waist. How could she still have the figure of a young women just stepping out into society? She was in her early fifties. Although Muriel was under no illusion as to the degree of engineering that must go into Elizabeth's bodices, it was a feat that she looked so well. Her hair was starting to show its age in colour, but she didn't take this as a cue to cease with fashionable styling. The effect of the dress was somewhat marred by the tangle of scarves and shawls that threatened to swallow up the woman. But she was only entertaining her sister and there was no need for decorum.

"Do you remember Anne Lister?"

Muriel raised her eyebrows. She doubted anyone who met Anne Lister forgot her. "I bump into her very occasionally, but we don't really move in the same circles. I hear more of her than I see her. She travels a lot these days."

"She saw me, and came bounding over with some young friend on her arm."

"You must have made an impression."

"Perhaps, although it doesn't look like it takes much now. The woman with her..."

"Well, from what I understand, Miss Walker doesn't have enough to do to occupy her mind. But the two are devoted to one another."

"Yes, well, they needn't draw attention to me," Elizabeth huffed, sweeping around the furniture to flop across a chaise, her skirts crinkling as the volume of fabric was suddenly crunched up in the dramatic gesture. "I want to be left alone. I think I will have to go on somewhere else, where nobody has a chance of knowing me..."

"Don't be so dramatic, Elizabeth. What does it matter if someone sees you?"

Elizabeth regarded her sister. They did not match, but they were of the same parentage. Whilst Elizabeth was allure, curves and raven dark hair, her sister Muriel had always been a skinny intense thing with a shock of red hair and far too many thoughts going on underneath for any woman. Even their lives were at contrasts, Muriel staying in Yorkshire, and a widow now, but working in the area of her husband's speciality: medicine. Elizabeth had been all over Europe, never married – perish the thought – but married men had made sure she was financially safe, in return for a few little favours along the road. She had indulged in life and enjoyed herself, but she was too old now to keep up with the young things stepping away from their mothers' apron strings. And those roving eyes wanted something young and fresh. It was felt that Elizabeth had been around too many houses.

"It has been some time since I was in York. People will remember me as a younger version of myself."

"So this is all vanity!" Muriel laughed.

"It's all very well for you to laugh when there's nothing wrong with you. But I do not need people's stares. I will have to go away for some time where no one will know me. I'll go to, I don't know Lincoln or somewhere."

"And would that be fair on Mairi when you've only just arrived?"

"Mairi won't mind."

Muriel raised her eyes to the ceiling and slouched back in her chair. Would it be so hard to suffer on in this apartment in the centre of York? She could see there was still a lot to be unpacked, and yet already the miasma of wealth was intoxicating. Porcelain, oil paintings, fabrics, furniture, a fine grandfather clock noting time in the far corner. People who could afford to live like this would want for nothing. Really, Elizabeth had lost all sense of self if she thought she had to flee York because she happened to have been recognised by Anne Lister. Besides, Anne Lister didn't even live in York, and from what Muriel had heard, would soon be on the continent again. The man who had bought this apartment for Elizabeth had died some years back and even if his family recognised his old mistress, Muriel was quite sure they would rather die than acknowledge the connection to anyone, even themselves.

"It must be all the stress," Elizabeth decided, answering a question that no one had asked. "I will go away somewhere no one knows me and nothing happens. Recuperate and get better, then we will return to Yorkshire in all our glory."

"Is there something wrong with you?"

Elizabeth paused, catching a suspicious look on Muriel's face. "Just some swellings," she shrugged. "They will go down, they are just taking far too much time about the business and in the meantime they love company and..." she was adjusting her scarves then caught the look on Muriel's face. "Don't give me that look, little sister. All of us suffer from ailments now and then, even I am not immune."

Elizabeth never spoke to Muriel of her health, regardless of the fact that Muriel was a trained doctor, or perhaps because of the fact, and that they were siblings. She may come out with flippant comments that she was just as every other crippled man on earth, but in truth Elizabeth relished her goddess status. She was fiercely independent, and although her wealth was garnered from the sexual satisfaction of very rich and extremely married men, she had kept her oath that she would never be married and bound to any one person for the rest of her days. Elizabeth decided what path Elizabeth's life would take. Muriel carefully ignored the knot of concern, and idly flapped a hand. "So this is why you're dressed like a scarecrow. A few spots blemishing your face."

"I do not get spots," Elizabeth hissed.

"Let me take a look."

"So you can laugh at my suffering?"

"I'm a doctor, Elizabeth, and my bedside manner is impeccable. Besides, I'm sure I have seen far worse."

"I'm sure you have, given the unwashed you tend..."

"Elizabeth..."

"Oh very well," She flounced up from her seat, secretly thankful Muriel had brought the matter up herself. She didn't dare see her usual medics, and the thought of a man looking upon her in this state was worse than the swellings themselves. Having a professional check it over and assure her that there was nothing seriously wrong would relive the problem and she would soon return to normal. "I've never had a medical consultation from you before. One should try everything once in life. Come with me."

A short while later, Muriel turned her back to Elizabeth to wash her hands in the basin on the dresser. Her reflection in the water surface rippled and broke as her fingers entered the water. It felt like her inner soul. She could feel a shake and pressed her fingers to the bottom of the porcelain bowl to steady them. No matter the diagnosis, a doctor must remain calm, present a face of professionalism, understanding and reflection that would quell any hysteria.

"I am quite sure it has been a vicious cycle," Elizabeth prattled as she pulled up the shoulder strap of her shift. "The more I worry the worse they are. They'll probably be gone tomorrow. My goodness, Muriel, you are washing your hands a lot. You don't think it's catching? You don't think Mairi would..."

"No," Muriel spoke, quite certain on this question, although she could not yet look at her sister. "It's not catching." Anymore.

"Well, thank goodness for that. I wouldn't want this to blemish a young girl's skin. Why, Mairi's only 17 and I have taken very good care of her, haven't I?"

"Yes." Muriel certainly couldn't fault the devotion Elizabeth had shown to Mairi throughout her life. "Tell me, do you recall having lesions in past times. Probably up between your legs but they could have been anywhere..."

"Mairi has never had any such problems."

"I was talking about you." Muriel turned and had a flash of memory as she regarded her sister. Sitting in these very apartments, but years ago, watching her sister scratching at a lesion on her hand.

"Oh, nothing in particular," Elizabeth waved off the query as insignificant.

"And what about rashes, perhaps across your back."

"Not for a long time. I remember getting some rashes, oh they were dreadful, and I can tell you that was all Georgie-darling's fault, for he had a similar problem. Naughty boy that he was. His doctor told him it was the pox of all things. Georgie sent me off to a spa for some hot herbal steamer treatments, and I can tell you they were vile, worse than the rash. But, I suppose one mustn't grumble, for they did cure me of the pox and I've been as fit as a fiddle since." Elizabeth didn't appreciate Muriel's silence. "Well, at least we know it isn't the pox. So what is the doctor's diagnosis? Will these swellings go down soon?"

"No."

"They're going to take some time? Please tell me I'm not going to need the herbal steamer again."

"They won't go away."

"How infuriating, well, it's a lucky thing my sister is such a brilliant surgeon. I suppose we'll have to have them removed, for I'm sure I can't go about with my arm looking this wretched for the rest of my life."

Muriel watched her sister as she trotted over to her dressing table and started messing about with her jewellery, holding up ridiculous earrings to her lobes. On some level this was starting to register, but Muriel knew she would have to spell things out for her sister. Elizabeth didn't like to be controlled by anything. Her eyes moved along Elizabeth's left arm, disfigured by these swellings as she called them, bulbous and twisting, pushing the flesh out at unnatural angles. Like a creeping pestilence these surface tumours were moving across her body, one at her collarbone, some appearing down the side of her ribcage. Attacking that thin, narrowed waist. Heading for the beautiful face. Looking at it clinically, she had lived for decades already with this disease, and now that she was in the tertiary stage, she would go for some time yet. Muriel had seen people much further on than this, their entire heads overinflated and malformed, barely able to see between the tumours. She remembered a colleague calling them abominations before God. Some might say they were lucky in the sense that their final stage took so long and manifested this way, than say the heart problems or the insanity that others suffered. This was essentially a nasty and very hard to cure disease. As far as the medical establishment understood, it spread through congress. That would make most sense given that it was especially prevalent throughout the community of prostitutes and street walkers. Some sneered down at it, as it if were an affliction of the poor and the immoral. As if poverty and morals went hand in hand, what rot! But disease took no notice of hereditary titles, of wealth or status in society.

Elizabeth had stopped her faffing and shifted on her seat to stare directly at her sister. "You'll cut them off?"

"I can't."

"Come, this isn't the time for modesty. Your talents..."

"No one can."

"You've seen this before?"

"Several times."

She had a nausea rising in her gut. She was quite aware of her age, but inside she was still that vibrant, self-assured young woman setting out from Scarborough. It was when she caught sight of herself in the mirror that she realised how much time had passed. Even more so when she looked at the young woman Mairi had become, and recalled the years of a baby and a toddler, seemingly like something she had once read about in a book. Yet it had happened, and it felt as only a moment ago. Ageing was one thing, but to consider disease, serious, potentially terminal disease, and a marking of the end, was an entirely different matter. It was inconceivable. Yet Elizabeth was not in pain. Perhaps Muriel only meant that she would have to accept her bloated and disfigured arm as it was.

"Elizabeth, this is going to get worse."

Her hand automatically went to her jawline. "Worse before it's better?"

"It won't get better. It will get progressively worse. These... swellings..." Muriel would stick with that word, it seemed less offensive than going into too graphic detail. "They will come up everywhere."

"My face?"

"Yes."

"I'm to look like a disfigured leper?"

"Elizabeth..."

"What is this? I don't understand."

"You're in the final stage of syphilis. The pox."

"The pox?" She scoffed. "I took a cure years ago."

"There are few effective cures, most people are never cured. You'll have gone into a kind of remission. It's a natural progression of the disease. With some it does take decades to kill."

"Kill?"

She had delivered bad news to so many people, far more times than she could remember. Telling her sibling that she was going to die, and that she'd resemble an ogre when she did expire, made it all feel like the first diagnosis. The first piece of bad news she'd ever had to deliver. "I'm sorry..."

"Never mind sorry," Elizabeth snapped, sweeping up and rushing to the window. She kept her back to Muriel and stared out at the rain. Pressed her fingers to the cold glass. "Do you know how long?"

"It's hard to say. Months to a year perhaps..."

"But Mairi," Elizabeth gasped. "I won't see." She shook her head and closed her eyes before pressing her forehead to the window. What wouldn't she see? So much. Mairi was only seventeen years old and had everything ahead of her. Perhaps she'd marry one day and have children and then Elizabeth could fuss over new babies. Babies she'd never meet. Oh god, if there was something she could use to negotiate. Some way to work around this. She wasn't ready to leave life yet.

"You need to reconcile with mother now."

"Mother? We've been reconciled for years. You know that. We've been writing for a good ten years or more."

"You haven't seen her for a long time. What, twenty, maybe even thirty years now."

Elizabeth huffed.

"Mamma has never met Mairi."

"That doesn't really matter to me right now."

"I am thinking more of Mairi." Muriel stared steadily at her sister. "She doesn't have much kin in this country. And it will not be easy. She has no acknowledged father."

"That's hardly my fault!" Elizabeth shrieked.

"Please." Muriel put her hand to her mouth. If only they would rewind, relive and correct the errors. Perhaps catch themselves at girlhood and leave warnings of traps ahead, of what was important in life. What ought to be ignored, what they should treasure. How different their lives would have been. "You must see mother."

The initial response of being 'mildly put out' in facing death did not last all that long. By the evening Elizabeth was wailing as a full force gale and refused to see anyone in her room. It was the injustice of it all, that she would be missing out on good years of her life, likewise countless good years of Mairi, and she was to lumber towards death as a blubber-ridden monster. For a woman so prided on appearance, this was hard to take. She looked in her mirror and considered how dreadful she looked. She would never look this good again. The march of decay would be relentless and then she would die. She took a trinket box and lobbed it at the mirror, smashing the glass.

At some point Muriel, with the aid of the maid, Suzette, managed to get Elizabeth under control to administer enough laudanum to put her to sleep for a good long time. Suzette stood at the side, an observer to the drama as Muriel got her sister settled in the bed.

"*Mon Dieu*," she commented, "You are like a real doctor."

"I am a real doctor," Muriel muttered tersely. She noted that Suzette did precious little unless explicitly told to do so in minute detail. It wasn't that the girl was stupid – far from it, she appeared to be learning a great deal of English – rather that she just couldn't be bothered. She was a long way from Elizabeth's old maid, Nolwenn. Muriel missed her, although appreciated that the woman had her own life to lead back in France. And she had been surly and opinionated as well, but she had attempted to help with things.

Muriel straightened and regarded her elder sister. Not for the first time, she wondered if it was better to have a relative idea of how and when or if it was better for death to come on swiftly and without any warning. Oh, everyone knew death was inevitable, and every day there were reminders of pain and suffering, tragic early ends, and constant funeral processions. Everyone knew they were to return to God and were supposed to be calm and accepting about it. Elizabeth always had been a bit of a drama queen, but then the women in their family often were blessed with good health and long life. The longer one had something, the more one became attached to it, and then it could be rather hard to let go. Goodness, their own mother was still spritely and going strong and their grandmother had lived into her nineties.

"She is dying, no?" Suzette spoke as they reached the door.

Muriel raised her eyebrows.

"Of the pox. I can tell. I've seen those lumps before. Old pox beggars on the streets, in Paris. Some you could hardly believe were human. The worst were the prostitutes. They couldn't work. None but the crazed would want to..."

"That's enough," Muriel interrupted. "Yes, your mistress is very ill." Another thought occurred to her. "Does Mairi know?"

"About the pox? No. She tells me all kinds of things, I would know. But she knows her mother is ill. She's not stupid."

"No. I had realised." The two women stepped out into the corridor and Muriel carefully shut the bedroom door. "She's going to sleep for a long time. Myself and Mairi can take care of ourselves this evening, you can retire from your duties now."

Suzette gave her a look as if to suggest nothing else would have happened, before slouching away to her own quarters.

Muriel returned to the sitting room where Mairi was working on a larger drawing based on sketches she'd made that afternoon before the rain had really set in. She set her pencils down, and looked questioningly at Muriel but did not say anything. She had seen her aunt on many occasions as a child, but then a gap of many years went by whilst she lived on the continent with her mother, and their only communication was by frequent letter. This was actually the first time they had met in person for years, and it had been more dramatic than expected with Elizabeth's theatrics after dinner. Muriel regarded her niece, a pretty young creature, and somehow more like her own cousin in looks, blonde and angelic rather than dark and luxurious as Elizabeth or red-haired and slender as Muriel. And what was she to tell the girl?

"How is mother?"

"She's sleeping now. Your mother..." Muriel paused. It wasn't her place to divulge the details of Elizabeth's conditions. "As we heard, her nerves are not good. I think now she is in York, all the stresses she has been holding on to have come out in a big release."

Mairi nodded as if this was explanation enough for now. There was something of a quiet, dignified control about the girl, which gave her an air of age far beyond her years. Even faced with bad news, it was hard to imagine her having a tantrum or a breakdown the way Elizabeth did. The mother was showy, but with the daughter still waters ran deep.

Muriel returned to her armchair, idly picking up her Blackwood's magazine. It was still open at the article about their new Queen, only into the second year of her reign. Muriel was too distracted to concentrate. She rolled the magazine up and walked over to the table where Mairi was drawing.

"That's Huntington Church."

Mairi looked up at her, suddenly the child again, pleased that her work was recognisable. "We went there in the carriage. You know it?"

"I haven't been there for a lot of years, but I have walked up that way when I've stayed in York."

"You walked all that way?"

"Oh yes, walking for distances, for hours, it's very good for the soul when one is troubled." The magazine abruptly unfurled in her hands, distracting her from memories almost twenty years old. "Or when one is feeling joyful as well. I do think it's one of the best preventative medicines we have. Doctors should prescribe it more."

"Would people take it if it weren't bottled?" Mairi set her pencil down. "Ah, it's evening and I do wish I could play something. It's been months but we still haven't unpacked the piano."

"Did your mother send it over from Belgium?"

"Oh yes, it's arrived in York. But I am not sure exactly where she wants it in the room and she's been distracted this week. Not as angry as this evening, but there has been something wrong. Of course, I have to pretend that I don't notice. That makes her happy but... is she very sick?"

Muriel was still disconcerted by how grown up Mairi was. She'd seen the development of thought over the years through her letters, but the last time she'd seen Mairi, she had only been a little girl. This was a great leap from the playful child to the sophisticated young lady of many languages and accomplishments who had returned from the continent. Muriel managed a smile of sorts and squeezed her hand. "I am going to take the very best of care over her. And remember I was married to one of the best surgical minds in the country."

"Yes, of course." Mairi looked back to her drawing and the two women looked to their activities without concentrating so that neither needed to try and convince the unspoken lie. Perhaps not a lie as such, but an avoidance of the question and the hard facts. "I found the book very interesting," Mairi spoke up again, unable to focus on her drawings. It was so strange to be back in her aunt's company. Somehow the woman was older than she remembered and yet younger, as though her child's perspective of every adult being ancient had adjusted slightly. She so wanted to understand this woman better, found herself drawn to her kin. She didn't have much actual family, never knowing who her father was, and as far as she was aware only having her Aunt Muriel and a grandmother she had never met but wrote to.

"Which book was that?" Muriel had sent so many books.

"The one by your late husband on anatomy. Oh, some of it was quite gruesome..."

"Gruesome?" Muriel almost shrieked. "But it's a scientific story, not a gothic horror."

"I know, but I'm not trained. I hadn't any idea of how much of the human body worked. I don't think us young ladies are supposed to think about those things." She laughed lightly. "But you and Mamma are of a mind. Mamma doesn't want me to be ignorant of some things. It makes me feel a little old around the other girls."

"Yes, my sister has always had her own way about things."

"The illustrations were very good," Mairi continued, not to be drawn into sisterly battles. "Such fine line drawings. I am not a student of medicine but I can see it is a masterpiece of a book."

Muriel didn't quite know what to say. "You think so?"

"Oh yes."

She felt flustered. "I think tomorrow we'll get the manservant to unpack the pianoforte in here. It will do us all good, your mother included, to have a little music."

Elizabeth did not emerge from her room until the afternoon of the following day. Shrouded in shifts and shawls, as well as a ridiculous white cotton bonnet one expected to see on wizened grandmothers of fifty grandchildren but not seductresses in their middle age. The untidy outfit achieved its goal in covering everything but her dark eyes, and left her as a shapeless, grumpy spectre haunting her own life.

She flopped onto a chair and closed her eyes as she listened to her daughter play. "Mairi, darling, play something more... soothing, gentle..."

"Shall I ring for tea?" Muriel asked.

"You could ring the bells of London but that Suzette will not come."

"The cook is in and I find her a very diligent woman."

Muriel watched her sister as she took a little refreshment, noting the short temper and being careful not to say too much. The sleep had calmed her to some degree, and although she behaved as though she was merely suffering from a bad hangover, really it was the shock of truth, as well as a sensation of otherworldliness. It was difficult to comprehend, or even accept such a dramatic finality when the dour everyday continued. Perhaps if one went to worrying over buttered toast, the bigger problems would disappear.

Once she had dined, she stood up and shouted at the top of her voice for her maid before disappearing to her room to dress. Muriel and Mairi looked at one another and Mairi smiled wanly, commenting that her mother was really quite fond of the maid and amused by her bad manners. She got easily bored of punctual, well behaved maids.

Elizabeth reappeared in a stirring dress of deep mauve, the shot silk reflecting the light and giving her a refreshing luminescence. She declared that she needed air and would be taking the carriage out for a drive. Suzette, already in cape and bonnet, stood sulkily in the background. Of course Mairi and Muriel would be joining them. Come now, it was thoughtless to keep the staff waiting.

The four women were packed into Elizabeth's carriage. The streets of York glistened brightly in the sunshine after the rain. Muriel sat back in her place so to allow Mairi full access to the window on their side. On the opposing window neither Suzette nor Elizabeth were particularly interested; the maid fiddling with her gloves, and Elizabeth hiding the bottom half of her face behind a hand-painted fan.

The carriage rattled down through Walmgate before bursting out into open cityscape close to the castle ruins and the River Foss. Carriages and carts rolled past, people milling here and there, tradesfolk shouting at one another over the din. The carriage departed from the cluttered build up of the city centre, heading down Fishergate and passing by the priory then Fishergate house with its fine gardens before the land broke down even further to fields and agriculture. Passing by Fulford Lodge, Elizabeth folded her fan and tapped it impatiently on the windowsill. She couldn't settle to anything. There was a furious energy within her that needed to be burned out.

"I need to walk," she decided, looking notably angry as though she had been forced against her will into this damned carriage. "Where are all the fashionable ladies taking the air these days in town?"

Muriel rolled her eyes. "You want to go back already?"

Suzette shrugged. "I hear they like to stroll round the new cemetery."

Muriel glared at the maid.

"You hear this?" Elizabeth asked incredulously. "How do you hear it? They don't speak French here, my dear."

"I know English."

"You were employed on the understanding you detested English!"

Suzette sniffed loudly as if that was answer enough.

"Tell him to stop." Elizabeth thumped on the roof of the carriage. "Where is this cemetery? Where are we going?"

After some confusion, the carriage stopped outside of the cavalry barracks much to the delight of the mounted soldiers and Suzette, who had suddenly decided that pressing herself to the window to fully experience England was now a marvellous idea. The carriage swung around by way of the parade yard. The light dragoon guards, currently on drills with the horses, came to an ordered standstill as the confused carriage ambled around like a doddering senile loon to their smart, ordered military lines. Mairi and Muriel shrank back into the shadows, feeling for the coachman who had been ordered by Elizabeth to take this route. Suzette was grinning for the first time since arriving in the country, happily waving to the cavalrymen.

"If that is what it takes to get you to smile, I shall have to invite the dragoons to tea," Elizabeth muttered.

"All of them?"

They were soon at the new cemetery, which was on the southern outskirts of the city, not all that far from the cavalry barracks. It was built on land purchased from a potato farmer whose family had been so blighted by tragedy, there was no one to continue the business. The work of the dead had seemed an apt change of direction. Suzette had not been wrong when she had said it was the fashionable place for an afternoon perambulation, for much of York society, all in its finery, were strolling along the neat gravelled pathways of the new garden of the dead. Much was unoccupied as of yet, leaving a neatly landscaped spread, contained within walls and fences, well established mature trees flanking the exterior, and within new plantings of shrubs and saplings which would, with time grow to be a delight.

Whilst it might be a novel new feature and a well-trimmed garden, the cemetery was a product of necessity rather than a need for aesthetics. The city's churchyards were bursting at the seams with the dead, and the recent cholera outbreak had seen a need for mass burial sites, if only to clear the bodies at an acceptable speed to what they were dropping. Things could not continue as they were and the city elders agreed that somewhere large, fresh and with plenty of vacant lots was needed to see the population through the next few decades of mourning. Cemeteries with angels and ostentatious stone memorials were becoming all the rage, with neat walkways and space for people to luxuriate in their grief. Something far more mannered and civilised than the jumbled, piled-up cluttering that the old churchyards offered. Construction had started in earnest, and it was only last year that the cemetery had been officially opened. Many still clung to the hope of going into their cluttered local churchyard, in the hope of keeping company with the ancestors, and enjoying a cheaper rate of burial, but the residents were coming around to the idea of a city cemetery.

The carriage pulled up at the lodge house, which served as offices and reception, and the ladies alighted. Great wrought iron gates announced the entrance into the graveyard, with a spread of high iron railings and stone pillars topped with urns creating the front facade. Elizabeth, keen to be vigorous and full of life, had clicked open her parasol, and was off marching, Suzette in grumbling tow, before the carriage had barely stopped. Mairi and Muriel followed at a more leisurely pace, noting the York citizens in their finery, parading as though they were walking down the seaside esplanade. Mairi was quiet, taking in the details of her surroundings, the goings on of the people, the business of the town. In the distance she noted the sexton and an assistant working on a new hole, for this was a business that would never dry up. Her nose wrinkled as an unpleasant, rotting scent wafted towards them and she stared in consternation at an open hole close to the path. Its dank, earthiness gave little away, for it was so deep as for the body at the bottom not to be visible unless one was to stand right up to the crumbling edge and stare straight down.

Elizabeth had stopped by the hole, and looked back towards Muriel. "Well, this is no good. They've left this grave open. In fact I see another unattended hole over there," she pointed. "Are the men not instructed on filling a hole afterwards?"

"It will be a public grave," Muriel commented idly. Although she was a student and a professional at the care of the living, it was inevitable that she had many dealings with the professions of death through her work. She had a good understanding of the nature of cemeteries.

"Open for any passing Jack to take a look?"

"They leave it open until it is full."

"No one is working here, it will never be full of earth."

"Full of bodies," Muriel sighed. "When the deceased are brought in, they will be added to the grave, and when it has enough bodies in, they will fill it up, close it off."

"As and when people die? You mean people are being buried with strangers? Any old dirty scoundrel?"

"Any old dirty scoundrel who paid for a public grave. Elizabeth, you know how these things work. No everyone has the spending power you do."

"So one would have to pay a higher fee if one wanted a room of one's own, so to speak?" Mairi said.

"I understand that is how it works. The richer families tend to buy a private plot. It will be opened up again as and when required."

Elizabeth listened to the prattle and stared into the hole. The rotting smell emanating up out of the open grave was really quite revolting; that they allowed such a thing to go on where fashionable, decent people were taking a walk was disgraceful. She put a scented handkerchief to her nose and felt a sweat break out across her forehead. She couldn't look away from that hole cut into the bowels of the earth, thinking of the strangers tossed into the ground, unknown body resting against unfamiliar limbs, one on top of another. The flesh decaying. Food for the worms. Her fingers started to shake and she lost hold of her parasol, the lace-covered contraption dropping unceremoniously onto her head. She let out a cry.

"Elizabeth," Muriel was at her side, holding her bad arm gently. "I'm not sure it's such a good idea to be here."

"I find I am not yet recovered," Elizabeth muttered. "Perhaps we could retire for the day."

1838 March
Lincoln

Elizabeth took another fortifying gulp of brandy to steady her nerves and focused on her feet. She would get herself out of this panic attack. She could feel her feet pressing into the rug, grounded and steady. The world was not about to topple over. The weather was clement, although a moment ago she had felt as though engulfed by an intense fever. Merely the heat of terror, she had experienced this before. It had been some weeks since her sister had confirmed that she was suffering from the final stage of the pox, and it had been even longer since these dreadful growths appeared, so really she ought to be used to it all. Yet the discovery of a new growth, such as the one on the side of her neck, disfiguring the line of her jaw, this morning had been particularly harrowing.

They were hiding in Lincoln, where they knew no one, whilst Elizabeth tried to work out a strategy. She did not want her sister here, or worse, her mother who had relocated back to Whitby, getting it into her head that she should come down to visit. She had fled further south into the country with her daughter. They had left a great deal of personal effects in York, including the pianoforte, which she knew Mairi pined after, but Elizabeth wasn't ready to return to her people yet. The truth of the matter was that she simply wasn't ready to die.

She moved back to her dressing table where the trouble had all started, and brushed her hair, careful to let it fall over her shoulders and not catch it behind her ears. She could almost deceive herself that there was nothing wrong. She put her hairbrush down on her childhood treasure box, and regarded the little wooden chest with a simple flower design carved into the top. Her father had bought it in London back when she was still a child and lived in the family home in Whitby. It was filled with ribbons and sea shells, pressed flowers and childish, girlish little notes and letters. A world that felt a thousand years ago. What had happened to that innocent girl, to become the woman who now sat here before the mirror?

Fresh air was what was required. Suzette was out playing chaperone to Mairi who had gone out sketching for the day. Elizabeth couldn't get her hair dressed properly on her own, but no matter, she would have that many scarves and shawls and hats to disguise her disfigurement that no one would be able to see her hair. At least she need not fear of being accosted on the street here. Whilst she could still do it, Elizabeth liked to get out and take the air, feel the sunlight against her clothes. Enjoy some simple pleasures of living.

She had plenty of experience of getting into corsetry and dresses without assistance. Soon she was dressed and ready to leave the building. She'd heard it said that Lincoln had its similarities with York, which she could see with the cathedral and the medieval buildings, but why they had felt the need to build on such a steep hill, Elizabeth couldn't say, as she puffed her way up to the cathedral. She was unfit and out of practice. True enough York was flat and one barely needed to lift a foot to keep moving, but Elizabeth had been born and raised in Whitby, a coastal port town clinging to the steep sides of the mouth of the River Esk. As children they had run up those 199 steps to St Mary's on top of the cliffs, passing by the coffin rests, as if it no effort was required.

Strange to think of her childhood now, she reflected, shivering despite the sweat she had put on post hill climb. Her state of mind was generally in flux, alternating between childhood memories that hadn't meant a thing to her for decades, to melodramatic whimseys of her funeral or the awfulness of no longer existing. Everyone said one's soul would live on, away up to heaven with the angels or down to hell with the devils. Elizabeth nodded away like every other good citizen, but secretly she struggled to believe that such things could even exist. It all seemed a little ridiculous.

Silly, it might be, the entire death business, but she was leaving nothing to chance. The day after their unsuccessful stroll around the new cemetery at York, Elizabeth had sent her maid off to the office to arrange an appointment for purchase of a grave site. They had seen her that afternoon, and the cemetery manager had shown her into a comfortable but not ostentatious office. Perhaps it was the sombre face practised in a thousand funerals, but he took her heavy load of attire as normal and did not remotely look surprised. Elizabeth swiftly dealt with the assumption she was here to make arrangements about a recent death, and explained she wished to purchase a private family plot now for future deaths. She would pay in advance for the interments of herself, her sister, her mother and her daughter and any future spouse or children, including additional engravings to the headstone once selected. She explained that due to a terminal illness she would be the first to use the plot, and wished to have all the arrangements made and paid for so that when the time came, it would ease the process for her daughter. She was still a young girl and there was so much to consider in mourning, even for older, more experienced citizens.

There was a question of religion and which side of the cemetery she would be entering. Church of England was situated on one side, and the non-conformists – essentially everything else – on the other. Elizabeth had only been to church as a society outing since leaving her girlhood home, and had spent as much time in Catholic churches as protestant. She did not even know which spiritual path Muriel took. Subscribing to the non conformists meant they could be planted next door to anyone, but at least with a private plot, she could be sure they would all be together again.

She had stared out at the grassy plains, the encroaching headstones, the gravediggers heading off to work with shovels nonchalantly over the shoulder and felt quite ill. With a perfected diplomacy, the manager mentioned that he found these offices could get stuffy and perhaps they could step out and get a little air. Madame may also like to view their headstones

A little shopping could distract one, and Elizabeth indulged her delusions of grandeur on her memorial. She chose a heavy slab on a plinth with a carved illustration at the top with the words "in remembrance of...". She had a moment of twisted glee to think as the first to pass away, she would be listed at the top in the biggest text, as the headlining act, with her family after her. All marked out in leaded writing, the slab upright for she could not stand the thought of the rain pooling on top of her memorial.

Despite the nausea she had experienced before and during the appointment, once everything was complete and paid for, Elizabeth departed as if she weighed little more than a cloud. The manager, employee of the York Public Cemetery Company had assured her that everything was considered and managed. Even down to the locking of the gates at night, and the employment of watchman and watchdog. Surely the residents did not try to escape, Elizabeth had scoffed. Not under their own steam, but the Company were adamant that resurrectionists would have no success here. When customers came for their eternal rest, eternal was what it would be.

She paused in thought, regarding her shrouded reflection in the window panes of a bookshop. When one was a girl, one had no comprehension of how quickly the years would go, how swiftly the regrets would accumulate. Or how one had utterly underappreciated the gloriousness of youth, how supple and stunning her body and her face had been. In life Elizabeth had made more of such assets than most women ever did, but even so, one didn't really appreciate it all until it was lost.

Elizabeth turned from the shop display, shaking her head to herself. What strange thoughts, from her girlish young flesh, and running up steep hills in Whitby. She thought again of those steps up to St Mary's, then all of a sudden she had a flash of Maria Argument's little face, just before she had passed. What an awful day that had been, and yet she hadn't thought of the young girl in years. And in bizarre coincidence, she looked up at a middle aged couple walking on the other side of the street and realised that she knew the woman.

Even though the couple had not noticed her, her first reaction was fury. She could not go anywhere without someone from her past popping up. Could she not be left alone? Was there no peace to be found? Then she calmed, remembering her disguise of shawls, and the fact that they had not seen each other for years, she ought to be safe. She found herself following the couple at a safe distance, to make sure it was really Jayne Argument she had seen – it was, as soon as she heard the voice, all the excess weight and age poured off the married woman and Elizabeth could see the young woman who had once been her girlhood friend. Jayne had gone off to be married before she was even twenty, and they had lost touch. Oh, Jayne had been a great one for professing eternal friendship and daily letters but she had soon dropped Elizabeth. It wasn't even due to Elizabeth's lifestyle choices, but the simple fact that Jayne had become a married woman. Although she didn't suppose her method of supporting herself as a mistress had fitted in with Jayne's new role as a curate's wife. She had heard vague updates over the years through the grapevines that the couple had prospered, with two or three sons and a daughter but that was all.

Perhaps it would be pleasant to sit and reminisce about childhood days one afternoon. To recall her youth, and the old days of Whitby. Elizabeth continued to follow the couple but dared not speak to them, uncertain of quite how to approach the matter or what she would say. As if Elizabeth MacCaskill had ever been known for being shy and retiring. She followed them across town, paying no attention to the turns she took, and tracked them until they entered what she later learned was a respectable boarding house. They must only be visiting the city. That was an irritant, for it did not leave her with ample time to plan what to do. They could leave at any time and as she did not know where they lived. Once they were gone, they would be lost again.

Elizabeth mulled over the issue that evening until she thought she might go mad, then decided she would pen a letter to Jayne inviting her to meet, and have it sent over to the boarding house first thing tomorrow morning. Now what was that drippy bore of a boy Jayne had married in the end? She couldn't recall his first name, but he had been from that ghastly Gaskin family. Yes, Mrs Gaskin would see the letter through to Jayne.

Already by the afternoon she had a response, but not the one she wanted. Although the letter professed not to know her, and begged politely that she would retire from harassing Mrs Gaskin's nerves, Elizabeth knew the moment she saw the letter that Jayne knew exactly who was in touch, and moreover that she hadn't told her husband about the letter. She was assuming that Elizabeth would remember her low place in society and not bother the good married woman again.

How like Jayne that was. Even as a youngster she had always thought only of herself, and assumed everything was arranged for her benefit. Elizabeth scrumpled the letter in her hand, furious that Jayne had the nerve to sneer down at her. She, who had lived in the continent, spoke many languages, had raised a fine daughter, a mother's pride and... she sat and watched her daughter work in her sketchbook and wonder once again what would happen to her when Elizabeth had expired. She might have dealt with the funeral arrangements, but really the most pressing issue was the rest of Mairi's life.

Elizabeth let out a dramatic sigh and put a hand to her forehead. "Mamma has one of her headaches."

Mairi glanced over at her. "Perhaps if you didn't wear so many scarves. It is not all that cold."

"I shall lie down for a moment," Elizabeth interrupted, not wishing to get into a discussion about her strange dressing habits. She left the room and marched to her own boudoir. Rather than laying down for a nap, she settled at her dressing table, to look herself in the eye and consider the problem of Mairi. She wanted safety, prosperity and health for her girl. Mairi was far too bookish and thoughtful to lead a career as Elizabeth had done, and quite frankly the standard of noblemen wasn't up to the mark these days. And she certainly didn't want Mairi being abused and cheated upon. As for these growths, the thought of something like that happening to Mairi put her in a cold sweat.

No, she would not follow in Elizabeth's footsteps, which really only left one path for a decent woman, and that was marriage. When Elizabeth was dead Mairi would inherit everything, so it was not as though she would be poor, but either condescending men in debt would say they would overlook her mother's dreadful reputation and marry her, or she would have to look to the lower levels of society who were not too hung up on these things. Elizabeth didn't want to think of her marrying someone lowly like a blacksmith or a baker. No, a gentleman's son was the thing for Mairi. A man who could give her a good life, but not one so rich that he would be able to afford a mistress. One that worked so that his mind was occupied and his life busy. It was easy to list a collection of ideal attributes, but where did one find such a man, and at short notice so that one could be sure a binding agreement was made before Elizabeth expired?

Her hands wandered over her dressing table and came to her childhood keepsake box. She opened the lid and took out the items one by one. Seashells and pebbles; an ammonite she had come across on the shore at Whitby. The artisans collected those strange coils engraved in rocks, and added snake heads to them to sell to tourists, claiming they were the petrified remains of snakes scared off the cliffs by blessed St Hilda in times long past. Elizabeth gave a little snort at how easily manipulated some people could be, and put the rock aside. She pulled out ribbons, an old feather, then at the bottom a letter long forgotten. She sat and stared at the handwriting, and thought how in all these years it hadn't really changed or improved, considering the note she had just now crumpled up. Back in the days when you would write to me, Elizabeth mused, as she unfolded the letter and read though. Her memory suddenly flooded with colour and detail as she read Jayne's young and honest outpouring. Neither detail nor open confession was spared. How could she have forgotten about all of this?

Elizabeth carefully put the letter down and looked herself in the eye in the mirror. Gaskin wouldn't still be a curate now, she betted. He would have climbed the ladder, surely a reverend at least. And Jayne so proud of her status, crowing to herself that she was the one Whitby girl that had made good. A revelation like this would be damaging to Gaskin's career and poisonous to Jayne's mental self. Why, Elizabeth could imagine if these things were known, Jayne would never dare show her face in public again. The shame and horror she would have to carry would be too great.

She got up and went to her writing desk to begin a new letter to Jayne Gaskin. Once again she suggested they meet, and mentioned a certain letter she had come across in her personal effects, summarising for Jayne the details within. Surely even Jayne wouldn't be so stupid as to not see what Elizabeth might do if she were denied a meeting. She passed the letter to Suzette for delivery, then lay down on her bed to consider how this new power might be played to best advantage.

The delicate chink of fine bone china sounded as the cup was replaced in the saucer. A twist of steam rose lazily from the surface of the tea. Jayne Gaskin eyed the hand painted design on the tea service, feeling her lips puckering in disapproval. She had always felt she had kept a refined and decent household, but they had never been able to afford goods like this on what her husband earned. Not that an expensive tea set guaranteed bliss in anyone's life, but oh how she felt her envy growl in the pit of her soul.

Her own cup of tea sat primly on the table, untouched. She didn't want to be here, but had decided it was better to meet the devil in its lair rather than deigning to meet in a public space, or worse still at her own lodgings whilst they were staying in Lincoln. It had been an unpleasant shock to receive the first letter from Elizabeth, shocking to remember her own youth, and also disturbing that Elizabeth would return to her life now, and knew where she was. She felt as though there were spies watching everywhere.

Elizabeth MacCaskill, she had muttered under her breath as she'd thrown the letter on the fire. She'd written a note declaring she had never heard of an Elizabeth MacCaskill, and would the writer kindly stay away, for Mrs Gaskin's nerves were delicate. She'd dispatched it forthwith – better for Elizabeth to know immediately rather than turning up at the lodgings looking for an answer. Her husband had asked who the letter was from, but Jayne had only shook her head dismissively and muttered something about nonsense.

Of course she remembered the MacCaskills. Oh, they had liked to think they were superior in morals and education to the rest of Whitby, but really, never had she met such a degraded family. Elizabeth had grown up to be a whore; the son a rough sailor who had died of gangrene; the little sister an ugly, scrawny thing; the father had been chased out of town on charges of bigamy, and the mother, well, she was little better than a fool for letting Elizabeth go bad and for allowing her husband disrespect her so. Jayne had heard her in-laws talk of Elizabeth's grandfather, long vanished and presumed dead. He had been another untrustworthy plotting rogue. Jayne remembered the mother, Eleanor MacCaskill, who had tried to buy Jayne's love, arranging tutors, and paying for her keep as a companion to Elizabeth. Even Jayne's goodness hadn't been able to save that hussy. Jayne had been lucky her dear husband had plucked her from that nest of filth and brought her to the good life.

That was where it ought to have stopped, as an unpleasant memory and nothing more. The second letter had arrived late in the evening. The tone had immediately changed. Elizabeth wasn't going to disappear, and she was bringing the knives out. Mention was made of a letter Jayne had written years ago, and an allusion to Jayne's younger sister, Maria. Elizabeth wished to reminisce, and if Jayne was not available, she would have to look for other people to talk to.

"Look at us two," Elizabeth twittered as she took a jam tart from the cake stand. "How many years has it been since we last met? Why, it must be thirty at least. Why did we not keep in touch?"

Jayne did not respond to the question. All she wanted was Elizabeth to name her price for that letter. When she knew the goal, she could work out if she could raise the funds alone or if she would have to involve her husband in the matter. She looked about Elizabeth's sitting room. "I did not know you lived in Lincoln."

"I don't. We're merely on a short holiday here. We live in York, recently returned from living on the continent. It is the only way to truly learn languages, you know. To get the accent right. My daughter has had many opportunities. She is a very accomplished girl."

Jayne looked horrified. "You have a child?"

"Well, she will always be my baby, but she's a young woman these days."

"Like you?"

Elizabeth almost tittered with delight that Jayne might be referring to her as young – certainly she had kept her waist whereas

Jayne had spread out like a yeasting lump of dough. The look of spite in Jayne's eyes stopped her laughter. "She's not a kept woman if that's what you mean. Mairi is a pure, honest girl.

Jayne sniffed as if it wasn't to be believed.

"And I believe you are only visiting in Lincoln also, or are you between houses, living in a boarding..."

"We are in Lincoln visiting my son," Jayne interrupted haughtily. "He is finishing up a contract here and then he will move to Yorkshire. We live in..." she tumbled over her words, horrified that she had almost given away their details in a rush of pride. "Lincolnshire," she finished.

"I remember you moved to Lincolnshire when first married," Elizabeth commented. "And you have built up a fine family for yourself?"

"Three sons and a daughter."

"How marvellous. Then you'll understand me, as a mother to a daughter."

"If there's one thing I'm sure of, Elizabeth MacCaskill," Jayne spoke haughtily, clasping her cloth handbag in both hands and rising from her chair. "I do not care to reminisce with you, nor do I care to discuss families with you. I beg you to get to the point. You have brought me here on a pretext of blackmail. How much will you have for that letter so we can be quit? Will you take twenty shillings?"

Fury rolled up Elizabeth's spine and she could have spat and clawed, but outwardly she held on to her calm. "I don't want your shillings, Jayne," she scoffed. "Now sit down."

The confidence was draining from Jayne's stature. She did not know where this was going, only that it was running out of the grasp of her control very quickly. She should have informed her husband of the situation immediately. He would have been able to deal with Elizabeth MacCaskill.

"I have contacted you as I wish you to help me with a problem." Elizabeth coughed awkwardly, and shuffled in her seat. "I find that I am dying."

Jayne choked on her inward breath.

Elizabeth scowled at her. "Not that quickly, you idiot. And I certainly don't intend to die until certain matters have been attended to.

I need to know Mairi will be well and safe after I am gone. I have attended to her education and she is an accomplished young lady, but I fear without my guidance, but with her inheritance, she could become pray to unscrupulous types."

Jayne tutted something about guidance.

"I do not wish her to have the kind of life I have led."

"I would think it a bit late for that."

"Jayne Argument!" Elizabeth roared. "I will not hear slander spoken about my daughter. Her reputation is beyond blemish. Quite frankly, I wish her married, to a decent, educated man. I am not looking for aristocracy or the insanely rich, but neither do I wish to see her in trade. I wish for her to have a good and comfortable life. Unfortunately, with my own contacts and reputation I fear the type of man I have in mind may be difficult to make connection with."

"Any decent gentleman would not touch the daughter of a..."

"And so," Elizabeth interrupted. "I find that I wish my daughter married and safe before I pass on so that I may be easy in my mind. This does put rather a time limit on an already taxing endeavour. Really in times like this one does have to turn to ones rocks. Family and old friends."

Jayne looked aghast. "You want me to introduce her to eligible young men?"

"No."

Jayne sunk back into the chair, experiencing minor relief.

"There's no time for all that unfortunately. Time is of the essence. I want to skip straight ahead to marriage, in fact I would like your husband to arrange for banns to be read this Sunday, to get the process properly started."

"Well, I don't know..."

"Come Jayne."

"I suppose if you could give me the gentleman's name."

"You will provide that."

"I know of no young man desperate to be married to a stranger before the month is out!"

"You have three sons." Elizabeth leaned forward. "It's quite simple, my first born and your first born."

"What, Wilbur?" Jayne shrieked.

"This is the son you are visiting now?"

"No. Wilbur is in Derbyshire. But you can't have him, no."

"May I remind you about the letter," Elizabeth said. "May I remind you about what you did to Maria. If you refuse to do as I ask then I shall take this letter to the papers, to the bishop. It won't just be your reputation, you know. Your husband will lose his job. Your children will be shamed."

"Wilbur is already married."

"Ah, a pity," Elizabeth mused. "And what of this son you are visiting here in Lincoln?"

"Stephen?" Jayne laughed. "He's not interested in having a wife at the moment, he's far too busy with his work. Although I do sometimes wonder if there is an understanding between him and Anna's friend Margaret."

"So he's not married, working, lives here and comes of a good family. That's perfect. Stephen it is."

"No, no, no." Jayne shook her head. "He'd never agree to something so ridiculous. Stephen has his own mind about everything."

"Well, don't tell him."

"What?"

"In fact, I don't think I'll tell Mairi about it either. She wouldn't be happy with the arrangements, and forewarning would give them chance to do something. I think it's best if they remain ignorant of the whole thing. We'll make all the arrangements, and all we have to be sure of is that they arrive at the church on the wedding day and say I do."

"This is ridiculous. You can't marry two people without them knowing. They have to be there for the banns. They have to..."

"I'm sure your husband can arrange that, pull a few strings." Elizabeth grinned. "You are going to have to get your husband to help you with this. And whilst we're going through the motions, you can work out how you are going to get your stubborn son to the church on time."

"You cannot ask this of me."

"If you do not do all that I ask, I will ruin you, all of you," Elizabeth informed her coldly. "Now, I find myself tiring so I must rest. I think you will have plenty to discuss with your husband. Oh, and Jayne," she added as her old friend rose to leave. "Do let me know which church the banns will be read at. I will make sure to have someone there to hear it."

1838 June
Lincolnshire

Mrs Gaskin, Mrs Mairi Gaskin to be exact, stood by her bedroom window for the light and examined the skirts of her newly laundered dress in her hands. A sigh escaped from her lungs, accepting that the iron burn was worse in the daylight than it had been when she had first seen it in the passageway this morning. The dress was ruined. Perhaps she could sew a large embellishment onto it to cover over the mark, but for that to blend in, she would have to create an embroidered border around the entirety of the lower skirts, and that would be a massive undertaking. Weeks of labour, and then an iron burn could appear further up the skirts.

Accidents happened and Mairi appreciated the volume of work staff had to get through but she was no fool and knew these things were happening on purpose. Most of her petticoats and shifts now had the stamp of disapproval on them, a red-hot iron held heavy on the cloth for too long, singeing at the threads and leaving its permanent tattoo. At least with those items only Mairi knew the marks were there, which was bad enough in itself, but no one else would see. This mark was a step up, boldly placing it where everyone could see, marking her out like a fallen woman who deserved public scorn. Yet Mairi had committed no crime.

She sat down on one of her chests in the little room and peered out into the garden. There was her husband marching out to the garden gate, with his coat on and work bag slung across his body. If he didn't look so stern and disapproving all the time, one could almost consider him handsome at a glance. Mairi knew that true beauty required a character of goodness to go with it, and in lacking that, her husband would never catch her admiration.

"Oh Mamma," she sighed, looking back into her room. "What have you done to me?"

Mairi's room was a small habitation on the first floor of a two storey cottage with garden set on the edge of a rather palatial landed estate. Had there been live-in staff, this may have been a room for the maids or housekeeper, but as all the staff came from the village, it had been unused until Mairi had arrived. It was simply furnished with a single bed, chest of drawers and a table and chair with a mirror propped against the wall in an attempt to create a dressing table. A small fire was the only source of heat, although not needed in the summer. At first she had made the mistake of trying to unpack what she could from her trunks into the room to at least make her refuge a little more comfortable. It hadn't even been a week before the iron marks had started to appear on her laundry, and one afternoon she had returned from a long walk to discover some of her sketches gently burning on a freshly lit fire that no one had requested. She had taken to storing everything that she could in her trunks, which were kept permanently locked. The keys were always upon her person. She noted that the door had a lock, but no available key. At night over a number of days she made a thorough search of the property and came to the conclusion that all the keys were on an iron ring the housekeeper carried with her during the day, leaving in her master's care when she headed home to her family. One night, on a particular moment of bravery, she had crept into Gaskin's room when she heard him snoring, and had taken the keys away. With a candle she sat patiently by her door and tested every single key until she was certain there was only one, which she removed for her own keeping. Now at least the door was locked and she felt as though she could relax a little in her small room, leave the bed more comfortable with some quilts and blankets brought from her childhood household. She was able to leave papers and sketch books out from the trunks on her table and even dare to hang a couple of pictures up.

Although the law said that a woman's everything became her husband's upon marriage, Gaskin had never shown the slightest interest in Mairi's possessions. Through his apathy, she had been able to retain her financial autonomy. More and more she did for herself, negating herself from the running of the household. She still had the problem of letters arriving for her always started off in the hands of the staff who would shamelessly open them and devour the contents before nonchalantly tossing them to her the following day. Mairi begged people to write to her in French or Italian, lying that she missed using the languages and wanted to practice, but really she was trying to hold on to privacy.

She looked at the iron burn on her dress again. It was intolerable. Mamma had hired all kinds of slovenly servants, but no one who had behaved like this had lasted long. Mairi lacked the age and experience to command the respect over women in service. In truth her very arrival at the cottage had set the precedence as to how she would be treated. She ached inside for her mother, wishing she could ask her advice or better still ask her to visit and aid her, but she knew her mother was too ill to do anything. No one would admit the truth to her in their letters. Shortly after Mairi had been sent to her new home, Elizabeth had quitted Lincoln and moved back to York. Judging from the fact that letters from her mother and her aunt now arrived together, she believed her aunt had moved into York to care for her mother. They never told the truth, and always had some story or alternative explanation if she asked.

Mairi picked up the dress and held it in her arms like a child. Any married woman and mistress of the house would fire a maid for such blatant insubordination. There was no point even trying now. She had attempted to assert her authority once, dressing in a rather dark coloured, severe dress, pinning up her hair to make herself look older. She had walked downstairs with her head high, asking the cook and the maid to step into the kitchen for a moment as she wished to speak to them.

Even as Mairi had said her peace the maid had struggled to hold back her laughter. The cook had rolled her eyes and told Mairi to get down from her high and mighty place. They were employed by Mr Gaskin and didn't take orders from blackmailing trollops, especially ones who were barely old enough to leave their mother's skirts. Although what with her mother being an old French whore, she probably didn't have her skirts on all that often.

Mairi wanted to cry. She wished she wasn't only seventeen. She forced her feet to remain planted and spoke, "How dare you speak about my mother..."

"We've heard plenty about you two, and we don't have a mind to listen to another word from you. You should count yourself lucky I'm prepared to feed you at all."

The maid burst out into gleeful laughter, her frizzy chestnut curls bounding out from the sides of her cap. "Go on, you daft cow," she cried as she pushed Mairi backwards so that she might slam the door in her face.

In any other marriage Mairi could have gone complaining or sobbing to her husband to have the matter rectified. Yet it was his behaviour that had started the insubordination and made it clear just how unwanted and unwelcome her presence was. She'd also heard the two women muttering about a Miss Margaret, and wondered if there had been another woman in the running for the title of Mrs Gaskin who had now been so unkindly usurped.

The day Mairi had arrived, all her worldly goods packed in trunks on a cart following behind the carriage, it had looked as though Stephen Gaskin was still getting over his hangover. It had been a blessing that his father had been present, for she was sure now, had he not, she would never have been admitted to the house. Given that her mother was so keen to be rid of her, she didn't know what she might have done.

As she had been helped down from the carriage by the footman, the front door had been wrenched open and Stephen Gaskin had appeared. "So you're continuing with this charade, are you? You clearly know no shame..."

"I..."

His father, the Revd Gaskin, appeared behind him. "Stephen, I think you need to calm yourself..."

"I'll have no whore's bastard prancing around here pretending to be my wife."

"Stephen."

"You're parasitic," he accused, pointing at her. "I'll have it annulled, you'll not set foot in my life."

The Revd pulled him roughly back by the shoulder into the house. "You need to go sit in the parlour and calm yourself. We've discussed this; it will destroy your mother, and our careers..."

"Blackmailing bitches!" He roared, staggering off into a room in the house.

As the father followed the son into an interior room, Mairi gained sight down the length of the corridor. Two women, who she would later learn were the cook and maid, were watching the performance with looks of horror on their faces. They didn't know the master was married. And he was making it sound perfectly scandalous.

The footman, who having worked for Elizabeth some time, was not so easy to shock, coughed awkwardly. "Miss MacCaskill?"

Mairi thought she was going to be sick.

The Reverend lurched out of the front door, an ill sweat upon his brow. "Yes, yes, welcome my dear," he said, taking Mairi by the forearm and practically dragging her into the building. His wife had terrified him with what their futures would hold if they did not comply with Elizabeth MacCaskill's demands, and although he did not know the details of the blackmailing, he knew enough that they could not allow this carriage to return to its mistress with her daughter on board. "Perhaps we could get a little room set up for you and your things."

She tentatively followed him upstairs, looking in horror at the closed parlour door through which she could hear Stephen Gaskin ranting about French papist blackmailing whores. She was neither French, catholic, a whore nor a blackmailer, but somehow in all of this who she actually was did not seem to matter to anyone. A deal had been struck and in order for order to reign, she would have to live in this house.

Her new father-in-law did not stay long to defend her corner. He did not return at all. Of the mother-in-law she saw nothing. Mairi had stood in the corner as the carters had carried up her trunks and piled them in the room. She then sat down on the bed and stared out of the window as she silently cried. She was an adaptable girl. She'd lived in several countries and spent her life moving around. It wasn't as though she'd never before been insulted over preconceptions about her own integrity either. Yet this was the first time she had been dumped into such a hateful situation. She listened as the cook went to speak to Stephen Gaskin. She asked what was to do about this new mistress, only to be told in a very loud tone that the slattern upstairs was no mistress and they were to make no adjustments for her benefit. Mairi looked at the gold band wedding ring her mother had given her. Something must have gone horribly wrong. Her mother could not have wished this for her only daughter.

Now she had been here a month, and a routine had settled upon the household to some extent. When in the building Mairi stayed in her room as much as possible, and she and Gaskin ate separately. He never spoke to her directly, and if he had the misfortune to come into her presence, he tended to scowl as if he had just bitten into something rotten, and leave quickly or simply slam a door to mark she was not to follow. That his staff had decided to respond as they had, coming to whatever stupid conclusions based on what they had seen and heard, spoke volumes for their own ignorance. These observations were all well and good, but sneering at their lack of intellect was hardly going to help Mairi in her miserable situation.

Summer was upon them, and for now it was possible to survive. She went out walking and sketching, and spent as much time as she could away from the cottage. Given the mild temperatures, this was easy to do, but it was hardly a workable situation for when winter arrived. She would have to leave him, citing cruelty or some such thing, not that he would miss her or anyone would really care for her reasons, but where would she go? Her mother had been adamant that this was her future and she could not leave. She would have to broach the subject with her aunt but she hardly knew what to say. In the first letter her aunt had been full of questions and suspicions. Given that Mairi had never so much as mentioned a passing acquaintance with this Stephen Gaskin in her letters, she found it difficult to swallow that Mairi was now a married woman. What had been going on? Mairi had ignored most of the letter and replied in French begging her aunt for language practice. Aunt Muriel had replied in French but with even more suspicions. Why in French? Who was reading her letters? Mairi hadn't been able to reply yet. What a little fool. If she wasn't such a docile lamb who followed her mother across Europe without question, perhaps she could have fought herself out of this mess before it had been created. The mothers seemed to be behind it, but why? There had been accusations of blackmail, but what would her mother be blackmailing these strangers about? It must be something terrible if they had agreed the son would marry her. Or perhaps they had blackmailed Elizabeth and something had got mixed up in the telling turning Mairi into the scapegoat. The more she over analysed the situation – for she had precious little else to do – the less she understood.

Her knowledge of the land she lived on grew rapidly, and she soon found that she could easily navigate the area from landmarks, stones and fallen trees, hummocks and grassy fields, a corner where a collapsed gatepost lay. There were patches of limestone woodland, openings of wild flower meadows, then flat open gasping fields. This was not a land of hills and drama.

On one of her early walks, passing by a copse of trees, she had met a tramp heading in the opposite direction. He had grinned at her, the stench of him reaching her first, then his gaping mouth with a few yellowed stumps left, gawping in the grizzled unshaven sag of his face. "Walking, madam," he boomed at her. "That will cure what ails you. You walk your land every day and you'll never be lonely!"

She paused in her walk, watching his retreating figure pass the trees, then skirt up the side of a field. Perhaps she could become a vagabond, just walk and never stop. No, she sighed, she was too fond of a bed and a roof over her head at night. That would never do.

As well as the land she learned of her own situation through these walks. On another occasion she came upon two men talking on the track. They each had a horse facing in opposite directions. The older man was taking a shaggy cart horse somewhere. The other man, who on closer inspection could only have been about her age, a lanky creature with dusty clothes and a red neckerchief around his neck, was leading a very fine beast, a riding horse that she couldn't imagine he could afford to own given how he was dressed.

They were in Mairi's path, and she had no option but to approach with the intention of overtaking on the grassy verge. The men's conversation faltered as they stopped to openly stare at the stranger. A well dressed woman with a satchel over her shoulder and a wide-brimmed sunhat pinned to her head.

"Who've we got strolling up here now?" the young called out to her, flashing the first smile Mairi had seen since leaving her mother. He had an Irish lilt to his speech and from his stance and his wink, looked as though he wouldn't mind trying his luck with her.

"I think I should know," the older man said. "This'll be the new Mrs Gaskin."

"That's her?" the young man was shocked. "I know they've been saying Gaskin's got himself wed, but it sounds like a rum do from what the gossips are saying..." he paused as Mairi reached them. "You this new Mrs Gaskin then?" he asked her bluntly. "Talk in the village is he won't have a thing to do with you."

"Diarmuid!" the older man exclaimed, slapping the lad around the back of the head. "You don't talk to respectable folks like that." He looked back to the young woman, guessing it must be her from the way she had blanched on hearing gossip about herself. What's more, some of it must be true judging by the expression on her face. No one could understand it. There'd been no engagement with anyone, only vague rumours about one of his sister's friends, then suddenly this young wife turned up. And looking about fifteen years Gaskin's junior as well. According to some of the worst gossips she was a French prostitute who had threatened to kill Gaskin's parents if he didn't marry her.

"You're a bonny looking lass, yourself," Diarmuid continued, oblivious to the warning. "I tell you what, if you were my wife, I wouldn't mind having a thing or two to do with you."

"Jesus, man alive, I don't know that you haven't been horsewhipped out of your job before now with such a tongue in your head." The man tipped his cap deferentially in Mairi's direction to try and erase the insult. "I'll have to apologise for the young man here, he was born without sense. Doesn't know how to talk to his betters..."

"From what I've been hearing, she isn't the better of anyone. But if this is how they do it in Paris..."

"Paris?" Mairi interrupted.

"Aye, we were told you were French," the unnamed man explained.

"No, I'm from Yorkshire originally."

"Oh well." The glorified balloon of Mairi's terrible continental history was deflating rapidly. Ugly she was not. French she was not. Old and evil was not looking terribly convincing either.

"Still a foreigner as far as these lot are concerned," Diarmuid said, scratching his straw-coloured thatch. "Don't you be worrying yourself about that. I manage all right and I'm not from round here either. Ireland originally."

"I can hear it."

"Indeed, from the beautiful hills of Connemara..."

"Give it a rest lad, we don't need your life story. Now, I need to get this old nag back before I'm in trouble. And I'll wager you're already late with this-un, so get a move on." He paused to tip his hat at Mairi again. "Mrs Gaskin."

"Yes, Good Day." She wondered what the gossips down the pub would be saying tonight. She worried what they had been saying before now.

"You needn't worry about those bitches in the village, mind, what with your man's contract coming to an end. I hear you'll be away by the end of the summer."

"Sorry?"

"Well, what with the survey complete and the mine up and running, I hear your man's got itchy feet. Ambitions and all that."

Mairi realised she had no idea what Stephen Gaskin did.

"Although I heard that it's only another land agent's job, but no matter. He'll be off to make his geographic finds and gather rocks. I can't make you out though, how he doesn't want to so much as look at you, I'll never know, I could look at you all day long. How did he catch a girl like you?" He suddenly grabbed her around the waist and spun her around sharply, making her yelp. "Buy you in a shop or something?" He laughed.

Mairi didn't know what to do with herself when he set her back on the ground. Etiquette suggested she ought to slap him for taking liberties and showing such a lack of respect but it had been exhilarating to spin around like that. Almost like being back at the balls, not that her mother had allowed her to attend any big dances, but she had allowed regular dance tuition. Music was when Mairi truly came alive.

Before she could make any definite action to mark her territory the horse leaned in to sniff her. Diarmuid laughed. "I tell you what, the horses know a rum one, and she's taken to you straight off. I reckon what they're saying is all wrong." He winked at her. "If you're fond of walking, perhaps I'll be seeing you again sometime."

And with that he was off on his task with the horse, leaving Mairi a little breathless and alone in the lane.

During the following weeks Mairi increasingly found herself coming across Diarmuid, at first by accident, but as time went on and she got to know his routines better, she would time her walks to cross his path. She looked forward to their short conversations, in fact there came a point when she was disappointed if she did not see him for a day. She felt more at peace with her situation and thoughts of writing to her mother or aunt to plead her case and be allowed to come home were put on hold. There was a lightness to her step, a turned up corner of a smile about her, and the words of the maid were barely heard when she was in the house. She went to sleep thinking of Diarmuid, and what they might speak of the next time their paths happened to cross.

Casual banter turned to more genuine conversation, peppered with personal details, descriptions of an idealised homeland long left behind. Strolling under green-leaved dappled tree avenues and across lush summer meadows, always just far enough apart for decency, but close enough to sense the other's breath on the air. They found common ground in their histories. Each was able to claim a heritage to a particular patch of land, yet neither had spent enough time there to truly know it. There was not yet a place that was home, and instead they had moved about a lot. Diarmiud had been born in Ireland, but the family had left when he was still a young boy. A string of ill-fed children led by a pregnant mother and a shamed father who had been evicted from his farm and was unable to support his family was his family portrait. There had been talk of America and great things, but they had travelled to Liverpool and gotten no further. Diarmuid had been lost part way through the medley of siblings and no one had paid him much attention. As soon as he was able, he was away into work and away from the family. He hadn't heard from them for years, although he made no effort to get in touch. He had worked his way across the country, west to east, taking employment as errand boy and servant as he grew in strength, to working on farms where it was found he had a particular way with horses. That was how he had come to work on the estate in Lincolnshire, poached from another estate when the lord and master had been staying to go shooting with his wealthy friend. Diarmuid didn't think he'd stay here all that long. It had already been a year. He was only waiting for the next opportunity to raise its head, then he would be off on the road again.

"And then, fair lady," he had said in a joking manner, bowing before her as if they were in a courtly romance. "Our paths will cross no more."

It had been said in jest, but Mairi had been sobered by the suggestion this summer of happiness was about to end. She walked home alone, feeling increasingly maudlin, and by the time she was locked back in her little room, she could not settle to anything. There were opened, crumpled letters from her mother and aunt arrived today, but she lacked the focus to read them. She could not lose herself in her sketching. She sat up late that night, furiously tapping the pencil to paper and staring into the candle flame. Was she to be discarded, the unassuming ghost that Gaskin would not so much as deign to look at, let alone speak to, for the rest of her life? She knew her mother was convinced this was Mairi's safety and well-being assured. She did not even know if her mother owed something to Stephen's mother, which was why they were all obliged to take part in this ridiculous charade, but this was not living. She was only seventeen. She couldn't accept this as the rest of her life.

She did not sleep well. In the early morning light she decided she would have to alter her future, and hope that her mother would forgive her. She would run away with Diarmuid. They would travel the country and make their future together, looking for the place they would call home. Perhaps Gaskin would get the marriage annulled when he realised he too could be free, and then she would be available and she and Diarmuid could... Mairi could barely keep the smile off her face as she walked downstairs.

She quickly ate some breakfast, leftovers as Gaskin had departed some time ago to involve himself in whatever it was that he did. She had her sketchbooks in her bag and was about to leave for her daily long walk when she was intercepted by the maid.

"Miss Gaskin is here."

"Sorry?"

"Miss Gaskin is in the parlour." The Maid grinned. "With Miss Margaret Sleight. They have come to visit."

"Yes, well," Mairi looked distractedly at the window. If she left now she could meet with Diarmuid as he was taking the horses to the new pasture. It would require a brisk walk but she could do it. "You'll have to send word to my husband he has guests..."

"They're not here to see him." The maid gripped Mairi's forearm. "And Miss Sleight is awful nice, we like her a lot here, you understand. We were disappointed she didn't become mistress. You need to go through and be polite."

Mairi felt weak. She couldn't play the role of the wife. Polite entertaining and conversation. Greeting the in-laws. She was no wife. She was openly loathed by the man who had taken her for a wife in name only. She was going to miss Diarmuid. She needed to talk to him about running away.

"Get your hand off me," she protested as she was physically dragged back into the house by the servant. The parlour door was wrenched open and Mairi was thrust bodily through, the unprepared fool stepping into the unknown. She stumbled in, tripping over the corner of a rug and making her entrance in the middle of the room, hair loosening from the pins and brushing around her face. Her artist's satchel was slung about her body, flapping out as she regained her balance. She looked uncertainly at her guests, who looked equally surprised by her entrance. The two women looked of a similar age, and had about ten years on Mairi. Well-dressed, refined country women of

Lincolnshire, collected in their manners and their place in society. The woman with lighter hair had a look of Stephen about her and was probably the sister she had heard reference to. The other must be Margaret Sleight, a dark haired woman with a square, sculpted face, a serious and analytical stare. She quite unashamedly examined Mairi as a specimen ready for the collection board, trying to work her out and classify her. Mairi forgot herself, staring straight back and wondering if this was the woman people hinted Stephen had meant to marry. Margaret's eyebrows abruptly popped up as if her assessment was complete. A smile twitched at the corners of her mouth.

"Did you not get my letter that we were coming?" the other woman burst out. "Really, Stephen should have told you, but he is still absorbed by his rocks as ever, I assume." She stood up and stepped to Mairi. "Well, will you not welcome us in? It must have been two months since my brother married and yet this is the first I get to see of the new Mrs Gaskin."

I will have to stay, she realised, wishing she were a child again and could run out of the room. "You are Stephen's sister?"

"Oh, but of course," she clapped her hands together. "None of us have been introduced. I am Anna Gaskin, the little sister of the family," she added in a titter. "And this is my dear friend, Miss Margaret Sleight."

Miss Sleight gave a formal bow.

"Well, I thought she was an even dearer friend of my brother, but clearly none of us were as dear as we thought. I'd never so much as heard reference to your name, then Mother was telling me he had married. Married? Well, bless me, he hadn't mentioned any engagement," Anna stopped for breath and looked pointedly at Margaret. "I wrote to Stephen of course, to offer my congratulations and ask about you, but he says nothing of his marriage in his letters. Men are quite hopeless, aren't they? So I thought there's nothing for it but I must come and meet you, even though Mother said I was best to leave it all be and wait until Stephen asked me. And Margaret said she would like to make your acquaintance, and it is so dull to travel on one's own, so I was glad of her company coming over here."

This was too overwhelming. I shall play hostess, I suppose. Mairi rang the bell, then regretted it. The staff took no notice of her. She would have to go and prepare the tea herself, then news would get back to the mothers that this sham marriage wasn't working on any level and they would all suffer the fall out...

"Why, Miss Anna," the cook opened the door, the picture of delight at the guests. Mairi witnessed a light and a joy from the woman she hadn't thought possible. "And Miss Margaret, why, it has been too long since you were both here. What a pleasure. Will you take tea and toast?"

"That would be lovely, how kind," Anna said.

Mairi may as well not have been in the room. Perhaps if she had hoped for a future here or felt the slightest shred of respect for Stephen, she might have tried to assert herself. Who was she fooling? She was a child trying to play a role she had not asked for and they all knew it. She started to pull the satchel strap over her head so that she might sit down.

"Oh dear, perhaps I am starting to understand," Anna spoke, looking to the bag. "Another outdoor work bag. You do look like Stephen's little mirror now. Are you terribly fascinated by rocks? Is that how you met, how you caught him?" She laughed a little, glancing at the silent Margaret. "Although my dear friend here is also a student of geology. Perhaps you will all have things to talk of. Myself I know nothing of these things. It's all rocks to me."

"Oh no, I like to go out sketching..."

"So you do not have intellectual pursuits?" Margaret's voice was measured and a little nasal. Her sudden question surprised ever her dear friend, who looked speechless as she stared at her peer. The tone of the question was clear to all of them, that Mairi was an imbecile.

"Well, you do look dreadfully young," Anna faltered, as if trying to excuse Mairi for her failings. "Perhaps you have not completed your studies. Not that any good lady has ever really completed," she added hastily. "There are always new things to learn. And accomplishments to keep up so that one does not become rusty. Why, myself and Margaret study French, we even practice our conversation together."

"Perhaps you know a little French, so you might follow?" Margaret asked.

Mairi sank miserably into her chair and listened to Anna and Margaret speak pleasantries to one another in dreadfully wooden accents. The only thing that could be said in its favour was that it slowed Anna's tirade of chatter down. But their vocabulary was childish and the grammar a little lacking. She could imagine what the women at court would have said behind their fans if they had had to listen to this. Still, Anna and Margaret lived in an agricultural community in the north of England and would have little opportunity to truly polish their French. If Mairi had lived their lives, she doubted she would manage anything but English. One must not be arrogant about the luck and opportunities one had chanced to receive. She stared at her walking shoes, the toes peeping out from under her skirts and wished she could get out into the sunlight. She could feel Margaret glaring at her, feeling vindicated by Mairi's poor hostess skills, and ill-educated, childish manner. It was unkind, but she supposed Margaret had expected to be Mrs Gaskin, and this young fool had slipped in unnoticed. It was all too ridiculous. Mairi didn't even want to be married to him.

So they continued for almost an hour, Anna prattling about trifles and Margaret staring in continued horror at Mairi. They all knew they were sitting in the wrong chairs, that something had gone very wrong. But no one would dare to speak the truth. The charade must be danced.

When it started to rain Anna announced they must be back in the carriage and heading home if they were to be in time for her mother. And so they were gone with promises of future visits by Anna, and nothing but a haughty stare from Margaret. Mairi returned to the parlour, dropped into the chair and picked up her sketching bag. She took out a sketchbook and flicked through her drawings. Gnarled trunks of rotting trees in grassland, landscapes of the sweeping estates, horses in movements, studies of Diarmuid, taken by stealth as he sat on a gatepost or lounged in the grass staring at clouds and considering his options out loud.

Her heart ached. She closed the book and looked to the window where the rain ran down the glass. I am about to burst apart, she thought. Picking up her shawl, she opened the door and walked out into the little garden. The rain thrummed down upon her body, her hair swiftly growing wet and heavy. She had missed her chance for today. What if she was going to have to play in this sick drama forever? What if she missed her opportunity with Diarmuid and he left her? Why had her mother tossed her away like this? Why was she treated with such distain by everyone under this roof? She stormed across the lawn, picking up a long stick that must have dropped from one of the trees. She stood at the end of the garden and stared at the fields. The rain grew torrential, the sound drumming in her ears. She had done nothing wrong. She was calm and controlled, polite and dignified and considered others' feelings in her behaviour. She did what was asked of her. She had caused no offence to anyone. Why were they so hateful?

Some fury bubbled inside as she thought again of Margaret's scowls. Of the maid's laughter. Of her sketches burning and curling on the fire. The vengeful burn marks on her clothes. Why? Of her opened letters. Of that man roaring about blackmail and whores. Unable to so much as look her in the face.

Mairi was stood in front of a particularly fine rose bush, spilling over with red blooms. Emblems of love. Was it supposed to be funny? She whacked lightly at the flowers with the stick. Rainwater ran in rivulets down her face. She ought to cry but she was so angry she started to shout instead. Italian sounded the best for an uncontrollable tantrum, and so she swore all the filth and frustrations at those flowers, whacking with her stick and growing ever more angry as the roses would not reply or justify their creeping insidious lack of response. Red petals bounced up and floated down, battered into the grass and the wet earth of the flower bed. Why could she not just be let alone to live her own life, to actually decide her own path? Why could she not have a little respect? Could none of these English bastards show her a little bit of kindness? She was not a bad person! Her temper eventually let go of words and she simply screamed, hammering away at the flowers, going in for the kill and feeling the thorns rip back at her fingers. Blood seeped out.

Finally a little bit of emotion, a response. No wonder they tittered at these cold fish on their wet, muggy island.

"*Figlio di puttana!*" she roared, flinging the stick away into the rain as if she were throwing a discus. It spun away into the distance and was lost.

Her shoulders slumped and her shawl hung from the crooks of her arms. She was soaked. Her hair felt flattened and the parts that had come unpinned from her face were now glued with rain to her cheeks. Her fingers stung. She turned, and numbly noted that the back doors were wide open, and the cook and her husband of all people were stood staring at her as if she had just descended from the heavens on a pair of great wings. Stephen Gaskin actually looked at her for the first time. She would not simper around them. Think what they will.

She returned to the house, dragging her shawl through the wet grass behind her, and pushed past them as if they were mere slaves, far beneath her in the social order. "The flowers needed pruning," she informed them flatly, before retiring to her room and locking the door behind her.

Mairi was awake as the summer light was only just starting to grey through the darkness. She couldn't slumber in anticipation of the rest of her life anymore. She had worked out every little detail. Every question for twenty scenarios was answered. They could stay in England, they could go to Scotland, perhaps Vienna and the horse schools, or perhaps they would get on a ship and complete the journey Dairmuid's family had intended to make. She would not be miserable, she would not be alone. Not again.

She quickly dressed and packed her art satchel. They would not run away today, but they would make their plans, then she could start making arrangements to move away from Lincolnshire. She would have all her trunks sent on to her mother's apartments in York. By the end of the week Stephen Gaskin and his vile household staff would be nothing more than a sour tasting memory.

Pausing at the top of the stairs, Mairi listened to the faded sound of Gaskin snoring further down the corridor. Below the sound of the staff beginning their daily work was dampened through the floorboards. There was a bustle as the back door opened and the maid brought in a pail of water, dumping it roughly on the floor. Water sloshed over the sides and splattered onto the flagstones.

"What's been happening to the roses?" the maid asked, her tone an affront as if they were her property.

There was the sound of movement in the kitchen before an answer was heard. "The mistress."

"The mistress?" the maid laughed. "When did you get all respectful? You're telling me that hussy destroyed those beautiful flowers?"

"It was a moment of fury. I and the master stood at the door and watched her."

"Well, that's just the proof. Not that we needed any, for it is as plain as the nose on your face what she is. And look at the mud on her skirts when she comes in from those long walks. You know she's taking her laundry out now? I heard it with my own ears from Mrs Yardly, whose sister knows the woman who lives nearby the laundry woman who's doing it. Paying for it with her whoring coin as well, I'll bet. No skin off my nose, I can't say I wanted to be dealing with her rags..."

There was a rattle of tin as tools of cleaning were removed from a cupboard.

"It is a shame the master does not move fast in the world of social engagements," the maid continued loudly. "If only he could not have wed Miss Margaret last year. Do you think he even thought of it?"

"Probably thinks he has all the time in the world," the cook muttered.

"Oh, and to see Miss Margaret yesterday. There is a proper lady. I would have been proud to serve her. Instead we're stuck with this creature."

"Won't be too much longer, you know he's leaving in a few weeks."

"Aye, but will we be asked to go to the next household? I'd thought it would be a lark to go up north to Yorkshire for a bit, but maybe not so much now if I have to accompany that little madam."

Mairi steadied herself at the top of the stairs. Thank goodness she would be gone by the end of the week. What a dreadful thought to think she would never have been quit of the maid and cook. She ought to walk out, for eavesdroppers never heard any good of themselves. Yet she lingered. One last insult for the road.

"And what did the master have to say when he saw the state of the roses?"

"Nothing."

"Nothing?" The maid shrieked. "That angry, were he?"

"He just stood and watched her."

The maid cackled. "She'll be for it now."

"I don't know. He's never been shy of speaking his mind, as you well know. I wonder if we haven't been a little too hard on her."

"Not hard enough, I'd say. She's a whore, believe me. You think she's just taking the air on these long walks of hers? I have it on good authority she's as thick as thieves with some stable lad on the estate. And her a married woman!"

"Well, I..."

That was enough. Mairi hurried down the staircase and fled out of the front door. She left momentary silence behind her as the gossips realised they had been overheard. They'd soon console one another with spiteful words.

Outside the air was still cool, the sharp sunlight only just rising and beginning to warm the atmosphere. It was late summer. A possible hint of morning dew, she wondered as she walked out into the grasslands, her heavy skirts brushing against the plant life. Seed heads waiting for release burst open as she walked by, scattering future generations to the breeze. She was out much earlier than she usually walked, and would have to second guess where Diarmuid might actually be.

Beyond a copse of trees he was slinging a bridle over a fence when she appeared.

"Jesus and Mary, the good folks of Lincolnshire are up early this morning," he called out, easily distracted from his chores. He sauntered across to meet the swiftly approaching Mairi. She was backlighted by the rising sun and looked like an angel sweeping to earth.

She felt her heart soar. What a drug it was to see a smiling face. To have one's gaze met by another, to see someone actually pleased to see her, to wish to engage. Someone who wanted to be with her. This is what marriage should be. Mamma had been wrong to be so fixated on security that she would sacrifice everything else.

The two young people met in a glowing pool of vibrant green meadow.

"And to what do I owe this early morning pleasure?"

Mairi couldn't keep the grin from her face. "Run away with me."

His face was open, a little bemused, but a positive reaction. He laughed in want of immediate words to say but when she gripped his hands he realised this wasn't a mere simple jest. He glanced about the vicinity to make certain there was no one but the horses to note their presence, before sweeping her across to the trees so they might not stand out quite so obviously.

"I thought I was just a lad you liked to laugh with now and then."

"Oh no," Mairi gasped, so giddy on the possibilities she paid little attention to what was happening as she was stood up against a broad tree trunk. "We have an affinity. I cannot tell you how much your attentions have gladdened me since I came to live here."

"You're certainly gladdening me," Diarmuid murmured, leaning in to her as he ran a hand up from her hip and over to her breast. "You're like the angels themselves, I've never..."

"No, wait," Mairi caught his hand and pushed it back. "We have to plan this."

"I find it works best if you take it as it comes."

"I'm talking about the rest of our lives. We can go away together. Find somewhere to work with horses..." she faltered as he abruptly stepped back from her. "You feel something for me."

"I'm not in a mind for running anywhere just now. I have a good position here."

"So what did you think I meant? A tussle?"

He grinned, "Come on, Mrs Gaskin my beautiful angel, we're both young and life is short. There's nothing wrong with a little bit of fun to while away the time. I understand you're not happy at home. Not everything has to be sanctified by God."

"I need more than a quick bit of fun."

"You're a married woman."

"Hardly," she scoffed. "That..." she pointed vehemently in the direction of the cottage, "is barely a marriage by any sense of the word. I'm leaving him. Running away, getting it annulled. I want to live with someone who actually cares for me, loves me. I've been working it all out, Diarmuid, we could do this..."

"Calm yourself, woman," he shook off her hands. "I'll admit you're a beauty and a man can be tempted. Perhaps in another life. But you and I are of different worlds. We'd never be together. A stable lad and a woman of the gentry? It would never work."

"I don't care about all that social status nonsense. We could go where we're not known, make our own histories..."

"Your husband would have me horsewhipped from here to London town if he caught us."

"My husband!" Mairi laughed. "He's not my husband. He doesn't so much as look at me." She stepped up to Diarmuid, careful to press her body as a feather to his side. She'd seen her mother do this when she was trying to get her own way with whatever rich aristocrat was taken to visiting them at the time. She spoke into the curve of his neck. "He's never touched me if that's what you're worried about."

"That would make it even worse!" Diarmuid protested. "I've heard about Gaskin's temper. I grieve for your situation, for you are too beautiful and too good to be left wasting as you are. But you and me..." he took a few steps away from her. "It would never work. "I am far from ready to be tied down, and certainly not with the trouble that comes with you."

Mairi pressed her hands to her face, covering her nose and mouth so he wouldn't see the ugly anguish coming to her mouth. "Am I to be condemned forever? None of this was of my choice. I thought we..."

He shook his head. "We were just having a lark. You and me, we're not naive. We've moved about a lot. We've seen how the world works. You've just retreated to your fairy stories to take you away from that miserable..."

"I mean nothing to you?"

He looked away from her. "I can't help you, Mairi Gaskin. I think it best we don't speak no more."

Mairi dropped to her knees in the grass as he stalked away from her. She threw back her head and screamed at the sky. No one would save her. All those fairy stories she had listened to growing up had been lies on the human condition. We are born, live and die alone. Love, of the courtly and the romantic was a fiction. One could only trust the love of a mother, and even that was lost with the placement of a wedding band. She placed her hands on her lap and gazed miserably down. So to return to that household, where the misery and the insults would follow her as she followed a man who loathed her presence but could not rid himself of the duty of her care.

"I will leave," she decided, standing up and turning back for the cottage. "I will leave on my own."

She reached the cottage just as the postman arrived. He looked at her curiously, as if they ought to be acquainted but he wasn't quite sure. He held letters in his hand, and she recognised the top one as being in her Aunt's hand.

"Mrs Gaskin," she introduced herself sharply. "I'll take those." At last she could be the first to read her own letters without the servants disrespecting her private correspondence. Paying for the delivery, she stalked into the house and directly into the parlour without checking if it was empty. Sitting down by the dormant fireplace, she raised her eyes to the ceiling. They were all here, she could hear their voices. In fact, judging by the creak of the floorboards, it sounded as though they were at the end of the house where her room was. Mairi closed her eyes, remembering she had forgotten to lock her door this morning. So sure she would be leaving. No matter, she thought stubbornly. The trunks were all locked, the essential items were safe.

She opened the letter from Aunt Muriel and opened out the letter, flattening it against her lap before holding it up to read.

My dearest Mairi, I am so sorry to write to you so suddenly without warning of this news...

There was shouting upstairs. Mairi raised her eyes again. Gaskin sounded furious. The maid was shouting as well. Were they angry that they could not look through her possessions? Tentative footsteps came along the corridor from the kitchen, and Mairi saw the figure of the cook pass by the open parlour door. She soon darted back the way she had come, as bodies thundered down the staircase, and Gaskin burst into the parlour with the maid directly behind him. He shook a fistful of fabric in Mairi's direction. "What is this?"

Mairi stared at him apathetically, then to the fabric. A long drop of cream, and as it shook she realised it was one of her night shifts. There were two distinct iron burns, one near the bottom hem, the other more provocatively burned at where her crotch would be. She really didn't care about things like night shifts, and she had arranged her laundry requirements elsewhere. It really was no one else's care. How bizarre it was that this would be the first thing he'd speak to her of.

"It is my shift."

"I know what it is."

Then why ask, she wondered.

He turned back to the maid. "And what do you say about these burn marks. Did you do them?"

The maid stretched herself a little taller. "Of course I did."

"These burns would take a long time. One would be stupidity, but to repeat the mistake..."

"I don't see why it matters."

"You don't see why it matters?" Gaskin scoffed furiously. "I pay you to keep my house in order. This is not order. Neither is it order when I see you lighting a fire where no fire is needed, and throwing correspondence that is not yours..."

Mairi looked back to her letter. She had grown beyond this petty torture a long time ago. There were far worse disappointments and insults in this world.

The maid had grown cocky in the last months, forgetting her place. Even the cook, hesitating in the background, could see that this had gone too far. "Well, I don't see what the problem is," the maid said, almost scolding Gaskin as if he were a child. "You said yourself she's a blackmailing whore..."

The cook pressed herself against the side of the staircase, in fear that she would be swept up in the fall out. Gaskin, a tall man as it were, leered over the maid in fury. He pointed at the door. "Get out."

... it is not even an hour since, and I sit to put pen to paper to implore you to come to York immediately...

"What do you mean?" the maid retorted stupidly.

"Consider yourself unemployed," Gaskin grabbed her by the scruff of the neck and bodily exported her thus out of the house, a screeching, thrashing fury.

Your mother passed quickly when it came. Dearest, I am so sorry to have to tell you by letter. Had the end come slower I would have course sent for you. Your mother did not wish for you to see the end, and was so keen for you to settle in your marriage...

"Mamma," Mairi whispered, the letter dropping from her fingers as her hand went to her mouth. It couldn't be so. Her only rock vanished and her heart sealed close. This wasn't possible. Her Aunt must be lying. Her mother simply could not be. "No."

The cook glanced into the parlour, then back to the entrance as Gaskin reappeared, still clutching Mairi's shift. He stepped into the parlour.

Mairi shook her head, abruptly lurching out of the chair. "No, no, no, no, no, no, no..."

"You want me to bring her back?" Gaskin scoffed.

She pushed past him and fled the room. "I am leaving."

The cook moved to the doorway. "What...?"

Gaskin stepped across the rug and picked up the discarded letter. There was an awkward silence. He folded the letter and passed both that and the shift to the older woman. "Her mother has died." The cook's face fell. "Make the necessary preparations. She leaves for York immediately."

1838
York

The journey to York had been conducted in something of numbed horror. Now she had arrived, she wasn't quite sure how she had managed it. She must have packed her things, for she had two trunks with her, and a bag that she had clutched on her lap the entire time. A solid anchor to stop her dissolving completely.

A cart had taken her and her luggage into Lincoln, and she supposed Stephen Gaskin must have been there because he had helped her up into the mail coach. Then he was gone and Mairi was travelling alone cross country for the first time in her life. She sat upright and prim like a porcelain doll, staring vacantly into space with tears streaming down her face. The male passengers had shuffled uncomfortably and stared out of the window or tried to feign sleep; the women fussed about her and cast looks at one another.

From Lincoln she travelled to Newark, then changed onto the coach heading north to Leeds. There was a final change to get into the historic city of York the following day. She had travelled through the night, quite unable to sleep and disinterested in food and water. Her appetite was lost. She paid a man to get her luggage to her mother's apartments, then walked the short distance to what she supposed she might have once been able to call home. It was bewildering to see York was just as she had left it, still busy with commerce and lives, everything continuing. It was possible that this world could still exist without her mother. There must be some mistake. Perhaps she had misread the letter. She searched through her bag, but realised she had mislaid it somewhere back in Lincolnshire.

Suzette's face confirmed it was true when she answered the door. Elizabeth would have been delighted to see her maid so devastated, but the appreciation of one's life's import is always denied until one is dead and no longer able to care. Mairi began to weep anew, and the two women embraced on the doorstep, all sense or need for etiquette discarded. Suzette brought Mairi into the home and shut the door.

"I will fetch Madame Must."

Mairi held both hands clamped to the handles of her handbag lest the shaking become too much, and walked slowly to the sitting room. She paused in the entrance, surveying the room. All of her mother's trinkets and expensive items, the pianoforte in the corner, Mairi's paintings hung on the wall. All of these objects were still here, pensively waiting for their mistress.

A sniffle alerted her to another's presence. By the window, on a plush velvet chair, sat an old woman with grey hair, hunched forward with a black lace veil draped over the back of her head. Her eyes looked dried out, her face lacking in days' of sleep. Mairi did not know the woman. She gasped and backed out of the doorway. There was a look of her mother about the woman, as if her mother had suddenly aged twenty years, lost all the colour from her hair and discovered a new humility in her approach to life. The skin was losing its suppleness. But she was not dead. It could not be so. The woman reached forward for Mairi, opening her mouth to try and say something. Mairi fled and ran down the corridor to her mother's room just as Muriel stepped out of the chamber.

"Oh, my girl," Muriel cried out, catching her niece in her arms.

"Oh, Mamma," Mairi sobbed. "What am I going to do?"

The two women stood and sobbed together in the passageway for some time. Suzette appeared at a point, miserable and staring at the floor, she stood sentry in case there was anything she could do.

The wave of distress subsided for the time and Mairi looked to her aunt. "May I see her?"

Muriel looked pained. "My dear girl. Your mother did not wish for you to see her, even afterwards..."

"But I..."

"You must promise not to move anything. None of the shawls or flowers," Muriel instructed. "I knew you would want to, she should not have kept you at arm's length, but Elizabeth was adamant, and I... well, I have found my courage enough to disobey a little and let you come say goodbye."

The room felt airless and unnaturally still. Suzette and Muriel had filled the room with strong scented flowers, but they could not completely mask the pervading sense of death. Elizabeth lay with a serene look on her face, nestled down in rich silken shawls and fresh flowers. She was waxen and grey, a wax doll that had no spirit. Her mother was gone. Mairi's tears dripped onto the shawls, leaving darkened spots like the first rainfall. She reached out to wipe it away then stopped, looking again at her mother's face. Her hair and the flowers had been arranged to shadow and disguise almost half of her face. It was bulbous and malformed, swelling out and hardened.

"What is this? Is this what happens when we..." she couldn't bring herself to say the word.

"It is what killed her," Muriel said quietly.

"Oh Mamma, you so treasured your looks." Mairi reached out a hand as if to pull away the flowers, then stopped.

"Keep your memories as they are," Muriel advised. Part of her wished that she hadn't needed to be there for the final weeks, but she was also glad her pig-headed sister had wanted her company throughout. Her training and experience had proved to be a great relief, and she had been able to ease her sister's passing. She had known what to expect, what to do.

"When will we bury her?"

"Tomorrow. It's all arranged. Months ago it seems. I suppose my sister didn't want us making her funeral too modest, so she'd already been to the cemetery and made all the arrangements."

"The one where we went for that walk?"

"Yes, that's the place." Muriel waited until Mairi was finished by the bedside, then naturally came away back into the corridor.

"She's gone," Mairi whispered.

"Yes."

"You can tell it's not her anymore. Tell me, where do we go when...?"

"You've heard the priests."

"Yes, I know all that but..." she paused, her mind jumping back and forth then across to more current subjects. "There is a woman," Mairi continued, "An old woman in the sitting room. Was she the woman who came to prepare Mamma?"

"An old woman?" Muriel was confused for a moment before she burst out into laughter. It seemed inappropriate as they all treaded water through grief, and yet it was all so ridiculous. "That is my mother. Your grandmother." She paused, realising that although the two had enjoyed a lengthy correspondence, they had never actually met in person. "Come through with me, let's go meet her properly."

"But you travelled all this way on your own? I don't understand. Where is your husband now?"

"Who?"

"Your husband?" Eleanor MacCaskill looked to her youngest daughter to question the confusion. Had she misunderstood something from their correspondence? "Mairi is married, you told me."

"Oh, him, yes." Mairi had forgotten about that charade. Her mother's legacy. "In Lincolnshire I suppose, at his work."

"He could not..."

"We're not really married," Mairi muttered as she stared into her cup of tea. She had only slept an hour or two at most last night. Coupled with the previous sleepless night of travel, she was not thinking clearly. Part of her so wanted to close her eyes and disappear into a deep sleep, but if she were to do that, it would bring a close to that waking period. The period of time covering when she had thought her mother was alive, and then she was not. After that there was only the rest of her days with nothing. That everything continued felt as an insult. Even that Mamma's fine possessions still lingered in the sitting room, existing and not evaporating into the air, seemed wrong.

"Not married?! But Elizabeth said..."

"Oh yes, we had a wedding ceremony in a church." Mairi finally picked up the cup and drank the contents in one gulp. She didn't feel any better for it.

Eleanor MacCaskill, an old woman in her seventies, with grey-white hair that had once been a lustrous black, looked a little lost. "I still don't understand. You'd never so much as hinted at a young man, and then suddenly you are Mrs Gaskin..."

"He's hardly young, past thirty I think."

"You think?" Muriel leaned forward. "You don't know?"

"I don't really know anything about him. He doesn't talk to me." Mairi stared pointedly at the teapot set beside her Aunt.

Her grandmother, Eleanor MacCaskill, whom she was still growing accustomed to as an actual person, looked aghast. "Why on earth did you marry him?"

"Mamma wanted me to."

"Elizabeth knew him?"

"No. I don't know." Mairi squeezed her eyes shut and pressed her fingers to her forehead. "She didn't really tell me anything. I just got whisked away to the church one morning and she told me I was getting married. I don't think he knew about it either. He was frightfully drunk at the time."

Eleanor grimaced. "Elizabeth..."

"I think Mamma knew his mother. They'd decided it between themselves."

"What was his name again?"

"Stephen Gaskin," Eleanor supplied.

"Gaskin," Muriel mused over the name. "Oh lord, didn't that dreadful friend of Elizabeth's marry a Gaskin?"

"Who?"

"You know who I mean. Her name was Jayne. The Gaskins were a big family in Whitby, Jayne was lucky to get to marry into them. You took her in after her younger sister died. I remember she and her mother couldn't stand to be in the same house together after the accident. Yes, I remember now," Muriel banged the table with the flat of her hand in the excitement, making Elizabeth's tea service rattle. "She was our housekeeper's niece."

Mairi felt the jangle and chink of fine china reverberate through her skull. "Might I take another cup of tea?"

"Yes, of course." Muriel leaned forward to pour out the tea. "Mother?"

"Not for me," Eleanor declined. "I vaguely remember the girl. She was a little bit precocious, not all that bright but there was no harm with her I thought. I can't imagine she would be clever enough to make Elizabeth do anything against her will."

"Unless this was all Elizabeth's doing," Muriel pointed out. "Mairi, my dear, I know you are only young but I don't understand why you have agreed to all of this. Why have you been living with this man for so many months, especially if he won't even speak to you?"

"Mamma wished it. She said she was worried about my future. She wanted me to be safe and not to live her life." Mairi stared miserably into her tea, watching the light steam curl off the top. Her Mamma. Already she had not seen her for months and now she would never see or speak to her again. It had been the day after the wedding when her mother had packed her off to her new husband, looking relieved as if to declare 'finally, I do not have a child in the house!' Mairi had been too loved a child to truly believe that so, and yet there had been obvious relief in her mother's face when the marriage had been completed. Perhaps part of her had assumed her mother knew best, and could see this was the right thing to do, whereas Mairi's youth was still blind to the sense of it all.

"My daughter loved you dearly," Eleanor started. "But she could have some funny ideas. You do not need to be bound by this marriage for this rest of your life. Why, we could have it annulled." She looked to Muriel for confirmation. "I mean, if it's not been..."

Muriel raised her eyebrows, amused by her mother turning prim.

"Well, I mean, Mairi did say they're not really married."

"The marriage has not been consummated, if that's what you're referring to." Mairi spoke bluntly. "Why look shocked? My mother was a courtesan, my aunt is a doctor. I'm still naive and innocent but I do understand the ways of the world."

"It could be grounds for an annulment," Muriel mused. "Mairi, you can't possibly want to go back there."

Mairi felt tears spring to her eyes. She hadn't really thought to tomorrow or next week, let alone next month. Quite frankly she didn't want the future at all. Her one stable pin point from her entire existence was gone. Everything else had been transitory. "Where else do I go? Mamma was so desperate for me to be married. She was so relieved when it was done."

"I'm sure Elizabeth had your best interests at heart, but my sister could be impulsive," Muriel spoke. "And you should not have to accept a loveless, nay, even worse, friendless marriage. You do deserve a lot better than this."

Mairi did not look convinced.

"I know women must do as they are bid and we do not have a lot of options or freedoms in this world. But you are not a poverty stricken wretch, and you do have the right to say no." Muriel reached out and squeezed Mairi's hand. "Don't let misery be her legacy."

There was a sharp rap on the door, followed by a shuffle, then Suzette, followed by the coachman dressed in black stepped into the room. Suzette pursed her lips. "The carriage is here. We have loaded her."

"Suzette, you have such a turn of phrase," Muriel muttered. She looked from Mairi to her mother, then down to her own black skirts. Three generations of crows, all in mourning dress, lingering around the tea things whilst waiting for the funeral procession to begin. It was starting to become the fashion for some women to attend funerals now – random remote country traditions aside – but an all female funeral procession, certainly all female mourners, was still an oddity and she knew there'd be some strange looks. Still, that hadn't stopped her in life before, and they were not going to let it stop them seeing her sister off now. She stood up as Mairi also rose from her chair, bringing the black veil across her face. "Let's get this done."

Perhaps Mairi had lingered a little too long at the grave after the coffin had been lowered. She could sense the gravediggers loitering by the tree, waiting to complete their work. The air was turning to mizzle, and an eternal dampness crept up from the ground. Mairi's face was drenched with tears and she probably looked dreadful. Not that she cared, even if people could have clearly seen her face from behind the veil.

How can you not exist? How could you just walk out on me like that?

At one point she had not been sure she would manage the funeral. Stepping out of the building and being faced with the funeral carriage, the mourners and undertakers waiting for the family, all dressed in black, a line of grave crows silently watching. Even the horses, blinkered and wearing black plumes, made the solemnity of the occasion stifling. Mairi had stared at the carriage, an elongated affair, with a wide front section placed just behind the driver, where the coffin had been loaded. Behind that was the seating for the chief mourners. Her mother was already on board. The carriage was just waiting for the female relations.

As the undertaker had helped her aged grandmother into the carriage, she had been sure her legs were going to give way. She couldn't do this. Muriel grasped her forearm tightly, as if she already knew what her niece was thinking, and took her to the carriage. The living entered from the rear and sat on either side, in a rocking darkened area feeling like livestock going to the slaughter. The space would have easily taken at least six people, and the vacant seats seemed to breathe their own hostile personalities. Were these the only living beings who would miss Elizabeth MacCaskill's presence on earth? Certainly there would be men across Europe who might have a nostalgic moment now and then to think of the fun they'd enjoyed, but even if they'd known of her passing, even if they'd been in the area, they wouldn't have attended.

Eleanor gripped the cushioning on the back panel as the carriage went around a corner. "You did not hear from Emmerline?"

Mairi looked to her grandmother, her brow wrinkled in confusion.

Muriel shook her head. "Rather I did, I got a letter, but she can't come. She has the family reputation to think of."

"From what I'd heard the girls are going a bit strange."

"I'm not sure. She worries mostly about her son. Mowbray's still very young really, and he's only learning the business. She's so desperate for it all to work, to prove a point against the other factory owners."

"Well, I can't fault her in her daily endeavours."

"She daren't risk any slur to the family name. It doesn't mean that she doesn't care. She sends her condolences." Muriel looked over to Mairi. With the black veil and the poised stillness, it was impossible to say if Mairi was even still awake. "A cousin of mine," she explained. "Emmerline Whitfield. I've been working at the medical practice at her village for years."

Mairi nodded slowly. Now she remembered. Muriel had mentioned the woman on numerous occasions in her letters.

The service had flown by. Mairi couldn't remember any specific details. Mourners had been few. Aside from the funeral entourage, there had been a few curious locals and random strangers. Suzette and the cook were at the back of the chapel, Suzette having refused the ride in the carriage, suddenly becoming very respectful and determined to keep the distance between them all. She was just the staff. Muriel had mentioned that Suzette had already handed in her notice and was planning to travel back to France as soon as possible. She slumped moodily about the apartments, saying she was just grumpy because her employment had ended, but truth be known, she was quite devastated by the loss of Elizabeth. No one had said her contract had ended, but even if Muriel or Mairi had decided they were going to live in York and would require a ladies maid, Suzette would not have stayed.

Mairi let the handful of dirt fall into the dank hole. "Mamma," she sobbed, "Please don't leave me. You're all I have."

Muriel put her arm around the young woman's shoulders. "Dear girl, we have to go now."

The family carriage was waiting at the gates to take them home. The wrought iron gates were closed behind Muriel and Mairi, so marking the line between before and now. Mairi stumbled trying to get into the carriage, almost lurching forward to bang her head on the step.

"Are you all right?"

"I feel strange," Mairi murmured vaguely. "My eyes are thumping."

"You have a headache."

"More as though they are thumping back and forth, my entire face trying to jump forward, or perhaps the side of this carriage is swaying..." She put a hand to the side, but it was still.

"Have you slept much the last few nights?"

"I doubt if it's been an hour." Mairi pulled herself into the carriage and slumped into the seat opposite her grandmother. She put her hands to her temples. "I feel as though I am going mad. This is all really happening? It's not some terrible dream?"

Eleanor looked concerned. "Is she not well?"

"Sleep deprivation," Muriel said. "You need to go straight to bed when we return. I'll get some laudanum..."

"I don't use those things."

"You can today, consider it special circumstances. Your brain needs to rest itself."

Thankfully Mairi hadn't had enough coherent fight in her to stop Muriel's prescriptions and doctor's orders. She was soon knocked out with a small dose of laudanum, and put to bed. Instead it was Muriel who struggled to sleep, and the following morning as she breakfasted alone, the dark smudges under her eyes paid witness to her troubled mind. She was still in shock at Elizabeth's passing, even though she was a doctor and had known it was coming. Elizabeth had been such a loud personality. Her elder sister had always been, at least metaphorically, there. Now there was only absence and silence, and horror at the situation she had left her only daughter in. What had Elizabeth been thinking, and to tie Mairi to that idiot Jayne Argument as well? It wasn't as if Elizabeth was poverty stricken. Mairi would be comfortably well-off, and she was a sensible, grounded enough girl not to need the kind of attentions that had pushed Elizabeth into the life she had chosen.

What a mess she had left behind for everyone else to attempt to pick apart. Perhaps the syphilis had affected her sister's mind more than she had realised.

Suzette appeared at the head of the table, a moody French portent of doom who merely raised her eyebrows at Muriel as if that was all that needed to be said.

Muriel put her teacup down. "I sense you wish to say something."

"I don't really work here now, and I was never the housemaid when I was. I am a ladies maid, I have ability and importance. I don't run about..."

"Get to the point Suzette."

"You have a visitor. If I had not gone to answer the door you wouldn't have one."

"At breakfast time?" Muriel was a little horrified. Surely no one ought to come visiting before ten at least. Even if this wasn't a house of mourning, it was far too early for callers. "You sent them away?"

"No, he is here."

Muriel put her hand to her forehead. One could tell Suzette wasn't a regular housemaid. She really was clueless. "Who is it?"

"He's just out here. I'll bring him in."

"But what is his name?"

Her question burst out in exasperation, but Suzette had already gone. Muriel raised her head as the visitor stepped into the doorway and looked questioningly at her. He was probably just as taken off guard by Suzette's behaviour as Muriel was. A tall man, well dressed but not in an overly showy or expensive way. He was a gentleman perhaps, but not a rich one. One that had to work for his living. Quite a square cut face, appealing to look at but easily turned to sternness. His chestnut hair was quite long, tied back but untidy this morning. He carried his hat in his hands, a bag strapped across his chest. Quite frankly he looked as tired as Muriel felt.

"I apologise for the early intrusion, but I have been travelling through the night and have not slept for some time," he explained, stepping into the room and assuming Muriel was acquainted with all the facts. "I felt it prudent to come here first before retiring to my lodgings in York."

"I'm afraid I don't know you."

"Neither do I."

"You don't know your own name?"

"Your name, I mean. It has been..." he took another step forward, unable to keep his stare from the breakfast table. "It has been a long time."

"Well, if you don't know me and I don't know you, I'm at a loss as to why you are visiting me at breakfast but I suppose I ought to invite you to sit down and take refreshment."

"Ah, I thank you." The man almost flung himself at the table, forgetting his manners. Muriel noted that he was careful enough to place himself at the furthest seat from her, also the one closet to the door.

"We are a little short on staff, you will have to serve yourself. You met Suzette. She is... well, she tells me she is not a maid, but anyway she has finished her employment and is to return to France soon."

"I doubt she is as bad as my former maid."

Muriel pursed her lips as she watched him pour tea. "We have staffing troubles in common. Anything else?"

"I have come to enquire after Mai... Mrs Gaskin."

"Ah, I see," Muriel said, not sure she did yet. "I can pass on your condolences, that is, if you would tell me your name."

"Oh, did your maid not..." He saw her shake her head. "I am Stephen Gaskin."

Muriel felt her slice of toast slip out of her fingers to her plate. This was the man Mairi had been forced to marry? And here he was at the apartments. At breakfast. Unnaccounted. Polite, and quite able to converse. Cautious as he entered the room, careful as he took food, but certainly not lacking in confidence in himself or his place in the world. He was not what Muriel had expected.

"Your maid who is not a maid did not say who was at home."

Muriel almost flippantly told him that he had found the correct property, when she realised he wanted to know her name. "I am Mrs Must," she told him, a little tetchily now that she realised she had invited the enemy to breakfast. Perhaps he was as much a victim as Mairi in this little plot concocted by Elizabeth and Jayne, but that did in no way excuse his treatment of her niece. "I am Mairi's Aunt; Elizabeth's only surviving sibling now."

"My condolences on your loss."

"Thank you." She raised her cup for a sip of fortification, horrified to find her hand shaking. This was not the showdown she had been planning. "Although it would seem my sister leaves in her wake more than the usual grief, which would be bad enough in any other circumstances. It seems my niece has been placed in a very unfortunate position. She is at present asleep and I do not know when she will wake, only that I will not bother her until she is ready. Grief is hard, especially as Elizabeth was the only parent she had. She has not slept for days, so I took the liberty of giving her some laudanum yesterday..." she caught a look flash across Gaskin's face. "I don't suppose you know anything about our family, but I can assure you I am a doctor and I know..."

"There are no women doctors..."

Muriel put her tea cup down loudly. "I can assure that there are. For here I am before you. Don't make the mistake of assuming that because we are weaker in body, we are also weaker in mind."

"I doubt the universities..."

"I have been trained by the best, and my years of experience speak for themselves. My late husband was Kaarel Must..."

"The anatomist?"

His surprise and obvious admiration for the name knocked her stability from the war path. "Yes, that Kaarel Must."

Stephen waved off any earlier disagreement. "Why, my field is not medicine, but even I have heard the name, and seen some of the textbooks by his hand. The illustrations are astounding. I can understand why so many in the profession see it as an essential addition to their library."

Muriel politely nodded deference to the compliment and secretly thought to herself maybe this Stephen Gaskin wasn't such an idiot.

"I must confess I was not expecting to find someone like yourself."

"Thought you were knocking on the door of York's littlest whorehouse?"

Stephen burst out coughing as he tried to breathe in the tea, Mrs Must's off-the-cuff bawdy remark so out of place for polite conversation.

"As I said, I'm a doctor. I'm not naive to the way of the flesh. My sister was kept by men, I won't deny it. Certainly she had the very best of English and European society. But she is an exception in the MacCaskills. The rest of the family tend to use their brains rather than their bodies to keep themselves. I don't know what your mother may have told you..."

"You know my mother?"

"Jayne Argument?" Muriel scoffed. "Oh yes, I know her from my childhood. We all grew up in Whitby."

"My mother has spoken very little of her girlhood in Whitby, and whenever she does say anything it tends to revolve around the town itself or Father's family. I confess the Arguments have been a bit of a mystery to me and my siblings. All of what I was told was post the..." he stumbled over his words. "If I may speak frankly to you, Mrs Must? I feel secrets are to no one's benefit now in this situation we find ourselves in."

"Of course."

"Post the marriage to your niece. I didn't know anything about it before, or during as it turns out. I can't remember the day. They'd gotten me so intoxicated so that I would not put up any protest. When my mother explained my new circumstance to me, I was told that Elizabeth was a blackmailing whore, to quote my mother. I didn't know the particulars of her life or how she lived, only that... well. Your sister held something very damning over my mother – I have no idea what – and I was obligated to honour the marriage to Mairi, otherwise ruin would be brought upon all of us. If it had only been my mother who had said this I might have wondered, but my father is quite convinced as well."

"Oh Elizabeth," Muriel groaned. "I had hoped this wasn't all of your making. I'm afraid I can offer no information on that cause. Jayne and Elizabeth were the greatest of friends as girls in Whitby, but it was my sister who went down a less respectable path. I can't imagine what she threatened your mother with. Mairi isn't even sure who has been threatening who in this entire ridiculous arrangement. From what she's told me..." she stopped, the flattery of good conversation falling flat as she recalled the sham of a marriage Mairi had described. "Either way from what I understand you have been less than a gentleman towards my niece. Mairi is completely blameless in this situation.

Stephen had the decency to look at the table and redden. "I cannot deny the charge. I have not been welcoming despite the necessity of us living under one roof. I did not know what the servants were about, unfortunately I only learned a few days ago, but I dismissed the maid immediately..."

"The servants?" Muriel sounded horrified. "Is this new torture I am unaware of? Mairi hasn't mentioned... My God."

"It is only in your niece's favour how well she had composed herself these past months. None of us deserved her good nature and manners. Apart from the rose bush..."

"The rose bush?"

"A minor moment, and completely justified."

Muriel waved it off. It didn't matter. "I will admit I have been disgusted to hear of what has been happening in Lincoln – even the circumstances of the marriage were told to me only on Mairi's arrival in York. Her letters all the time were evasive at best. But I am a little relieved to see you appear to be an educated and reasonable gentleman. I think it would be prudent to discuss where we go from here."

"Yes, of course."

"But my niece is still asleep and I think enough has been arranged behind her back already. Perhaps you could call back later in the afternoon, that is if you are still to be in York?"

"I intend to be in York a few days at least before going on to Scarborough. I will call later in the day. That will give me some time to rest."

Muriel nodded. "I'll bid you good day for now. I hope you don't mind the rudeness of asking you to see yourself out, but I'm sure you can appreciate it's better than me calling for that French demon."

Stephen Gaskin managed a slight smile. "Until this afternoon."

Muriel slumped back in her chair when he had gone. What an odd breakfast interview. At first impressions, he seemed like a decent man, thoroughly good husband material. And yet word-for-word, she must have heard him speak far more in half an hour than Mairi had in all their months of marriage. The entire situation was ridiculous, but she was hopeful he would be amenable to breaking off this sham marriage as easily and as quickly as was possible.

Mairi woke in a dark mood. She took a full pot of tea from the kitchen, and along with a cup – no saucer – she placed them on top of the piano. She did not speak to anyone. Mairi might have sketched and painted nicely, but it was through the piano that her fingers and her communication really came to life. She had started to learn as a small child when they had still lived in York, but it had been on the continent that she had really been taught, by an Italian master working in Vienna. His pedagogic style had been that of passionate eruptions and expletives, and utter joy when things worked, something Mairi had passively taken in her stride. From an early age she had grown used to the more passionate of lifestyles and the constant changeability of her mother.

And now you are dead.

She stared levelly at the oil portrait of her mother, sat at an angle as if to move away from the viewer, yet her face looking teasingly outwards, as if to say, yes, I will stay a minute more if you can say something engaging to me.

You who could come across so frivolous and scatterbrained, everything happening with good luck and mere chance, yet it was all planned.

She started to play, her fingers powering across the full length of ivories on the piano. It had been well placed in the room, the music vibrating down the length of the floorboards and along the corridor. The fluid sound, not notes tapped out but a true flow of music saturated the air. The teacup remained still but the steady ripples across the taut surface of the tea noted the vibrations. This was no polite parlour ditty that young women were taught to impress suitors, in fact Muriel had no idea what the piece was, but then she wasn't a music connoisseur. It was deep and thundering, a repressed passion rolling out of the bass line. Muriel lingered in the corridor, peering in at her dishevelled niece. The music was so loud and intense that it grasped at one's consciousness. No, don't think or do anything. Listen. You are mine. This was more than husband hunting accomplishment, she reflected. If Mairi had been a man she would have been able to work in the great concert halls of Europe.

Mairi glared at the portrait.

Well mother. You have always planned my life and kept things constantly moving. What now? We are stagnant. What was the plan for the rest of my life?

Elizabeth's stare remained coy, but she began to look as if she wished to run to the other side of the ballroom and talk to someone else on a pressing matter.

Are you saying I am to decide for myself for the first time? I have the immensity of all possibilities and no guidance? May I say no now?

Muriel's eyes closed, the irritation of reality returning as she heard someone knock at the front door. Now was not a good time. She had just left Suzette howling in her servant's quarters – where this grief and emotional display had suddenly sprung from Muriel couldn't say, but it left the household with only herself to manage everything.

Her mother was out for a walk. She needed time to reflect alone. Muriel wasn't sure how she coped with all of this in life. Oh, she'd seen enough death and suffering through her own medical work, but grief and the torments of the reality of life, the mortality of all men and the loss of those personalities and souls was something she wasn't sure she had come to terms with yet. Plenty of people would smile benevolently and say they were with God. At peace. With the angels. But were they? Muriel was disinclined to believe anything she couldn't see proved, and even then, with age she had learned to question even the most convincing arguments. Early in her career in Edinburgh she had done a lot of work with the phrenologists, something that had been all the rage at the time, but was now increasingly poo-pooed by science. Even she felt that declaring the shape of a man's head denoted his personality was nothing more than rot. Back in the day there had been convincing arguments and such passionate talkers. As for heaven and hell one was just simply expected to believe and do as one was told.

The door knocker went again.

Muriel headed towards the front door accompanied by a crescendo of notes echoing down through the building. She opened the door to a waiting Stephen Gaskin, on a back drop of slowed pedestrians, some openly gawping at the building and listening to the music that could clearly be heard on the street.

"There is the most amazing concert being given somewhere," Gaskin explained as if Muriel couldn't hear it herself. "I don't know..." he paused, his brow lowering and he leaned forward slightly, a great oak trying to bend to the breeze. "It is louder now you have opened the door."

Muriel, dressed in her black mourning dress felt very much the spectacle. She shouldn't even be having to open the door. "Do come in, please."

Stephen Gaskin followed Mrs Must up the staircase to the apartment, the music growing louder all the time. He was a man of science, not of the arts, but he could appreciate there was some skill in the music being played. Not perhaps appropriate for a house of mourning, which ought to be swathed in black and silence but nothing associated with this family seemed to be as society deemed it ought. They reached the sitting room and stood side by side in the doorway, Gaskin a little shocked to say the least that his silent blackmail bride, now in black, hair dishevelled, was the source of all this music.

Mairi could not see them from the angle she was sitting at, but Muriel could see that she sensed they were both there. Her back seemed to arch up a little in aggression, rather like that of a cat. And her fingers jumped more, diving violently down onto the keys. Her old Italian tutor would have slapped her knuckles and told her to keep her personal anger and affront at life out of matters. "You think it is not fair? You think you have been treated unjustly? You think you are special in this? We all of us suffer and labour and then we die. Hardly anyone acknowledges who we are or what should have been right or wrong. Life is pain and suffering. In music we can find the righteousness and balance. Here we can ascend."

The music started to calm and slow, Mairi bringing the piece to a natural conclusion. She took her time about it and made everyone wait a full five minutes before the music ended. She sat for a moment, her fingers hovering over the silent keys as if debating whether to start up again. She straightened her back a little, reached up and took her now-cold cup of tea.

Muriel cleared her throat and Mairi swivelled around her seat, the grain of her skirts pulling taught and drawing a distinct line against the side of her thigh in all those volumes of flounces and skirts. Mairi didn't look in the slightest way surprised or apologetic for her messy appearance. No cap or veil, her hair unbrushed and hanging out of her hair style. The top of her dress looked a little loose around the shoulders, and Muriel suspected that the top couple of buttons on the back of the dress hadn't been fixed. There was no maid in any sensible state to help with dressing, but then Elizabeth always had the little tools of the trade about the home – hooks that one could reach down one's back to catch a button or hook one couldn't quite reach with one's own fingers.

"Mr Gaskin has come to see how you are," Muriel said weakly.

Mairi merely stared directly back at her husband, who was actually looking at her for perhaps the second time since their marriage. She would not be moved, and was pleased to note he was the first to look away.

"And perhaps we need to speak of the future," Muriel continued. "I think although we honour my sister's memories, not all obligations need to be kept. You have both been placed in a most unfair situation. I think we could all agree that any necessity has now been dissolved and we can take control of the future. I am not sure how these things work, but perhaps an annulment..."

It was so like her Aunt to be this direct. Mairi stood up abruptly, shocking the pair of her visitors. She took the teapot and cup and carried them over to the armchairs, placing them on the small table. She didn't offer anyone anything, but then who would have wanted cold tea? Mairi sat belligerently and drank her cup dry.

"I think first I need to apologise," Gaskin tried. He found himself in a dance no one had thought to teach him the steps for. Muriel swept around, gesturing to a seat whilst settling herself in another armchair. "The past few months cannot have been easy for you. I behaved abominably. I realise now that none of this was of your making. I neglected to manage my own household. Had I realised earlier what was happening under my roof I would have dealt with it..." he faltered, unsettled by Mairi's lack of response. Ought she not to graciously accept the apology at some point, assure him that she ought to have informed him of the staff's appalling behaviour? "I dismissed the maid on the spot when I saw what she had done. And the rest of the staff, well, I am no longer at that house. My contract there is completed and..."

"And next to work in Scarborough?" Muriel said with forced brightness.

"No, to Rosedale; that is my next contract."

"Rosedale, but I thought?"

"I go to Scarborough first on invitation from a correspondent of mine."

"I see." Muriel looked to Mairi for some input but the girl remained mute. "Well, I don't suppose annulments can be arranged in a couple of days, but perhaps we can all remain in communication whilst we work out the particulars? Mairi can stay here, these apartments will remain available..." she picked her words carefully, thinking that she did not wish Gaskin to know just how rich Mairi had become with the death of her mother. "I will stay here with you of course, or if you prefer we could go to West Yorkshire. Perhaps even a stay at Whitby with my mother..."

Gaskin shuffled awkwardly. Without the chief puppet master, no one seemed quite sure how this was going to play out now.

"You must excuse me," Mairi burst into life, rising from her seat. "I have a prior engagement. I need to go now lest I be late."

"Of course," Gaskin stumbled up as Mairi headed for the door. "If I can accompany..."

"That won't be necessary. I know my way around York."

1838 Late Autumn
Scarborough and Hackness

 Mrs Jennifer Burton-Waugh turned on the track to look back up the valley. She gazed at the mighty trench of sunlight she had just walked beyond. "Why, this has been a most invigorating walk. So much to see, so much landscape. I can see why Mr Smith did such good work here."

Mairi merely nodded, not really that sure about what good work Mr Smith had completed in this region. It was hard to imagine him completing anything, for the older gentleman seemed to be constantly distracted by his own curiosity, either that or questioning others on their studies. Still, he seemed pleasant enough, and the invitation extended to her had given her opportunity to get away from York, well-meaning family and questions on what she was going to do with the rest of her life.

"This was all formed by ice, you know," Jennifer continued as she started to walk again, waving vaguely at the walls of the valley they had entered. "Slow-moving glaciers cut through the rock and created this. It's really quite amazing to think about. You look at the sides, dig into it and you'll see the strata of different ages," she laughed, not unkindly. "Mr Smith is a great one for strata. I think it must be one of his favourite words."

Mr Smith was the previously mentioned correspondent of her husband. The connection had been made through a Mr Phillips, who was Mr Smith's nephew. After much travelling about the country, Mr Smith now lived in a small but well set up cottage in the coastal spa town of Scarborough. They must have been discussing Stephen Gaskin's upcoming employment in Rosedale, and the older man, rheumatic and slightly deaf but still full of enthusiasm for study and exploration, had invited the Gaskins to stay in Scarborough before heading out to the remote dale. So they had come to a three bedroom cottage, high up from the shoreline and situated behind fine tiered gardens that were groomed to ambling promenade perfection. It was a carefully planned and packed visit, for between Mr Smith and his wife and the Gaskins,

Mrs Jennifer Burton-Waugh had also been invited to stay – an enthusiastic woman who had become known to the Smiths through her husband's connection with Mr Philips, the said nephew, who lived in York. Mrs Burton-Waugh had a man's mind, Mr Smith had commented on the first evening, and it was invigorating to find that ladies could be invited to understand fossils better. Mairi had almost choked on her mouthful of food when he had made the comment, looking adoringly at his little wife whilst petting her hand. She wasn't sure to which fossil he referred. Those dug out of the ground, or the old bones of aging men. He himself was a curiosity; a broad, tall figure who could have been an ex soldier, and yet Jennifer had informed her over tea that day that he was one of the most underappreciated minds of the age.

Mrs Smith, or rather 'do-call-me-Mary-Ann', was a short, slight dark-haired woman with a flushed countenance, a merry smile and well-attended dark ringlets about her face. She was open and talkative, and regularly laughed, even when no one had made a joke. It was as though the very being of life caused her amusement, and yet she did not seem to follow the deeper conversations on science and learning that automatically took over the dinner table. Neither did she seem bothered that she was ignorant to of what they spoke. Her eyes sparkled vacantly, she admired her husband's posture, a man in his sixties who must have been twenty years her senior, and she seemed happy to simply be.

Mr Smith had looked from Gaskin to Mairi and declared that she reminded him of his dear wife when they had first married. Jennifer had looked horrified, having already quizzed Mairi from the moment they met over tea that afternoon and having made the assessment there was intelligence that could bloom in the right directions if only it was encouraged. Mairi, taller, slender and distinctly blonde, had merely looked politely quizzical. She had always found herself more of a quiet observer rather than the light-hearted chatterer Mary-Ann appeared to be, and watching the woman wondered if the glassy-eyed look wasn't something from drunkenness. Perhaps he only made the observation for there was also a distinct age gap between her and Stephen. But she very much doubted the circumstances of their matrimony would match.

The two men stayed up late into the night talking of rocks and pouring over Smith's papers and maps that he kept in his parlour-cum-study. He had mentioned something about showing Gaskin a paper, or rather an appeal he had written entitled *The Case of the Founder of Geology*. The three ladies had retired to bed, retreating up the creaking stairs in order of age, Mary-Ann, Jennifer and finally Mairi, each to retreat through a separate doorway. As she was nodding off, Mairi wondered momentarily where Stephen thought he would be sleeping. He'd better not assume that he would be in this bed. The fact that she had accompanied him to Scarborough meant nothing. They had barely spoken in the journey across to the coast, not so much out of animosity but more that Mairi was so drained as to have nothing to say to anyone, and if anything Gaskin was at a loss for words in her presence. Meeting Jennifer Burton-Waugh had changed that, for the woman was a whirlwind of words and questions, constant observations and a delight in the world. She was quite infectious. She was a widow of ample financial means and a bubbling interest in a great many things. Although she was older than Mairi, she radiated the fascination and energy one might have expected in a small boy. Jennifer had a great number of acquaintances and contacts within the fields of science and history, and a deep breath of knowledge over everything that was happening in Yorkshire. It felt as though Mairi had made the first friend of her own in the county.

Stephen had slept in the study, claiming to William Smith that he did not wish to disturb his wife. They had been talking to the small hours, and running on adrenaline from good conversation, were promptly at breakfast with plans to walk down to the rotunda museum in Scarborough that Smith himself had helped to design and plan. Such a place to display the order of fossils he had suddenly boomed as Mairi and Jennifer had come down from breakfast. It was a tragedy that he had been forced, on account of personal misfortune to sell off most of his own collection years ago. It would have looked very fine in the rotunda.

The men were off to talk yet more science at the rotunda without a single thought of asking the ladies. Jennifer had smiled wickedly at Mairi. "I hardly think we should sit around here stitching handkerchiefs. How about a jaunt in my little trap? I brought it over with me. I think we should go to Hackness. It can only be six miles from here and Mr Smith had often told me of its beauty." She felt from her talks with Mrs Gaskin, she had found a fellow appreciator in the way of the foot and long walks, and was keen to properly stretch her legs. Walking was always the more pleasant with someone to talk to, she found.

Mary-Ann chose this moment to appear, and although not on the original invite agreed it would be very pleasant to take a trip over to Hackness.

Jennifer faltered. "I had thought of walking there for some hours. Your dear husband has spoken so much of the hills, and of the great valley..."

"Oh, I'm not one for walking," Mary Ann sighed.

"Well, no, of course."

"It would be nice to go and visit our previous home," Mary Ann continued. "We were very happy in Hackness." She made it sound as though this had not always been the case. "I should like to call on some old acquaintances. We don't keep a horse so I find I do not travel so often these days." She paused, looking a little uncertain of herself with the younger women. "If you would not find it offensive, we could drive to the vicarage, and you ladies could take your walk from there whilst I talk to my old friends? We used to live in the vicarage, of course it wasn't a vicarage then," she tittered. "I don't think the men of the cloth have always been so happy with my husband's findings."

Jennifer looked visibly relieved. "Not the old stick in the muds, but I find some of the younger reverends these days have a fine appetite for science and study. Why, I wonder sometimes that they ever find the time to tend to their flock!"

Travelling inland from Scarborough, the trap had left the spa town by the north west, through the village of Scalby, over the hills and dirt tracks, solid and frozen for now from the early morning frost, before sweeping down into the parkland of Hackness, past the finery of Hackness Hall and seat of Smith's old employer and sponsor, past the church, then down a wooded lane into the hamlet and out to what was now the parsonage, where the Smiths had once lived when he was employed as a land agent by Sir John Vanden Bempde Johnstone. It was a finely situated white building, now with an added wing according to Mary-Ann, that overlooked a field running down to the small, busy River Derwent. They had briefly met with the reverend's family, who had been happy to stable Jennifer's horse for the few hours they would be in the village. Mary Ann had gone in to pay a visit, holding a hand to her forehead and declaring that the rattling ride had quite taken it out of her. Mairi and Jennifer had started on their walk, Jennifer's eyebrows rising in amusement, stating that she hoped she had a stronger constitution when she reached Mrs Smith's age.

Although Jennifer said she had not been to Hackness before, she had a route in mind, in fact Smith had even drawn her a map of a suggestion of walking in the area. Mairi realised that this had been in the planning for some time. They walked a short distance the way they had come, past the hall and strolling alongside a clear-watered brook before they left the main cart track and went up to the hill through a delightful little wooded tunnel, a pathway heading upwards with deep sides, drifted with autumnal leaves, criss-crossed above with the lattice work of tree branches almost prepared for winter.

From the low, wooded hills and sprawling fields of the Hackness area they had headed into Forge Valley, a deep sided and narrow passageway heading down towards the village of East Ayton. Whilst the sun across hill and field had melted away the morning frost, here in the deep valley the temperature was still noticeably lower, and frost clung on yet in the shadows. The scent of smoke from the charcoal burners deeper in the woodland clung thinly in the air, the smoke barely moving. Mairi was glad of the woollen shawl she had brought out with her for the walk, pulling it more closely about her head and face.

They walked down past the charcoal burners' cottages, following the plumes of white smoke towards the charcoal ovens. Jennifer was soon in conversation with one of the charcoal workers about the process. The man was taken aback at first, but as Jennifer ploughed on, he gradually relaxed then enjoyed being the great expert in charcoal production. Jennifer mentioned something about burning wood, and the collier had laughed, saying that if the wood burned, the entire day's activity was wasted for all he would have was ash at the end of the day. They were there to make charcoal, which meant heating everything else out of the wood until you were left with the black, wizened remains that were so excellent for burning, or in Mairi's case, sketching with. Only what they burned to heat the kiln should truly burn, and the burn itself was carefully regulated by how much air was allowed into the centre.

The domed pile of turf, with carefully piled and layered timber underneath, would be the collier's focus for the day. His great creation. Whilst it may not be smoke as one would expect from a giant bonfire, there was still a distinctive scent of the outdoors, and a comforting warmth radiating outwards. The charcoal pyres threw off a bit of heat, as well as a comforting smoky, almost chocolate scent. Mairi lingered close by to feel the warmth. The smoke would infiltrate her clothes and she and Jennifer would return home that evening smelling of woodcraft. She thought of this time a year ago, and the polite high society she had socialised at the edges of. It was a world away from this practical, earthy woodland work, out in the cold, in muddy walking boots. No delicate silk slippers, carefully styled hair and fussing over how the skirts of a dress fell as one sat down. No society gossip, no flicking of fans, no discussion of the latest fashions from France. If her mother had still been alive, she would have stayed in the parsonage with Mary Ann, Mairi reflected. Her dear mother. In a confused faltering way, her mother had been right in getting Mairi ready with her own life away from Elizabeth's courtesan society and travels. She had certainly not been right with the secret and forced marriage, but it was essential for Mairi to be and do something that was her on her own. Out of the two very different lifestyles, she was finding she liked this one better. Of course, there had been plenty of learning and exploration back on the continent, and she couldn't deny that the chance to study languages and her dear piano had been a joy. But she did not miss high society, the sideways sneers at her, for they knew what her mother did to earn her money. Everyone assumed she was the same by association, whilst laughing at the young English woman's dreadful ineptitude at flirting with the dandy young men.

Beautiful but far too serious and dull. How could she be Elizabeth MacCaskill's daughter?

Mairi wiped at her eyes with the back of her hand. Oh Mamma, she thought. You would not believe the way life turns out.

"Are you well, Mairi, my dear?" Jennifer appeared at her side. "Am I neglecting our walk too long? I find you crying."

"It is just the smoke," Mairi forced a smile. She couldn't bring herself to explain about her mother. "Shall we get started again? I feel my feet are growing numb."

"My dear, I have a gift for you," William Smith declared at the dinner table that evening.

Everyone, not in the least Mairi, was a little surprised by this announcement, especially when she realised the 'dear' in question was she. Smith placed his hands upon the table to push himself onto his feet, then creaked over to the sideboard to fetch something down from the top shelf. He returned to the table, and asking Mairi to hold out her hand, plopped something cold and round into her palm.

"That is a Chetworth Bun."

Mary Ann laughed. "Oh my dear, it's far too late for tea and cakes. We're to have soup shortly."

Mairi stared at the object in consternation. It was hardly something one would eat, for it was a round stone. Raised up in the middle, like a small dome, and with five pairs of almost undulating lines running up from the exterior to a centre point. She didn't know what to make of it. Mary Ann seemed to think it a prank. Jennifer was leaning unapologetically across the table, a touch jealous as Smith had never given her such a gift. When Mairi dared to look across at Stephen Gaskin, he looked passingly interested in the way one was who said, seen-that, been-there before.

"Also known as a pound-stone. They pick them up just as you see it now from the fields where I grew up. They all weight about the same, so the dairymaids have taken to using them on the scales to weigh out the butter. As if a gift from God for the righteous slicing and serving of butter for sale."

"A rock."

"Ah, a rock in consistency now, but that was once alive," he said, waggling a finger as he sat down.

"A rock that lived?" Mairi ran a finger along one of the ridged lines. They did not look man-made, and in truth she could imagine them undulating in time. Running like lights, directing to the centre.

"Have you spent much time at the coast? In particular rocky shorelines?"

"No, I'm afraid I haven't." Mairi answered distractedly, turning the rock over to look at the underside. "I spent a lot of time growing up on the continent."

"A diplomat's child?" Jennifer asked in all innocence.

"Something like that."

"Then you won't have seen its living counterpart."

She looked back to Smith. "These are alive in the sea?"

"A great many years ago."

"It's a fossil," Gaskin joined the conversation. "It was alive a long time ago. Then it died, sediments piled upon it and it became fossilised."

"It turned to rock."

"In this case, yes. Many fossils are actually the imprint of the thing, in the formed rock. But in this case, and those of bones..."

"And so fossils are found in the ground, and we can use these to identify and date the strata from which they come," Smith finalised.

"Ah, Mr Smith," Jennifer beamed. "I was waiting for your beloved strata to make the conversation."

"It is a very beautiful concept. I have travelled the length and breadth of the country in my years. Studied the very ground..."

"I thought you sold all your fossils off," Mary Ann muttered. "You had to. For the bailiffs. I hadn't realised you'd hidden some."

Smith waved her frown away. "These are forever popping up when the plough takes to the field. These were my first look at fossils when I was a boy. Of course science back then did not understand what they were. I picked this one up on my way down to London this summer. I stopped off in Oxfordshire, that is, where I grew up, on the way. I was requested to assist in a survey this summer. I'm sure you all heard about the damage at the parliament buildings. We were to select a quarry for the rock for the new Westminister buildings..."

"It's been selected now?" Stephen asked.

"Oh yes, we trawled through Derbyshire, visited so many places. It will be a place called Woodhouse, a wonderful magnesium limestone. The buildings will be stunning when completed."

"And would you say that has been the most exciting commission you've taken on?" Jennifer asked.

Smith raised his eyebrows.

"Well, the highest prestige," she amended.

"Perhaps, although services to discovery, to the birth of geology as a true science must be the ultimate in calling," Smith started. "Although for society ladies, perhaps saving the springs of Bath will be of more interest. Did I ever tell you about that, Gaskin?"

"No, that's not come up in our correspondence."

"It was some time ago, why it could be thirty years now. Have you been to Bath, Mrs Gaskin?"

"I'm afraid not."

"Ah, the continental upbringing."

"You shall have to go sometime," Jennifer advised. "Stunning place. They say the waters are very good for your health."

"Certainly potent," Smith laughed."And there are hot springs for bathing. But imagine the horror of the Bath Corporation when the hot springs suddenly stopped. And all those paying customers lining up, and not a drop of heated water to be had. Some of the members of the board were of a mind that a nearby coal mine was to blame. Nonsense of course, but they would not be told, even after I had discovered the root of the problem. I had to go to the coal mine to prove what was already obvious."

"Was it sabotage?"

"What a mind you have, Mrs Gaskin!" Smith burst out, amused by her innocent question. "But no, only sabotage by nature. The cause of the blockage was a bone."

"Someone had dropped a bone?"

"No. It was already there but had shifted. It took some time to get the corporation to agree to me having a bore dug."

Jennifer looked horrified. "You dug up the Bath hot spring?"

"Well, just a bore. And the spring wasn't working, the cause had to be found. Oh, let me tell you, it was hot down there as we dug down, down, down past limestones and clays, working down through time. We got to the spring and found a large bone, something from an ox or some such creature. It had been down there all that time, and had become crystallised. Anyway, for whatever reason it had moved and rolled into the channel and blocked the hot water. The spring water was going elsewhere and the great and the mighty..." Smith paused for a moment, a scowl crossing his face. "Well, those people who are our betters, they could not take the waters. But the bone was removed and the day was saved."

"You saved Bath."

"One could say that. It's a fine city. I drew my first map of the area." His chair creaked as he lent back to reflect on the incident.

Mairi looked at the fossilised sea creature she held in her hand. The candlelight flicked on the table, making the warm light dance across the lines of the dome. Once alive, washed by salt water and beating to the back and forth of the tide. To be turned to rock and dug up in an Oxfordshire field and given to a dairymaid to weigh out her butter. She snapped out of her thoughts and looked up abruptly, finding herself staring directly at her husband on the opposite side of the table, who had been quietly observing her illuminated by candle light. Her question fell from her thoughts momentarily. "Why were there... rather why are there dead sea creatures in Oxfordshire? It's no where near the sea."

"Ah ha," Smith boomed, ignoring the fact Mairi had been speaking to Stephen. "When they were alive, the world was a very different place to how it looks today."

"Like a glacier in Forge Valley?"

Everyone but Mary Ann perked up at this comment. Jennifer looked pleased and the men were perhaps a little surprised that this girl trained in languages and accomplishments was beginning to ponder on questions that usually engrossed men with little hammers and bottles of acid, striding out in the countryside.

"You did suggest a route for our walk around Hackness," Jennifer reminded Smith.

"Indeed. And so you see, Stephen," Smith continued, looking to his fellow geologist. "This is a good start. I know you are only just newly married, but for a wife to take an interest in her husband's studies, why it is a good thing. What will be started with a Chedworth bun..."

"You never gave me a Chedworth bun," Mary Ann muttered. "Although we had other diversions to bring us together." The select dining group looked up to her seat at the table, where she sat with her soup spoon in her mouth in a slightly suggestive manner. Jennifer hid an amused smile behind a napkin. She'd heard some gossip about Smith's wife. Mairi looked blank, but she'd spent enough time on the periphery of her mother's world to know what Mary Ann meant. What kind of woman had Mr Smith married?

Thanks to a previous late night of talking, and much fresh sea air and hearty walking today, no one wanted to stay up till the following morning discussing the very origins of the earth they walked upon. It was decided naturally that all would retire after dinner. It was rather ridiculous how playing a charade for virtual strangers took precedent over everything else, Mairi reflected as they went upstairs. It wouldn't do to be rude to their hosts, and she supposed in coming here she had accepted by default that the man she had been married to would be able to share her bed. She didn't want to, and in fact the position she had stupidly put herself into only really dawned on her just now.

She was glad that they were the last to ascend, so that no one would see the awkwardness upon the landing and wonder, gossip, or worse still feel as though they could question it the following day. Stephen carefully shut the door before looking to her. "I'm not..."

Mairi raised her eyebrows.

"That is to say, I will sleep on the chair," he gestured to an armchair squeezed in next to the window. "This is only a marriage by legality, but Smith isn't to know that and their invitation and accommodations were offered as such. I don't know where..."

She almost felt affronted, perversely, as if to demand to know what was wrong with her. He was being a decent person, and she nodded demurely.

"I am not sure how you see things going forward. I confess I don't know myself, but I am confused even if you intend to come to Rosedale as my..."

"I do not know. I can't think beyond a day or so at the moment."

"Of course."

As she placed the fossil Smith had given her on the dresser, there was a thump against the wall. She raised a hand toward it, thinking of which direction every party had taken at the top of the stairs. "The Smiths..."

Stephen nodded.

There was a muffled gasp, some words indistinguishable through the wall, only sounds of speech, then some giggling followed by repetitive creaking. The silence in their own room only seemed to amplify the noise, and their own awkwardness. Lord, it hadn't taken long on getting upstairs, and William Smith an old man at that. Mairi had seen them of all ages chasing her mother and was not all that surprised.

Stephen Gaskin grew increasingly uncomfortable. Curse their mothers for getting them into this ridiculous situation. He was too much of a gentleman to take advantage of the situation, but to have to listen to the Smiths like this, and when they had guests in the house. He had heard talk that Mrs Smith was a bit wild, highly strung and needy, but given his connection to the family hadn't wished to take gossip too seriously. Hopefully they would go to sleep soon. Who knew what Mairi thought was happening; a young woman...

There was almost a whoop from the neighbouring room. Mairi coughed to stop herself laughing and couldn't help but look across at Stephen, who was trying to be the mature English gent who didn't react to this kind of nonsense. The whole thing was really rather comical. "Don't worry," she told him. "I've heard worse."

His eyes widened and he looked as though he didn't know whether to be horrified by her unladylike behaviour or laugh along with her. She didn't suppose Margaret Sleight would have ever come out with such vulgarities.

"My mother kept me apart from that world, please don't misunderstand me. She was very keen for me not to follow her in her line of... lifestyle. But it was unavoidable that I heard some things growing up. I'm not an innocent supping tea and tittering over needlework. In fact I'm sure I rather failed when your sister and Miss Sleight..."

The mention of her name made him look uncomfortable.

"I'm sorry, I speak out of turn and embarrass you. Perhaps if we could just aim to get along civily until it is decided quite what is to be done?"

"After Lincolnshire that's the very least I owe you, but please don't apologise. Whilst I have found aspects of you... alternative, shall we say, I've not been offended, despite what my mother may have ranted when this all started." He was interrupted by a thump on the wall and an audible exclaimation of 'goodness me!' by Mary Ann.

They looked at one another and the smiles were infectious.

"A truce perhaps?" He suggested.

"I was never at war with you."

"I understand, but..."

"Yes," she agreed. "We can be civil and get along. But goodness me, it is late."

"All the walking?"

"And the fresh sea air?"

"Indeed. Perhaps we should retire."

Mairi pulled one of the blankets off the bed, and with a pillow passed it across to him with no guilt that he would take the uncomfortable night. He turned his back whilst she loosened her stays and took her dress off, getting down to her shift and hoping neatly into bed. It had been aired and warmed by the maid whilst they had been at dinner, and the warmth from the hot water bottle still lingered. Mairi rustled down into the bed and curled up to sleep. She only had to close her eyes and she was gone.

1839
Rosedale

Dark, short days with low temperatures cut the mood of the first weeks. The colour palette contained grey skies and vegetation mostly browned off and stark, sleeping for winter. It was not the best introduction to a landscape, but it was the one the Gaskins had taken when they had moved into the small hamlet of Rosedale Abbey. Situated in the bottom of the great valley of Rosedale, the village sat on the banks of the River Seven, at a joining point between two small rivers, the Seven and Northdale Beck. As well as the waterways, Rosedale Abbey also marked the point where the valley head split into two parts. The major part of the valley rose up directly north, with the high top moorland of Blakey to the western rise. Beyond Blakey lay Rosedale's mirror valley, Farndale dipping down again further to the west. The minor off shot of the main Rosedale valley went up north-east, providing the source of Northdale Beck, and eventually steeply shooting up to the Rosedale Moors. South from the village, the valley continued following the path of the river, passing through wide tracts of open moorland past Hartoft and down to the village of Cropton. On the moorland tops the land was covered in heather, a scrubby tough shrub that would flower a delightful purple in the height of summer, but in winter was either brown or snow covered. Coming down the steep valley sides, Rosedale would become greener, with agricultural fields and small farms dotted here and there. Farmers tilled the earth of their land with horse drawn ploughs, to the dramatic background of sleep slopes, overlooked by the moorland and the beginning of open skies.

The lands, considered an estate of gentry, were owned by the Vanden-Harden family, who owned land and fine houses in several parts of the country. Varden Hall, in the centre of Rosedale Abbey, was a smart, and for them, relatively small property. It was used as something of a summer house and hunting lodge suited for outdoor pursuits. Stephen Gaskin had been employed by the family as land agent and surveyor. They were quite caught up in the mania for exploiting the mineral content of one's estates. Land agents employed on such a basis was something that William Smith himself had done, and undertaken many surveys in his younger days. The Vanden-Harden family was concerned they had neglected their more northerly estate and there was money to be made. Not that the family was short of funds, despite grumblings now that the free labour out in the West Indies had come to an end with the Abolition Act. No mind that the compensation paid out by parliament had been great. A fine folly and water feature had been built on their more civilised, lower-lying estate, but there was still a great deal of compensation money burning a hole in the patriarch's pocket. That and a desire to dig up the earth and sell it for whatever could be had driven him to consider if one ought to take more seriously the employment of staff managing the Rosedale estates, and a geologist-minded land agent had been sought. He still worried about money as if he were down to his last shillings, concerned that even if minerals were there, it would cost much to extract. His agent advised on leases of the land should mineral wealth be found, for there were always companies keen to mine who did not have the landownership to match the desire. That way an income could be generated with no hassle or work.

The Gaskins had a small cottage just to the south of the main village, with a fine view across the small River Seven, to go with the job. The couple's possessions, Mairi's being in the majority, were taken by horses and carts from the train station at Pickering, and up into Rosedale that way. With the short cold days and snow-white of the moorland tops, she did not dare to go out for her long wandering explorations as she had enjoyed in Lincolnshire, and restricted herself mostly to household activities. Mairi was living a very different lifestyle to the one she had enjoyed with her Mamma, but she had some financial flexibility, and had no intention of dragging herself through days of laundry every week. She had her dirty linens promptly in baskets and sent to a washerwoman in the village. She managed the cleaning of the upstairs rooms – perhaps in part to keep any outsiders from prying, for she and Stephen naturally had separate rooms and rather separate lives – and also as she was enjoying her privacy. For a little work, it was a pleasure to avoid having a household of staff about the place at all times. A local woman came in regular to help with the management of the kitchen and some cooking, but even in this Mairi learned and worked at herself. She would smile when kneading bread, wondering what her mother would say about her situation. This was perhaps not the married dream she had been aiming for with all her conniving and plotting, but this was how things had worked out.

Despite all this seeming bliss and simplicity, Mairi was lonely. She was neither rude nor haughty, yet she was different from the other women, and outsiders always had a hard time settling in. She was not born to the area, spoke with an educated accent and clearly was considered a lady to their farmer's wives and dairymaids. Not so high up as to be aristocracy, for she was only married to a land agent, but she was not like folk round those parts. Far too beautiful for one, and as some husbands watched her walk by, wives would scowl and fold their arms and nod, clearly it was just the looks that had caught such a sensible fellow as Mr Gaskin, for what would such a young woman know otherwise? Talk had it that the couple had been married in the summer just gone, so they supposed there was still time for children to start appearing, but a woman without children was to be regarded with a touch of suspicion, especially one whose background seemed incomprehensible to them.

For a time Mairi felt as though her only friend in Yorkshire was Mrs Jennifer Burton-Waugh, who was a delight in her long letters that came and were replied whenever the weather allowed for movement. At times when the snows came, it felt as though Sowerby, down in the Vale of Mowbray, where the widow lived, was in another country and another time to the world Mairi now found herself in.

She had unpacked most things into the house to arrange for comfortable living, although there were some of her mother's personal items, including a keepsake box. The very sight of it brought back so many memories that she couldn't face to do anything with it. She kept that and some other objects on a small table in the corner of her room, unable to touch them, and wished she could get in touch with her mother, if only for one last time, to tell her of all that had happened and to let her know just how much she was missed. The apartment at York still retained some of the furniture, but nothing personal or too valuable, as it was rented out for the time being with local solicitors acting as agent on her behalf.

As well as her letters, her reading and her sketches of indoor still life, Mairi also played a lot on the piano. It was, admittedly, a great luxury and had been a burden to transport to the cottage. It was an indulgence she blessed every day. Word soon got around that a pianist had moved into the village, and there was some discussion as to whether she ought to be asked to be the new organist at church, especially after the proposed rebuild. Mrs Drying, a wrinkled woman of undetermined age had been playing at church in her own stodgy way and intended to continue thus until her fingers no longer moved, said that no foreign young slip of a lass should be making a spectacle of herself in God's hallowed corridors. And so Mairi remained a mere member of the congregation on Sundays, quite happy to pay lip service to it all, whilst lost in her own thoughts.

Now the days were growing longer, the earth was greening up and new shoots were appearing on the trees and hedgerows. Birds made busy selecting nesting sites, snowdrops were already past their bloom, and other spring flowers were powering up to take over. Out in the fields in the bottom of the dale the sheep, heavy with lamb were at the point of birthing. There was still snow on the moor tops, but it was hard, encrusted old snow lain down weeks, if not months ago, and becoming all the more patchy.

With the laundry outsourced, Mairi was able to plan the chores she did take up in order to leave herself with good blocks of hours to do as she pleased. And now that the days were longer, the skies bright with sunshine, and the snow from the lower levels all gone, she took her walking boots out once again and set to exploring. For here was an entirely new world she knew nothing of.

At first she walked up the main valley head, Rosedale, and the source of the River Seven, past green fields with farmers dofting their caps to her and the wives given her bewildered and slightly suspicious stares. They all knew who she was, this strange woman, not in a position of idle gentry, and yet educated and from a different world to their own.

She went out walking for hours, with a bag across her shoulders, and some of the shepherds had made mention of seeing her up on higher ground, crouched in the rough heather, sketching out the landscape before them. Vanden-Harden had picked a fine class of folk to work as land agents, not the usual educated farming stock, but perhaps that would be a change for the better, they whispered tentatively amongst themselves. Maybe improvements could be made. They made a pair, despite the fact they were rarely seen together, setting off on long, lonesome walks, bags slung across shoulders and eyes to the ground, looking for some illusive thing.

As she repeated the walks, her confidence for the land grew, and Mairi took herself out onto the tops above Rosedale. Striding out onto Blakey Moor, she came upon the well-churned cart route over the moors, thinner with snow and thicker with slush. At first she was almost blinded by the white brilliant snow mounds battering the sunlight directly at her. The air was thin, cold and crisp, and distinctly brilliant. There was nothing higher. Here were great spreads of open moorland on top of the world, seemingly going on forever.

The slush soon soaked into her skirts and chilled her feet and she found herself shivering. Little fool, she was not dressed properly for these conditions. And out far from the village or any farm. Squinting along the skyline, she noted what first she assumed to be great piles of snow, then realised was what looked like a farmstead. Right out in the moors, open to all elements. Mairi increased her pace, hoping the farmer's wife might let her sit by the fire for a little while. As she grew closer she realised it was an inn, and not a farm. There was a great, steaming cluster of ponies, all togged up in their baskets of coal, gathering for a rest and a feed before they continued on their journey. The drivers stood together, mugs of some hot beverage steaming, as they talked to a tall young man. As Mairi approached, the cluster of men turned to observe her, baffled and amused to discover a lone female wandering the moors in the melting snow. The bottom of her skirts were sodden with the slush and peaty earth she must have trudged through.

"Afternoon, Miss," the younger man left the group, striding out to help her through the shovelled pathway up to the inn. "Are you lost?"

"No, no, just out walking."

"It's just we don't see many walkers out this time of year."

"What, people don't care to get out and see the stunning land they live in?"

Mairi almost looked fevered with her rosy red cheeks and glittering eyes. The young man looked a little wary of her, worried for her health, as if she might be quite mad.

"I reckon yon be Gaskin's wife," one of the pony driver's commented, his pipe gripped steady between keen teeth. "I heard tell you and yon husband were fond on wandering in circles."

She was surprised she was so easily identified, but then she supposed strangers stood out, and gossip moved fast. "I'm not lost, I assure you. I hadn't thought that there might still be so much snow on the tops."

"Aye," another man sucked in breath. "Best way to learn your land is to walk it."

"I didn't mean she were lost," the man with the pipe grumbled. "Only that they go walking without a destination. They end up back where they started."

"Oh aye."

"Mrs Gaskin," The young man caught back her attention. "Perhaps you'd like to take a break and warm yourself by the fire in the inn before you head back down to t'Abbey? My wife is just inside and I'm sure she'd be glad of someone new to talk to."

"You run the inn?" She was a little surprised, he hardly looked older than herself, and to be running such an establishment.

"Apologies, Callum Iredale," he introduced himself. "Just this way."

As they approached the front door, two little matching girls of three or so came pelting out of the building, squealing and laughing. One of the girls' hats came loose, revealing a head of thick dark curls. The other ran for a mound of shovelled snow, grabbing a fist full and throwing it at her sister. Horrified that the other had the better of her, the hatless child ran at the other, and like a charging bull, flung them both bodily into the snow.

A young maid ran out of the door, still pulling shawls and boots on, a stumbling hazard as she focused on feet and shoulders simultaneously. "You two, will you watch yourselves. I only just got those coats dry from last time!" She lost her breath as she ran into Callum.

"One thing at a time, eh, Annie?" he suggested as he helped her back onto his feet.

"Yes, of course." She nodded, not meeting his eye, before running off after the two little girls.

Inside and down a corridor, the temperature increased dramatically and Mairi was swiftly greeted by a roaring fire. Close by a little boy, perhaps a year or so older than the girls, sat playing with a spinning top. On a wooden spindle-backed chair sat a plump young woman who clearly was mother given by the matching dark, curly hair. She was dressed in cheap but respectable dress with apron and mop cap, a woollen shawl about her body and crossed over her chest for warmth. On her knee she bounced a giggling one year old, who held a rag doll in one hand and with the other kept trying to grab fistfuls of her mother's hair, which spilled out from her cap as if it had a mind of its own.

The woman, Mrs Iredale, looked up as Mairi entered, her eyebrows popping up sharply, and she burst out with no thought of propriety: "Goodness me, Miss, you look a fright with the cold. Come site by the fire."

"This is Mrs Gaskin," Callum introduced her as Mairi took the seat opposite the woman. "I think she could do with a bowl of stew. "She's been out walking and the weather got the better of her."

"Oh yes, I've heard about your wandering."

Mairi looked horrified. "Has the entire valley been discussing me?"

Mrs Iredale laughed gaily. "Of course. But nothing bad, don't you worry. And don't mind those old men out there. They've nowt else better to discuss. To be fair, nothing of note has happened for the last six months."

"I'd best be back out to see to those old men," Callum said, catching a smile and a slight nod from his wife. "Mrs Gaskin, it was nice to finally make your acquaintance."

Mrs Iredale pulled herself up from the chair, already feeling her next pregnancy trying at her back. "Would you just mind Sonneta Jane whilst I fetch you something," she said rather than asked as she thrust the tot at Mairi before disappearing into the depths of the inn.

Mairi looked in horror at the small child, clearly a girl from the name but it was hard to tell from appearance only. The grubby cream, worn-out layered clothes she was in offered no distinct clue either. Mairi had no more experience with small children that viewing them from a distance as they were taken out in perambulators. She felt as though she was holding dripping laundry, from the way she held the child under the arms, grasping it by the chest, and all its clothes hanging loosely down. The little girl, a head full of thick flowing golden locks, was quite different from the twins she had seen earlier. How incapable and unwomanly I am, Mairi thought. Surely children were the natural premise of women and yet she didn't know what to do with the thing. Little Sonneta Jane giggled warmly at the stranger.

"Aye, she's taken to you right enough," Mrs Iredale declared as she returned, setting a bowl of stew onto the table near to Mairi's elbow, blind to the slopping over the edge. She added a hunk of bread to the side. She straightened up and stretched out her back, laughing as she saw how Mairi held Sonneta Jane. "Why, you look like me when our Daniel was first born. But then you don't have children yet, do you?" She took the tot from Mairi. "I can't say I was that good with babies, even though I'd helped my mother with all my siblings. Before, my mother was always there. With Daniel I was quite alone. Callum's mother passed a long time ago."

Mairi leaned forward, surprised and hopeful by a patch of common ground, no matter how sad. "Your mother has passed as well?"

"Oh no, she's away in Canada," Mrs Iredale explained.

Mairi hid her disappointment.

"They went, my mother and my father and all my brothers and sisters, when me and Callum were wed, and I've never seen them since. I get letters from my sister, and she swears she's coming back, but well, the passage isn't all that cheap and I wonder if sooner or later a young man will catch her eye, and then that will be that. It does make me sad that my mother has never met all these little ones. Maybe she never will." She hugged Sonneta Jane close to her. "But then I have four little ones and the inn to mind, so I don't get all that much time to feel sorry for myself." She looked wistful for a moment before her eyes turned to the table. "Eat it up, you'll feel better for it."

"Yes, of course." Mairi turned to the food. It was hot and mostly vegetables with a little meat in it, but it was good. Her body flamed back into life with the warmth.

"How are you liking Rosedale then, Mrs Gaskin?"

Mairi chewed on the bread. "I am liking it more now that spring is coming."

Mrs Iredale laughed. "Yes, I think winter time is a bad time to move in somewhere new. That why you walk about so much? Getting to know the place?"

"In part, yes."

"Well, enjoy it. You won't have the time nor the energy when the babies start coming." Illuminated by the fire, Mrs Iredale sat and stroked her daughter's hair. "Not that you aren't all a joy to me," she cooed.

Mairi turned back to what was left of her food. She did not know what to say in response. It was not the first time she had felt a fraud. She always quickly pushed the sensation down and ignored it, for the alternative was far worse: reflect on how she was going to run the rest of her life. Make a decision. Both her grandmother and her Aunt had pressed the point, perhaps a little too much for Mairi was avoiding replying to their letters now but the fact of the matter was she couldn't hide from her grief and the rest of her life as Stephen Gaskin's extremely bizarre houseguest posing as his wife. It wasn't fair to either of them, and they would both miss out on life's opportunities the longer they continued in this charade in penance for who knew what.

Increasingly it was harder to just swallow down the worry and think distractedly of something else. A week after she had taken respite at the Iredale's she was still worrying about the sight of the children, and what a traditional marriage was supposed to entail. Did Gaskin not wish for that? Or was it a case of children and domesticity would bring about too much mess and distraction from his good work. Perhaps having a false wife served him well as he could be left alone to his geology. Aside from his paid employment as land agent he worked on mapping and writing papers for publications and societies. Things that only brought one off payments and could not sustain someone wholly, but things that were his true calling in life. Perhaps Stephen was reaping great benefits from her mother's odd arrangements, with an unpaid housekeeper installed and a shield from any potential matchmaking.

And what of Mairi? She did not know. This could not be right for her, but the simplicity of this new lifestyle was suiting her very well and she did not miss the Continental courts and their finery. A light breeze came up the valley and rustled through her hair as if to question her certainty. She closed her eyes. Very well, perhaps there were some things she missed. She could still play the piano here in Rosedale, but lessons with great musical minds were an impossibility now. Such things would have been enjoyable. The great feather beds had been more comfortable than how she slept in the cottage. An image of her mother throwing her head back and laughing at some comment Mairi had made suddenly flashed into her mind. The sunlight bounced off her mother's lustrous curls. It all seemed very real and Mairi gasped out in pain. Like a great unexpected wave, it came from behind and brought her to her knees with the reality that her mother was actually dead. Not only dead but gone from existence. Wiped out.

Knelt in the heather, Mairi leaned forward, shackled with gasping sobs that wretched their way up through her body. The tears poured forth and she could hardly see through the deluge. Oh, her poor Mamma. How could she abandon her at this point? She was only just eighteen years of age. It hardly seemed any age at all, even though she knew people married before eighteen. Sometimes she felt older, aged as the earth. Something about losing a parent forced a sudden maturing.

She remained like that for some time. As the waves of grief subsided, she was able to sit back on her haunches, wipe at her face with her shawl and see clearly back down the valley. This morning she had followed the eastern split of Rosedale, heading up Northdale Head, ambling by the beck and following tracks up between green agricultural fields. The track had then started to pull up the hillside towards the beginning of the heather moorland. Towards the head the beck had split into its two originating tributaries, and Mairi had gone up the steep sides of the eastern slope. Behind her the ground continued to rise, albeit at a gentler pace, and the horizon was open; a sea of hibernating heather scrubland. Close by there was an empty, small stone building that looked like a shooting hut. Something that would be used by the landed gentry, most likely the Vanden-Harden family and associates during the hunting season, but at this time of year it was left cold and empty. It would perhaps only take her forty minutes to hike back down to the village, yet it felt so remote up here, isolated and cut off from humanity.

Mairi let out a great sigh, took a handkerchief from her bag and emptied her nose in a most unladylike but necessary way, before wiping her eyes again and looking about her. The clouds in the great open sky shifted and the sun suddenly fell unrestricted upon the dale. The heat from the rays was delicious, Mairi closed her eyes to savour the sense of being warm and protected.

Somewhere a little further up the slope from her she heard a shifting movement in the heather, and assuming it was just a sheep or a grouse looking to take flight, paid it no more mind. There was a pause then the movement started again and transformed into most definite footsteps accompanied by the sound of bristling heather stems pulling and scratching at passing fabric.

Mairi twisted to look over her shoulder and was shocked to see a woman standing a few mere metres from her. A few moments ago she had been certain she was alone on this hillside. How could this woman have gotten so close in a few footsteps?

Mairi twisted in her seated position to better face the stranger and nodded cautiously saying a good morning. There was something odd about the woman, and not only her appearance. The woman had neither cap nor bonnet on, nor had she so much as brushed her hair let alone attempted to pin it up. Her silvery-blonde locks, and very long they were as well, floated gently on the upland breeze, weighted down by what looked like the occasional moss green ribbon tied into the nest merely as decoration and to serve no function whatsoever. The woman's dress looked layered, tattered and patched and undeniably of none of the fashions Mairi knew of. Her very presence made Mairi look intensely normal, conservative and unadventurous.

She opened her mouth to speak to the woman, then wondered if she might be one of these gypsy people she had heard about. Maybe she didn't even speak English.

"You don't look like her."

The woman's voice had an almost childish lit to it. It sounded local, and yet... the question was out of Mairi's mouth before she could consider herself. "Are you a vagabond?"

This sparked off a series of giggles, and the woman took her hands from the deep pockets in her skirts as if showing her hands would prove she was safe. "Oh no, I've lived here a long time. Well, I don't live here, I'm from one of the dales over that way," she waved idly off at the horizon. "But I like to come here from time to time."

"To Rosedale?"

"To the well."

"The well?" Mairi was perplexed. "But there's no well here and surely there's water in the other dales. Which one is it you come from?"

"I come to Job's Well," the stranger said, ignoring the questions. "It's just down here. Follow me." She strode boyishly through the heather, striding confidently down the slope. Mairi staggered up onto her feet, and without a thought to her personal safety or what could be further down the bank, she obediently followed the stranger.

She did not get far before she jumped down off a small ledge hidden in the heather. Mairi followed her route and came around to the mouth of a small secluded spring. The water seemingly came off the ledge and pattered down as a miniature waterfall into a little drop pool where vibrant green mosses clustered around the edges. The water seeped into the undergrowth, leading a boggy wetland track down the slope towards the little beck.

"This is Job's Well," Mairi said quietly, reaching out and putting her fingers to the clear water. It was icy cold.

"It turns things to stone."

Mairi snapped her hand away. The stranger giggled. "Not that quick. It takes a few weeks. Look."

What had first looked like plants caught up in the pattering water, or merely part of the rock and earth at first glance, now showed themselves as what looked like mud sticks dangling in the waterfall. They had been tied with string to outcropping stones or branches of heather at the top of the ledge.

"I hung these last year," the woman explained, cutting one down with a little knife she had out of a pocket like a flash. "Lucky rabbit's foot." She held up something that just looked like a turd-shaped rock, before placing it on the moss. "Or this."

She took down a long slim piece and passed it to Mairi. It was stone, and slick and wet from being in the water so long. Mairi turned it upside down, or perhaps the right way up depending on how it had been hung, and looked at the forms, and how the stem split into parts towards the top. An almost bushier centre piece and slender strips. "A grass head," she breathed.

The woman grinned. "Yes. I hung it last summer."

"It's a petrifying well, isn't it?" she realised. "I've heard about these places. They turn things to stone."

"That's what I told you. Here, you try."

The woman had taken a ribbon from her hair and was tying it to the ends of one of the strings that was left. With a sudden spark of child-like joy, Mairi wanted to add something to the collection, and was searching through the contents of her bag for something small that might hang well. She pulled out a pencil and brandished it like a flame.

"Yes, we can hang that," the woman said, taking it from Mairi's fingers and hanging it in the well mouth. Mairi offered her the petrified grass stem back but the woman waved it off. "No, you keep it. That way you'll remember to come back."

The two women moved a little from the spring, and sat side by side in the heather staring back down the valley. Mairi was so intensely curious about this individual, yet was too polite to plough into her many questions. And so they sat in silence, watching the atmosphere and the bursts of sunlight moving over the patchwork of fields hemmed in by acres of heather.

Something occurred to Mairi and she looked sharply at the stranger. "You said I don't look like her."

The stranger looked straight back at her, her expression blank as if it should have been obvious. "No, you don't."

"Who are you talking about?"

"With your hair and your face you look more like her younger sister," she added illusively. "Although I can see you're nothing like Clara. You don't have the sight."

"The sight?"

"But I can see something of her in you."

"Who is *she*?"

"Eleanor."

"Eleanor?" Mairi paused to mull over the name, thinking over the women she had fleetingly been introduced to, those ladies who had come to call when they had first moved to Rosedale Abbey, the other characters she had only heard mention of. "I don't think I've met..."

"Eleanor Hurst."

Mairi shook her head slowly. "I've not met a woman by that name."

"You'll know by her Scots' name. MacCaskill."

"Eleanor MacCaskill? What, you know my grandmother?" Mairi sounded shocked. "Are you talking about my grandmother? You know her?"

The stranger looked straight ahead again. "I knew her as a girl."

"As a girl?" Mairi laughed. "That's not possible, you're nowhere near old enough."

"I'm as old as the hills," the stranger said in a joking manner, wiggling her fingers. She stopped, then hopped to her feet. "I must away now." She said, turning and looking up to the top of the valley where the moorland proper stretched off. Mairi followed her gaze and for a moment was sure she saw a little figure watching them from the distance.

"Will I see you again?"

"Perhaps."

"Here at the well?"

"Perhaps," she shrugged. "Or if you find yourself at Commondale I can show you my moors." She said it in such a way, possessive and proud of the delights she held over that way.

"Perhaps I will. I'm only new to the area and I'm sure I'll explore..." Mairi darted up as the stranger started to stride away from her through the heather. She held onto her petrified grass stem. "And who should I ask after?"

"Ask after no one."

"But what is your name?"

The stranger stopped, and grinning looked back at Eleanor MacCaskill's only granddaughter. "I am Atheleys," she said.

There was a small desk in the corner of Mairi's room. It was the depository of her writings and sketches. Increasingly her room felt more like a study than a place of sleep, and she guarded the room and its management jealously. No one was permitted to enter to clean it or enter to fetch bed linens that needed to be washed. Sleeping was one thing, but it was her sketches and her notes on explorations that were absorbing her attention. She sat at her little desk by the window, gently lit by spring time sunlight, and pondered on the things she was learning.

Shelving was fitted to the back of the desk, where pens and ink, along with small, seemingly insignificant treasures could be stored. Mairi had ceased in her writing for the day, and had taken down the Chedworth Bun William Smith had gifted her last year in Scarborough. She turned it about in her hands, thinking that a long time ago it had actually been a living creature. Now it was stone. Placing it on her letters as a paperweight, she reached across and took the petrified grass stalk.

The seed head at the top was almost formed as a great drop, but then as the lowest point when hung, this was where the water had dripped off. The slow, final point where the sediment had been left behind. It was smooth like water flow along the shaft of grass. She wondered if she cracked it open, what she would find inside.

She was so absorbed in her rocks that she did not hear the creak on the stair. Stephen had returned home, it being late in the afternoon, and had found himself drawn away from the study and upstairs. The door to Mairi's room had carelessly been left wide open. She formed quite the picture, illuminated by sunlight, her blonde hair tousled from the walking, and her mind and attention completely absorbed by the contents of her desk. Despite their pitiful start together, Mairi and Stephen had fallen into something of a respectful routine, something akin to being fellow lodgers. Mairi stood as something of an unpaid housekeeper for her right to live in the property. Nothing had been spoken of or agreed, and whilst it was fine for the short term, he was still at a loss as to broach the subject of what they were going to do about their futures.

Framed by the doorway, it could have been a Dutch painting of quiet study. He wondered what the long stick she held aloft in her fingers was, and couldn't help himself but to go to the room.

Mairi jumped a little as she came out of her thoughts, and looked to the doorway where Stephen Gaskin stood. He filled the space, having to hunch his head down into his shoulders for the frame was low set. "Oh."

"You have made a discovery?" He nodded towards the stick, which now on closer inspection looked like a stone.

"Atheleys gave it to me, up at Northdale Head the other day."

"Atheleys?"

"Yes, she said she's from over Commondale way. Bit of a strange woman, but she was very nice." Mairi paused, her eyes back to the grass stalk. "She'd hung some things up in Job's Well."

"Job's Well?"

Mairi broke out into a smile. "Everything I say seems to cause you questions just now."

"I've heard of neither Atheleys nor Job's Well."

She reached out with the grass, offering it to him to examine. Stephen stepped into the room, able to straighten fully again and accepted the slender rock. Cool and incredibly smooth. "It feels like flowstone."

"It's a grass seed head. Job's is a petrifying well."

"I see." He held it upright and he could see how it may once have been a slender-stalked grass head, with thin blades of leaves coming up the sides. It had bulked out and lost its definition as the sediments had quickly layered on over its form. "I've not heard of Job's Well. I haven't explored this region as much as I would have liked for personal interest. There is the job of the land agent and also the mineral surveys I am working on in the main head of Rosedale."

Mairi lowered her eyes. "I know I am in the lucky position of not following a profession." She abruptly gasped and put her hand to her mouth. "But I have neglected my own meagre tasks. I haven't started on the supper yet."

He smiled lop sidedly. "No matter. I found something today, nothing petrified but man-made of a sort. Let me fetch it from the study."

He was gone for a minute at most, then returned with a dark, hard piece of rock in his hand. It looked like a splurge of lethargic fat bubbles frozen in time. Placing it in Mairi's hand, he stepped back and seated himself on the side of her bed, too busy in discussing finds to remotely think of the impropriety of the situation.

It was surprisingly heavy, and overall an unattractive piece.

"It is the by-product of an industrial process."

Mairi held it up to the light as if that would help. A piece of slag then. "I didn't realise there were metal furnaces here."

"It's not metal, although I confess I first thought it was from iron smelting. It's a by product of glass production."

"Glass?"

"Three hundred years ago there was an illegal glass furnace here. A French one."

"The French were here making glass in secret?" It hardly sounded credible.

Stephen hadn't taken it that seriously either the first time he had been told. He had been walking south of Rosedale Abbey, first to visit one of the tenants who had submitted a complaint about a barn roof. Once the inspection was complete, he had continued south along one side of the valley before randomly deciding to head down through fields and broadleaf forest to the river. He had decided he would walk up the other side of the river-cut valley to stretch towards the open moorland. Crossing over the river, he had seen a young lad, perhaps eight or nine whom he later learned was Alan Fletcher. The lad had been at a loose end, avoiding chores whilst tossing pebbles and twigs into the river. Stephen had provided a fresh distraction, and he had cheekily hopped up from his rock and followed the tall land agent across the river, chattering that he was going to be the man's local guide, and a very good one he would be too, for his grandfather had told him all the tales of the valley.

Stephen had tolerated him, although not engaged that much, hoping the lad would grow bored and wander off. The tactic didn't work. They had started up the other side of the valley, wading through a wide swath of fresh bracken. The old chestnut-brown bracken boughs from last year still lingered within the mass. Coming out to a grassy clearing, Stephen decided to take a break, and also to test the earth a little to see what was here. He had not dug all that deep before he had come across the piece of slag Mairi was now examining. Knocking the dirt off, Alan Fletcher had grown excitable and told him that they were digging in one of the glassholes.

"Glass?"

"Aye, glass. They used to make glass here. It were right illegal and the law came down on them and chased them all away."

"Nonsense," Stephen had told him. "There will have been metal smelting here at one point. Look, there are plenty of trees about to keep the fires going."

"You need fires for glass an'all," said Alan. "Me Granda told me all about it. You come and ask him if you don't believe me."

"Your grandfather? And what name does he go by? Where does he live?"

"Carter Fletcher's the name. We live over in Hartoft End. It's not far, come on!"

And with that the scamp was charging back off through the bracken.

Stephen straightened up from his freshly dug pit. "I didn't mean right this moment."

The boy ignored him, disappearing from view. The only sign of the child was the crashing through the bracken. Sighing, Stephen kicked the earth back into the hole, gathered his items and strode off after the lad.

Hartoft End, as the lad called it, was really only a couple of stone cottages by Rigg End Farm. The Fletchers rented the cottage shunted out the back and around the corner, with a well kept front yard upon which chickens scratched and rustled at one another. There was a small vegetable garden around the back. Food prices were on the rise again, and although country folk managed a little better than town people in that they could grow some of their own, no family could be self sufficient for every need. There was always something that needed to be purchased. The father and older sons laboured on the farm to earn the keep. Mother ran the house; looked after the still-growing brood of children; sold eggs and took in extra laundry when she could. Alan probably ought to be helping someone or doing something, but had an uncanny ability at disappearing just at the moment of command issuing.

The grandfather, Carter Fletcher, was dozing by the fireside when Alan clattered in without a moment's thought to etiquette. The main room in the cottage was small, with a large open fire gently crackling, surrounded by a frame of blackened wood stocks as thick as railway sleepers. On top of the rustic fireplace stood a couple of pieces of green glassware that caught the sunshine from the window, drawing them out of the shadows. Over the fire directly hung a turf-pan, rather like a large round metal skillet with lid. It was suspended over the fire by its own oversized handle on a hook. To the side of the fire stood a tea kettle on a metal stand, with a long pair of black fire tongs propped on the side. The old man was lame in his right leg, on account of an old farming accident that had not improved with draughts and cold winters. These days he tottered about with a stick. Walking any great distance was too much. He woke with a snort and start to the noise of his grandson, and raising a gnarled, vein-embossed hand to his forehead, he leant forward in his chair.

"Alan, you young good-for-nothing!" he exclaimed, more tenderly that the words might have signified. "Your mother was hoping you'd help her carry t'shopping. She's been away up to Rosedale this last five minutes or so. Can't have been long, I'd just closed my eyes..."

"You were snoring away. More like half the hour," Alan laughed.

"You rascal! If had my young legs I'd be after you, and that's without a doubt."

Carter lent forward further out of the chair, trying to reach for his grandson to clip him around the ear, but Alan was sat just out of reach.

"Grandda, I've brought a man to see you."

"A man, what man?" Carter looked horrified as if he had been caught with his hair unbrushed, and suddenly sat rod-straight in his chair, patting his waistcoat down. He saw the tall figure in the doorway, and leaned forward again, squinting at the figure. "I don't believe we've met before, have we sir?"

"Might I come in?"

"God bless me, of course. I thought the lad had shown you in. Alan, what're at? Go fetch that chair and bring here round fire so we might talk. No, don't you bother, I'll do it..."

Stephen had seen the chair the old man was gesturing at. When he saw how the man would struggle to walk when he stood up, he went and fetched the chair himself. "Mr Fletcher?"

"Aye, that's me, Carter Fletcher as is."

"I'm Stephen Gaskin, I..."

"Oh, I know who you are," the old man interrupted. The land might be sparsely populated, but there was generally not a lot doing, and anything from a man falling over in the street to a new purchase of sheep was gossiped up and down the length of the valley. Carter would be talking of his distinguished visit for weeks to come. "New land agent for the Vanden-Harden family, am I not right? And I'm told you have an interest in the rocks."

"That is correct," Stephen nodded as he sat down opposite Carter Fletcher by the fire.

The old man sucked on his teeth. "And a pretty young wife to go with it all."

"I didn't know about a pretty wife," Alan spouted petulantly.

"Away with you and fetch those mugs," Carter scolded lightly. "You're too young a lad to be worrying about pretty young women, especially those that are married. Our Clare, that's the daughter-in-law mind, tells me fine music can be heard at times when she walks up to the village. Mrs Gaskin has a talent with the piano I understand. And she's French?"

"No," Stephen wondered how these rumours built up to change one into a very different person. He supposed there would not be much to talk about, so their arrival would have been something of an event for the locals. "My wife is an Englishwoman, in fact a Yorkshire woman. She was born in York," he explained, keen to remove the sense of the foreign. He'd travelled enough to know how country folk could be around those from another county, let alone another country. He didn't want Mairi being ostracised. It was not exactly high society in these parts, and although she had taken and returned some calls when they'd first moved here, most of the women in Rosedale Abbey and the surrounding valleys were busy with families and homes and farm life. There wasn't the idle society of afternoon tea one found in the towns.

"How odd folk mention France."

"She did spend some years growing up on the continent."

"That'll be right then," Carter nodded. "Not that there's any French folk left around here these days, they were chased out a long time back. But perhaps the Vanden-Harden women will enjoy her company when they come up. They'll be into all that French and music talk and what no, I've no doubt. Mind you, they only come up for a bit in the summer, so they won't be much company. From what my son says, yon wife of yours is settling in. Little strange and taken to walking, but friendly with the Iredales up on Blakey. He said he's seen her up there a couple of times when he's been up to fetch a bit of salt or sell something."

"The Iredales run the inn up on the ridge," Stephen half guessed. How strange it was to talk to people who knew more about his wife's doings than he did. People who had even met her.

"Aye, that's them. Bonny young family. Happy times now, good to hear of, for Callum's a good lad, and it were hard on him the way his father died like that." Carter paused to scratch his chin, trying to decide if he would need to shave later that day.

"Grandda, I brought him here because he didn't believe me about the glass holes."

"The glass holes?"

The old man sounded a little confused. Perhaps all that talk of glass had indeed been a young lad's imagination. "I was across from here, the other side of the river," Stephen explained. "I'd dug up some iron smelting slag. Your grandson was under the impression it's glass."

"Was he now? And what were you doing down at the river?" Carter asked, his attention focused on the boy. "You knew your mother was wanting help."

Alan scuffed his feet moodily on the floor. "Nothing."

"Nothing indeed. I know you and yon water. But aye, there were glass works across the way there at a time. People dig up bits of the slag now and then. Even now the odd bit pops up. None of this was in my lifetime, you understand. It was hundreds of years ago. My father told me as his father had told him. It were the French that came, master glass makers."

"What on earth brought the French all the way up here?"

"I think it's the very reason it is a long way from anywhere," Carter laughed. "There was only one man down in London who held the licence so they couldn't work down there. They'd come over to England to flee persecution. You know what the French are like for always fighting. Well, a man has to eat, has to learn his keep whatever his faults may be, so they headed north and found this quiet valley. Good site for a furnace, plenty of wood and off they went. They were at it for a good few years before those that make the rules and take the taxes found them out and chased them out of the dale."

Stephen took the dark piece of slag out of his bag and turned it over in his hands. "I stand corrected. I could have sworn this was a by-product of metal production."

"It does look very similar. You're not the first to have thought so, of those that even realise it's left over from industry and not a rock of the earth." Carter smiled. "Now, look here," he said, pushing against the wooden arms of his chair to bring himself to his feet. "By-products are all well and good, but it's the product that's of interest." He took down one of the glass goblets from the rough wooden mantelpiece and passed it to Stephen. "They were masters at what they did. Most of it were shipped out, but we had a couple of pieces in the family, like."

Stephen accepted the piece for examination. It was a well crafted goblet, glass of a deep forest green. Such a hue spoke of thick lush moss and dense foliage.

"They were all that colour, I'm told." Carter informed him as he took the goblet back. "We got a couple in the family and they're passed down. I always tell the stories of where they come from, so the children know. Folk don't know or aren't interested now, for there's no one living who remembers, and as there's no sign of the old furnaces, or no benefit, I don't suppose they feel it signifies. I doubt if they mixed much with the locals either, for there's no families with French names about the place. Although reverend tells me there's a few French listed in the old parish records he minds."

"It's an interesting story to know."

"Aye, I reckon you'd have liked it, enjoying your old things such as the rocks."

"Yes, although the rocks I study are far older."

"Can't be that much older," Carter reflected. "For it were hundreds of years ago that the French were here, and the world as the Lord himself made is only of a certain age. Not that I'm saying this glass is of an age of the Garden of Eden, you know."

Stephen shifted awkwardly in his seat and did not attempt to contradict the old man. He'd studied, seen and discovered too much with his own eyes to believe the world according to the Bible in a literal sense. It was an exciting age to be in for all the time great men of science were making discoveries. Enlightenment put into question the literal facts that the theologians dictated from the Bible. Outside of the scientific community people still followed their religion to the letter, and Stephen had learned from experience that sometimes it simply wasn't worth the effort nor the fall out to try and persuade them otherwise. Carter Fletcher was an old, traditional man quite certain of the material nature of the world and he would have just taken Stephen for a fool if he had tried to explain the geological timeline. So he said nothing.

He did not think he had yet found any like minds here in Rosedale, and was very grateful to still have his multiple correspondents with across the country. It had been something of a revelation to come home and discover Mairi pondering over a calcified piece of grass. Her focus on that and the Chedworth bun Smith had given her in Scarborough had been so absorbing. Stephen wondered about how she saw the world and how open she was to understanding the true nature of things.

At some point, a point that Mairi had missed, she had become a pupil. Not just a housekeeper but also someone to be taught. She stood with the little rock hammer in her hand, her brow creased, and wished she could remember what had first been said about sedimentary rocks. She would have to find those books in the household library and read up on the matter at night. If only William Smith was here to explain. She had liked the man, and he had a down-to-earth way of talking and explaining matters. Not that Stephen was confusing or overly elaborate in his speech, and Mairi was no dunce either, but he had a more polished, formally educated way of talking when he got into his subject matter. William Smith had been of the very earth he enthused over.

Stephen had not walked much in North Dale Head. It was the shorter and more easterly dale head coming off from Rosedale Abbey village. The tract was part of his remit and he needed to visit the farmers there, although more pressing on his mind was following Mairi out on one of these walks he kept hearing about. It felt wrong that he knew the least. He was also keen to see the petrifying well she had spoken of. He'd gathered up his usual kit when he was going out to survey the land, but on looking through his boxes, he had noticed an old rock hammer, in fact one of the first he had purchased when studying geology in the early days. He'd hesitated, wondering if she'd think him foolish in bringing something for her to use. Finally he picked impulsiveness over awkwardness and went all in for this expedition to the hills.

Mairi hadn't viewed the walk with such seriousness. Over the weeks of wandering on her own, she had found that she generally preferred the solitude. It granted one permission to go at an appropriate speed, stop when one wished, and also to be utterly disinterested and pass things by. There was a little more compromise required with a companion. Given that they soon would have been married a year, it was a little strange to reflect that they had never been out walking together. Two walkers very consciously walking in opposite directions.

Stephen proved to be a pleasant walking companion, even considerate enough to slow down so that Mairi didn't have to run. At first he had set off on his normal striding pace, but the man was a good deal taller than the wife. Mairi had found she had to break into bursts of jogging so that she didn't fall too far behind. Stephen had apologised, a little sheepishly, as he waited by a gate for her. His enthusiasm had gotten the better of him, but he would slow his pace. He managed the promise with his feet, but not with his words. The more he talked about the rocks in the dale and the make up of the earth beneath them, the more enthusiastic he grew. Mairi lost much of the gist early on, unfamiliar with a lot of the terminology. There had to be much variation beneath the surface for there to be so many words and so much to study. It couldn't all just simply be a uniform 'rock' and 'mud' that formed the ground.

When they reached Job's Well the sun had come out unobstructed. There was only the lightest of breezes. The disturbance through the heather set a skylark up ascending, twittering its summertime tune that formed the background of sun-blessed summer days. Mairi pointed out where the well was, and they headed across towards the spring. She held back as she thought she saw movement out of the corner of her eye, but when she looked back there was nothing there, neither man nor sheep. Yet she did not quite feel as though they were alone. She remembered Atheleys' vague promises of returning to the well, and perhaps they might meet sometimes. She wondered if Stephen's presence would put off the strange Commondale woman. She considered lingering back when Stephen had finished at the well and the call of his employment forced him back to his duties, but the idea was almost forgotten as they sat together in the grass and ate the food they had brought whilst looking back down the dale towards the village. Conversation meandered onto more general themes, and Mairi learned that although Stephen along with his siblings had all been born and raised in Lincolnshire, both of his parents in fact came from Whitby. His mother was not so fond of the town but there had been some trips back to the sea port to visit his father's side of the family when they had been growing up. He knew that his maternal grandmother was dead, but beyond that his mother was always so vague that they were never really sure if there were any living relatives from that side.

"My own grandmother lives just outside of Whitby," Mairi said. "I've only seen her since we came back to England, although I've written to her all through my childhood."

"You should go and visit. You're not all that far from Whitby. There's a horse drawn train from Pickering you could take. Get across to there and you'll have quite the journey."

Mairi pursed her lips. She wasn't sure if she was ready to see her own family yet. Letters came and pressed the issue that her mother had been dead a year and she could not remain in limbo. She needed to make a break from her false marriage and start her own life. Such observations were easy to ignore in letters and in written replies, but not so easy in person. "Perhaps in the autumn," she said vaguely. "I want to stay for the summer here in Rosedale. I'm waiting for the heather to bloom. I'm told it's glorious in August. I don't want to miss it."

"My parents have talked of going to Whitby in the summer. I will perhaps visit them then. I could always accompany you to your grandmother's..."

"We'll see." Mairi murmured. She pointed to a building in the near distance below them. "Is that the farm you needed to visit today?" she asked, drawing attention away from the subject of Whitby. She did not wish to see any of her family until she knew herself how she was going to resolve this situation.

"Yes. In fact I should get down there now, or there will be complaints I'm neglecting the tenants." He stood up, paused, then looked back to Mairi and offered his hand. "Will you come with me, come and meet these tenants? They're Longbottoms, I'm told a very jovial bunch."

Atheleys was all forgotten for the day as Mairi took Stephen's hand and allowed him to pull her to her feet. It would be good to meet some of the women away from the familiar blocks at Sunday church when Mairi was often left feeling as an outsider. Things had gotten easier with time, although there were a number who were uncomfortable with her odd ways. And more importantly that she did not behave as a wife ought to. Galivanting about across the hills like she was a wild hare. What an odd sort she was. And it had been a year, some wives muttered, looking pointedly at Mairi's neat waist, since the Gaskins had been married from what they understood. And that girl was no more with child than maiden Aunt Dixon over Glaisdale way. It wasn't right; it wasn't right at all.

Mairi was unaware of the worst of the gossip, but she picked up on enough to know that her circumstances made some of the villagers uncomfortable. Had they been pressed, they would have struggled to explain exactly why. She tried not to create a spectacle of herself, or give them cause for concern, yet she could not lock herself into the kitchen either and needed to be outside. And no matter how she tried, circumstance continued to stick a foot out to trip her up.

It was strange how a habit of going out for long walks in solitude could lead to so many conversations and acquaintances. The next time Mairi got away on her own, she had walked up to the far distant height of Rosedale, wondering as she puffed her way up the steep slopes to the heather tops, whether it would be far from here to Commondale. Perhaps she might be able to walk there one day and find Atheleys at home. The woman intrigued her, not in the least as she seemed untroubled by domesticity and children, but also that she was a wandering soul. Mairi wondered if they might not have matching thoughts and ways.

Not today though. For reasons she did not quite know herself, she had come out with her sketching items and the little geology hammer Stephen had gifted her. It had been handed over in an awkward manner, as if she had now decided to become a student of science. Geology was still beyond her. She had read a couple of books intended as introductions, but grew increasingly lost in sediments and strata. She had closed the books with a weary hand and wondered if perhaps she would do better being out on the land and examining such things in person. And so here she was, settled down upon the heather. Noticing a rocky outcrop with some tumbling loose rocks, she got up and went to make good an attack on one of the smaller pieces. Rocks and pebbles became so worn and smooth from the elements that they became difficult to identify. One needed to look at the raw fresh material inside to begin to understand it. Perhaps she would find a fossil, she laughed inwardly as she whacked the rock with the hammer, making not the slightest impression on the stone.

She went at the rock with a fury, knocked a few chips off and created some dust, then abruptly stood up, declaring herself a fool and stretching out. Her hands on her hips, the hammer stuck out at a jaunty angle, she stared out down the length of Rosedale.

"I say!" A voice called out from close quarters behind. "I wouldn't say you're a fool, but you are a curiosity."

Mairi twisted her torso to look back and see a man leading a horse towards her. She did not know him. She was uninterested until she noted the bright look of his eyes, and the saddle pack on the horse. There were tripods tied on the exterior. She thought to herself that here was a curiosity. Then she realised in horror how ridiculous she must look. Her bonnet hung down her back, her head too hot for the contraption as she had marched up the bank. The feel of warm sun on her hair had been too delicious and so she had left the bonnet to bounce against her back in a rather scandalous manner. She was aware that her neatly pinned hair had become a little dishevelled in the walking, and she probably looked like a wild little ragamuffin.

"A lady geologist, I see," the man said as he reached her rocky site. The horse stopped as if understanding they would be here some time, and took the opportunity to stand restfully.

"Hardly. My husband gave me this," she explained, brandishing the hammer. "And a book as introduction, but I feel none the wiser. I've yet to make a crack in a rock. I don't think I'm cut out for it."

The man had a moment of mentally stepping back on mention of a husband, then his interest got the better of him again. She did look so enticing, stood there a little hustled and natural, bonnet off, and sunshine gleaming through her blonde hair. What husband had she who gave her hammers and books and sent her off into the world alone? He laughed, not unkindly. "I think you may have hit upon the nub of the subject. Rock crackers the lot of them, geologists I say. And I do believe there may be more of them out there than we realise, breaking their rocks."

Mairi's eyes widened in horror. "My husband's not in prison."

"And I should hope not as well, for he would be a fool to keep himself so apart from so lovely a wife."

The breeze washed over the moorland tops, circling around the pair before rushing between them. Mairi felt the isolation and the fact that he was the only person she could see for a mile or so in any direction. The Blakey Ridge road was not all that far away, but the pack pony trains had already been past for the day and there was a lull in traffic.

The stranger cleared his throat. "I do apologise. I am so frequently unfit for polite society, I do not always phrase my thoughts as I mean, and things can come out sounding very wrong. I meant no insult to yourself nor your husband. I think this is the problem of being out in the wilds so often; one doesn't get much practice to refine the art of good conversation."

"Please don't worry," Mairi smiled, an unconscious need to meet his apology and confession, however light it was, with understanding. "I can't say I am always the best at fitting in with what is expected of me."

"We have had a poor introduction here, and indeed there's no one to oversee the introductions other than my trusty stead. Charlie Gibson is the name."

"Mairi Gaskin."

"Mrs Gaskin, then?" he said with a twinkle in his eye as though Mrs were a naughty secret between the two of them.

Charlie Gibson was a tall, gangly man, perhaps around Stephen's age, and simply buzzing with energy. He carried his hat in his hands, and his sandy blond hair looked wind-brushed and scruffy, yet naturally arranged in such a pleasing manner. The thinness of his figure, which spoke more of abundance of energy and movement than starvation, lent a rather sculpted formation to his face.

"And you are a local of the dale here?"

"I've not yet lived here in Rosedale Abbey a year, so I suppose I would still be classed as a visitor," Mairi smiled.

"Well, we are kin in this, for I've only been in the county for a handful of weeks. I'm newly arrived from Ireland. And I feel I've landed very well in my next assignment," he breathed as he looked about him. "I decided to take a day to get out on a good ride across the area, cover a few of the dales and the moors, see what I'm about."

Irish again. Mairi had a flash of memory of Diarmuid from Lincolnshire. What a curious infatuation. She had so loved to see him and since coming to Yorkshire she hadn't given him a second thought. "You don't sound Irish."

"And I'm not. I'm a Yorkshireman, don't you worry. I was over in the country for three years, only just sent back."

"You're with the military?"

He smiled, amused by the thought. "No. I am with the Ordnance. Most of the staff was shipped over to Ireland with some urgency to get the country surveyed in its entirety. It is a beautiful country, and say what folk will here about the Irish, I found them to be a delightful people. But the work is coming to an end and so I have been given my next assignment, and this parcel of Northern Yorkshire is to be my domain for the next couple of years. I will get to know every inch of the land with time."

"I see. This is to do with tax?"

"My dear Mrs Gaskin, I am here for noble reasons, for I am a maker of maps."

From a chance meeting on the wild, summer-sun-kissed moorland, Charlie Gibson swiftly became a feature in their lives. It was only a few days later when Stephen told her that he had met a cartographer. The man was working for the Ordnance Survey and had just moved to the district. Stephen had invited him to supper that evening if that would not be too much trouble to her. He was an interesting fellow and he though Mairi might enjoy some different conversation.

When he turned up at the door that late afternoon, his face broke out into a wide smile as he dofted his hat. "I did wonder if it would be the same Gaskin. There was only a little doubt as I had been expecting a geologist Gaskin rather than a land agent, but it would make sense to combine the two."

"It is not easy to make enough of a living through geology if one does not have private incomes," Stephen said, suddenly finding himself a little off kilter. Gibson appeared to have prior knowledge of him, and as an incomer he had invited with philanthropic thoughts of helping another professional man of science settle into the sparsely populated wild region.

"Indeed, I appreciate that issue as well," Charlie laughed good naturedly. "And I do not have a wife to support. Keeping her in food and clothing and small hammers."

"Excuse me?" Stephen's stern brows lowered.

In contrast Mairi raised hers, and gestured towards the dining room. "Mr Gibson caught me on the moors trying out the hammer. We have already met the once."

"Don't ever send her to prison, Gaskin," Charlie advised. "She's no good at rock breaking."

Charlie Gibson's easy way and sense of humour was something that could easily and unintentionally cause offence, and yet he was too gaily involved in life and discovery, and too enamoured of meeting kindred minds to ever try to curb his humour and cease his prattle. There was no malice intended and as the evening wore on and they grew to understand his nature, the Gaskins both independently felt that he was a positive addition to the area. He was not one for formalities and quickly swept aside notions of Mr Gibson, stating that they must call him Charlie, and never Charles, for only his mother said that and only in displeasure.

They fell into an easy trio of conversation, and remained at the table a good time after the food had been finished. Charlie was an open source and a great talker. A well travelled bright spark who had an uncanny ability to take genuine interest in whatever life threw in his path. His mind would absorb the details, minor and major, to long term memory. The vivid conversation brought back some of the experiences of being on the continent for Mairi. She had met so many different people, representing countries and lives she had never thought of prior. Although this little supper was hardly the formal and courtly world she had grown up on the shadowed edges of, for her mother's love interests had been rich and well heeled if nothing else, there was something far preferable to this homely, simple country gathering. Although Charlie was the focus of discussions, Mairi's gaze wandered to Stephen more often, feeling a warmth as she watched him relax and become bright and enthusiastic, forgetting society formality and polite restraint. The expectations of society usually put a stern cap upon him and left him with a thoughtful yet uncommunicative look. He lent back in his chair, his legs kicked out to a stretched length under the table. So far they reached, unconsciously knocking up against Mairi's feet and remaining there. She watched how he picked up his glass to take a drink, then replaced it on the table, allowing his fingers to loosely surround the stem, fingertips barely touching the smooth stem of the glass, side of his hand resting against the table cloth.

"Of course, getting to know the land one is to map is not always the easiest project," Charlie was speaking at length upon his passion of cartography. "If inclined, landowners can refuse us access to their land, and I've found some of the tenant farmers to be to the worst. Why, if one wanted a truly effective guard, chase out the dogs and geese and hire one of those men!" he chortled. "But the boys down in the London offices are starting to push parliament. We can't continue as this ineffective speed if they want a detailed a total map of the country. It's not as if we do any damage, but it seems very much that it needs to be written in law that we may not be denied access."

"You don't think this denial of access is just because you are an incomer?"

"No indeed. In some cases I think it is sheer stubbornness, and in others, a suspicion, as if I am a tax man in disguise wanting to go about and count what their assets really amount to. But I am no foreigner. I am a Yorkshire man myself. I hail from Tunstall originally."

"Tunstall?" Stephen mused over the name. "That is on the Holderness coast is it not?"

Charlie was delighted that his little village was known. "Indeed it is. I come from the coast of East Yorkshire; a coastline so ever fluctuating as it crumbles away into the sea. Why, Mrs Gaskin, we have a bad storm and lose another village. It is the cartographer's nightmare as you can imagine. I'm quite glad I am on the sturdy, reliable hills of the moors. Some aspects are still the same, it's all little village communities. But one doesn't have to worry that after a spell of bad weather, half the map one has just committed to paper will no longer exist."

"Whereabouts are you staying?"

"Over in a very little hamlet known by Gerrick. It's north of here, over some dales and high moors."

"Is it at all close to Commondale?" Mairi wondered.

"Yes, Commondale is the next village, south over the hill from where I am. That's another little out-of-the-way place. I am curious. You have connections with Commondale?"

"Not really, only I met a woman from there. I'd like to try and meet her again. She's called Atheleys, have you heard of her?"

"That's a curious family name, one that would stick in the mind if I'd heard it. I'm afraid I've not met anyone from that family."

"I think it was her first name. I don't know her family name."

Charlie shrugged. "I do not know it. It sounds a rather old fashioned name. She could come from anyone of a hundred families from the moors!" he joked. "If I come across her, I'll be sure to remember you."

"Thank you," Mairi nodded. It was odd that she did not really know Atheleys, and on reflection it was a rather odd name. Perhaps they thought she was mad. "I'm not familiar with Tunstall," Mairi commented, standing up with abruptness then as if having only just remembered her place and her wifely duties. She wanted to move the conversation on, and she was feeling awkward suddenly about having mentioned the strange woman she had met on the moors. She gathered up the plates, her bare arms reaching across the table. It was a warm evening and she was in a light dress with sleeves that only covered the shoulders. The smooth, soft length of her arms glowed in the late evening light. It was only the other day she had laughed about the brown tone of the skin on her arms, and how her mother would have been horrified, for ladies were bound to remain pale and interesting, not brown and swarthy like a land labourer. Mostly Mairi did not care, only with her pale complexion she found that she would sometimes burn. She personally did not worry over the deepened tanned shade, but red was not a pleasant sensation.

As she gathered the plates, Stephen had contained himself from reaching out and taking one of those arms in his hand.

"It's a small village on the coast, pretty enough I suppose although I'm sure I'm home blind," Charlie began on his home turf. "But of little to no consequence to the rest of the world. Not a lot happens. Why, I remember when I'd just become a young man, we had the biggest drama I suppose the place will know in a lifetime until it is washed away into the sea. A whale came to us."

"A whale? We're talking of the sea creature now?"

"Yes, those mighty beasts as are hunted out of Whitby. Well, we are not a coastline for whales, and the creature for whatever reason came up to the shoreline and was stuck there. Out of water they have no mobility, and they are such an enormous bulk. Truely, I don't think we can really appreciate the size until we see them in the flesh."

"What happened to it?"

"Why, I'm sorry to say it died. But that is the fate of whales that become beached. And what a drama it was as well. All the locals came down to see it. It was a great bull of a sperm whale, a terrible beast. And this being the scientific age, there were men all over it, measuring and sketching. It was there for a good week, growing more putrid by the hour... why, I say, it's good I didn't come to this subject before we had finished our meal! But the men of science, we do not care for trifles such as rot. They came down, up to the elbows in rotting blubber, to make their discoveries and observations. I do wonder if that enthusiasm started me off in my own desire to mapping. Although I have always had more interest in the earth beneath my feet than the flora and fauna of the land." He paused to muse over the point. "Dr James Alderson conducted a dissection of the beast right there on the beach for all to see. I stayed and watched it all. It was the science of it, you understand. Well, I don't know what became of all the parts, only old Lordy of Burton Constable claimed the bones as his own. I believe he has them laid out somewhere in the parklands like garden ornaments."

"What an end for such a creature," Mairi murmured.

"What an end?" Charlie questioned. "How many individual whales can say to be the subject of scientific papers? And his good bones will been seen for decades to come. Don't mourn too long, the creature had signed its own death warrant by coming too close to shore. But in this way, our understanding of the whale has greatly improved."

"I'm sure there's plenty of Whitby men who know much about the whales," Stephen commented. "They've been sailing north and whaling for over a hundred years."

"I don't know that the rocking ship on stormy seas and pressures of further catches for commercial profit provide the best setting for a considered study."

"I concede your point."

That night Mairi dreamt of oceans and whales, as she imagined them for she had only ever seen the creatures in illustrations, drifting currents and gently lapping waves. It was dark and the illumination came from the stars above and the phosphorous in the water. She was washed and lapped beyond herself. She was left breathless.

It was hot in July. There was not much cover in Rosedale, and the higher one climbed the less there was until one was at the complete mercy of the solar heat. Stood on the moorland heights, only one's ankles gained shade from the heather. Mairi had neither the complexion nor the constitution for intense heat, and stayed indoors during the height of the day, concentrating on her letters and books, and increasingly on the piano as she found herself beginning to compose. Her appetite, the same as Stephen's, dropped, and they would leave it hours later than usual before eating. That in itself was a blessing for she had no desire to start cooking whilst it was so hot.

It must be dreadful having to do the laundry at this time, she reflected. Water was always refreshing in summer heat, but hot water was needed for a good clean, and of course there was all the physical effort involved in cleaning cloth. Yet more clothes were in need of cleaning, for the sweat seemed to pour from their bodies. Mairi had smiled, imaging how horrified her mother would have been if she had heard Mairi putting sweat and herself in the same thought. Ladies did not sweat. They might glow a little with the afternoon heat, but that was all. If that was the case Mairi didn't know what she was to be classed as, only that these well fitted bodices and dresses of yards and yards of fabric were not good for air circulation. Some evenings Stephen turned up with his shirt fair pasted to his back. Then there were the other things that brought the heat out upon her that she couldn't quite explain. She wondered if she had caught something, for sometimes, it was almost as though she had shakes. The condition tended to disappear when Stephen was not in the building, so perhaps it was just quiet that she needed.

Since moving to Rosedale Abbey they had fallen into companionable ways, most meals could be taken with interesting conversation and even some walks had broadened their repertoire. Mairi liked Rosedale, despite feeling as though she still existed on the periphery of the community. She could have claimed to have found a place in the world. But these things are not static.

She was growing increasingly awkward around Stephen. She dropped things when she was trying to cook. It was nothing more than pure clumsiness. More days than others, she felt like a foolish child, desperate for him to leave the building so she might sit and calm her nerves. One evening he had talked of going to visit one of the farms, then of a clumsy dairymaid who had knocked over two of the churns somehow as he was stepping across the yard – this anecdote had been inspired by one of Mairi's own accidents – and how he had been able to catch one churn before it hit the ground, although at an awkward angle that now accounted for a bruise on the side of his hand. The next day Mairi had ventured from the house to go to the store in the village for a few items. At a distance she had happened upon the said dairy maid, coyly swinging slightly from one foot to the other, her wicker basket clasped in front with both hands, a winning smile and fluttering lashes directed upwards as she spoke to Mr Gaskin. They were too far away for Mairi to hear what was spoken, so she could not have eavesdropped if she wished to. Yet she darted into the shadow of the side of a building as if she were somewhere she ought not to be.

Mairi watched the young woman, who could only have been a couple of years younger than herself. Her focus was intent upon Stephen and yet there was something about her expression that said she did not hear a word the man said. Mairi had seen the look many times, caught in a group of young ladies swooning after smart young men dressed in military uniforms parading by in Belgium. Mairi stood in the midst of it all thinking there were better things to do than stare at men who had barely ceased being boys. The ladies gushed as if the young men were the most beautiful thing that had ever been seen – for they weren't. Infatuation and lust. The maid and Stephen were of two different classes, even if one ignored the fact that he was a married man, so it would never have happened, but watching the scene Mairi could see the imagination flittering through the girl's eyes. In her mind all kinds of things were happening.

Her attention shifted to Stephen, her gaze unconsciously running up the length of his body. He was in his early thirties, broad and well-formed. A finished article, she supposed, and long past the era of a naive eager boy. She found herself growing hot, despite the shade and the coolness of the stone walls. Flushed and feeling a fool, she hurried into the store, completed her business and then rushed home, terrified someone might spy her, and know better than herself what was in her mind.

So it was that she found herself seated at the piano, looking for a mental distraction. She needed the hours when she was housebound to fly by. She started to play. At first she was still composed of nerves and her fingers slipped, missing notes and stumbling part way through a piece. She slammed all her fingers onto the keys, closing her eyes and thinking what her music tutors would have had to say about her careless playing. An hour of scales? Solitude and silence for the afternoon? What would her mother have advised? Something quite different, for Elizabeth had always seen straight through much human behaviour and pretence. Mairi wasn't ready to face up to it.

She closed her eyes and started to play a waltz she had learned in Vienna. Polite, formal and well-bred, it would do nothing to make anyone feel awkward. It was boring. Mairi continued to follow the waltz time signature but found her fingers jumping in a layered way, building layers of music on top of one another in a heat-induced, gliding fantasy. She closed her eyes and felt the colours that burst out of the sounds. She played the melody on repeat, building up the sequence of notes, her fingers flying fluidly across the keys of the piano. It wasn't a waltz she had heard before, but something that might have come from the forests, from the sea perhaps, and a choir of a thousand voices. And she was back at the balls she had seen. Spying from doors open a chink, from balconies at a distance, dancing on the periphery on the few occasions she had been permitted to attend. The society and the gossip, as well as the marriage hunting had not interested her, but the music filling up the very air, and the graceful swirl and twist of the dancing had been nothing but pure intoxication.

"I never saw anyone look so far away as you do now."

Mairi gasped, her eyes snapping open and her body lurching forward. Her fingers lost coordination and she stumbled through the final notes before coming to an abrupt and undignified stop.

Charlie Gibson the cartographer lounged in the open window frame, casting a shadow across the body of the piano that she had not noticed. Outside he was perched on the edge of a tub of wilting flowers, his arms loosely folded across the base of the window opening to provide a resting place for his head. He had arrived in the village an hour or so ago, leaving his cartography equipment at the inn. He had decided for some foolish reason to take a stroll in the heat of the day. He levitated towards the Gaskin's house.

Mairi sat up straight, a little too primly for the temperature, and set her hands in her lap. "How long have you been there?"

"Longer than you would have wanted me here incognito, I'm sure," Charlie assured her. "But you do play exceedingly well. It's rather hypnotic." He paused, hoping she might blush at the attention, but his compliments did nothing to upset her balance. Neither did she look overly flattered, rather more disinterested, as if she was confident in her playing, and that was enough. "A waltz, but not one I've heard before..."

"I just made it up."

"You compose?"

"Not as a habit."

"And will you be playing this evening?"

"This evening?"

Charlie burst out into laughter, leaning back from the window a little as he removed his hat to waft at his face with the brim. "I think the heat must have addled your mind, Mrs Gaskin, for surely this evening is all and everything the women of Rosedale Abbey have been twittering about these last weeks?"

"It's you who look addled by the heat," she countered, considering the sheen on his face. People's bodies were slick with sweat this week.

"I'll admit I have been feeling it," he smiled. "But don't distract from the main point. There's a dance in Rosedale Abbey this evening. I made a point of booking a room at the inn for it. Don't tell me the Gaskins won't be attending?"

"Of course we're going," Mairi said quietly, flicking back through her recent memories to talk of the dance. Yes, she knew of it, but hadn't given it a lot of thought and certainly hadn't wished to bring up the subject with Stephen. She supposed as land agent to the area it would look very bad if he and his wife weren't in attendance. "And they're still going ahead with it in this heat?"

"Naturally. I heard the innkeeper's wife and his daughters twittering about it and what they'll wear, and what everyone else will wear and who will be there. I myself have struggled to select which pair of boots will show my ankles to best advantage," he joked. "But Mrs Gaskin, don't tell me you've not been worrying yourself silly over dresses this past fortnight?"

"Oh, I'll get something out," she sighed, closing the lid over the piano keys.

"Just throw on whatever comes to hand?" He set his hat back on his head. "Your lack of hysteria disappoints. Although perhaps with your time on the continent, a little country ball is like water off a duck's back. And you don't strike me as a woman who twitters."

"I'll take that as a compliment."

Charlie regarded Mrs Gaskin thoughtfully. It wasn't for the first time he wondered where on earth Gaskin had found her, and furthermore how he had caught the woman. He did not strike Gibson as being well versed in the art of seduction, being a little too quiet and serious for all that. And Mairi Gaskin was too much of a speciality not to know her own worth. This was not a woman who would have to take the first fumbling proposal she received.

"They're coming along splendidly with the new church building, you know," he broke out, seemingly moving on to polite conversation of the village. "In fact, as I was passing, they had just finished installing the organ."

The old chapel, connected with the priory of the middle ages which the locals had been using for worship had been knocked down as it was no longer fit for purpose. The population had grown and it had been agreed that the village should have a purpose built church which would amply fit everyone with room to spare.

"I think the acoustics need testing before Sunday. It would be dreadful if the reverend leads you all out in song for the music to fail. And the place was empty. Far too hot for working, the men have all gone on a break."

"Mr Gibson, are you suggesting..."

He reached through the window for her hand. "I most certainly am. I bet you've never had a go on the local organ."

Mairi hesitated. She really shouldn't. It would be quite unbecoming behaviour and would only cause all kinds of gossip and upset. The organ was Mrs Drying's domain, and as long as there was life in her body, no one else would play. But it would be such a pleasure to try a piece of music other than the dry old hymns on such an instrument.

"You could play that new waltz."

I shouldn't, Mairi thought. She caught Charlie's eye, the mischievous glint of the naughty younger brother she never had. "I'm not coming through the window."

A cat lay in the road, rolling pleasurably about on its back in the dust, enjoying the heat of the sun. Mairi and Charlie had fallen into a silent, swift walk, not daring to look at any passer by or one another as they marched through the sunshine in a direct line for the new church. Passing by the stores and the little village green, they stepped through the open doorway of the soon-to-be-completed church, a rectangle of heavy grey stone, with small, open bell tower at the far end. The windows were still to be glazed, but the roof was on and the organ installed at the head of the church. Great lengths of wood were installed, ready for the carpenters and joiners to begin work on adding the rows and rows of pews.

The temperature change was instantaneous as they stepped into the church, the old earthy coolness of the stonework radiating the atmosphere. Mairi almost felt herself again as Charlie Gibson led her up the centre of the room, seemingly consciously open and large without the expected seating arrangements of a church. There was no seat in front of the organ but Charlie graciously pulled a barrel across then draped his jacket on top for Mrs Gaskin to sit on.

Mairi set herself in front of the instrument, marvelling at the keys and pulls in front of her.

"Have you ever played one of these?" he asked, almost whispering.

"A few times, but not this one and not here." She pressed a key and automatically jumped back in surprise at the volume. The sound moved pleasingly throughout the room. Mairi raised her eyes to the ceiling. She could feel it already. The acoustics here would be good.

"Do you think we'll be in trouble for playing the devil's music in a house of God?"

"This is not the work of the devil," Mairi spoke defensively and started by playing the introductory bars to her waltz. There was laughter from behind them, and she stopped abruptly, almost ready to dart away from the organ if Charlie had not stayed her by a touch on the forearm.

The Iredale twins, Dorothea and Anita, had scampered into the building, led forth by the music. They had grown a lot since Mairi had first seen then, in fact every time she saw them she wondered if they were not half a foot taller than the last, although she knew such growth wasn't possible. The little girls, three years old apiece, stopped hand in hand and stared at Mairi. They knew Mrs Gaskin well, and did not feel timid in her presence.

"Can we dance?" Dorothea asked.

"Anita!" Mrs Iredale shrieked, making a third at the doorway, as she hurried after her children. "You two girls will not listen. We're not to be coming in here." She grasped at Anita's hand, then straightened, realising there were other people present. Mrs Gaskin and the new map maker, Charles Gibson, were up at the organ. No one else was here. It seemed a little odd to find them in solitude, and although Mrs Gaskin wasn't some innocent maid unchaperoned, perhaps it was worse somehow. "What are you doing?" she asked before she could stop herself. "I don't suppose Mrs Drying would like to see you there."

"No," Mairi admitted, smiling shyly. "But it is such a temptation."

"Well, I can understand that, given you play so fine. I hear all kinds of folk tell me, and I've heard myself once or twice when I've had reason to come down to the village... Anita!" she huffed as the little girls broke free and started to skip around the open room together.

Mairi watched Mrs Iredale straighten. She had probably left the other children with one of her husband's sisters, who worked in the village. She'd had another baby recently, a little boy called Seth, and it was good to see her looking so well and being back out and about. Mrs Iredale, or rather Ewat as the woman was keen for Mairi to call her as they got to know one another better, was not that much older than Mairi. Even now with four children she was only twenty-two to Mairi's eighteen. Yet Mairi couldn't help but feel as though they still lay fathoms apart in lives and experience.

"Mrs Iredale," Charlie broke the awkward silence, striding off towards the wife of the Blakey Ridge innkeeper. "I don't believe I've ever had the pleasure."

"I used to dance as a girl," she laughed, as if she were an aged crone. "I don't seem to be one for dancing these days, unless it is the merry dance those two lead me."

Charlie stood in front of her, heels tapped together. He bowed before straightening and offering the good lady his hand. "Might I have this waltz?"

"Waltz?" Ewat Iredale looked horrified. "I'm not sure I'd know what to do."

"You'll be fine. I happen to be very good at waltzing." He looked back to Mairi. "You'll have to play now, there's a waiting audience."

As if on cue Dorothea and Anita stood in front of one another and held hands, suddenly still as they waited for the music to begin.

Mairi turned back to the organ and flexed her fingers. It was a heavier instrument to play, in comparison to the piano one had to hammer at the keys. But it had been some time since she had been able to play an organ, and it did make such a beautiful sound. She placed her fingers in their starting position, closed her eyes and breathed deeply. Then she began.

The two girls squealed with joy and began to prance about the church, paying no attention whatsoever to rhythm or pace. Mrs Ewat Iredale looked horrified as the lithe cartographer took her in his arms and started to twirl her easily about the floor. She was aware of his feet neatly pacing out a beat, following a neat pattern of dance, but all she could do was scrabble about and try to keep up. She was up and about since the baby, but she certainly didn't feel as she had been before. Since children she did not find she had her girlish vigour anymore. But part of her still wanted to let go and enjoy the moment, for the music was heavenly, and she could almost fool herself that she was a fine lady dancing at a ball. As they moved about, Charlie found himself looking longingly at Mairi Gaskin's straight back, and wishing he could pluck her from her seat to dance. But of course if he did that, the music would end.

They were heading for a third circuit of the room when Charlie first saw a tall figure in the doorway. He chose to ignore it, but as he swung Ewat Iredale around, she caught sight of the man, and was immediately embarrassed that she had been caught out playing truant. "Oh my goodness!" she shrieked, pulling Charlie to a halt and surprising even herself by the strength in her arms. Mairi stumbled to a stop in her music, but remained calm and turned in her seat to gaze at the church entrance in a dignified manner. The two young girls giggled together then charged at their mother's skirts.

Stephen Gaskin was in the first shadows of the entrance. He had heard the music as he had walked through the village, noting a couple of open doors with curious villagers looking out towards the church. The building project wasn't complete yet, and everyone was hoping the dry weather would hold whilst the leaded glass was fitted into the open window openings. He soon recognised the music although he could not put a name to it. It was something he had heard being played at his own home the last few days. His thoughts caught in the back of his throat as Mairi sat calmly at the organ, and looked directly at him for the first time in what felt like an age. Then she seemed to become aware of herself, her eyes suddenly widening and she looked away.

"Gaskin!" Charlie Gibson was the first to greet him, freeing Mrs Iredale from his arms. "You've caught us out. It's the fever of the coming dance. I take complete responsibility," he added, glancing back at Mairi. "I tempted your dear wife to come out from behind the piano. I'd just seen that the organ had been fitted."

"It sounds very well," Stephen commented.

"Although I hope she won't be playing tonight," Charlie continued in his chatter. "For I do want to see if she waltzes as well as she plays."

Mairi stood up from her music. "I should be getting home."

There was an awkwardness about the space. Stephen felt a little irritated that he appeared to be the cause of it, for it had not been his intention. Although why Charlie Gibson should be here enjoying music and dancing with his wife whilst he barely seemed to be in good favour with Mairi these days did not seem fair. "I've not come here to banish you all; you needn't look so guilty. Only that the gossip is moving outwards across the village and Mrs Drying is possessive of the organ. She will be coming."

Mairi bit her lip and told herself sternly not to cry. She inhaled through her nose, regained her equilibrium and turned to face the hall. "I should go home."

"I'll walk with you," Stephen and Charlie spoke in unison, before looking at one another in consternation. Charlie broke out into laughter. "I'd forget my own head," he said, slapping Stephen on the back as he left the church. "I'll see you all this evening."

Mairi was at a loss as to why it all felt so wrong. Why she felt shamed, awkward, penitent, and somehow as thought she was in the process of loosing something very precious. She'd walked home with Stephen, accompanied by meaningless pleasantries about the heat and how dry the earth was becoming. She'd disappeared to her room as soon as they'd returned to the cottage. Sitting on her bed, she had sat for some time, crying for no apparent reason, before telling herself off and setting to the task of the day. Appearance at the dance was something other women would have been planning for weeks. Mairi had not given it any thought, but she would need a dress for the dance, and to fix her own hair. One of her mother's legacies was that she had plenty of fine dresses and could always be sure to be well dressed. Only that she didn't want to be too well dressed for this occasion. She had no wish to stand out.

She soon settled on a silk gown of a deep sea-green blue that was not too showy, but pretty enough to make her feel happy by the glow of colour. It was also a lighter weight gown so she ought not to be too hot, she hoped. Sitting at her desk, where a mirror was propped up, she worked with her brush and pins, fixing up her hair before adding a few ornaments. Not too much, just a little something, for she was sure her mother would have disapproved if she had gone with nothing. It was like a stab to suddenly think of her mother, and all that she was missing out on. Elizabeth had adored balls and parties. It was a chance to dress up, glitter, and admire her tiny waist in the mirror. A waist Mairi had not inherited, although she was sure such a look only came from years of dedication to a strict and brutal regime of tight corsetry.

Her mother should go to the ball however, Mairi decided as she thought of a pearl necklace her mother had passed on to her the night before her wedding. Yet where was it? When Stephen knocked on her door, they were already a little late and Mairi still hadn't found it. "I'll be there soon," she called out, a little flustered as she worked back through a trunk of dresses she had already searched through twice.

Stephen tapped the door open, and stood in silence for a few moments, watching Mairi scrabbling through fabrics. She was beautifully dressed, but it hardly seemed to register as his eyes moved up the back of her neck.

"I just wanted to find Mamma's necklace," she said, slamming a trunk lid down. "I know it sounds silly, but I wanted to take her to the dance."

"It doesn't sound silly."

Mairi stood up and turned to look at him. They were silent, then she felt awkward under the attention, her eyes searching for a distraction, and she noticed her mother's old keepsake box set on her desk. She hadn't looked in it very much, it seemed too sacred, but now she lifted the lid to flick through the old letters and ribbons, dried flowers and brooches, and there it was, the pearl necklace.

"Here!" she pulled it out, and quickly fastened it around her neck. "Now I am ready."

Shade was starting to pull in over the village at the bottom of the narrow valley. The dancing was held outside, for no one could face gathering in mass within a building to overheat. Assembly halls would have functioned well in other towns where money was more abundant for social constructions, but here, in the clear country air, the land itself was as good a venue as any could hope for. This was a high point in the local calendar and no one would consider postponement, or worse still cancellation. All the farm labourers and dairy maids turned out in their best apparel, blankets were set out on the edges of the grass for folk to rest. Benches had been brought out from the inn and some of the nearby houses to provide seating for the older folks. Tables held the refreshment for the evening. And so a small field on the edge of village was decked out for a chance for all locals to gather and dance, eat, gossip, and simply take pause from the labours and worries of life.

There was a small band comprised of locals, with guitars, fiddles, whistles and recorders along with the beginnings of a brass band. It felt as though a few brass instruments had been included to give some power to the sound. One of the old shepherds stood at the front of the musical gathering and proved himself a very tuneful singer of the old folk songs. They were all portable instruments. This was not the venue of the pianist, nor the organist. Mrs Drying made a comment, not directly to Mairi, but in hearing, hoping that people would remember their place and that she had not quit the church organ despite its recent relocation. Mairi pursed her lips. As if she wanted to usurp the old woman's right to play dusty hymns. She saw Charlie Gibson laughing away with the publican, and felt irritation grow for a moment. It was all very well for him to enjoy his mischief and capers, for he did not have to live in this village. Besides, people always seemed to be more forgiving of a man.

Charlie Gibson soon spotted the arrival of the Gaskins, and with the briefest of apologies to the publican, was gone, weaving his way through the ambling crowds towards the new comers. Some of the younger people were getting up and gathering to begin the dancing. Charlie flashed one of his healthy smiles, beguiling to all, and put on his best cheeky young brother persona as he took Mairi's arm even before he had begun to talk.

"Don't mind, do you Gaskin?" he said, pulling Mairi away. "I have an urge to dance with your wife."

She didn't know if Stephen said anything, or if his face betrayed a thought, but she was lost within the medley of villagers, taken as Charlie's dance partner. She felt her nerves dissolve again, submerged into familiar good will. Here was no worry of future impact, only the immediate now. Dancing upon the grass demanded more of a jump to the steps rather than the graceful glide of the European ball rooms, and she found this meant that one was positioned far closer to one's partner. She soon adjusted to the new ways, and found herself laughing as she and Charlie danced about the arena, making quite the pair. They danced straight through the first few dances, much to the envy of some of the young unattached women who felt they had enough of a status to make a serious play for Mr Gibson the cartographer. And there was Mrs Gaskin keeping him all to herself, and she, a married woman.

Mairi took a break, much to the complaint of Charlie, to take some refreshment and sit a little while on a bench and watch the dancing. Charlie hovered about her, ignoring the mooning eyes of the village daughters. The moment Mairi stood up, he had taken her hand, ready to rejoin the dancing. He was about to sweep her around and back into the melody of summer dance, when another figure stepped into their path, cutting in between Mairi and Charlie with some comment that Gibson wouldn't mind, would he? Something sparked up Mairi's hand as it took its new partner, and she looked up at her husband, not really knowing where to look all of a sudden. She'd never danced with him before. Stephen was not the fluid dancer Charlie was, but Mairi found she must be tiring, for she tripped up a few times, only caught by Stephen, from tumbling into meadow grass. After a couple of dances she found herself relaxing, and she was able to speak again, the breath no longer caught in the back of her throat. They even managed a joke or two, and the smiles broke the ice that seemed an impossibility in such heat. Later they sat down to eat and watch the dancing. Charlie sat with them for a while, and talked in his usual easy manner, but he did not suggest a dance with Mairi again. One of the farming families came to sit with them, and Mairi fell into conversation with the wife, a drowsy infant languidly sprawled half asleep over her lap.

People started to disperse as twilight fell. The Gaskins wandered amicably home together, a little drunk on the elderberry wine one of the farmer's wives had been forcing on anyone who would listen to her. Mairi almost fooled herself that whatever it was that had been setting her nerves on edge these past weeks had gone, but the easy feeling between them broke as they walked through the cottage door. No one knew where to put themselves, and they were swift in retreating to their respective rooms for reflection and solitude.

In the following days Stephen avoided her more and more and a strange silence settled within the home. Perhaps he would have disappeared entirely into the landscape had it not been for the coming of August and two visitations from the outer world that brought it all to a head.

Her fingers curled around the rough, knobbled stalks of heather, recently ripped off the plants. Mairi had been walking over the tops, picking heather as she went, for the scrubby bush was in its most beautiful phase of the year. Those woody, scratching branches that tugged back at boots and skirts, clawing off tufts of wool from sheep that would sit in hollows of the upland plant, had now burst open into a vibrant purple bloom of tiny flowers. One heather plant would have been pretty, but imagine an undulating open landscape, mile after mile, with nothing but heather to be seen. There was only the blue sky above for contrast. When the sun shone, the plants heated up and the scent of the blooms was intoxicating.

When one examined the landscape, different shades of purple were discerned. Mairi had soon gathered an armful palette of purple. She walked along the Blakey Ridge road, nodding to passing horse and carts, pony trains transporting goods across the moorland communities, and other travellers. As she started down a rough track, only fit for feet, to head back to Rosedale Abbey, she came across Stephen who seemed to be heading in the opposite direction. They faltered as they met one another on the track. For a moment she thought he might pass her without saying a word. The distress must have flickered across her face, for he relented and said he would accompany her home, if that was where she was going. They went with occasional comments but not the old easy conversation of before. She wished she could ask outright what had changed, for this avoidance was deeply saddening. She could not find the words. Perhaps he was just worried about his work for there was too much to do. As well as the responsibilities of the land agent, there was also the surveying work in Rosedale to be conducted. The intensity and urgency from the landowner was increasing as he heard more of Stephen's convictions that there were enough deposits under the ground to make mining a viable concern. Vanden-Harden's mind drifted on a happy cloud of impending wealth, but carried no desire for involvement in the necessary work to earn the money. Stephen didn't think he could manage mines as well, and he certainly didn't have enough experience. He was considering suggesting to his employer that the land be leased out to organisations more able to take up the work.

They reached the valley bottom in a state of awkward silence, and walked into Rosedale Abbey. In the village an older man leant against the trunk of a tree in the little green, smoking a pipe. Stephen had almost walked past before he stopped to take a second look. Mairi didn't notice he had paused until she heard him say, "Father?"

She stopped and turned, holding up a hand to angle the brim of her hat better to shade her gaze. Stephen had stepped into the shadow cast by the tree, and the other man had stepped forward. She hadn't seen the Gaskins since Lincolnshire, but she quickly recognised her father-in-law.

"We're on holiday in Whitby just now," The Revd Gaskin said. "I did write to say. Did you not receive my letter?"

"About Whitby, yes, but you never mentioned coming to Rosedale."

"Ah, well, we hired ourselves a gig and a local guide and thought we'd come over. Surprise you a little. It was your mother's idea."

"And where is she?"

"Resting," the older man looked a little abashed as if he would rather not explain further. "I think she caught the sun too much and needed to rest in the parlour. I said I would take a walk around the village whilst we were waiting for you."

"The parlour? Do you mean at the inn?"

"No, at your cottage."

Mairi felt her guard rise as the two men approached her. Mr Gaskin senior looked surprised as he realised firstly that she was waiting for them, and secondly that it was she, the young creature they'd forced their second son into wedlock with. Sign away the younger generation's future to save something for the aging population. She could tell he wanted to ask her why she was here, but couldn't find the courage to do so. She thought back to the cottage and the door they never locked.

"Very strange that you have neither housekeeper nor maid," the older man commented as the three of them fell into step. Never had three walked together who were so separate and isolated. "But the door was unlocked and your mother had a headache. We didn't think you would mind..."

"No, of course," Stephen said.

Mairi was silent.

Mr Gaskin cleared their throat.

Clearly the headache was passed, for when they arrived Mrs Gaskin was the picture of activity in the parlour. She had even lit a candle, although as it was neither cold nor dark, no one could immediately discern why. She had a look of vindication as the arrivals joined her in the parlour, and thrust up a piece of folded paper. "I've found it," she shrieked. "I can set you free."

"My dear," the reverend started. "I fear you are not recovered yet."

"I am more than recovered. And I have recovered our family honour." She shook the folded paper, which on closer inspection looked to be a letter, at Mairi. "This little scheming madam can no longer blackmail any of us. I have found the letter Elizabeth had kept all these years. I have it here in my hand." She darted back as if Mairi had made a move to snatch it. "I only waited until you had returned so that she could witness that I have it and know that she has failed. I will burn it now."

In front of her dumbfounded audience, Jayne Gaskin dipped a corner of the letter into the candle. The flame burst in brilliance, consuming the paper and leaving a blackened crisp wake. Jayne tossed it into the dormant fireplace to leave the flames to conclude their work.

And so in a blackened puff of smoke, off went the thing that had been controlled their fate. That something as simple as a piece of paper with some words written upon it could force people to act despite their better wisdom seemed bizarre. Prior to her death Elizabeth had explained so little, Mairi reflected, and now that she was dead, there was no possibility of asking. She stared at the fireplace with its little paper corpse. "What did you do?"

"What did I do?" Jayne huffed, giving Mairi a disdainful stare. "I would have thought that was as plain as the nose on your face, or were you not blessed with your mother's cunning wit? I have burned the letter."

Darkened stretches of shadow moved as emotions in the room. The reverend went with calming hands towards his wife, as if to try and pat down the clouds of agitation that were rising about her. Stephen appeared to grow in height. "Do not take this tone, mother."

"What did you do?"

"Ha!" Jayne shrieked, shaking her husband off her arm. "She is a simpleton. I have already explained what simple action..."

"What did you do in the past?" Mairi spoke slowly, her words well enunciated and her eyes on the floor. "What did you do that made you so afraid of my mother?"

"It was a lie," Jayne Gaskin hissed.

Mairi let her shoulders sag. What did it matter? No one apart from Jayne had given that letter a second thought for months. Whatever it was, it was gone. She did not have the energy to concern herself with it.

"We can throw her out of the house now," Jayne started.

Mairi sank down into one of the armchairs.

"She has nothing over us. You could get it annulled," she added, crossing the floor to her silent son.

"My dear, it has been over a year, I don't think that would be possible," the reverend said quietly.

"It doesn't matter, I've been all over this house. You," she pointed at Mairi. "I know you don't live as a wife. It surprises me given what your mother was like, but we should be grateful for small mercies..."

The tension in the room was pounding. Steven strode out of the parlour, the atmosphere as it had been in the beginning back when she had first moved into the property at Lincolnshire. Mairi remembered the shouting and the insults, and worse still, the heavy, disapproving silences. The distain on the faces of the staff. She looked up at her mother in law, who had the expression of a cocky school boy, a bad winner, who had triumphed in the game and would make all his peers suffer. Her husband, the reverend of distinctly ineffectual action, was talking quietly to her, but she did not listen. She has been everywhere, Mairi thought. She has been in my room. Her eyes moved back to the burned letter in the grate.

The front door slammed against the passageway like a gunshot. Mairi abruptly wrenched herself up from her seat and fled upstairs, Jayne Gaskin shouting after her that it was too late now, there was nothing she could do. Stephen's shouting overpowered the other voices, but Mairi couldn't focus on the words. Noise of disagreement and disgust. Movement downstairs. Protest. Mairi stood on the threshold of her room and surveyed the mess. Even the maid in Lincolnshire hadn't been this thorough. The chests were all wrenched open, with clothes and books scattered across the bed and floor, trampled down with disregard, then scattered with a confetti of drawings. On the floor by her table lay her sketchbooks and paints, as if brushed off the tabletop by a busy arm. A chip had been broken out of a glass paperweight. Her Mamma's keepsake box was empty and standing on its side. Upon the table was a messy array of letters, necklaces, pebbles, a little cloth purse opened with a scattering of baby teeth pouring out. A shiny brooch. A couple of miniature portraits. Locks of hair tied in ribbons. A book with pressed flowers coming from the pages. A fine lace handkerchief dotted with foxing.

These were the things that had been precious to her mother. Items embroidered with memory reference. Now her mother was dead and these things only hinted at memories and experiences that were lost forever, unexplained, and growing more and more meaningless as the years went by.

My mother is dead, she thought.

It was silent in the house.

A soundless cry of distress left her mouth as her knees buckled. Her mother did not exist. She was blinded by tears, overcome by her grief, and twisted as she dropped to the floor. Her descend was softened as Stephen caught her, and they crumpled up together in the doorway. Mairi soaked a side of his waistcoat in tears, thinking of her mother, who would not see her in her last months of life. A mother who had abandoned her to hateful people. She missed her dreadfully. She was embraced for the first time she could remember in over a year.

Outside a silent couple approached the gig. Jayne Gaskin was red-faced and tight lipped. She could not look her husband in the eye. She got up into the gig and sat sourly, glaring out at the village, her hands primly held together as she waited for her husband to go fetch the guide so they might drive back to Whitby immediately. She could hear the faded sound of sobbing from within the cottage they had just been forcibly ejected from. It was all an act, she told herself. Stephen was no fool. He'd see through it soon enough.

Mairi walked up the road towards Rosedale Abbey with a dark green glass goblet in her hand. The cool damp of river water had long since dried off during the walk north. The sunlight of early September was warming, and starting to take on that slanting golden slide of autumn.

The morning had taken a surprising turn, for she had left the house feeling aimless and incomplete. She did not feel like walking anywhere, but as Stephen was working on correspondence and accounts for the estate, she had been unable to sit in the house. It was not all that long since his parents had arrived unannounced and his mother had ransacked her room. Neither of them seemed to know what to do with the other. It's coming to an end, Mairi had realised sadly. It's all coming to an end.

Instead of taking her favourite route on the moors, she had headed south, following the main track down towards Cropton. Before she reached the little village, she had veered off down the slopes and into woodland by the river. There was something soothing about the sound of moving water, and the idea of being hidden away under dappled light in solitude suddenly appealed.

Holding onto a lichen-encrusted tree trunk to keep her balance, Mairi took a deep step down the final section to the river bank. Her foot crunched down on a build up of washed gravel. Larger rocks and boulders burst up out of the drifts of pebbles. Mairi flopped down, then looked upstream and for a moment was horrified to realise she was not alone.

Atheleys grinned back at her. Like an imp, she was crouched on top of a half-submerged rock at the side of the river, the skirts of her dress wet with river water. She wore no bonnet, in fact it didn't even look as if she had brushed her hair this morning, and the ribbons half tied and hanging in her hair were from weeks ago. Messy. Her entire appearance would be shocking to society and yet somehow it was just right for the strange woman.

"I haven't seen you in months."

Atheleys shrugged as if it was of no consequence. "Job's Well needs some time to work."

"And today you are down here. It's even further from Commondale."

Atheleys looked up sharply at her.

"That's where you said you came from?" Mairi faltered.

The woman pursed her lips and looked up to the tree canopy as if reflecting on the question. "I have a home there."

Mairi looked miserably at the moving water. "I don't know how much longer I will live here."

"Human life is but fleeting," Atheleys murmured vaguely.

"Yes, but I..." Mairi stopped herself. She couldn't spill her woes to this relative stranger. She had no idea if she could trust Atheleys to keep her secrets, and who knew who she might tell. Gossip spread like fire through these remote communities, and through long winter nights folk had nothing better to do than reminisce over every tale they ever had heard, from their own lifetimes back to those of their grandparents.

"You'll just have to do what you want to do," Atheleys announced, her advice coming out of context and referring to nothing. "Oh, look," she leaned forward, somehow managing not to fall into the river, and dipped her hand into the bubbling water. She pushed down, shifting stones out of the way, sunlit-diamond splashes leaping up to her arm. The water frothed up as she dug with some fury, then she wrenched her find up and into the light, water pouring down her arm. For a moment she wavered as if she might lose her balance and fall head first into the river. Then she was on her feet and poised wonderfully, holding a goblet aloft.

"It's a wonder that has survived in the river so well," Mairi commented as Atheleys walked across the gravel bed towards her.

"There's a crack in it now," Atheleys observed. "But it was well made. Thick glass. He made it for his betrothed."

"Sorry?"

Atheleys sat down beside her. "You should have it."

"I couldn't. That's your find."

The goblet was dropped nonchalantely into her lap.

"Will you see her soon?"

"Who?"

"Eleanor."

"My grandmother?" Mairi could not follow the thread of Atheley's thoughts. She came across as though she might have escaped the lunatic asylum and yet there was something ancient about her, as if there was nothing she did not know. "I should go soon," she mused.

Atheleys nodded. "I must go."

"Back to Commondale?"

"Back that way." She stood up, lingered for a moment, and then like a startled deer darted across the river, leaping in a sure-footed way from rock to rock and landing neatly on the far bank.

Mairi stood up, holding the goblet and waved goodbye but Atheleys had already disappeared into the woodland.

So here she was, goblet in hand as she entered the cottage in Rosedale Abbey. There was a strained silence inside, and she hesitated for a moment, worrying that some more of the Gaskins had arrived to cause problems. Cautiously, she entered the parlour to find Stephen in one of the armchairs, a hand to his forehead and a letter hanging from his fingers. I have had enough of letters, Mairi thought.

She set down the goblet on the windowsill, the chink of movement alerting Stephen to her presence, and he raised his head. The sunlight came in through the window, cutting through the glass and creating a moss green glowing shape on the ground at Stephen's booted foot.

"I've had a letter from John Phillips," he told her, answering the unspoken question. "It's not good news."

"John Phillips?"

"William Smith's nephew," he explained.

"Oh." Mairi sat down in the armchair opposite him. It was nothing to do with his family, or hers, yet she knew how Stephen looked up to Smith. She still remembered that visit to Scarborough fondly, and the poundcake he had given her still sat...

"William Smith is dead," he spoke bluntly.

"Dead?"

"It was very sudden, unexpected. He'd been down in Oxfordshire looking at gardens or something, I don't suppose it matters anymore, and caught a cold travelling up to Birmingham. Just a cold, but it took hold and it took him. It was last week. Philips has only just had chance to write to associates just now..."

Mairi didn't know what to say. "I'm stunned," she finally managed, looking at Stephen who was staring at the reflection on the floor. "I'm so sorry, I..." She thought back of that poundcake. Of the visit to Scarborough. Of all the thoughts and work that had happened in that old man's head, through his lifetime, and now it was all erased. Gone. She wondered on his strange wife, so much younger than him, and so different, yet they seemed to be devoted. "How is Mrs Smith?"

"Distraught."

"It's expected."

"Philips thinks it's worse than that. She always had a delicate constitution and they may have to..." He stopped abruptly, suddenly not caring at all what might happen to the strange Mrs Smith. Everyone had their own troubles to attend to. "This cannot continue."

"It may take her some time..."

"I cannot live like this anymore." He looked up for the first time and met Mairi's eye. "I bear you no ill will and will not leave you in a compromised position. I make no claim on your mother's money and property, so I think you will be very comfortable."

Mairi put her hand to her mouth. Her stomach gagged. She felt a sense of nausea rise up. She had been expecting this and yet hoping it would never come. Please don't send me away.

"I cannot live this way anymore. It is incidents like this that make one reflect on how short and sudden life can be." He waved the letter about in an agitated manner, until Mairi pressed his hand to his knee, the death notice of William Smith held within. She didn't know what to do, only to calm him, try to stop him making a bad decision. As if her touch would compel the plea don't-send-me-away through skin. Her heart rate was increasing.

He looked down at her hand. "I have reached the point, where under normal circumstances I would ask for your hand."

Don't forget to breathe.

"And yet that is impossible for the situation we are in. I can't..."

"I would have said yes," she interrupted him. Her chest felt so tight as if her heart had frozen in surprise. "If we were in a position now that you could ask."

And where should one go, when one is already married in the legal sense. They had already passed by the first year. There was no need to speak to parents. No ceremony needed to be arranged. They did not even need to set up home together, for it was already here. I don't know what to do with myself, Mairi thought, me, the daughter of courtesan. How utterly ridiculous. She cautiously raised her eyes, and wondered for a moment if he would know any better. It was hard to keep her increasing breathing level. They both shifted at the same moment, leaving their seats to meet in the space between, dropping to knees in a much delayed proposal. She felt fingers through her hair, then his mouth on hers and as the urgency rose, an old anxiety she had been carrying with her for months started to break apart.

The 1840s

Elizabeth MacCaskill Gaskin, forever to be known as Eliza, was born in the summer of 1840. It was a fine summer, following a harsh winter. The snow took its time to melt, and coupled with heavy rain in July, the deluge became too much. In Rosedale they suffered with the water, but the rivers there were not long and the valley coped. Across the moorland hills their neighbouring Esk Valley flooded and those who lived deep in the valley, close to the river were forced from their homes. In Lealholm, the Wesleyan chapel, only constructed the previous year was washed out thoroughly. The building stood strong but with a new inner and outer coating of muck. At the height of the flood it was noted how many stones high the waters reached, and a local stone mason made a mark to commemorate what would be the first of the floods the chapel would have stand strong against.

It meant that Mairi's Aunt Muriel stayed with them a little longer than originally intended, for travel across to Whitby to stay with her aging mother grew more complex. Not that she minded, for Muriel was quite taken with little Eliza. When she had learned from Mairi's letters of the coming birth, she pressed for details so that she might know the expected arrival date. She told the Gaskins she would come to stay a month before, and although appearing calm, bolstered by years of experience in delivering babies, she was nervous under the surface. Her thoughts would twist with worry over the worst case scenarios, recalling occasions when things had gone wrong, for it was always a risk to a woman to give birth. The locals were bewildered by the idea of a female doctor, and decided Mrs Muriel Must was simply a midwife giving herself airs and graces. Stephen knew of Muriel's late husband's work, had heard of Muriel's own work in the field of medicine, but as his wife grew ever larger and the inevitable grew closer, he found that he couldn't completely relax with the idea that only a female doctor would be on hand. He felt that the safety net of a male doctor on standby would settle his mind that all would be well. Muriel wouldn't hear of it, taking the suggestion as an affront to her experience and professionalism. Besides which, she wouldn't let anything happen to Mairi. No one seemed quite to understand just how dear Mairi was to her. A compromise was reached that was not particularly satisfactory to anyone, in that a local midwife would attend as well. The poor woman felt her own abilities under question when she learned that this woman calling herself a doctor would also be present. Yet Mrs Must let her get on with her usual work, only adding some new fangled ideas about pain relief at certain times. Towards the moment of birth, things did not run smoothly, and given the family's status, she normally would have called for a doctor, but instead was impressed by how the aunt dealt with the situation, delivering the baby and then proceeding with nimble surgical skills to save the mother as well. It would seem this Mrs Must called herself a doctor for good reason.

And so Mairi gained her own little dark-haired soul to love and carry about on her walks – admittedly shorter than they had been when she ranged solo. At home she had a busy social life through paper conversation. She read letters from her grandmother whom she had visited last autumn in Whitby, and promised to visit soon. There were also letters from her friend Jennifer Burton-Waugh, who had taken the adventure upon herself to visit Rosedale Abbey last autumn and was ever eager for the young family to come down from the hills and visit her in Sowerby soon. Muriel's letters were full of requests on the latest updates on the infant's progress. Charlie Gibson's visits grew more sporadic, and whilst he was still his usual charming self, something had cooled to a memory of past summer fun within him. There was a young lady in Castleton, rumour had it, who had caught the young cartographer's eye. He only came for the conversation in Rosedale now, from both the Gaskins if they were present, or Stephen on his own, but he no longer sought out Mairi. She missed what she had felt to be brotherly comradeship, but Eliza soon filled up her life.

So the land agent's cottage in Rosedale Abbey became a happy site of domesticity. Mairi sat and played lullabies on the piano. The maid kept order in the entire house. Now that they did not feel they had things to hide from the local community, and with a new baby coming, it was agreed that they could easily afford, and needed a maid to help in the home. It was something the locals had been expecting for a long time. Some of the local young women had been a little irritated that such a good position had not yet come up on the market. It was agreed in local circles that Mrs Gaskin would be an easy going mistress to work for.

In October when Eliza was just past three months the Gaskins took a short holiday across to Whitby to stay with Mairi's grandmother, Eleanor MacCaskill in her Whitby home. Although Eleanor still owned property down in the old town from her younger days living in the whaling port, she now lived in a more recent build. She said she preferred the clearer sea air up top, but perhaps some memories lingered on in the narrow streets of the old town that she did not care to revisit.

Her new home was a smart two storey house, up on the east cliffs with fine views out to sea and down to the topsey-turvey clustered town tumbling down steep valley sides to the river mouth. There was a clump of scots pines, long grown in twisted distortions to lean with the winds, along the sea-facing side of the house. To compliment the windbreak of the tree there was also an embankment that had been built up by one side of the cottage garden. It gave a little protection from the sea winds. The house was close to St Hilda's cottages, and not that far from the ruins of Whitby Abbey, the old seat of St Hilda herself. Eleonor's new home had been built in the early 1800s, had no name but on purchasing it Eleanor had declared it would henceforth be known as The Pines, muttering about some connection to her childhood, and thus it was ever known.

Eleanor, who was now in her late seventies, was quite content to take naps out in a sheltered seating area in the garden when the autumnal sun still had its power to warm them. When she went to rest she would have the baby with her, snuggling down into the corners of her shoulder whilst Eleanor reminisced about her own babies from decades ago and how strange it was that time could go so quickly. These familiar moments could pull memories out of reality and into a bizarre dreamlike quality of episodes one might have once lived through. Watching Muriel working on creating a well-stocked herb garden, it was difficult to believe her fifty-year old daughter had ever been a sobbing little baby. Or later the earnest little girl clutching her books as other girls clutched dolls, devotedly sitting by her Mamma's skirts as the two of them worked in the office. Days long gone and lost to the relentless passing of time.

Stephen stayed with them for the first two weeks. Although the time in Whitby was supposed to be a holiday, he spent some hours every day working on correspondence for the projected mining that might one day be set in action in Rosedale. The maid at the house in Rosedale Abbey was forwarding any correspondence on to Whitby whilst the family was away. What with Muriel also staying long term at her mother's home, the delivery of letters to the property was weighty that autumn. It was a blessing for household finances that the penny post had recently been brought in, turning the responsibility of payment to the sender rather than the receiver.

"Oh, good Lord," Muriel's knife clattered onto the plate. The gathering at the breakfast table seemed to disappear to her as she read her letter. The noise coincided with Mairi entering the dining room, a beshawled and snuggled Eliza in her arms. She had been awake early, and after feeding Mairi had decided they would take a walk in the fresh sea breeze across to the abbey ruins. From there she had ambled along to St Marys to stare down the steep incline towards the town. Mairi's stubborn and constant care of the infant confused a great number, given the Gaskin's earning and financial independence. Surely such a wife ought to employ a nursemaid to care for the infant. To Mairi's mind, with the running of the household now the domain of another, she had ample time for her daughter, and really where was the point of having a child if one was going to pass it over to another? Mairi's own family were of the mindset that whatever suited Mairi would be best. Stephen's relatives followed more traditional thinking following standards expected of social class. Although he had restarted some communication with his father, the main flow of correspondence went via his younger sister. This was how Jayne Gaskin had learned that she had become a grandmother. She disapproved of the lack of a nursery maid, and had written to Stephen to let him know that such behaviour would ruin the child. They might even expect Eliza to follow in her grandmother's footsteps.

Stephen had tossed the letter on the fire in the dining room, which had raised an eyebrow on Muriel's face. It had been another morning when only the two of them had been at breakfast. The old and the young seemed to be particularly early risers, and Mairi, Eleanor and Eliza had already set off together for a morning walk.

"Not good news, I assume?" Muriel had commented.

"A letter from my mother."

"Ah, dear Jayne."

Stephen had sat down at the table again and stared moodily out of the window. "She made a comment that Eliza may turn out like her grandmother for the lack of a nursery maid."

Muriel had looked confused. For a moment she almost asked what was the problem with Mairi's lineage. "You mean my sister," she acknowledged, setting down her tea cup. "Well, nurse maid or not, some of our character is set from our inheritance. And my sister did have her good points."

Stephen had given her a sharp look.

"I don't think you really ever knew her."

"I know what position she put her daughter in. That she blackmailed..."

"Not her finest moment," Muriel had acknowledged. "Although some things worked out regardless. I know her choice of... profession, was not ideal. But a lot of these things are merely the circumstance of life..." she had held up a hand as he had opened his mouth to contradict her. "I have worked with the poor and seen too much to think otherwise. It is easy to presume that vice and poverty are merely a matter of choice, or the result of a bad character. Especially when one is born to comfort and has opportunities in life. But I believe every person has a breaking point, and given the right set of stimuli, any one of us could crash. Now, I would never suggest that the way Elizabeth chose to live her life was the result of desperation – for I know how her life worked – but she was young and naive and confused about what would constitute excitement. Mairi is a very different character. Calmer, certainly more considered in her approach to life. An analytical mind..."

"Perhaps she takes after her father. Not that anyone knows who he was."

"A Scot."

"Pardon?"

Muriel had looked shocked that she had so easily divulged such a secret. She took a deep gulp of tea, as if to busy herself or suggest this was not the revelation it appeared to be.

"You know?"

"Please understand that Mairi does not know. As far as I am aware, Mairi has never shown any curiosity as to her parentage." Muriel had stared fixedly at the table. "But if you are worried as to Mairi or indeed what may be passed on to Eliza, I can assure you there is no need. Mairi's father is the best of men. A doctor in the Highlands. Dr Erskine MacKenzie. He doesn't know of Mairi, he was never told. He is married, you see."

"And you knew him as well?"

"Well, yes, of course..."

"And that was how Elizabeth came to meet him, through you or your late husband?"

Muriel had looked utterly confused for a moment before she nodded in agreement. "Yes, I suppose that would have been the case."

Revelations and letters at the breakfast table. Stephen recalled their conversation of a week ago, when Muriel had told him of Mairi's paternal heritage. She had not explicitly told him not to speak to Mairi of the matter, but it was unspoken that unless Mairi ever asked, the matter was not to be raised. Rather it was a passing of a truth, lest it be lost in the one surviving memory. And now another letter was causing more shock.

"That's a fine greeting for an entrance," Mairi spoke lightly as she entered the room, noting her aunt's pale face. She passed Eliza to her father as she went to sit down and get something to eat. "Are you quite well, aunt?"

Muriel shook her head and placed the letter on top of her toast. She felt lost, glancing at the butter as if she would continue in her automatic actions. She looked up again as her mother entered the room.

"Muriel, you're very pale."

"Anne Lister is dead."

Mairi looked at Stephen. He was equally out of the loop as to who this dead woman was.

"My God," Eleanor spoke. "She was only your age, and in good health the last I heard. What on earth has happened?"

"She died in Georgia. A fever or something, it's all rather vague here," she shook the letter open again to re read its contents. "Well, I knew she and Ann had gone off travelling to Russia months ago. Those two were always off gallivanting. Ann was stuck over there trying to get the body back and... how dreadful."

"I don't understand," Mairi said. "Anne's with Anne? You mean there's two Annes?"

"Ann Walker. They were companions."

"I always heard she was rather weak of character," Eleanor commented as she sat down. "How did she cope with all that?"

"I thought the travelling was the making of her," Muriel said. "The last time I saw her in Halifax there was a spark about her. It's true she's suffered with nervous episodes in the past, but really I think Anne has been the making of her."

"And now she's dead. Halifax society will be the less for it. Anne was a character."

"I wonder if Emmerline knows," Muriel mused, thinking of her rich cousin in the west of the county. Emmerline had hosted Anne Lister at her property on many occasions. She abruptly stood up from the table. "Excuse me, I need to think, rather I should write or do something."

Mairi put a hand to the table as if she were about to push herself up and follow her aunt, then desisted and turned back to the table. There was a sombre silence, a reflection on the dark traveller that followed them all, before the atmosphere was broken by a baby burping in her father's face.

"Babies at the breakfast table," Eleanor scolded without meaning a word of it, a bright twinkle in her eye. "I'm sure there's an etiquette book somewhere that tells us children should be kept in the nursery. Lucky for us I never did pay any heed to such things. I'm sure your mother would be horrified, Stephen."

"All the more reason to do it," Stephen commented. He set Eliza down on his lap facing the table. Eliza promptly reached out for a piece of toast and proceeded to suck the butter off it.

"You'll turn into quite the eccentric," Mairi jested.

"What can you expect, living out in the wilds?"

Eleanor felt excluded from some ongoing joke.

"But Grandmother," Mairi turned back to the older woman. "This Anne Lister, she was a friend of Aunt Muriel's?"

"Not an excessively close friend, but she has known her a lot of years. We lived in Haworth, in the west for a long time. Anne lived at Shibdon Hall over at Halifax. She knew Emmerline, my niece as well. She may have been at some dinners at Emmerline's mansion house when Muriel was there..." Eleanor paused in her wandering recollections to turn directly to Stephen. "We have a bit of a complicated ancestry, and some extremely rich relatives, as well as some very humble ones. Emmerline was wealthy before she married, but she married one of the industrialists, a Whitfield. When he died that left her an extremely wealthy and desirable widow, but she's never remarried. She had her children and didn't want anymore. Besides, I always thought she rather enjoyed being able to move into a position of control. She's done very well for her workers. It's a shame not more industrialists haven't followed her example."

"So the Whitfields are the other line of the family?" Mairi was surprised to hear this. "Mother never spoke much about family."

Eleanor mused over that piece of information. It didn't surprise her at all. What little Mairi must know of her own roots. "One of the lines. The other is now scattered about these moors. I was born in Commondale, you see," she added, looking over at Stephen and assuming her granddaughter would know at least this fact. "And from that point our family has spread outwards over the North Riding."

"You were born in Commondale? I've met a woman from there. I should like to go and visit her one time, for I keep meeting her when she is walking in Rosedale. She's a little odd in her manner, but a fount of knowledge."

"Oh? Which family is she from?"

"I don't know," Mairi admitted. "She can be vague with details at times. I only know her first name. But she's very kind. It's a curious sort of name, Atheleys..."

Eleanor spilt her tea across the table. She gave a gasp, as Mairi gave a little worried cry and leapt up as if to tidy the table. Eleanor's housekeeper, a Mrs Sarah Argument, bustled in to tidy up the mess, mopping up the tea with a cloth and telling Eleanor not to worry about it. She'd soon wash any stains out of the tablecloth and it would all be good as new by tomorrow.

Eleanor's hand had a distracted shake to it as she placed it firmly down on the table. Sarah Argument swept back out of the room as quickly as she had appeared. Eleanor sighed. "It has been such a long time."

Mairi watched her cautiously. "Atheleys is about the same age as I."

Eleanor smiled sadly. "Yes that's true." She felt her eyes welling up and carefully dabbed at them with a corner of her napkin. "I find myself growing wistful for my girlhood, and would almost suggest a trip over to Commondale."

"That would be wonderful," Mairi started.

"But I do not think one can go back," Eleanor continued. "Those days are so far in the past." She coughed, then set the napkin decidedly upon the table. "You'll have to excuse me, I feel a headache coming on. I will go and rest, see if I can stop it before it takes hold."

"Yes, of course." Mairi watched with a frown as her grandmother left her breakfast, then turned to her husband. And like that there was just the three of them, her family upset and retreating to solitude. "I feel as though I've upset them."

"You haven't done anything," Stephen assured her. "The passing of time is not always kind." He smiled at her. "You're too young to have felt it yet."

"And you're at such a great age now?"

"I wouldn't say that although I sometimes feel an inkling of what it must be." He turned his attention to the baby who was kindly pasting soft mushed toast into the tablecloth. "We must focus on the here and now. Make the most of what we can."

"Of course, you'll have heard from your old university friend, Jacob, that Margaret married him at the end of last year," Anna Gaskin prattled on as she twirled her parasol in the crook of her arm. She ambled along the Whitby seafront, cutting quite the fashionable young lady. This was the seaside resort to be seen at. In her new dress with new parasol that she managed to hold in every position that would not shade her face and stop the sun tanning it a country bronze. Her mother always complained that her complexion was from her father's side and was stopping her attracting the right sort of man. Anna liked to think that complexion wasn't at the forefront of any man's list when approaching matrimony, but she was almost thirty and without so much of a whisper of a suitor. Of course, neither of her brothers had married until they were past thirty, but somehow that seemed preferential for men. For a woman it felt wrong, and worse when she compared herself to her latest sister-in-law, who was not yet twenty. Of course Margaret was a good six months older than Anna, and she had only just married. But Margaret's mind was like that of a man, and if not desirable as a woman, more studious men may see an unpaid assistant in her. Anna was certain that was why Jacob Mallinson had married Margaret. She's only seen Margaret twice since marriage, and something had changed between them. Margaret had pulled away, as though her knowledge had mushroomed and she had attained true adulthood. She smiled down at Anna in a slightly patronising way, and Anna found herself uncomfortable in their chatterings, even when practising French. Margaret said she didn't have time for any of that, now that she was married.

Mairi felt the mention of Margaret's name like a stab at the base of her spine. Old insecurities and miseries lurched up at her. Memories of her time spent in Lincolnshire. Of the feelings of animosity and hate. Of accusations unspoken, when protesting her innocence was futile. She did not think that Anna mentioned the news as a way to score points against her sister-in-law. In fact, Anna had been the same friendly gush of words as she had been at their first meeting in Lincolnshire. Mairi wondered if somehow she'd been kept ignorant of all the unpleasantness surrounding her marriage.

So here was Anna, the happy-go-lucky, trusting younger Gaskin sibling. She was quite the same, and yet at a loss, now alone without her intellectual friend. Anna had wanted to come to Whitby for a holiday for so long, but her mother was refusing to set foot in Yorkshire after an incident last summer that she would not speak of. Their neighbours, the Bensons, were coming to Whitby and had offered to take Anna with them. Their mother had not been keen, but Anna had been so excited that she had pestered their father into overruling what mother wished. And so she was here. Quite frankly, it had been a relief for her to escape the house and the locality. The dynamics of all her relationships had changed so drastically in the last couple of years. She felt at sea.

Meeting her little niece for the first time was a joy. Thus far she only had two nephews, who were fine little fellows, but had soon grown out of their baby curls and love of cuddles. These days they were more taken to striding off through the grass on their little legs in search of adventure. Eliza was a delight, and Anna was disappointed to think that essentially no effort had been made to bring her down to Lincolnshire to visit the family, or indeed that the grandparents had not travelled north. She had tried once to broach the subject with Stephen but his face closed, and she knew she wouldn't get anywhere on that matter.

As luck would have it, Mairi and Stephen were already staying in Whitby with Mairi's grandmother and aunt, when Anna's letter had arrived saying she would be in Whitby by the time they read her note, and perhaps they could meet? They had popped Eliza in the perambulator – a new fangled device that had Eleanor shaking her head and watching with wide eyes, wondering when babies had needed their own carts – and walked down into the steep-sided port town. They crossed the River Esk and headed up to Anna's guesthouse to meet her.

Mairi had been anxious on arrival. She had yet to have any real positive experience with Stephen's family. Previously Anna had filled the air with nothing but friendly pleasantries. Mairi had spent too much time with the political backstabbing games of young women, and couldn't keep the worry completely at bay. Yet there was hope that Anna was innocent to the entire drama of Mairi and Stephen's marriage.

They came to the end of the road, Anna leaning forward to take a deep breath of salt-infused sea air. "It does do the lungs good, doesn't it? Doctors are always prescribing a stay by the sea for the sickly, aren't they?"

"Are you ill?"

"Who, me? Not likely," Anna laughed. "Bless me, I doubt I've ever been ill a day in my life. But I did need a change from home. Mother is always finding fault with this and that, and the fact I am so dreadfully old and not married yet. Margaret's marriage hasn't helped. She was sure I would marry first because she says I get along with people so well, and Margaret's so clever and off-putting to most men. And she went and caught Mallinson. What has he told you about it all?"

"Nothing," Stephen answered simply. "I've not heard from him for years."

"Oh, I always thought he was a friend."

"Just a colleague from when I studied, but I found him too competitive for discussion." He stepped up beside Mairi, and she felt his arm slip about her waist. Such a public display. She saw Anna turn away out of the corner of her eye. Eliza began to gurgle and Mairi leaned in to tickle her nose.

"Shall we go back to my boarding house?" Anna burst out, turning away from the seafront and striding a few steps away. She had been taken aback. Her brother had never been particularly demonstrative about any emotion for all the time she had known him.

But worse, it felt like an exclusion, to mark out her own solitary nature. The way Margaret had looked down on her, noting the different between girl and woman. "My landlady does the most wonderful tea and scones."

"Of course." Mairi shifted the perambulator around. It was not the easiest contraption to push about on the cobbled and steep streets of Whitby, but it was very useful to keep Eliza, her blankets, spare clothes and toys when they were out of the house. "Perhaps you'll come and dine with us tonight, at my grandmother's? I'll send her a note from your guesthouse."

"That would be lovely," Anna gushed. "And perhaps another day we could take a ride across to this tranquil little village you live in?" She glanced across at Stephen. "And see the abbey ruins? I'm assuming there must be the most frightful gothic abbey ruins with such a name as Rosedale Abbey. Are there terrible ghosts that haunt it?"

"You've been reading too many silly novels," he told her with a smile on his face.

The trips and the dinner were not to be. The landlady, a most courteous and well dressed lady of some fifty years, was ashened and both relieved and in dread as they returned. She gestured vaguely to the sitting room at the front and said they had a visitor. She didn't know where the Bensons were yet, they must have gone for a long walk, but she had sent a boy out to find them.

"Well, I'm sure we're quite capable of greeting a visitor, us three," Anna declared as she pulled her parasol to. "Oh, I'm sorry, little one," she added as the baby started grumbling. Mairi had picked her up out of her cosy nest of blankets. "I'm sure you'll see off any unwelcome guests."

A tall man waited in the sitting room, straight and still as a formal painting, with his back to the door. He looked out on the fine views down into the old town, without appreciating any of it. At the sound of their arrival, he turned in expectation, looking from Anna to Stephen. Anna let out a little gasp and automatically held on to Mairi's forearm.

"I, er..."

"Wilbur," Stephen spoke his elder brother's name aloud. "I feel this isn't good news."

He shook his head. "I'm afraid it's not. Mother collapsed yesterday."

"Oh my," Anna gasped.

"She's not come round. I've travelled through the night to find you, Anna..."

"She's still in a coma?" Anna asked, "She's not come round?"

Mairi felt sick. She knew what Wilbur was actually telling them. Jane Gaskin was dead. She looked to her husband, whose face was like stone. He saw nothing. He turned on his heel and walked out of the building without saying a word. Eliza started to tug at Mairi's hair.

"She passed on," Wilbur explained, wishing and hoping that he would not have to put it so bluntly as dead. "I didn't want you to read it in a telegram, so I travelled through the night to see you. It's lucky coincidence that I find Stephen here in Whitby as well. I...."

"Oh no." Anna's knees buckled, and Wilbur caught her by the arms and helped her to one of the chairs. "Mamma's dead?"

"Yes, I am afraid..."

"Oh no," Anna buried her face in her hands. "And we had such a disagreement before I left."

Wilbur looked desperately around, wishing he had brought his wife with him to help with these female woes, but she was expecting their third child and had not been prepared to travel through the night. He looked at the young woman carrying the baby and realised this must be the girl Stephen had married in secret. The woman that his mother had been so furious about. On the surface she looked rather calm and dignified, nothing of what his mother had described. Perhaps he would hear the truth when she opened her mouth and proved herself ignorant and common. "I am sorry we first meet under such circumstances. You must be Mairi, and this Eliza?"

"Yes, that is us. I am so very sorry for your loss." Mairi grimaced as Eliza started wriggling, growing grumpy over a missed nap.

"Would you be able to pass the baby to the nursemaid and help with my sister? I'm sorry for the urgency, but we must get her packed and back home."

"I don't have a nursemaid, I..."

"No maid? Surely my brother can afford..."

"I prefer to look after Eliza myself."

"Ah, first child, I understand it." He nodded. "You'll feel differently when you have more."

"They can both come and help me," Anna sniffled. "In fact I think it would be a comfort. Would you mind, Mairi?"

"No, of course we'll come up with you."

As it worked out, Mairi attended to all the packing whilst Anna sat on the bed and played with Eliza. Mairi had moved about enough and attended to her own packing frequently to get the work done quickly and neatly. She would have made an excellent ladies maid, she reflected as she brought down the lid on the final trunk. Had the money not been there, there were all kinds of things she could have done rather than being forced to go into her mother's profession.

When they returned downstairs, Stephen had reappeared. Anna had cried a little, but was red-dry eyed now. It was only the shock and the worst was to come. Stephen went up to Mairi and embraced her, kissing the top of her head but giving no explanation before turning to take his daughter from Anna.

"You are packed? I have a handcart ready to take your luggage down to the station. I've written a note of explanation for the Bensons. We must head off today." He looked to his brother. "You will come?"

Stephen exhaled, suddenly looking incredibly weary. "Yes, of course. I'll go across and pack a few things then meet you both at the station. If you prefer to get away as soon as possible, take the first train if I'm not there. I'll soon follow. Mairi can stay here with her family. I think it best with Eliza being so young."

"Indeed." Wilbur agreed. "My wife is staying at home. She's awaiting the third, you understand," he added for Mairi's benefit. "And of course, she wouldn't be expected for any funeral anyway. Mairi, it has been a pleasure to meet you. I confess you're not at all what I had been expecting, and I'm only sorry it's taken this long and under such sorry circumstance."

She nodded her mutual feelings, but refrained from saying anything. What could she say? She didn't want to know what he had been expecting – clearly family ranting had reached his ears. Thank goodness the Gaskins followed with current tradition of no women attending funerals. She didn't think she could have born to stand in a church where that woman's remains were, given the things she had said, and how she had ripped through her mother's memories last year. And so she was alone again, just her and Eliza, pondering on her mother, and now Jane Gaskin gone as well. The two architects of trouble expired from this mortal plain. Only the pawns were left to make their own decisions without anymore judgement to be passed.

Mairi crouched down by the edge of the lake and watched the greater crested grebe paddle gracefully across the still waters. The colours of its crest were glorious, brightened for springtime dancing and attraction. She wrapped her arms around the body of her daughter, just one year old and tottering, as they quietly watched the bird together. Eliza had a stick in her fist and was increasingly desperate to go poke at the water. The bird spun around as if on ice, then suddenly disappeared below the surface.

"Mairi, my dear, you've not drowned in the lake have you?" Jennifer Burton-Waugh called out in her clear voice. She strode across hummock pasture land, rushing her skirts through clumps of reeds and sedges. "Mrs Mayskew has unpacked the lunch. She is a wonder. Do come along and see."

Mrs Mayskew was Jennifer's accommodating, understanding and highly adaptable housekeeper at the property in Sowerby. She'd been with the family for years and either out of necessity or flexibility, was used to eccentric ways. Since Jennifer's husband had passed on very suddenly, leaving her a widow only in her thirties, the housekeeper had been indispensible to Jennifer. She had a calm eye for detail and the unexpected, and managed exceedingly well with the mistress's various excursions and multitudes of houseguests. Dear visitors who came with their own personal set of complications. This month's feature was Mrs Gaskin with her young daughter, Eliza, who was quite a treat to look after whilst Mrs Burton-Waugh and Mrs Gaskin went out on one of their walks. Mrs Gaskin was like a younger sister to Mrs Burton-Waugh, with a similar curious mind. From what the housekeeper understood, she lived in Rosedale Abbey, up in the moor country, with her land agent husband. He had currently gone off to Cheshire on some business and rather than be alone, Mrs Gaskin had taken a trip of her own. Jennifer had wanted Mrs Gaskin to visit for the last two or three years, and finally she had her wish. Jennifer always wanted someone to visit, something to do or had some hair-brained project to keep her occupied. Anything to avoid the solitude and the quiet, the inactivity that might signal a dread that there was nothing left in the world worth contemplating.

Mairi picked up her daughter, carrying her on her hip, and followed Jennifer through spring-green meadow land, around the lake edge towards flatter grassland. This small plain was a flatbed section that seemed to take a slow, dignified wade out into the lake. There was something curious about this place, still and silent like holding one's breath in anticipation of thunder. The lake was set in a carved out bowl of land, surrounded by pastureland on three quarters of the circumference, the land of varying degrees of steepness. Ahead of them was the longest and steepest section, and the only one that was forested. The canopy of the trees reached up towards sun-golden outcropping of cliffs that could be seen for miles away across in Sowerby and Thirsk.

A large tartan blanket, bigger than some cottages it seemed, had been spread out upon the grass, and a most marvellous lunch of tea, bread, cheese, cold meats and fruits, along with a selection of appetising cakes was on display. The wicker baskets were neatly stacked to one side and would have served as a neat windbreak, only there wasn't a puff of air on this spring morning. Eliza's eyes grew round at the sight of so much cake. Jennifer could be quite the equalitarian when it came to good staff, and had insisted that Mrs Mayskew share in their picnic, on the same blanket no less. It would have housed a platoon, but Mrs Mayskew lingered between her two places, being outdoors and knowing her place as a servant, she knelt in the far corner, aware of the cart man smoking his pipe and minding the horses a hundred metres or so away.

Jennifer already had a cup of tea in her hand, the proper rituals observed even out in the woodland, as she sat holding her cup and saucer to the backdrop of reeds and glittering sunlight on a still lake as if it were the most natural thing. "I do so love it here at Gormire," she spoke. "It's a frequent place we visit, and I know the landowner."

"I shouldn't be surprised to hear you know every inhabitant of the Mowbray Valley," Mairi joked. "You are quite the font of knowledge for this part of Yorkshire."

"I know society declares that a woman ought to mind her needlework and her home, and the contentment of husband and children. That ought to be enough for her attention. But really, there is such a big, fascinating world out there, I wonder at people who are never straining at the window, wondering what is over that hill, or why is the earth just so, or indeed, who walked down this road five hundred years ago."

"I can't imagine this place has changed all that much in five hundred years," Mairi mused. "If I didn't know better I would almost say time has stopped here. And those must be the cliffs I've seen in the late sunlight from my bedroom window."

"Indeed you have," Jennifer nodded. "Whitestone cliffs, or some call them the White Mare Crag. They are very fine sandstone cliffs. You must bring your husband here sometime. Take him walking up through Garbutt's Wood to the cliff base. It's the place for someone with a geology hammer."

"I would like to, but he is very busy with the mining proposals."

"Ah yes," Jennifer nodded. "What riches can the earth supply us? It is quite amazing the wealth one can get out of the dirt with just a little elbow grease. I wonder what will happen when we have extracted it all? I don't suppose we ever will reach the centre of the earth. So you think there will be mining in Rosedale?"

"Sooner or later." Mairi sighed. Progress was inevitable. True, in times past the valley had been witness to more industry than currently worked the land, but large scale mining felt like something the remote moorlands weren't ready for. Mairi certainly did not wish for it. She did not want any break to the tranquillity. She did not want to share it with any more people. "He's meeting with others who have worked in the industry, managed start up mines. He has to work on the viability and the costings, although I don't know if there will be some delay. The landowners have vested interests in industry..."

"I thought your lot were the old landed gentry type."

"They are, but there's been a couple of marriages of financial advantage to prop up the finances," Mairi said wryly. "A lot of the money, money not locked up in land and property I mean, is tied up with the textiles industry. The English cloth is out of demand and not making the profits it was previously."

"Yes, I'd heard about cheap imports. Well, it's all on a slow down. Mrs Mayskew is always shocking me week by week it seems with how much prices have gone up, haven't you?"

"Indeed, Madam," Mrs Mayskew nodded. "Why, I say it is daylight robbery and I would go somewhere else for the tea and flour, but they're all just as bad."

"But we shall count our blessing that we are able to afford these rises. I have friends in Manchester," Jennifer paused, catching a glint of amusement in Mairi's eyes. "I know, I have a great many friends. They tell me that people are struggling there. Children are going hungry. And of course now that the mills can't afford to employ so many people, there's simply not enough work for the number of mouths that need to be fed."

"There are hungry children in these parts too," Mrs Mayskew muttered to herself. "I reckon folks should try on some other employment rather than moaning on."

Jennifer smiled in conspiracy with Mairi. She had tried to have this out with her housekeeper, that sometimes no matter how hard one tried, circumstance battled harder and one could not win. Mrs Mayskew, who had worked in service since she was eleven, and had five children die before they reached the age of five, would have none of it. If she had gotten herself through life under such woes, no one else had cause for excuse. Jennifer did not like to argue too deeply with a housekeeper she respected and had genuine affection for. But despite Mrs Mayskew's tragedies, she had been blessed in other ways, and when one had not starved, nor gone without a rag to sleep under on a sewage-glistening cellar floor that was meant to be called home, it could be sometimes difficult for anyone to have true empathy for those who suffered. And Mrs Mayskew was a busy woman who didn't have the luxury of time to worry about folk on the other side of the country.

Mairi moved Eliza to a different part of the blanket so that she wasn't quite so positioned as though the dish of cake was her own personal platter. Mairi gazed across the water's surface, that deep endless pool of silent water. Her eye focused on where Garbutt's Wood slalomed down the slopes with its array of trees to meet with the lake shore. It looked fresh and green, the spring leaves glowing vividly in the branches. She listened to the sound of her daughter burbling, to the delicate chink of china as Jennifer set down her tea cup. How drastically and differently life could turn out, from what one might have expected. For the better in her case. Yet she wished her mother, for all her failings, could see this, to know that it had worked out. Even that Eliza had come into existence.

A movement in the shadows of the trees made her jump, then lean forward, squinting across the lake to see what it had been. For a moment she could have fancied she saw her mother stood back in the shadows, watching from another world, but it was nothing but a mere fancy. Her mother was gone.

"Are you all right? You gave a frightful jump there."

"Yes," Mairi laughed, feeling a little foolish. "Just a trick of the imagination."

"Well, have a scone with some fortifying jam." Jennifer passed her a plate. "It's a curious place I think. It could play tricks on the mind. I'm told there's fairies in the wood. Perhaps that's what you saw."

"Hardly. Nothing small and spritely. I was just thinking about my mother."

"You thought you saw your mother?"

Mairi waved the idea away as if it were an irritating fly. "Just a fancy of the imagination, that's all."

"Or perhaps is was Abigail you saw."

"Abigail?"

Mrs Mayskew chortled to herself as she heard the name.

"Ah, Mrs Mayskew thinks I'm merely encouraging children's stories and nonsense. But I am convinced she was real. Abigail Craister, you see. Oh, she's long dead now, she lived a long time ago."

"I wouldn't question whether she lived, rather if she did what they say," Mrs Mayskew explained.

"She was fairy?"

Jennifer laughed. "Hardly. She was a witch. Lived in a cave on Black Hambleton, a hill over in that direction," she waved vaguely in a northerly direction. "There are various stories about her, and to be honest I don't think she was all that bad. She did help a young woman on the moors who was in trouble with an overly, shall we say, amorous young man?"

"And what was her connection to Gormire? Did she die here?"

"I have no idea where she died, but they say she jumped here." Jennifer leaned back on the picnic blanket and pointed up at the cliffs. "She was up there on the moors, being chased by hounds. Men could treat women, especially those rumoured to be witches, as they wished back then. Whether things are much better now is debatable. Chased she was, and she came to the cliffs. It was a choice of jump or be torn to rags."

Mairi gazed up at the cliffs. It was sickening to imagine oneself on the cliff edge, crumbs of sandstone loosening under foot and tumbling down into the forest. That sound of clatter and snap. Feeling that great void of nothing behind and thinking one would plunge to ones death. It was that or the furious jaws of hunting dogs. Even in such a dire moment, would she have had the courage to step out?

"She jumped and landed in the lake."

"The lake? Here? No, that's not possible," Mairi exclaimed. "The distance between the cliffs and the lake is too far. She would have fallen into the forest and been broken and crushed."

Jennifer grinned. "She didn't re surface in the lake. Story has is there's a tunnel, a sink hole if you would, that spat her out nine miles from here."

"That's very convenient."

"Indeed," Jennifer laughed. "Oh, these tales are to be taken with a pinch of salt, but it's interesting non-the-less. I wonder if there's a grain of truth somewhere in the fairystories, a connection back to real history and real people, that's gotten lost somewhere in the mist of it all. It's not so fantastical to think that there could have been a real Abigail Craister at one time."

"A mad old crone who would rather live in a cave than earn her keep," Mrs Mayhew muttered.

"Indeed," Jennifer nodded. "But it's a nice name, I think. Abigail. I don't know anyone by that name."

Eliza clambered across to stand in her mother's lap, her fingers sticky with cake crumbs and her eyes ready for a nap. Mairi pointed up to the cliffs and held Eliza's soft cheek to hers, so that they might look in the same direction. "Look," she said, "What a big jump. I don't think you or I would be brave enough to take such a leap."

"Or mad enough," Jennifer added. "She must have gone a little mad, living out in the wilds."

The 1840s had been a maddening time. Looking back at the worst of it, Mairi sometimes was in a depressed awe that her mind hadn't given way completely, like the mind of a very distant relative had done. Living out in the wilds. Living with personal loss and tragedy alongside the woes of a nation and the suffering of the common man and woman. It had been hard enough in Rosedale and the other moorland villages. As farming communities, there was a certain amount the locals grew for themselves, but food prices had rocketed. A bad harvest in 1846 had only exasperated the problem, and there was news of a terrible potato disease in Ireland. Pleas for help for the starving masses. Industry had seemingly collapsed, and the industrial working class were out of work and out of money. Some turned to tramping, and took up any work they could, turning to the railways as navies, so that they might earn their keep to fill their bellies.

The winter had been particularly hard. The Gaskins had stayed over at Girrick with Charlie Gibson and his young family, and what a packed house that had been. The heat from so many bodies, and plenty of company in the freezing beds had been welcomed. The snow was endless and continually piled up and drifted. One morning they had been forced to dig their way out of the house. Girrick bank had been lost, quite literally buried in a phenomenal depth of snow. When they had climbed out and stared out across the white landscape, it felt more of a flat and even plain, where there had once been a steep incline down towards the Jolly Sailor's Inn at the bottom. Charlie Gibson had shook his head and repeated the same old line about how ridiculous it was that the main highway had even gone down that steep bank, only to immediately come back up to the same level almost as soon as it had gone down. No one needed to be a cartographer to see the road should have been swung around towards the village and kept up high on the level moorland. But an inn could not be ignored and the coaching post was set down in a dell, rather than following common sense and building something new in a more suitable position.

The situation may have given ample fuel to Charlie's grumblings, but for Mairi it was a worry as the family had been planning to catch that coach in two days' time to get further across the moors. They had intended to drop down into Danby, then onwards to Rosedale. Sheer bloody mindedness and determination saw that the post would not be stopped, and a tunnel large enough for a carriage and horses was dug through the snow at the bottom of Girrick bank so that the highway could reopen. Mairi would not have believed it had she not walked down with Stephen to see it herself, her breath steaming and frosting on the woollen creases of the thick shawl wrapped closely around her face.

The winter had been cold, money was counted a little more closely, and they did not take quite as much meat, but the Gaskins did not starve during those years. They were kept well-clothed and healed and in comfortable accommodation. On fireside afternoons Aunt Muriel had ranted about Engels' studies on the industrial poor in Manchester, and how disgusting it was that man could treat fellow man in such a way. That the rich, the industrial rich who would employ and abuse these people when it suited, felt no duty of obligation when times were hard was shameful. She would return time and again to the subject of the few socially and morally decent industrialists, including their own cousins headed by the matriarch Emmerline Whitfield, who built up communities and had a respect for human life.

Had it only been a year or two since those social reports had come out, Mairi wondered? And only this week it had all been dredged up again, Muriel furious after reading a novel recently released. A romance and a murder, but also a damning social commentary on Manchester's suffering. Muriel had marched into her mother's dining room at breakfast, waving her copy of *Mary Barton* at anyone who cared to glance at her. Nothing changes, she despaired. The troubles of Manchester and the people were hardly new. There had been protests in the past. Peterloo. And did they care? No, they had ploughed peaceful, working class folk into the earth, and after these decades nothing had improved. People were still treated with contempt. Muriel sat down heavily at the table. She had been there, she told them all, her wide-eyed great nieces staring at her in bewilderment. She had attended the rally at Peterloo, and she had seen what they had done.

"I remember it well," Eleanor had sighed, glancing down at her hands as she picked up a butter knife. Age spots seemed ever more vibrant on her wrinkled hands. She did not recognise them. Inside she was still young and these were not the fingers of Eleanor MacCaskill.

"You were never there," Muriel muttered.

"I heard all about it. A lot. You and Emmerline dressing down and sneaking to the fields as though you were a couple of factory girls." She smiled to herself. "I'm sure Emmerline's children wouldn't believe it of her now if you told them." Eleanor looked over to her one surviving child. "But please calm down Muriel, I don't want your furious face on the portrait this afternoon."

Four-year-old Tilda looked very gravely at her own mother. "May I have a furious face, Mamma?"

Mairi had told her daughters that she wanted no angry faces. But what were they to do when they had to sit still for so long for the photograph to develop? Eleanor was still unconvinced that a good portrait could be created in such a short time and without artist wielding pencil or paint. She had agreed to come if only to keep Muriel quiet. The family group had been told to keep very still until Mr Stone said otherwise. Eleanor wondered if he was furiously sketching away under that cloth. And so they remained as ice. No one could keep up a smile that long, so instead they all stared solemnly at the camera, and Mairi hoped that the baby wouldn't wriggle too much or that Adelaide wouldn't start picking her nose at an inopportune moment. Eliza, now a thoughtful eight year old, wore a questioning gaze as she stared at the lens of the camera. It was a strange box like an accordion on stilts. William Stone, the proprietor and photographer at the Whitby Studio on Church Street, was hidden under a cloth cape at the back of the camera, as if their family portrait was so terrible he didn't dare look at them.

It was awkward having to sit still for so long, and worse not to allow an expression to cross one's face. Eight-year-old Eliza retreated inwardly to her thoughts and the half-finished drawing she'd left at her great-grandmother's house that she would finish later this afternoon. She was aware of the group effort around her; her Mamma sitting with baby Charlotte on her lap, her father stood just behind. Her great-grandmother had a seat just beside Mairi, and Aunt Muriel (technically great-aunt Muriel, but she had informed the girls in a rather grave tone that she was no old crone and would not be called great anything) stood like a man about the house, alongside Stephen. Eliza's younger sisters, the figidty Tilda, and Adelaide who loved to please, in her neat little pose for the camera, were also present.

There was one unmentioned person who was not present for the photograph. So rarely mentioned Eliza sometimes wondered if he had been real, and if her memories of him were somehow mixed up with those of the births of her sisters. William ought to have been six years old now, but hadn't even made it past seven months. Eliza thought she could recall him, although if her memory of the boy was uncertain, she definitely remembered how his death destroyed her mother. There were months when she had barely managed to get out of bed, and even then, all she would do was lay downstairs and weep or stare vacantly out of the window. She would perk up for Eliza, and play with her, but there was always something distant about her. She was looking for someone who was not there.

Business had to be the key, her father had decided – silently terrified he was going to lose his wife as well as his son. Mairi had taken on a number of children from the village to teach piano to. She had to be up, dressed and motivated when her students arrived, and this habit broke the spell of grief and brought her back to living, as much as anyone could return when they had lost a child. It also saw the start of Eliza's early musical training as she sat at the piano with her Mamma and began to learn how music was constructed. In later years a violin master moved to Rosedale for a year and Eliza took lessons with him. He said he had come for his nerves, and the need to work on his masterpieces, but gossips whispered there was a society scandal left in one of the big cities behind him, and he had come to the back of the beyond to wait for the controversy to die down.

Eliza hadn't immediately taken to the violin. It took a summer holiday in Whitby to unleash her joy for the instrument. Her younger sisters were pestering her mother in the garden, Aunt Muriel was off reading and Pa was in town. Eliza, like a good girl had been set to practice her scales on the violin – such a handy instrument as it could be easily transported. Her great grandmother, an old white-haired lady who must have been over a hundred years old by now, and was as fond of afternoon naps as the babies were, had hobbled in and asked her if she knew anything livelier. Eliza had told her that it wasn't a tune but scales, then played a melancholy piece that Mr Swales had taught her. He was fond of reflective pieces, and didn't have much time for any of that giddy, working class nonsense. Eliza wasn't sure of quite what he meant as she recited what the violin master had said.

Eleanor had rolled her eyes at such nonsense, and opened the cupboard at the dresser, taking out a precious bundle she'd neglected for a year or so. Eliza watched in surprise as it was opened to reveal an old, but well-loved fiddle. Even more so when her great-grandmother popped it nimbly under her chin and began to tune it with the manner of someone with both a keen ear and decades of experience.

"Now," said Eleanor, "Here is one a dear friend once taught me when I was not much older than you are now." And she broke out into a fast-paced reel that eagerly tumbled over itself. Eliza's spirit soared and she discovered the music of her soul. Soon the two of them were playing together, feet tapping in time on the fine rug in the sitting room. Eliza spent the summer learning the tunes of the moors of Yorkshire, reels the length and breadth of Scotland where her ancestors came from, and even across the seas from Ireland. Eleanor had met so many fiddle players on her travels. More than once Muriel would come into the room, worried that her eighty-six-year-old mother might be over exerting herself.

And so the childhood of the Gaskin girls panned out. They grew up in a happy home, vaguely aware of the mutterings of adults and worries over the state of the world, rising prices for food that far outstripped the slow rise of wages. How would some families make ends meet? But they were fed, had a happy home and a child accepts what is before it as the natural state of things. They played with the other local children, attended the village school and gained extra schooling at home from their father. Without the male protégé to take an interest in geology, and bolstered by the fact that Mairi had proved how women could be more than pretty accessories to the sitting room, he broadened his daughters' minds, adding to what the school provided. He even took them to task over being able to swim, having once watched a man drown for the simple lack of a basic paddling ability. Under the watchful eye of the White mare Cliffs, they learned to swim in Lake Gormire on the way to and from holidays at Sowerby with their honorary Aunt Jennifer Burton-Waugh, a stately and eccentric widow in her forties, whose network of intellects and personalities across the county brought them greater opportunities for exploring the world. Bobbing about in

Gormire, Eliza would gaze up at the cliffs and remember the stories of Abigail Craister, the witch who had jumped to escape persecution. Her parents said it was just a story, for no one could leap such a distance between the cliffs and the lake. Even so, Eliza imagined being up on the precipice and what courage would be needed to actually make that leap. Or if not courage, then terror of what remaining on high ground would mean.

The lessons in geology from their father were taken to varying degrees of interest. Eliza was fascinated by the fine-lined maps and scientific drawings of fossils, taking it to her own illustrations of plants, delving into the most minute of detail. Their father's work and passion both brought them into contact with other such minds from across the country, as he worked on proposals for mining on the Rosedale estate. A favourite had been a man from Cheshire had come just before Christmas to regale the Gaskins on his mining experience. His speciality was the mining of salt, and for Mairi he brought, rather than flowers, a many-pronged tree branch, which had been taken down the mines and left to crystallise. It was covered it white salt crystals, like hardened feathers stretching outwards. He told them that many of the miners did this for their own families before the festive period. Mairi had been delighted with the crystallised branch. It brought back memories of petrified grass stalks from Job's Well and her own musings and explorations into geology before motherhood had consumed her attention. She delighted in her children and watching them grow, an almost perfect antidote to the hopeless grief that came with the loss of a child, but there were times when she thought back to her early days, free of responsibility when she had wandered for hours at will.

William remained with her, like a little ghost full of the memory of baby laughter. She'd never seen him ill. Eliza had caught scarlet fever, the symptoms coming on suddenly one morning whilst Muriel had been visiting. The toddler had become feverish and languid, and the doctor had soon made her diagnosis. The maid had been out with William on a walk, and as they returned to the house Muriel had advised that they should go stay somewhere else. Scarlet fever could kill, and whilst Eliza was a more robust child of two, and had a better chance of fighting off the infection, William was only a few months old and needed to be kept safe. The maid had not reentered the house but gone back to her own family to live with the boy until it was safe to return. Mairi had been torn between the two children, but seeing her sick little girl in bed, she couldn't leave her, and had remained in Rosedale. The tactic had succeeded in some respects as William never caught scarlet fever. But as Eliza was recovered, news came that measles had broken out in the maid's family, and the little boy had gone very fast in the night. By the time word had reached the Gaskins that could they please send their clever aunt, it was too late.

The rock was taller than either of the girls. Their father would have been able to tell them about the type of rock it was, but to Eliza and Tilda, it was just rock. Rivlets had been hewn out, as if it had been half formed of thundering rain. The pinnacle almost disappeared into the growing mist that surrounded them.

Tilda was only seven, and although usually quite bold and forthright in her thoughts and her speech, she was severally regretting agreeing to come up here to Wheeldale Moor. She could only see a few metres of ground away from her feet. The visibility was worse than five minutes ago, and dreadful compared to when they had first climbed up the steep hill east out of Rosedale Abbey. Puffing their way to the top, they had been able to see for miles. That was then, but now the mist had fallen. She wasn't sure if it was the low visibility or the creeping damp chill that was the worst. She shivered, pulling the shawl about her that she had taken from the parlour when she and Eliza had first tramped off. No, it was definitely the mist that was worse, for one couldn't see what was out there. What was making the strange noises. Who might be watching.

She turned back to the standing stone where her sister was hunkered down with a geologist's hammer and pick that she had stolen from home. Who cared what stupid Daniel Iredale said, she thought. "Do you think he's out there?"

"He doesn't exist," Eliza muttered through a clenched jaw as she focused her energy on her work. When inclined, Eliza could be quite a ferocious eleven year old. She experienced the world with an intensity that unsettled folk, made the lads a little self conscious. In retaliation they liked to tease her all the more. Eliza didn't tend to mind what the local children said, she wasn't one for lots of friends and quite happy with her books and drawings, but Tilda had seen how Daniel's words bothered her, brought out a little blush on her brow. That was why they had come up here, to prove something to Daniel Iredale. Tilda was only here for the glory, but now she wished she'd stayed in by the fire in the parlour.

"They said he'd come out of the mist."

"They were making it up."

"They said if you say his name three times..."

"There isn't even a man. Pa says it's just a boundary stone."

Tilda rubbed her hands together. She could hear something moving through the heather out there. Her eyes welled up with tears of fear as she looked at the insubstantial grey-white walls of billowing mist. She didn't want to admit to being frightened, but she wished her sister would hurry up so they could go home. She jumped when a sheep stepped into their arena, equally surprised to find the girls, and twisting nimbly round with a bleat to disappear again. Tilda's heart dropped back down from the top of her throat, and as the beat calmed, she wiped at her running nose with the back of her hand. "Eliza, I want to go home."

"I'll soon be finished. I've already got two numbers in."

"What do you mean?" Tilda scampered around to her sister, where she was single-mindedly on her knees before the standing stone, oblivious to the peaty dampness soaking into her skirts. She was carving something into the stone's surface, and it was surprising how much she had done already. There was a rough letter E, then the numbers 1 and 8. She'd started on the number 4. "The year you were born?"

"Exactly."

"But why are you doing this? We'll get in trouble."

"I said I would go up here, that I wasn't afraid."

"And we've come here."

"I have to leave proof."

Tilda huffed, and turned away, skidding over a hummock of grass. She put her hand to her head and was surprised to find her hair damp. It must be mizzling, so fine they didn't even notice it. "Daniel said he never has any clothes on, the blue man I mean," she added with a giggle, putting her hand to her mouth. "He's blue 'cause he's as cold as death, and they brought him out here and murdered him and when the fog's down he looks for revenge. He's buried out here somewhere, under the moss."

"They're just making it up. Besides, if no one knows where he's buried, how would anyone know he's here?" Eliza pointed out.

Tilda's eyes were round. "Folk talk."

"Now you're just being stupid." Eliza leant back from her work. She had completed the 4. Just a 0 left to do. She looked over at her sister and was shocked to see the mist for the first time. It was so close.

"If you say his name three times, you can call him forth."

Eliza started hammering again.

"Blue Man in the Moss."

Bang.

"Blue Man in the Moss."

Bang.

"Blue..."

"Stop!" Eliza shrieked, dropping the chisel. "You mustn't say it."

"I thought you said it was just made up."

The sisters stared at each other, and listened. Even the sound of the wind had gone.

"Do you want to chance it?"

Tilda started to cry. "No. I'm scared, Eliza, I want to go home."

"I just need to finish this."

"I want my Mamma," Tilda suddenly rushed away, blinded even to the right direction back to the track that crossed the moors.

Eliza groaned, looking at the rock. She'd only started the zero, so at the moment it looked like 1841, rather than the year she was born. She was almost finished, but she didn't want to stay here on her own. "Tilda?"

No answer.

She hesitated, then decided it would do, throwing her tools into her bag as she got up and ran after her younger sister.

Tilda hadn't gotten far, and had veered off the little earth path, which could be wet and boggy enough at the best of times, and stepped into a real bog. She was sobbing in heaving, shoulder shuddering gulps now, her foot stuck in the dank peaty earth. She screamed as Eliza ran up and clutched her shoulders, thinking the blue man in the moss had come to get her.

"I'm stuck," Tilda wailed.

Tilda was worried her Mamma would be cross about the dirtied shoe and the sopping, muddy dress hems. Eliza realised she was going to be in trouble with both her parents for coming up here in such bad weather, and worse still taking her sister with her. And taking the hammer and chisel without permission. "It's all right," she said, feeling the chill creep through her clothes. "I'll get you out." Putting her hands under her sister's arms, she tugged, and with a sucking slop, Tilda's foot came unstuck and the two girls went tumbling into a bank of heather. Tilda rolled over and clutched at her older sister. "Can we go home now?"

"Yes. Let's go." They stood up, and holding hands started down the track Eliza hoped was the path they'd taken from the moorland track, and not just some sheep track. The moorlands were crisscrossed by a strange network made by the beasts through the heather to get to shelter, good grazing, or wherever it was sheep thought they were off to when they herded. Eliza didn't even know if they were headed in the right direction. But they kept going, Eliza sometimes pulling at Tilda as she stumbled against the scrubby arms of heather that pulled back at her skirts. Nothing looked familiar, but of course it was open moorland for miles with no points of reference other than the tall standing stone they had long since left behind in the mist.

"What if we never get home?" Tilda sobbed.

Eliza didn't dare speak. They kept moving forward. The chill worked its way into their limbs, and both girls grew weary. Eliza wasn't even sure if they'd already passed the moorland track, and their route down into the village. Perhaps they were wandering aimlessly in circles.

"I can't go on," Tilda whispered.

Eliza pursed her lips. Either through her feet from the vibrations, or the sounds in the air, she could tell something was approaching slowly yet heavily. She felt Tilda creep up right behind her and clutch at her skirts. She felt a little sick herself. What if this was the blue man, out looking for a meal or a victim, or whatever it was he was after when he rose from his chilled bog grave. They would simply disappear, and no one would even know what had happened to them. They'd see her initial and the date and wonder if the names of victims were added to the rock. Or laugh because even then Eliza Gaskin didn't get it right, with the wrong year for her birth. If only she'd stayed a little longer to finish the 0.

A horse led by a tall man appeared out of the mist, colour and form solidifying from a ghost-like quality to real living beings. Tilda let out a little shriek and squeezed her eyes shut, burying her face in her sister's back. Eliza didn't worry about the future scolding, she just felt relief as she saw her father, his boots bog-splashed, his long coat hanging damply around his frame. "Thank God," he breathed as he clutched at his little girls, enveloping the pair in a deep, warm embrace. "I feared you were lost."

"We know these moors," Eliza scoffed meekly with a poor attempt at bravado.

"No one knows these moors in mist like this. Come on, get up with you." He first helped Eliza, then Tilda, sheltered in the arms of her sister, onto the back of the horse, then helped the beast turn around whilst avoiding the worst of the peat bogs. They started on the slow tramp home to a frantic mother who couldn't bear to lose any more children.

The three of them carried their own fearful memories, remembering the mist and the low temperature, the feeling of being watched somehow, but of no help coming. Other villagers shook their heads. Girls of a land agent ought to know better, having grown up here. Worst, girls of their status ought not to be wandering the moors like that in any weather. The other children thought it was hysterical, and Daniel Iredale, older than Eliza, went up onto the moors the following week and saw what Eliza had carved into the rock, laughing at her when he next saw her, how funny it was that girls were so desperate to impress the lads and do whatever was asked. The other children laughed at her and Eliza felt a burning shame. Her fascination with Daniel, who was a beauty, turned to something closer to repulsion, and she realised that this longing that was starting to awaken could be a woman's undoing. Perhaps that was the thing that drove women to jump from cliffs into lakes and men to take other men to the moors and bury them in the bogs.

1854

Talk of witches was never far away. The girls were growing up and out of their childish fairystories, reason and enlightenment noted folklore as a fiction, and yet there was intangible inner sense that somethings could not quite be explained away. Even Great Aunt Muriel could delight in tales of the old world, and she was the first to see only the science in any given situation. Eliza, now fourteen, stood and silently regarded her aunt, now in her sixties but still with the energy of a wiry young boy. In society's eyes she was aged, but in truth she was still youth, but creased and frowned from burden of living. Muriel had survived beyond many of her peers. A great population of white strands twisted through her hair, but the redness still shone through. Her eyes darted to the ten-year-old Tilda who was captivated by Muriel's story. Tilda hadn't taken on that boyish look that characterised Muriel, but she certainly had the family red hair. Eliza had been told that she looked like her grandmother, a woman who had died before she had been born. In appearances at least, although Muriel said her personality was more considered and thoughtful than her ancestor. Whatever that was supposed to mean. The details of their grandmother, a lady called Elizabeth MacCaskill, could be a little patchy at times. All the girls had seen the miniature portraits that their Mamma kept, and the shocking amount of jewellery – she must have been very rich and important Eliza supposed. Mamma said she had been a very clever women, underrated because of her sex. Elizabeth MacCaskill had spoken a great many languages fluently, and had been a natural diplomat. They had grown up on the continent, and Mamma had lived in a number of countries, and was just as canny with the languages herself. But beyond those scant facts, the family did not speak. Who her husband had been was not discussed, and there was always something pressing to attend to when questions on husbands and grandfathers, and what old granny had done with herself for pleasure came up.

That summer the family had returned to Whitby for a long holiday. It was not simply that it was a fashionable place to be that drew them there. It was a charming place with a rugged prettiness. The town was filled with yards: no-through alleyways where houses clustered up against one another like frightened birds. The settlement was multilayered, clinging to steep sides of the mouth of the River Esk as it into the briny sea. The whaling boats were an industry on the wane now and nothing of what it had been in Granny Eleanor's girlhood. The family had a great number of connections. There was the maternal side up in the fine house at the cliffs, beyond the abbey ruins. Father's side had a great many Gaskin relations, mostly distant and forgotten, or married into new names, scattered all over the area. Some of the cousins, a little older that the Rosedale girls, would visit sometimes. Then there were the friends, and Eliza had made friends with a quiet, bookish little girl, Mary Linskill. Mary's mother, a religious woman, had been impressed when she had heard mention of Gaskin, and realised the potential status and lineage of the family. She encouraged Mary and Eliza in their friendship, and girlish correspondence when they were parted as the summer's sun sank ready for autumn.

That summer morning, three generations of women took a stroll through the old town. They walked by the River Esk, where the narrow streets winded and lurched up sudden steep hills. Muriel had stopped outside a fine yellow sandstone building at the bottom of Chubb Hill, and was pointing at it as she continued to talk to Tilda. The building was formed of three storeys, with arched, gabled ends, and windows made up of long, narrow rectangles of darkened diamond-shaped class. It was a gothic manor house born for flickering candle light and ghosts haunting the uneven passageways. There were iron crosses fixed to the walls, whether to buttress the stonework, keep out the devil or merely for decoration, Muriel couldn't say when Tilda pressed for finer details.

The youngest sister, Charlotte, only six, was tugging on Eliza's hand and talking about the sand. In her small fist she clutched a little cloth bag of digging implements, pilfered from the various kitchens she'd had chance to enter in the last six months. Charlotte was eager to attend to business. Eliza ignored her requests and dragged her closer to Aunt Muriel so she might hear what they were talking about.

"Bagdale Hall," Muriel said. "They used to try witches here hundreds of years ago. They held the old courts here."

"They used to kill witches here?" Tilda's eyes were stretched wide in delighted horror.

"No. They tried misunderstood women here then took them elsewhere to execute them."

"And there were a lot of witches in the olden days?"

Muriel raised her eyebrows. "There were a lot of misunderstood women. We still live in unenlightened times and we can only dream of the day when women are treated as equals..."

"Aunt, they're only girls," Mairi spoke, not wanting to hear another soapbox lecture on the common rights of women just now. She'd heard someone say that as folks grew older they let things go more easily, but with age Muriel only became all the more furious with the state of society.

"And they should be prepared for the injustice of the world they are growing into."

"But there must have been some witches," Tilda piped up, not paying attention to the political discussion. "Abigail Craister never could have jumped into Gormire from those cliffs without a bit of magic to help her fly."

"Abigail Craister?"

"She was a witch who jumped into the lake from Whitestone Cliffs," Mairi explained. "Jennifer delights in the story every time we go there and the girls have become quite taken with it."

"Why did she jump into a lake?"

"She was being hunted by hounds."

Muriel tutted. "That sounds about right."

"But no one could jump that far," Tilda tried to get back to the main point. "She should have fallen into the wood. She must have been magic."

"All legends start with a little grain of truth, but they're not to be taken literally," Mairi advised.

Tilda huffed. Witches were real. Sprites and hobs and other strange things still roamed the moors. She still wondered about the Blue

Man, even though a couple of years had passed since their misty stone carving adventure. Eliza didn't like to speak of the Blue Man. The local lads would still occasionally bring it up and laugh at Eliza, and how she'd carved her initials in the standing stone. Gone up in the mist. She was lucky she hadn't been swallowed up by a bog. The Iredale lad had even gone up to the stone to see if she really had carved her initial there. He had laughed at the crude work she had left, then neatened the job up for her, turning the rough final line into a proper digit of one. He returned laughing at Eliza that her workmanship was no good and he'd had to repair it. It now properly said 1841. Tilda looked at her sister and said she supposed she was a year younger now. Eliza had grown guarded with the local children, and became increasingly reclusive, keeping company with her botanical drawings, sketches of old buildings and life observed from a distance. Tilda on the other hand delighted in the fantastical. "But there must have been hundreds of witches," she preserved. "We must have had witches in our family?"

Mairi laughed lightly, but a dark look crossed Muriel's face.

"Do you think grandmother Eleanor (so named as she didn't like the addition of greats either) will remember any?"

"Your grandmother is old and you mustn't upset her," Muriel said sharply. "There's no such thing as witches, just misunderstood women. We've certainly had those in the family; women who haven't fitted in with what's been expected."

Eliza felt a chill on her back and looked up at Bagdale Hall. Would that be her? A girl who was awkward and scorned by the lads, teased and mocked, who went off looking at plants and herbs and would not make a good housewife. As for not upsetting grandmother Eleanor, why, the old woman was always keen to talk of the past. She'd taught Eliza hundreds of jigs, reels and folk tunes, hailing from the length and breadth of this island nation: both the mainland and communities on small islands. She's told stories of hobs and trowies playing their fiddles on late summer evenings. When she wasn't sharing the rich history of the folk music, she sometimes wandered into her own past, and told Eliza about her own children, of whom only Muriel survived now. Some days she would go back to her own siblings. She had once talked about her twin sister Gillian who had struggled to fit in and had been the victim of a lynch mob. Of a wicked sister Clara who had eventually been caught out by her own mischief. A brother lost to underground ghosts. Then a dark look would cross her face and she might vaguely mention the stepfather who had given her the original family name of Hurst. But she did not care to speak of him. Some things were best forgotten.

Charlotte had changed tack and gone to her mother. "Mamma, might we go to the sands?"

Mairi looked down at her youngest daughter and smiled. "Yes of course, let's head that way."

"Yes," Muriel sounded decided. "We'll take a meandering route and I can show you the house where we grew up."

They climbed up the step lanes to the north of the river, following Muriel's fast pace, until they reached a smart town house. The girls were bored at this point, Charlotte desperate to start digging in the sand. Elizabeth wanted to sit down somewhere and sketch. Muriel was enjoying her ramble in the past and ignored the grunts of protest.

"Of course, we still own it. But it's been rented out for decades."

"Why did you ever leave?" Mairi idly questioned, looking up at the fine building. She'd never been to Haworth but she'd heard her mother's descriptions of the cottage the family had lived in, and it was nothing in comparison to this. Elizabeth had always rolled her eyes and been grateful she'd moved out before Eleanor had decided to take the family home across country to the west.

"My grandmother was back in Haworth, my mother wanted to be closer to her."

"And my own mother grew up here. It's a shame she could never have brought me here." Mairi let out a long sigh, and watched as Eliza started to lead the girls back down the lane so they might get to the seafront and the sands. Everyone was getting bored of Charlotte's complaints. "I do still miss her, even after all this time."

Muriel touched her hand gently. "We're not meant to ever get over grief. Not completely."

"I feel disconnected sometimes. Oh, I have you and grandmother and I'm very grateful. But I look at what my girls have and I think there's so much I missed. I have no idea who my father is."

"You've never said..."

Mairi shrugged it off. "Where's the point? The knowledge is gone with my mother. She never wanted to talk about it, so he must have been very cruel. I don't even know which country he came from. We went to so many places and met so many people. I could be an Armenian princess for all I know!" She laughed.

Muriel turned away. "He was not cruel. You must never think that."

Mairi's chest tightened on itself. "You know who he was?"

"He never knew about you, do you see? He never met you."

"He died before I was born?"

"He came from Scotland," Muriel offered up a scrap of information, avoiding all the other incorrect assumptions. She didn't want to have this conversation. "The girls are disappearing round that corner. Come along, I think we should go to the beach."

Mairi lingered back, watching her aunt march down the lane. You know, she realised. Her aunt knew her history. Her parentage had never been unknown, as she sometimes wondered in less charitable moments about her mother and her wild parties. No one had told her in all these years. Was it right that she was the only one who did not know, when it was she who shared this man's blood? Suddenly possibilities bloomed before her. Where did her bloodline go? The warrior highlands of Scotland, an Edinburgh academic, an island farmer? She smiled to herself, as if her mother would have come into contact with islanders, so remote from the life they had led as to have been on the other side of the world. She would get at the information gradually, realising that Muriel did not wish to tell her. It wasn't just for her, but for the girls as well, to understand where they came from. More Scots, she mused to herself. Now there was a father and a grandfather who came from north of the border. She wasn't quite sure if she knew herself.

Down on the shore Charlotte was digging in the wet sand with a soup ladle. It was a furious scurrying action, almost animal, as sand sprayed up in a frenzy, grains catching in her hair and the lace edging on her dress. Smart women strolling above on the promenade tutted when they saw the girl, judging by her dress she was not one of the scruffy uneducated poor one could not expect any better of. They looked down in distain until they were caught by the glower of an older, dark-haired girl close by who held a cloth bag and was obviously keeping an eye on the little urchin.

"Raised by ruffians," one of the women muttered as she twirled her parasol and turned away. "When I was her age I'd never dare stare at my elders and betters like that."

"I wouldn't even now," her walking partner commented. "I was raised with good manners."

When the women had gone - snooty, judging brainless things fluffed with lace, Eliza thought - she turned her attention back to the promenade steps where Adelaide still lingered. She was waiting to see her Mamma. Of all the girls it was Adelaide who didn't like to stray too far from home or Mamma.

"I found a rock!" Charlotte shrieked, flicking the soup ladle up with dexterity. A black, sandy blob hurtled out, and Tilda leapt forward with the grace of a cricketer to catch the missile in both hands.

"Nice catch," Eliza applauded.

"Why, thank you," Tilda gave a curtsey.

"That's my rock." Charlotte brandished her ladle.

Tilda rubbed the sand off with her skirts. "It looks like a piece of jet, do you know? We could sell it. Don't you think?" She looked to her sister. "They make jewellery and things out of this. We could be rich. Go travel the world."

"I'll be rich," Charlotte corrected, snatching the rock out of Tilda's hands.

"So I can't travel the world?"

"You can come as my maid." Charlotte trotted over to Eliza and deposited her find in the cloth bag. "You can look after my rock."

"Oh, Eliza!" a voice called out. "I thought it was you." An earnest-faced young girl, the same age as Eliza, ran up to the group, coming via the rock-hard wet sand accompanied by the slap-slap of footsteps. Wet tracks were left behind where seawater bulged up in the footprints. The Gaskin girls paused in their play and turned to meet the arrival. She was a neat and primly dressed girl, dark-haired with very carefully brushed hair, not a strand out of place, with a central parting and tightly worked pigtails hanging over each shoulder.

"Mary," Eliza waved to her friend. "I was going to call on you tomorrow. We came over to Whitby yesterday for our holidays."

"Oh, I'm so glad to see you," Mary said, breathing a little heavier from her outburst of speed. Mary wasn't one for showing emotion, despite her love of poetry and her artistic soul that felt things so keenly. She had been carefully brought up as a respectable child, by a pious and slightly snobby mother who was keen on social standing and family history worth bragging of. Not that Mary came from a high-landed family. But they were hardly destitute, her father a police constable of the town. Her mother came from more humbler beginnings, up from one of the moorland villages, but was happy to ride on whatever she could learn of her husband's roots. Mary, their eldest child, had been brought up to be an earnest, grave little thing. The same age as Eliza, they had met a couple of years ago, and when not on holiday in Whitby the girls kept in touch by letter. Mrs Linskill was happy for the friendship to continue as the Gaskins were a renouned family in Whitby, and Eliza's own father was a land agent on the Rosedale estate which was no slight thing to be scoffed at.

"We've come a little earlier than we planned, or what we were thinking of," Eliza added. Maybe she should have written and told Mary of the change of plans, but had decided to enjoy a few days incognito before she would see her friend. As much as she liked the girl, she could be a little intense.

"Come with me," she asked, taking Eliza's hand then pointing across the beach, back the way she had come. "There's a man telling stories. It's all free."

They looked to a cluster of people, a few adults, a man perched on a rock and a great number of children, all gathered in a loosely formed circle. There wasn't always so much entertainment for children here in the town. Sometimes there would be a Punch and Judy show, or a donkey ride, but that was all. Story telling was something new. Eliza nodded. Tilda was already marching off towards the group. Charlotte stuck her bottom lip out and told them she was digging.

"Oh, there's lots of sand over there," Eliza pleaded, "And you've not dug there yet. Think of the big rocks we might find."

Charlotte ran across and took her sister's free hand, then the three girls ran off after Tilda to the storytelling group. As they neared, the man's voice became clearer and they could make out the words as he neared the end of a tall tale. He stumbled over a word now and then, with a touch of stutter, but he clearly relished the role of storyteller as much as the children were in awe of so much attention from the young stranger. He looked as if he came from the same mould as young Mary Linskill, with his grave and earnest countenance. Hooded, thoughtful eyes glanced about his young audience, dark hair ended in curls that were carefully pomaded to the side of his face. Neatly, and well-dressed, he had the look of a wealthy, thinking man.

"I heard they are scholars," Mary whispered excitedly to Eliza, nodding at the man on the rock and the equally young and well-dressed men, all waistcoats and pocket-watches, that lingered at the periphery, amused to see this other side of their colleague. "Mathematics, from Oxford."

In the natural pause between stories, and the arrival of a fresh audience, he looked at the new comers. His lofty stare first reached Tilda, skirting over the older girls Mary and Eliza, blossoming young woman, then down to the little one, who stood brandishing a sand-riddled soup ladle in the air. He broke into a smile.

"And whose presence are we graced with here? The lady of the ladle, I presume?"

Charlotte looked horrified that a strange adult was speaking to her, and blushed. "I'm me."

"Of course you are, and you shouldn't be anyone but yourself. Have you just come from the kitchen?"

"I'm digging for treasure."

"And will you go to the end of the sand for your treasure?"

Charlotte looked confused and looked at her shoes as if they might have the answer. She'd done a lot of digging before but had never managed to get so deep that she had found where the sand stopped. "I think I'm too small to dig that deep."

"But the end of the sand is that way." He pointed to the north. Charlotte's brow creased up in utter puzzlement. Someone in the background snorted, and said, "He means the village Sand's End."

Tilda stepped behind her sister and held her shoulders gently, sensing she looked as though she was near to tears. The man on the rock was being very kind, although some of the adults in the background were tittering in amusement at the conversation and Charlotte was getting lost in this play of words. "We heard you were telling stories," she said, distracting him from the focus on Charlotte. "Will you tell us one?"

"Oh yes, another story!" cried out some of the other children.

"Regrettably I have just come to the end," he sighed, pausing and placing his hands together. "Although since coming here to Whitby, the beginnings of a new story have been taking form in my mind. Something about a carpenter..."

"Oh, come on Charlie, let's have a break from this!" One of the scholarly men in the crowd interrupted. "We're already late for tea and I'm parched."

The man's face fell in irritation. "Charles," he muttered, knowing no one would take any notice of his request. He wasn't quite so confident in these social circles as some of his colleagues. Oh, he could lecture, which was part of the reason why they'd come north, to give lectures. And a little story telling in his free time, for stories and verses were occurring to him all the time. This he did enjoy, spinning tales for youngsters, and watching the believing, delighted faces that attended his words were such a charm.

"Will you be back tomorrow?" one of the young lads asked.

"No, he'll be on a tour of the moors or there'll be trouble from me," a bearded man said. "I've gone to the trouble of getting these carriages arranged for our tour, and you'll all be attending upon pain of death."

"That's a bit extreme, old man," someone else said.

"Regrettably, not tomorrow," Charles said as he stood up, dusting down his coattails. "But I will be back."

"I say, that's Elizabeth Gaskin, isn't it?"

Tilda turned around to stare accusingly at Eliza, as if to ask who she thought she was being recognised on the beach so often. Mary looked questioningly at her friend. "I thought you were Eliza?"

"Everyone who knows me calls me Eliza," she muttered, watching as a young woman who had been flirting with the mathematicians, twirling a tiny lace parasol that was neither use nor ornament as far as Eliza could see, came strolling across to the little girls, radiating womanhood. She was only eighteen, a mere four years older than Eliza, but tightened into her corsets, her hair styled up and her flashing smile, she was of another world.

"Why, Elizabeth, I thought it was you. This is good fortune."

They'd met once last year sometime. One of Pa's cousins's children or some such connection. Emily Gaskin: that had been her name, Eliza recalled. She hadn't been interested in meeting her distant relatives, for they were rich townfolk with delusions of grandeur and small minded conversation. They'd been off to some cultural gathering at the assembly rooms, and had met their distant cousins in town by chance. Five minutes if that. Emily had a good memory for a face.

"You live up in the moors, don't you? Johnathan," she twisted around, waving to the man she'd been circling, "I've got us a guide now, see, this is my cousin who lives up on the moors. Now I simply have to join you all tomorrow."

"I'm not going anywhere tomorrow," Eliza looked horrified.

Emily turned her back to Jonathan and stepped closer to her cousin. "You simply must. I can't not go but I can't go on my own."

"I'm sure you'd manage."

"It wouldn't be decent, stupid," she hissed. "I need an escort. And you've been enjoying Mr Dodgson's stories, so really it would be rude not to come."

"Can I come?" Tilda asked.

"Certainly not."

"I want to come," Charlotte protested, gazing up in awe at the rich lady. She'd looked like a watercolour painting of youth on holiday from a distance, but she wasn't as pretty when one was almost standing on her feet.

"She's the lady of the ladle, she has to come," Tilda persisted.

"Absolutely not," Emily hissed. "This is not a children's outing. Now, dear Elizabeth," she turned her attention to the elder girl, glancing up and down Mary Linskill and wondering who the dour little puritan was. "I'll send a note to your mother and we'll pick you up first thing tomorrow. Make sure you're ready."

"I don't think I want to go."

"Of course you do. Who doesn't want to go out with Oxford men?" Emily twinkled.

Charlotte stuck out her bottom lip and felt a huffy crying session coming on. She was always left out of things for being the smallest. Tilda stuck out her tongue at the retreating back of Emily Gaskin. "What a snob," she sniffed, irritated that she hadn't been invited either. They vaguely knew of all of Pa's distant relations, for there were a lot of Gaskins about the area, coming from a wealthy shipping family. Their little Rosedale enclave came from the second son of a far-away-down-the-line son, and seen as the poorer, inconsequential relations. A bonus to this shabby sideline was that they had never been forced into all that polite socialising they might otherwise have had to commit to. Living in the back of beyond, not being too rich (as far as the Gaskins were aware, if only they truly knew the money behind Mairi, Muriel and Eleanor) or important did have its advantages.

"Don't worry," Tilda consoled Eliza. "Mamma will get you out of it."

Mamma did not absolve anyone from their obligations. In fact it seemed that in Emily Gaskin's panicked haste to accompany the Oxford students on their moorland excursion, the wider family was drawn into a number of obligations no one particularly wanted to follow through. On hearing that the distant relations were in town, and that his middle daughter was so oddly keen to socialise with one of the children, Mr Robert Gaskin felt duty bound to invite his cousin, Stephen and wife to an evening's supper. His wife rolled her eyes at him and asked if they must have the poor relations over. It would probably just embarrass them not knowing how to properly hold a knife and fork. The wife would feel ashamed for being underdressed for decent society. They would manage to put their simple relatives at ease, he assured her. Robert remembered some vague mention of an interest in rocks or history or some such thing, and he'd show the man his collection of ancient flint arrow heads. Mrs Gaskin tutted and turned back to her needlework. How to make a dull evening even worse.

Mairi was the best dressed and attractive of the Gaskin wives that evening, youth naturally taking a large percentage of the glory in the achievement. But good living and outdoor exercise nourished her youthful spirit, despite being five children into the game, at thirty three, she still shone with vigour. Perhaps it was the continental upbringing, perhaps everything else she had endured, but she held her head up as though it did not even occur to her that she ought to feel inferior. The wives gossiped over her dress and jewellery the following day, and concluded she must come from money, for none of that was anything Stephen could afford. What was he, a farmer's agent or something of the sort?

After dessert Robert had taken Stephen and the other cousins off for port and a lecture on his growing collection of ancient flint arrowheads collected from the area. He already had two glass cases full of the things.

"I don't know whether they were prolific or just poor shots up this way," Stephen had grumbled when they had finally managed to escape the evening, and were walking up to the cliff tops back to Mairi's grandmother's house. "But it seems thousands of the things have been dug up in the locality. A fellow by the name of Simpson has a knack of finding them I'm told."

"Arrowheads?" Mairi asked. "There was a battle here?"

"Hunting arrows I think. They're made of flint, not metal. Neat little things, with flakes chipped off. Of course, they could have been made last week as a thousand years ago, there's no way to date them unless there is a record of the strata they're removed from. Details of which Robert is utterly clueless on. When I mentioned strata he thought I was showing off and speaking Italian."

Mairi giggled and tightened her arm around his, pulling herself closer in to his side. "It wasn't the most scintillating dinner evening you've ever taken me to. Quite dull really. Think of the people we've met with. You remember when we visited William Smith in Scarborough?"

"He was one in a million. I still miss being able to bounce ideas off him. It's over ten years now since he passed."

"Really that long?" In some ways Mairi felt old, with so much time having passed. She had a hoard of growing children about her, she was the head of her own family. She did not even have a mother or a father to defer to. And yet, now that Charlotte was ever growing more independent, and no more children had appeared, she had a glowing hopefulness that her own girlhood was returning and she might find a moment now and then for some of her own beloved pastimes and solitary walks. She thought back to that little house in Scarborough, the odd dinner evenings with William Smith and his seemingly unsuitable wife. Yet they were so much in love. "What ever happened to Mrs Smith?" She suddenly wondered.

"She died a few years ago," Stephen said. It had only been mentioned in passing to him, but he was still in sporadic communication with the nephew, who had written it as a final afterthought in the letter at the time. "It was quite sad. She had a mental collapse when William died. They had to commit her in the end."

"It must be very hard when one's husband dies. I suppose all women must be lost for a time."

"This was much worse I understand. Not something you will suffer from when the time comes. You're too strong for that."

She pulled away from his arm. "Stephen, don't be so morbid. Don't talk like that."

"I am older than you."

"No. I'm not talking about this now, or ever," she muttered. "I've lost enough people."

"I'll be fifty in two more years."

And don't I know it, she thought, hugging his arm tightly and pressing herself into his side. She might be blossoming for the second time, but she could see her husband was well into the phase of maturity, with greying hair, lines deepening about his face, and a little more width around his middle. Of course people could go at any time of life; she only had to recall her own precious little son to understand that. But for healthy folk who had gotten safely through to adulthood, it felt as though a distant bell could remind them of time due at any moment in that middle age. Her own dear mother had gone at fifty-two. On the other hand, her aunt was in her sixties and still vibrant, and her grandmother, although slow, white-haired and generally a recluse at home these days, was still keen in mind and walked about the gardens. Eleanor MacCaskill was in her early nineties. When the family came to visit, Muriel said Eleanor burst to life, and was ready with her freshly stringed and tuned violin, waiting for Eliza in particular.

The moorland outing with Emily and a collection of well-educated Oxford academics with over inflated opinions of their own marvellousness was pending. Eliza hadn't been certain of what to mark the day down as far as experiences went. It had given her opportunity to escape Charlotte for the day, who had taken on the title Lady of the

Ladle since that storytelling man had bestowed such a name upon her. She marched about the house with that blasted soup ladle, annoying everyone. That morning had been no different, and even through the dramatics about the ladle had barely started, she'd almost felt her heart leap when Emily Gaskin had arrived to collect her.

There had been that many additions and alterations to the trip that two carts had been arranged in the end. They were to jaunt up onto the moorland roads, crossing miles of heather moorland, before dropping down into the villages, and taking refreshment at Commondale before heading back to Whitby. Eliza was plonked in the cart with a number of unfamiliar faces, equally uninterested in her as she was with them. A few were known to varying degrees. There was of course Cousin Emily and the current obsession of her eye – neither with any time for anyone else; and the shoreline storyteller, Charlie Dodgson as the other fellows called him, although it was obvious from the prickling that he preferred Charles. He had pondered on Eliza for a moment from under his hooded eyes, making a short comment that Eliza's sister wasn't there, then dismissed her from his attention. Eliza rolled her eyes at no one and shifted so that she could watch the scenery and ignore her fellow passengers.

Their cart was second, and due to passengers wanting to stop and look at this and that, they soon lagged behind. Somewhere on the high moors above Commondale the cart started to judder violently, the horses shrieking and the driver swearing at them, before a collective cry came out as the axel broke. The cart stopped and lurched deeply to one side. Eliza fell onto her cousin who screamed and clutched at her neighbour. There was much cursing and scuffling, followed by apologies to the ladies present, as the group, unhurt and only embarrassed and muddled, scrambled out onto the track and surveyed the damage.

"Bugger it," the driver muttered, kicking the cart as he unharnessed one of the horses. "I'll ride on down and sort summat."

"What about the rest of us?"

"Wait here or walk on down to Commondale," the driver shrugged as he hoisted himself onto the horse. "It'll be half an hour at most, even for the likes of you."

"See here now!"

"What about the cart?"

"It's going nowhere."

"Perhaps we ought to stay and guard it."

"Nonsense," Emily snapped, her words as sharp as the flick of her opening parasol. "I'm not sitting up here in the dust. We'll go down and take refreshment. You," she added, speaking as if to a servant as she turned to her cousin. "You come from these parts. You'll be guide."

"You just follow the track," Eliza said, a little bemused how someone could not work out how to get to Commondale. She felt herself groaning inwardly as the party merely stared expectantly at her. "This way," she spoke surely, scuffing her heels in the dust as she started after the driver and his horse. He'd been no fool in getting away quickly.

"I'll stay with the cart," Charlie Dodgson offered, not inclined to have to make conversation today. It would be the perfect opportunity to take his notebook out in peace and work on the verses he'd started yesterday.

"Good man!"

"Will he be all right on his own?" Emily asked, not particularly caring, as she took her beau's arm.

"Don't let Charlie's looks fool you," he laughed. "I remember him from Rugby. He stands up for himself."

Charles Dodgson went to sit at the side of the road in the heather, watching the party walk away for the first minute or so before he took out his notebook and pencil to return to his work. He read the verses out loud and shook his head at the second verse. It didn't flow smoothly. A couple of words needed replacing. He tapped the pencil to his chin, lost in thought to his stories and verses. Who needed the simplicity of real life when one had one's imagination? He didn't notice the cooling of the air as the clouds shifted and gathered, blocking the sun, and making the moorland vista a little dull. The colour quality took on a silver sheen.

It was as he was crossing out and rewriting a line that he experienced that creeping feeling that he was being watched. Not only that, but that he had been observed for some time now. Charles lowered his pen and raised his head confidently.

On the opposite side of the road stood a woman. She was impossible to age. She could have been a hundred from the long silver hair, messily loose but with the remnants of ribbons intertwined. Yet her skin was clear and uncreased, her figure trim and yet definitely adult. Oddly there was a childlike innocence about her. She stood in her long, tatty skirts, with a very calm rabbit draped over one forearm as she gently stroked the wild creature. He would have assumed her to be one of the moorland girls, yet she was dressed badly even by their standards. Her head was completely uncovered, and her dress looked like something from an historic play. Something that had been torn and tugged at by traipsing through deep moorland heather. Quite simply, he was taken aback.

"Can I help you?" He finally broke the silence as they stared at one another.

"No," she replied. "I am Atheleys." As if the second statement were explanation of the first.

"What an odd name," Charles commented before he had considered she might be offended by his opinion. Yet it was an odd name, so antiquated. What was it, old English? Anglo Saxon? He ought to have studied harder with those old dead languages, but Latin and Greek were of more interest, and nothing compared to the blessed state of mathematics.

"Lughaidh."

"I beg your pardon?"

Atheleys looked down at the rabbit. "He'll be sleeping soon. But we'll have to let him go. Mustn't follow him down the rabbit hole."

Charles opened his mouth to ask her what nonsense she was talking about but was abruptly taken aback when she looked up sharply, meeting his eye and startling him.

"You mustn't follow him into Freebrough Hill," she warned. "They're sleeping."

"Look here, you'll have to explain..." Charles stumbled over his words, then dropped his pencil in the heather. Irritated by his clumsiness, embarrassed by the brain freeze on his vocabulary, he stood up and quickly retrieved his pencil. Straightening, brushing down his coat, he went to question the stranger about her odd comments, but was perplexed to find he was alone on the moors, with only a broken cart for company. Even the rabbit had disappeared.

The group had taken their refreshment quite happily. Emily seemed to have forgotten the need for a chaperone, so Eliza had wandered off to find the driver. The man was at the village blacksmith's, discussing the damaged cart and pondering on where to get a joiner or a cart man to fix the damned thing. He'd rented another cart that would take the rich folks back to Whitby as soon as they'd finished supping, but his boss wouldn't be happy about the loss of a cart. Hardly lost, the blacksmith had said, just needed bringing down to the village to be fixed. If he could be assured of payment, he'd take his own horse up and fetch it back down to the village and arrange the repairs.

Eliza stood listening to the business arrangements, wishing someone would notice her and ask what she wanted. She wanted to go home now, she would say, no more lingering. She watched as an old, rather stately woman came out of the cottages and walked over to the blacksmith, asking if his customer was in need of refreshment.

"Not right now, Magda."

"Oh, and what bonny lass is this?" The woman was the first to acknowledge Eliza, and walked over to her. "You have a familiar look about you. Are you from the village?"

Eliza shook her head. "I'm from Rosedale."

"Rosedale!"

"She's with the Whitby group," the driver muttered. "That's all I care about, where she needs to get back to."

"Been a lot of years since I was last at Rosedale," the woman sighed. "I sometimes went over, if my husband had a special commission. Of course he had to stop the smithing a few years ago, no spring chicken anymore, and then he passed away last year, dear man." She smiled sadly, then clapped her hands together. "I'll go in and fetch you something to eat. Can't leave a young girl starving out here."

"I'm not starving..." Eliza started, but the woman had already retreated into the cottages.

The blacksmith raised his eyes to the sky. "Dear man, my arse," he muttered. "I was apprenticed to Longbottom. Decent fella, let me take over the smithy when he went feeble. His wife was always off with him. Don't know what she's been on since he died."

"Sounds like most wives," the driver laughed coarsely. "You should meet my missus on a bad day."

"Aye, I know," the blacksmith chortled along. "But villagers say Magda never forgave him for her babies dying. As if that were his fault in the first place. Sounds more like she were no good with the children. She lost another girl she was supposed to be looking after. Never found again. I only keep her on out of pity you understand. She keeps house well, cooks a hell of a lot better than my wife. Anyway, she's busy with all the little'uns..."

"Here we are," Magda reappeared with a plate of scones, oblivious that her long life had been so quickly and callously dissected and spread before random strangers like a spectacle for the passing tourist trade.

Eliza looked at the plate of scones. They were freshly baked. She could smell them, and felt her stomach growl. It had been a long time since she'd eaten. The old woman offered the plate at her, and she took two, one for her pocket and one to eat now.

"All right, away with you, lass," the driver waved her off, looking up at the sun and realising they were running late. "Go tell them southerners I'm coming to fetch them now. We need to be away now if we're to get back to Whitby in time." He broke out into a leering grin. "Any complaints and tell them we don't want any moorland beasts after us."

The two men burst out laughing, mocking old beliefs in witchery and spirits. The local people were scary enough when they wanted to be. Eliza glanced back at the old woman, wondering why she stayed here. It didn't seem she was particularly liked, but then perhaps she had nowhere else to go.

"Thank you for the scones," she said, then darted away back up the beckside path to return to the daytrippers. Time to head back for Whitby. As she ran up to their outdoor tables, she wondered for the first time how Mr Dodgson had been passing all this time in solitude. He struck her as someone who would manage on his own. Perhaps he was like her, with a bit of paper and a pencil tucked away in a pocket in case a sketching opportunity arose. Or maybe being a scholar he would sit and work out clever algebra in his head or whatever it was scholars did.

Emily Gaskin happened to look up at Eliza stepped up to the head of the table.

"Time to go home."

Their stay in Whitby was nearing an end. Mairi sat at the seating area near the French doors of the house, looking out to the garden. Adelaide knelt upon the grass threading daisies together. Stephen was crouched nearby trying to fix a kite for Eliza and Tilda whilst Charlotte continuously tried to scramble up his back. Hardly lady like behaviour, even in a girl so young and yet no one wanted to pull her in line and leave a sombre little shadow of a child in her place. Their little Lady Ladle, as they had taken to calling her. She'd been so excited when a poem had been published in the Whitby Gazzette entitled *The Lady of the Ladle*. Charlotte had been certain it was about her, and penned by the storyteller on the sands. Tilda said it couldn't be because his name had been Charles Dodgson, and the poem had been written by 'B. B.'. The arguments grew worse when the poem was read aloud. The tale followed the strutting of a young man through Whitby, only for him to reach the sands and lament his lost love, a cook called Matilda, which had sent shrieks of fury and laughter flying across the breakfast table. At one point Tilda had stood in the doorway and stamped her foot, saying it was all a lot of nonsense.

Mairi shifted in her position and looked across the metal garden table to her Aunt. "Muriel," she spoke, bringing her aunt out of her daydreams of seafaring adventures. The woman had a thing for reading the journals of old sea dogs and explorers. "I want to ask you something and I'd like you to be as truthful as you can."

Muriel had stopped paying attention to the words in her book a while ago, and had been half-dozing in the late sunshine. Mairi's voice sounded grave, and so she gave up the pretence and closed the book, setting it on the table. "This sounds rather serious," she commented, sitting up. "I'm not prone to lying. What is it you wish to ask?"

"Who was my father?"

"Ah."

"You must know something for you mentioned he was a Scot a few weeks ago," Mairi leaned forward, picking up enthusiasm for the subject. "And Mamma never told me a thing."

"I always thought you weren't interested," Muriel said, knowing it was half a lie. Just because a thing is not spoken it does not mean that no one cares, or that no one feels it. Or that it is not true.

"I hardly know some days. But when I watch Stephen with the girls," Mairi shuffled, lowering her eyes. "Well, I never had that. And when you mentioned Scotland I found myself wondering. I'd always assumed he would have been from the continent, maybe France or Italy. I don't know that Mamma ever went to Scotland, but then the Scots travel as much as anyone else, don't they? Perhaps he was a laird, travelling in France..."

"Not quite," Muriel sighed wistfully. "If you are hoping for glamour, I cannot provide it. He was a doctor."

"A doctor? Like a celebrated surgeon or someone like your husband?"

"Not quite. He was a simple country doctor, up in the Highlands. Near a place called Plockton. I've never been there. Perhaps your grandmother has. She did travel a lot in the country with Pa. But she never knew your father, you understand? She wouldn't be able to tell you about him."

"What was he called?"

"Erskine MacKenzie," Muriel said, having hesitated for a moment in fear that she might not be able to get the name out. "I met him in Edinburgh, at the university..."

"And you introduced him to Mamma?"

Muriel's brow creased for a moment, then she nodded slowly. "We could say it was so."

"And did he not love Mamma?"

"Mairi, life is not so simple as we might like to hope. He was due to be wed before.... well, before all of that." She looked away from Mairi and stared out across the garden. Mairi was in her thirties now. Could it really be over three decades since those days? She didn't think she could look at her niece whilst she spoke. "You see, he was never told about you. He was wed and then you came. Elizabeth was protecting you, from upset and disappointment I suppose. We didn't know how it could have gone, and it seemed better this way than rejection."

"And news of an illigitmate child may not have been acknowledged." Mairi concluded, looking away herself.

Muriel nodded slowly, looking to the sky. The rest of the story was on her tongue but she couldn't force it out. Erskine MacKenzie, she thought. Where was he now; was he even still alive? He probably had a hoard of children himself, and grandchildren. She dared to look back to Mairi. "What will you do with it? The knowledge, I mean?"

Mairi shrugged. "I don't know, probably nothing. But thank you for telling me. It feels good to know a little of where one comes from."

"Wake up; you promised!"

Tilda had been out of bed for some time. Like a fiery beetle, she scuttled about the room, harvesting the supplies she had been secreting in readiness. Earlier she had peered out of the window, glad to see it was a cloudless August night. The moonlight would help them find their way. Even so, she was glad of the little lantern she had managed to discreetly borrow from Mrs Burton-Waugh's stable.

Eliza groaned in her sleep and rolled over. Infuriating. Tilda whipped back the bedcovers, which would have found a quick reaction in winter, but in the height of summer it was probably nothing more than an improvement in comfort. She leapt into the bed and violently shook her sister's shoulders. "Eliza, you have to wake up!"

There was a moan in response. Eliza pushed her younger sister's hands off her. "What is it?" She rolled onto her back and pushed her dark hair off her face. She had plaited it before bed, but it was coming lose. "Tilda, we ought to be asleep."

"You promised!" Tilda hissed. "They start digging tomorrow. This is our last chance."

A resigned look flashed over Eliza's face as she did indeed remember. "But it's just a silly children's story," she grumbled, referring to the local folktale their hostess had told them at the dinner table. "Must we?"

"But I got a knife," Tilda scowled, holding up a rather vicious looking carving knife she'd taken from the kitchen after supper.

"Tilda!" Eliza sat upright abruptly. "You should be careful. What a thing to have in a bed. I really don't think this is a clever idea."

Tilda sat back on her haunches and stuck out her bottom lip. Eliza was growing boring, so bogged down in her drawings and her music, being an adult lady and acting like she was all grown up. She was only fifteen. Fifteen was an age, Eliza would counterpoint. There were a couple of girls her age in the village who were already engaged. Not that

Eliza was getting engaged to anyone, she wanted to become an illustrator, and children and household management would only get in the way. Mairi would look worriedly at her eldest when she made announcements like that at the breakfast table. It was frightening how quickly her girls were growing up, and yet they still seemed a lifetime away from adulthood. When Mairi had married, she had only been two years older than Eliza, so she ought not to be so shocked.

Tilda held the knife up before her face, twisting it a little to and fro to reflect what little light streamed from the open window. "You promised me, and besides, I went up to the Blue Man in th' Moss with you."

"Yes well, that was just a silly childish game," Eliza huffed.

"And I'm still a child and I want to be silly." She narrowed her eyes, then pushed herself off the bed and hurried across to her clothes, rushing to pull her dress over her shift. "Oh, be old and boring then. I'm going on my own."

"You can't."

"Can too. And I'll hear the fairies and maybe I'll hear them playing their fiddles." She paused to stare at her sister. "I might learn a tune you've never heard."

Fairies didn't exist and Tilda wouldn't hear a thing and yet... Eliza hesitated for a moment, then hurried out of bed and quickly dressed. The girls pulled on their stockings but carried their shoes so as to make as little noise as possible. They crept down the servants' staircase at the back, having already played on there to be sure they knew where every creak could be avoided. Mrs Burton-Waugh's home was a red brick townhouse with ridiculously high chimney tops, which the girls had used on many an occasion as a navigation point when ambling about the village. They'd easily find their way back when they were done with their late night mischief.

Unlocking the trade entrance, they slipped out into the night, full of giggles that were held within tightened lips. Shoes in one hand, knife in the other, Tilda with her loose red locks led the way. They skipped down the garden path like imps, out of the gate and onto the little road into Sowerby.

It was a smart village just outside of the market town of Thirsk. Smart was the operative word. A smart little village full of smart but not so little buildings, for this was the place where all the businessmen of Thirsk liked to live. It was somewhere beyond the hustle and bustle of a busy market town, where only the very respectable could afford a home. The village was essentially a single street of fine properties lined up on either side. Stretches of tended village green provided a partition between the properties and the dust of the road. A fine old church and a couple of inns punctuated the residential, but this was a place of domestic calm and fine society of the nouveau riche. Mrs Burton-Waugh, widow to the high ranks of the navy and general eccentric, managed to navigate the social strata, and was equally comfortable conversing with tradespeople as she was socialising with the local aristocracy. Through her network of connections she had arranged an invitation with the local aristocracy for them tomorrow. Best behaviour was required. Here in the lowlands, deference and behaviour counted for more, and the social differences were more acute. Compared to Rosedale, it was a different world. As the children of the land agent, they were technically in a different social strata to the farmers' broods, but playmates and schoolmates were all one and the children of the village had all played together. The rules were a little different here.

When they reached the Crown and Anchor Inn, the girls slipped down a side lane which took them out of Sowerby and into the farmlands of the Mowbray valley. The little road took a sharp turn as it crossed Blakey Bridge over the River Codbeck. "Blakey Bridge," Tilda snorted with a laugh. "Blakey Ridge is better."

The lane took another sharp turn and headed away from the little river. The girls left the road and followed a track that continued alongside the river until they reached their goal. It was a small but abrupt mound – great hill to the local children – covered in meadow grass, yellow with buttercups in early summer, but now with thick lush grass and flower heads of seeds for next year's blossoms.

The girls stood at the base of the hill and stared up at the top.

"Pudding Pie Hill," Tilda whispered. "It's a silly name."

"It does look like an odd pudding in all this flat farmland."

"Do you think they'll find custard in the middle when they dig it up?" Tilda joked.

"You never know."

"Come on, we have to start running. You remember what she said. Nine times."

"Which way?" Eliza mused. "I don't remember anyone saying. Should we go clockwise or anti clockwise?"

Tilda looked a little lost. She set down the knife and the lantern in the grass. "I don't know. Do you think it matters?"

"It could do."

"So what should we do?"

Eliza shrugged, looked at her younger sister and broke into a grin. "Run of course, silly. Come on."

With a whoop of joy they started to run around the mound, counting each time they passed the knife on the ground. With each loop they were a little more breathless, the deep grass pulling at their skirts, dew moistening the fabric. Nine came out with a gasp as they reached the knife again. Tilda picked up the implement and they ran to the top of the hill. She felt giddy, full of magic and expectation, and gazed up at the moon as if to receive its blessing. "I suppose I just stick it in," she said. "And then we'll hear them. Do you think we should make a wish?"

"No one ever mentioned wishes in the story," Eliza replied, thinking over what Mrs Burton-Waugh had told them at dinner. She was a great fan of folk stories, in fact she'd been the one to introduce them to Abigail Craister and her leap into Lake Gormire. She was always careful with the details, perhaps embellishing more than she needed to. No mention of wishes had been made when she had spoken of the history of Pudding Pie Hill.

"Maybe we should say one just in case," Tilda suggested. "Hold the knife with me and we'll do it together."

Eliza clasped her hands around her sister's. They met one another's eyes, checked their feet were placed well back, then plunged the blade to the ground. It seemed to barely glance off the ground, and they dropped to their knees so that they could push it further in. Eliza wasn't sure how much hold in the ground it actually had, probably propped up by all the grass.

Tilda squeezed her hands around the handle. "I wish for a pot of gold."

Eliza giggled. "Is that the best you can come up with?"

"All right then, a pot of custard."

The girls tittered with laughter, feeling bold and silly as a twilight breeze curled around their bodies on top of the hill.

"And what do you want?"

Eliza stared down at her fingers, still curled in their ball of accessory after the fact with her sister's. A feeling tightened in her chest. "I don't know. I don't know the word for it only that I feel very much that I want it. I hope I get it."

Tilda snorted like a little donkey. "That's not much for the fairies to work on."

"It's something wonderful. Something worth stepping off the cliff for."

"You're still obsessing with that Abigail Craister story?"

Eliza pulled her hands away sharply, feeling foolish.

They knelt before one another, listening to the sounds of the night. Across the fields the ghostly form of a barn owl glided soundlessly away. Tilda looked about, waiting for magic lights to appear that did not come. "I can't hear them," she eventually said. "She said we would hear the fairies."

"Maybe they're sleeping?"

Tilda dropped to the ground, pressing the side of her head into the grass. Desperate to see or hear something. Find the magic of the hill before that lady and her men ripped it all up. All she heard was the wind moving through the grass. No noise and she'd wasted her wish hoping for a pot of custard. What a fool.

"Come on," Eliza nudged her shoulder gently, getting her to sit up again. "We'd better get back before we're missed. Put that knife and lantern back. I don't want to get in trouble and Mamma say we can't go tomorrow."

"Suppose not." Tilda stood up. "Maybe when they dig it up, all the fairies will come flying out. Do you think that might happen?"

Eliza took her sister's hand as they started down the hill. "It might. You never know what is coming next."

"Of course, Mr Jefferson told me that the hill was an old watch tower from centuries ago," Jennifer Burton-Waugh told Mairi as she surveyed the dig from their more genteel set up in the meadow. "He said there'd been some bones found here a while ago, but essentially that we're getting ourselves excited over nothing." She looked across at Mairi with an excited twinkle in her eye. In part it was that something directly on her doorstep was to be excavated, and here she was, a mere woman, to be ahead of some of the local historians in discovering what might be unearthed. Coupled with the fact that she had personally been invited by the instigator of the dig, aristocracy of Thirkelby no less, had added extra spark to her step for weeks. Although she had a great many friends and contacts in the scientific world, often it came back to the point that she was a woman, and might well be 'interested', in the same way she would be interested to view the flowers in a garden or work on some needlework; but the actual work and graft, and theoretical investigation of a matter would be beyond her. People like Jefferson didn't think this dig was worth attending, but then a woman was directing it, and a foolish aristocrat at that. Even worse she'd gotten an outsider to come and supervise the dig: a man who lived over ten miles away.

What rot, Jennifer thought. Some people let their egos get in the way. They were so pumped up with the notion that they were the county expert, that if anyone else showed independent interest, they were immediately labelled a fool and dismissed to be watchfully observed over the shoulder from a distance. Just in case they did find something.

Mairi, with a parasol perched on her shoulder that was providing no cover whatsoever from the sun, watched the dig with interest. Stephen would have liked to have been here. Of course it was more the rocks than the human history that interested him, but it was all of the earth and one never knew quite what one might find when one started digging. But Rosedale was growing busy. The iron ore mining had begun, and as in its infancy, there was much to supervise and liaise on. Not only with the mining, but the tenant farmers' worries and the influx of workers who needed somewhere to live. He could not be spared for a month.

By her side stood Adelaide, who was quite content to hold her doll in one hand, her mother's in the other and merely dreamily watch the world pass by. Charlotte, the youngest, had been in a sulk this morning and had been left in the care of cook, who was probably feeding her extra treats at this very moment. Eliza and Tilda, ever confidents in each other's games and mischief, had been a little cagey at breakfast, and did not linger with the main group. They had taken little stools to sit off on their own, where Eliza was hunched over her sketchbook and Tilda was pulling at long stalks of grass seed heads whilst chattering at her sister.

The workers, supervised by Mr James Ruddock of Pickering, had made swift work and dug a trench straight into the side of the hill, heading for the heart of the mound. They had removed the turf and placed it in a pile off to the side. At the end of the excavation period they would be able to replace it and allow the grass and meadow flowers to weave their rooted mesh back over the surface of the hill. The labourers carted wheelbarrows of soil off to a spoil mound twenty meters or so away from proceedings, forming a neat and regular line of industrial back and forth.

The instigator of the dig was Lady Louisa-Anne Frankland Russell. She was a fine lady and widower in her sixties of Scottish descent, who according to some local gossip was growing bored in her riches rattling about on her own, now that her husband had been gone these recent years and her girls had all grown up and gained lives of their own. It was a shame she couldn't have just picked up her husband's old paintbrushes to keep herself busy. Rich widows didn't need to get involved in matters of the historian. But she was rich, and had a lot of sway, and here she was, keen on her dig to get to the bottom of the mysteries around Pudding Pie Hill. Naturally she wouldn't get her fingers dirty, but she had surprised some by turning up in her carriage to see the start of the dig, and to remain for the day. Blankets, chairs and tables, all the fittings for a lavish picnic had been decanted from the horse-drawn transport by servants, and the good Lady herself, accompanied by maid, had gone for a gentle stroll about the meadow and down by the river.

She was now making her way back to the small collection of people, both the workers and observers, and brushed her way through the long grasses in her fine gown. "Mrs Burton-Waugh, I am delighted to see you were able to attend my little dig," she spoke as she approached the ladies.

"My Lady," Jennifer bobbed a curtsey. "It was so very kind of you to think of me."

"Anyone who's ever heard of Mrs Burton-Waugh knows of her obsessive nature in all things historical. I knew you'd be interested in getting to the bottom of what's really in this delightfully named Pudding Pie Hill. And I am so glad to see you have companions with you."

"This is Mrs Gaskin, of Rosedale Abbey, my lady," Jennifer made the introductions. "She's staying with me in Sowerby with her daughters this summer."

"Ah, daughters, they are a blessing. I have a fine brood myself. So nice to make your acquaintance. And this young lady here is one of yours?"

"My daughter, Adelaide, my lady," Mairi made the introductions, all with a bob and a nudge to get Adelaide to curtsey. Adelaide looked a little star struck, as if a character from a storybook had stepped down off the pages to say hello. They didn't usually meet such glamorous people up in Rosedale. For Mairi, it was like a jolt back to the old days, travelling the continent with her mother and socialising with the upper levels of society, or at least the male half. With her mother's way of earning her keep, they always remained in an odd liminal space, with plenty of money and etiquette and yet looked down upon by so many in a great many levels of society.

"The girls over there are yours, I assume, although they don't have your colouring. I couldn't help but take a look, incognito you understand. I don't think they realised I was just behind them... Oh, no, no, not to worry," she brushed off the pending apologies, misinterpreting Mairi's expression and assuming she was horrified that Eliza and Tilda hadn't jumped up to curtsey when the Lady had been by. "I must say, your dark-haired daughter has a talent. Why, if she were a boy I could say she could make a career at it. But for women it is not the same. Although times do change, and there's always a great woman out there to catch us by surprise, so we shall have to keep an eye on..."

"Elizabeth, my Lady," Mairi said. "We tend to call her Eliza."

"We shall get her to illustrate some of the finds, I think," Lady Frankland-Russell decided, her eye twinkling. "We ought to have all the proper documentation and reports. Do things properly, as it were."

Lady Frankland-Russell looked as though she was going to say something more, when an exclamation of male voices, followed by the dull bang of shovels being dropped to the ground broke through polite conversation. Eliza ceased in her sketching. She and Tilda shared a look before they jumped up, rushing over to see what had happened. The foreman, Mr Ruddock, was ushering his men back, warning them to take it steady now, lest they damage anything. The men made a hallowed semi-circle around the head of the trench. Eliza and Tilda came to the edge, having to go up the unexcavated bank a little in order to see.

"What is it?" Tilda asked.

Eliza squinted in the shadows, noting the brown heavy lines of a protrusion from the earth. "Looks like bones."

"Girls, get back down," Mr Ruddock told them sharply. "Your weight may destabilise the trench wall."

Eliza felt a flush of embarrassment rush up her neck, thinking really that common sense ought to have already told her it was foolish to scramble up here. Tilda merely scowled and followed her sister back to where they had been sitting, out the way of the working men, who knew best. She directed her best girlish scowl at Mr Ruddock's back as he beckoned her ladyship across to inspect what they had come to. Potentially the internment, he said.

"An internment?" Tilda repeated curiously.

"They've found a dead body," Eliza told her, setting her sketch papers on her lap again. "You do know what this means, don't you?"

"What?"

"That you did it."

"Did what?"

"Killed him."

"I never did a thing!" Tilda shrieked.

"You stuck a knife in the hill."

"It never reached as far down as there."

"Silly," Eliza giggled, making a quick sketch of Tilda's horrified face. "I was only teasing."

"This is extremely exciting," Lady Frankland-Russell declared from across the way, where she inspected the bones from a safe but curious distance. "I always knew there was more to this mound than a watchtower base. Well, get them excavated and out on a sheet and the dig's illustrator can get to work."

Mr Ruddock looked bemused. "My lady?"

"Miss Eliza Gaskin over there in the buttercups. She is documenting everything through her sketches. I must say, I am looking forward to seeing the daily updates. Now, you must excuse me, but this sun can bring on a headache and I feel it's time for luncheon in the shade."

The excavation crew all dofted caps and due deference to the local nobility. Tilda looked furiously at her sister. "You never told me you were the official illustrator. When did you start getting jobs?"

"It's the first I've heard of it." Eliza looked across the breeze-wafted array of meadow grass seed stalks and sedges to where her mother stood. Mairi gave her an encouraging nod and a smile.

"Well, lardy-da!" Tilda sniffed. "At this rate you'll be doing the Queen's portrait by the end of the year!"

These ancient remains had set Eliza thinking. Material signifiers of lives long since lost beyond memory. Not that she was at an age where she seriously contemplated mortality for herself too greatly. Even so, death was something that always hung around at the side lines. It stepped forward, wishing to be remembered at every farming accident; each time a small coffin was taken to the churchyard; news of a young mother taken in the childbed; or the anniversary of her younger brother's early death, when her mother would retreat into melancholy for several days.

The dig had produced more finds than perhaps any of them had expected. After the first body, of which many bones crumbled away upon removal, two more similar burials with burned bones, bits of broken crockery and a few coins were unearthed. The sum hardly amounted to a great treasure, but it was plenty for Eliza to busy herself with particular and exact illustrations. She wanted the proportions and the details just so, in order that a record as good as photograph might be kept.

The final find, and the greatest, was discovered right in the centre of the hill at a great depth of sixteen feet or so. A skeleton lay at rest, with remains of his tools of warfare: boss and rivets of shield and handle of sword. Mr Ruddock declared it to be the burial of a great warrior, commenting on the uncanny size of the limbs of the man. A couple more bodies and some cow horns were later unearthed, but it was the great warrior, later upgraded to clan chief as the find was discussed, that lay at the forefront of people's memories in connection with Pudding Pie Hill.

And what became of the fairies? Nothing more than a childish notion, Eliza thought wistfully, worrying that her childhood was long behind her and yet she had no great urge to move on into womanhood. She turned sixteen the following year. Her female peers of Rosedale Abbey talked of their work on the farms, thinking of what farmhand they'd like to marry, or the better off girls who didn't have to labour wondered about eligible young gentlemen and whether they could catch one who would take them away to somewhere more exciting like Whitby or York. Or perhaps they might find their fortune as the mining around the dale expanded. One didn't even have to focus on a dirty miner; there were corporate men, engineers and railway staff as the railway around the top of the once wild dale was expanded to transport the rock ore away. There were always engineers and surveyors who came out to Rosedale on contracts. Pickings felt rich.

Eliza didn't particularly want to grow up and she certainly had no wish to marry. Her illustrations of the Pudding Pie Hill excavations had been greatly praised, and Lady Frankland-Russell had even purchased a number. A financial earning from her drawings lay new possibilities upon the table. The great Lady implored her to take further tuition, whilst she would look to London contacts for future commissions. Eliza felt breathless. Was it possible to hope she might be able to earn a living from her art? Then she could keep her own house and not have her future dependant on having a husband to look after her.

That autumn and winter she stayed with Aunt Muriel and Grandmother MacCaskill in Whitby so that she might have access to a better level of drawing tutelage. When she had told her family how her illustrating was progressing, Muriel had sounded very keen. Of course women with brains could and should do things other than having babies and keeping house. They had a legacy for it in the family. Her own dear father had been a drover, and a good man but the family fortunes hadn't come from his hard work. Rather it was all the profit of Eleanor MacCaskill's business dealings in Whitby, coupled with wise investments. Whitby was a town that could better deal with women doing business, Muriel informed her, for with the men out at sea for so many months at a stretch, there was no alternative.

Eleanor had not been quite so gushing, and had shrewdly observed her great granddaughter that evening as she listened to the possibilities of illustration. Botantical illustration was something in particular that publishers were looking for. She looked over Eliza's drawings, and agreed she had talent and potential. "I certainly think you could do it," she finally said, setting a batch of sketches down on a side table with a shaking hand. "But it will be hard, do you understand?"

"I am working hard with my tutor..."

"Oh, no," Eleanor waved it off. "I'm not talking of the technical aspects but rather of life. You must understand that you will walk on the edge. As much as Muriel boasts of Whitby's forward thinking status; an independent working woman is viewed with suspicion. Women don't feel comfortable around her, and many men would not consider such a burden as a wife."

"But with my illustrations I wouldn't need to marry," Eliza said. "I would earn my own money."

"That may be, but you may find yourself not wishing to be lonely. There are other reasons for matrimony other than financial security. Many men may not wish to be married to such a woman, and you will have to chose."

"Oh that's easy, I'll just never marry."

Eleanor smiled gently. "That's easy to say now, but you may feel differently when you are asked. What I am trying to warn you is that society is not kind to women, and especially those who step away from tradition. It will not be easy and you must harden yourself."

"It almost sounds like you don't want me to do this," Eliza muttered, moodily scuffing the back of her heel against the rug and thinking she wouldn't go fetch her fiddle later and play with her grandmother this night. She'd sit alone in her room and answer her letters, and read over all of Tilda's grumbles another time – how dare she go off to Whitby and leave Tilda with the 'little girls'!

"Quite the contray," Eleanor chuckled. "I just want you to go into it with your eyes open. Now go fetch that fiddle and let's see if I can manage a couple of reels before I retire for the night."

1856
Rosedale Abbey

Eliza jumped as the brass band commenced and a communal whoop of joy reared up from the villagers. Dancing would soon begin on the green. She ought not to have been surprised, for she was sitting so close to their makeshift stage and had idly watched the musicians gathering and preparing for the early evening's entertainment. They would play as long as the light held. Given it was September that meant it wouldn't go on as long as the regular summer fetes, but Eliza had heard her father saying Mr Maw was planning to invite all those who were still interested at dusk to come and dance at his house. He was desperate to show off his fine, large living area. Whatever the motive, it was a generous gesture.

She leant back into her perch, kicking her heels as she observed the festival ongoings with a dispassionate nature. It was as if she wasn't even really present. She hadn't been able to focus since the letter this morning. She had sat through an entire cricket match and couldn't say who had won or what the score had been, although any player from Wrelton would have made it abundantly clear had she asked. Those Wrelton boys always behaved as though they were coming up north from a worldly-wise cosmopolitan world, although their village wasn't any bigger than Rosedale Abbey. But they were close to Pickering, and therefore close to the railways and the rest of the world. Although their hometown wasn't anywhere near as beautiful as Rosedale Abbey. Nowhere could compete with the beauty of this place, even if the mining was starting in its tentative form. Besides, from what father said, they'd soon have a railway of their own. Charlotte had grown overexcited about the prospect of travel straight to Whitby, and he'd had to point out it was doubtful the trains would head in that direction. This new railway probably wouldn't even consider human traffic. Charlotte had looked rather glum. So it was only to be for the sheep? Not even that, just for the rocks.

They'd begun with an open cast mine to the south of the village, above Hollin's farm. They were taking the ore away in horse-drawn wagons, lumbering down the valley towards Pickering where it could then be transferred to the railway. The road to Pickering was hopeless. It was a clay-dirt route full of holes, some of them two foot deep, and if the weather had been anywhere near wet, it was like fighting a losing battle getting the horses and the wagons anywhere. The industrialists behind the mining, who mulled over geological maps prepared by her father, and calculations of what else could be dug out of the hills of Rosedale, were in the planning stages of getting a railway to come in to Rosedale from the north. A lot of money was to be made, but profits would not appear in the bottom of deep, muddy pot holes that swallowed up wagon wheels and horses' legs.

Eliza gazed across the melee of people, to where her mother was sitting talking to Mrs Iredale of the Red Lion Inn up at Blakey Ridge. The way the two of them talked, one would think they must be related. Yet they were not obvious companions, neither from class nor lifestyle. Mamma always maintained that Mrs Iredale had always been very kind, ever since she first came to Rosedale. She had always made her feel welcome. At home. Just as Adelaide was, snuggled into Mamma's side. Not that she was being greedy on purpose, she was a homely child who was content with the home and hearth and didn't strain to see what was around the far corner. But the other girls had to make their own bonds, and Eliza sometimes felt as a substitute mother for Tilda and Charlotte.

There was a fine young lady sitting beside Mrs Iredale. She must be one of her eldest daughters. Eliza had never really managed to tell Anita and Dorothea apart that well, although it must be Anita she was looking at now, for this was a smart woman who would match the stories of a daughter who had gone away to be a school teacher no less at some other village Eliza wasn't sure where it was. Dorothea hadn't been seen for years and wasn't spoken of although within the local community now and then eyebrows would be raised and aging faces shaken to the tune of a sad yet foolish end.

Tilda shrieked with glee as she dragged her Pa into the dancing and made him twirl her about like a diminutive lady. Charlotte scurried around their ankles, desperate to be included. Charlotte almost hadn't been allowed to come to the Gipsy party, as this day's revelries were being referred to, had Eliza's stubborn nature not given way to their mother's blackmail. Eliza had received a letter from Mrs Jennifer Burton-Waugh that very morning, advising her of a small commission she had secured on Eliza's behalf. It was only for a set of six ladies' note cards, to be of botanical illustration, and the pay would be next to nothing, but this was beyond words could describe for Eliza. The start of her artistic career. She had wanted to start on preliminary sketches immediately. Her mind was racing over compositional ideas and coloursheets, and had told her family off hand that she wasn't going to bother with the cricket match and dancing. Her mother had protested that the entire village and surrounding area would be there, no one could bow out for any reason other than the death bed, but Eliza said she didn't mind missing it all, honestly. As if that was the point. So her mother had said if Eliza wasn't going, she wasn't sure if she could let eight-year-old Charlotte go, in all good conscience. Everyone would say she hadn't permitted Eliza to go and one could hardly ban the eldest daughter, and then allow the youngest child to attend.

Charlotte had been furious, running up to Eliza and kicking her leg in a fit of tantrum. After a scolding, she had soon returned to haunt Eliza at her drawing desk, complaining and alternately sobbing until Eliza had thrown down her pencil and begrudgingly agreed that she would attend. But she wouldn't enjoy it and she certainly wouldn't dance. Besides, a brass band playing the music? Where were the fiddles? Everyone worth their salt knew that the best music for dancing was arranged for fiddles. But Rosedale Abbey had their brass band, and play they must at every party and formal event. Eliza loved it when she was over in Whitby, and able to hear such a variety of music. There was such vibrancy to be heard walking down the street on shopping errands with her great-aunt or the housekeeper, or on other occasions sneaking down into town with the shadows when it was assumed she was asleep in bed, to listen outside to the sea shanties and folk tunes of the world playing in the inns and at the harbour side.

A couple of cricketers from Wrelton ambled by, slowing down with no attempt to cover their reason as they brazenly stared at Eliza with smirks on their faces. She lowered her gaze and her head, glad suddenly for the wide-brimmed hat her mother had made her wear for this party. They had decorated it with fresh flowers and ribbons, her younger sisters taking greater joy in it than she. She wished there was a flower one could wear to denote one had no interest in courting. Please just leave me alone. The stares grew tiresome, the scowls from some women worse, as though she was not to be trusted around their husbands nor their sons. Did no one understand that she was to become a working artist and earn her own way through life? She didn't want the drudgery of matrimony. Mamma had commented more than once how much she looked like her own mother, the grandmother Elizabeth MacCaskill who had passed away before Eliza was born. She wondered if her grandmother had found this unwanted attention as infuriating as she did. She didn't know all that much about the woman, although her mother had shown her some of the old lady's belongings, and Aunt Muriel occasionally told some vague childhood stories, but on the whole the woman remained quite illusive.

Thinking she might dare to show her face to the sun, Eliza looked up and her heart sank when she saw Daniel Iredale heading her way. He was on the cricket team, and along with the rest of the village she had been obliged to cheer and clap at his efforts. He had grown somewhat since his days of taunting her as a child, and was now in his early twenties, carrying his father's easy charm and his mother's dark eyes. He worked down at the mine near Hollins Farm. They'd been taking stone out of there for years for road stone, but now with the discovery of the ironstone ore, the miners, masons and other workers had been redirected to a more valuable industry. Although Daniel was not shy about saying he was only doing this to earn some money until his father no longer wished to run the inn and he would take over. Some of the local girls fluttered around Daniel like moths, hoping they might be the next Mrs. Red Lion Inn. Perhaps if one was born up there one could find a romance in it, but it seemed like a constant hardship to Eliza, and being snowed in regularly every winter must be hard as well. Imagine working so closely with so many travellers and so many connections across the county, and yet never to budge an inch in one's own life.

"Eliza," Daniel dofted his cap to her, interrupting her rambling thoughts on lives she felt a horror of ever having. Eliza looked at him, already defensive. She hadn't interacted with him much the last couple of years, and whenever she had been to see the Iredales, she always made sure to keep out of his way if he were to appear. She hadn't quite forgiven him for meddling with her carving in the standing stone.

She nodded to him. "Daniel."

"Fine afternoon of a party we're having."

Was this the starter to some saucy comment or gesture, perhaps a way to get to cold men lying dead in bogs, she wondered. But when she looked at him properly she was surprised to see he was quite serious, almost nervous in behaviour.

"You're not dancing."

She had missed something here. "No."

"Well, why not? You should be. I say, rather, will you come and dance with me?"

"I don't dance all that well," Eliza declined. "I prefer to be playing." She glanced over at the brass band, as if her stare would make them think twice about their choice of music and ask her for advice.

"It's not exactly three fiddlers three at the moment, is it, lass?" Daniel almost laughed, flashing her a grin to which Eliza only scowled. He stepped forward reaching out with a hand. "Come along now."

"No thank you," Eliza said, folding her hands in her lap. "I don't feel like it today."

"Aye, but I'm here about more than the dancing. I'm wanting to be stepping out. I think you'll find I'm a good..."

What part of no was hard to grasp, Eliza huffed to herself as Daniel started to rattle off all his best traits to her. It made no difference. She was content to watch, and later at some suitable point she intended to sneak away home and get some sketching done. "I'm no dancer and you know it. If this step-out is a new dance I don't know it so you'd best be asking another lass."

Daniel laughed loudly, amused by Eliza's manner. She always had been a little odd compared to the other girls. In any other young woman, such a comment would have been coyness, but with Eliza, it was easy to believe she was clueless. "Stepping out is the oldest one there is. It's not so much about dancing as courting."

"You're off courting now?"

"Aye, with you the hope is."

"Me?" Eliza looked stricken. "I'm only sixteen."

"Plenty of lasses your age are engaged, a couple are already married as well. You know that as well as I do. There's nowt wrong with it, and I have plenty of good prospects." He took her hand. "A year or two and that could be us."

Eliza jolted up as if some beast had bitten her from behind. She snatched her hand away. "I'm not getting married."

"I hadn't quite proposed yet, I only talked about stepping out. Give it a year or two and you'll..."

"No, no, no."

"You stepping out with someone else?"

"I don't want to get married at all," Eliza hissed. "I don't want to get tied down with housekeeping and babies. I'm going to be an artist, an illustrator..." she felt her frustration grow as he stared blankly at her. "Draw pictures."

"No one's saying you have to stop drawing. My mother was always drawing little pictures for us..."

"I mean as a way of earning my own keep."

"Now you're just talking daft."

Eliza waved off his lop sided smile and started to walk away. There was no point in trying to explain this to him. She didn't really care anyway, Daniel Iredale had only plagued her throughout her childhood so she was in no need of his good opinion.

"You think you're too good for me, Miss," he shouted after her, his tone turning sour. "I can read. I read my books as well as you do. You won't ever get a better offer than me. You'll end up an old spinster. Old Spinster nanny for your little sisters' families. Bloomed too early..."

Eliza felt tears unexpectedly well up in her eyes. Suddenly he switched to the personal attack. Why could folk not just accept her as she was; what she wanted to be? She meant no harm to anyone else, and really it would be as easy as anything just to ignore she even existed.

She posed a threat to no one. She twisted as she walked away, to look back at his dark stare and angry stance. "My answer is no, Daniel Iredale," she told him. "Now kindly leave me alone."

She knew that she should not be chased away from where she wished to be by the comments of idiots, but she couldn't stand to remain at the party any longer. As she walked away, she grew increasingly aware that their altercation had been witnessed and noted. Of course it had, the entire valley was in the village, packed in together a hundred times over, and local gossip loved nothing better than a bit of heated drama. Especially if it meant knocking that round peg that would not fit in its designated hole down a place or two. She felt shamed. She'd never realised Daniel had viewed her in such an adult manner. If she had realised earlier she would have kept out of his way and made it perfectly clear she had no interest in marriage and certainly not in him. She was only sixteen. No one got married at this age. Well, they did, she knew her own mother was married at seventeen, but now that she was at this age she didn't feel ready or interested for matrimony. There was too much to be done in life.

The family house was quiet, empty and sleeping when she returned. Eliza hurried up to her room, took out fresh drawing paper and tried to start on some compositional ideas that had been forming in her mind. Her hand and her imagination were refusing to engage and everything she drew looked childish and twee. She started to cry out of frustration, scribbling through a rose and flinging the paper to the floor. Why could people not just leave her to be as she wished?

As the light was fading, Mairi walked back to the house with the three younger girls and the maid. Eliza was dozing, tear-stained and sprawled over the bed covers. She woke with a start to the noise of over-tired footsteps charging about downstairs and the maid's shrill complaint asking Charlotte to calm down, for that was simply not lady-like behaviour. Eliza wanted to shout down to let Charlotte be, for she would have precious little time in this life to be herself.

The door was flung open and Tilda charged at the bed, lobbing herself on top of her sister. She breathed into Eliza's face, and Eliza wondered if Tilda hadn't managed to get at the punch. "They're all talking about you," she said gleefully. "Is it true that you're going to marry Daniel Iredale?"

Eliza groaned and rolled away from Tilda, pushing her face into a pillow. "I'm not marrying anyone."

"Oh, that's right, you jilted him and you're going to look after my children now!" Tilda laughed, bouncing on the bed.

"Tilda, that's unkind."

The bouncing stopped. A red-faced and flushed Tilda looked sheepishly back to the doorway where her mother stood.

"We don't laugh at other's misfortunes."

Tilda's mouth turned down and she stared at her knees, lost under the long skirts of her pretty party dress.

"Go through to Charlotte and Adelaide's room and get into your nightdress. I want to speak to Eliza."

"But..."

"Off you go."

Tilda begrudgingly sloped off to her younger sisters dragging her feet across the floorboards. Mairi sat down on the edge of the bed. "I had been going to send the girls back with the maid, but when I heard all this chatter, I had to come back and find you..."

"Oh no, Mamma, I haven't done anything wrong," Eliza wailed, sitting up. "I didn't mean to spoil the dancing for you..."

"You haven't, don't worry. Gossips are... well, unkind would be the best way to describe them. I know this hits you hard now, but it will be old news within the week and everyone will have forgotten about it."

"Are they saying very dreadful things?"

Mairi shook her head gently. "No, and there's plenty who have empathy in their chatter as well."

"What are they saying?"

"Don't worry about it."

"So it is very dreadful."

"Can you tell me what has actually happened? There will be some grains of truth in there but..."

"You won't be angry with me?"

"Why would I be that?"

"Because Daniel said it's the best offer I'll ever get. And if my drawing doesn't succeed, then I'll just be a spinster burden to the family for the rest of my life and, oh..."

"He said all that?"

"Not quite," Eliza admitted. "He just thought my drawing was something to entertain children. I don't suppose he understands what I want to do. I don't really have anything to do with him so he doesn't really know me." She wiped at her eyes with the back of her hand, feeling a little calmer. "I didn't know what he was talking about when he was talking about stepping out. I thought it was a dance. Then he was talking about courting and getting married. And I don't want to, I'm too young, I'm only sixteen, and not to him even if I was a hundred. But then I can't stay here and expect you all to pay for me."

"We manage well enough for money and are hardly starving," Mairi stroked the tousled hair back from her daughter's face. Too young. Yes, perhaps all girls ought to be allowed to go to twenty until they had to marry, she reflected. Although so many did it out of financial necessity, a desperation to get away from busy cramped homes full of children and a desire for attention for themselves. How ironic that eventually they found themselves back where they started. So many marriages without choice. Everyone knew she had only been seventeen when she married, but she and Stephen kept the messy circumstances away from the girls. They had been lucky, it had worked out for the best, but Mairi wondered for every forced occasion that did eventually work, how many never found a balance and just spiralled into misery and anger? "You marry when you want to, to someone you want to."

Eliza's mouth was a hard line. "I never want to marry."

Mairi let it go. "Besides, your father thinks you're too young as well, so there is no one in this household who thinks ill of you."

"Pa's heard of it all?"

"Of course. Everyone has by now... it'll burn out quicker this way, don't fret so. He would have come now but he has to stay. His standing in the community demands it. I said I would come and see to you."

"They're still dancing?"

"And merry making," Mairi confirmed. "But the light has gone and we've moved on to Mr Maw's. You know how pleased he is with his living room. I don't think we could have said no, and the party is going along very well. Would you like to come back? The other girls need to be in bed now..."

"No, no, no." Eliza shook her head. "I'm not going back out there."

"Try not to worry about what people say. None of it changes who you are." As she spoke she wondered how true that was. Even when one stayed strong to who one was, the very battle of standing up to gossip and popular opinion created new facets and armour to the personality. She thought of her mother and the path she had willingly taken. For her mother it wasn't just gossip, but the demands of society that permanently ruined her reputation for ever socialising in respectability. For ever being really accepted.

Eliza got up and went to the bowl of water on the dresser, splashing at her face to wipe away the tear tracks. She picked up the linen to wipe her face dry, then turned back to her mother. "I think I'll go to bed now. You should go back to Mr Maw's, keep Pa company."

"If you're sure. I don't mind staying longer."

"No, I'll be fine." Eliza forced a smile, looking upon her mother's angelic features, light and blonde, still youthful and so different to herself. She suddenly felt as though she were the old matriarch encouraging the young, unmarried daughter out to enjoy herself before the woes and responsibilities of life became too great. "I'll see you tomorrow."

1857
Rosedale

As days stretched longer, the reign of sunlight in the atmosphere felt near to endless. Mairi would rise earlier and earlier and flee to the hills. Her hills, whose wilderness had provided solace in the early years. Landscapes that were changing. Because of Stephen's job, and his fascination in the earth, in science and discovery and technology, she heard everything that there was to hear about the increasing mining in Rosedale. Not only that but the future plans put forth by the industrialists. They had not even begun on creating the empire. Her remote hills would soon be but a memory.

A new mine had opened that year. It was different to the open cast mine south of Rosedale Abbey. The new enterprise was worked on the principles of a coal mine, with a shaft plummeting deep into the earth. The ironstone was mined and lifted straight up and out. Sherrif's Pit they called it. It could be seen from the lower valley from parts of the village. The red brick buildings up on the surface stood out in sunlight. Great clouds of dust and grime erupted from the belly of the earth. Trains of horses and wagons lumbered away under heavy loads. Snakes of the uniform slump of the miners walking to and from shifts went up and down the valley slopes. The noise as the ground was blown open was prelude to old man earth's sneezes. High up on hills to the west of the village, it loomed over Rosedale Abbey. The presence was worse still for the little cluster of buildings that formed Thorgills. There was talk of building a line of kilns just down from the mine, so that they might roast off the water and impurities from the iron ore. The roasting process would make the ore lighter and therefore a full wagonload all the more profitable. Of course in the longer run the horses would become redundant, because initial proposals were being put forward for the iron roads. The railways were coming.

Railways out here, in the wilds of the moors, far from anywhere. The rail connection was not envisioned to transport the small local population of people, but the very earth. Even the very population of

Rosedale was starting to change. More workers were required, and the agricultural folk looked on in consternation as outsiders charged in eager for the work. She'd heard there was even a family from Cornwall of all places here now. If one had empty rooms, it would soon be no hardship to find lodgers and earn a little extra money. She'd listened to some women gossip excitedly about the boom times for all coming. Why, if one could persuade the chickens to share the nests, one could sell the space in the coop for a young lad starting his career. The shops and inns would reap the benefits, the village might get more investment, why they might even aspire to things like better schools and reading rooms. The possibilities were endless.

Progress. Improvement. Development. Discovery. Civilisation.

Mairi had made the mistake of walking an old favourite route, along the bottom of the main valley, up to Blakey Ridge then across the tops to head back down by the steep western road to the village. The final part of her walk took her past the pit. The walks she remembered from her girlhood days were gone. She was a different woman now, and life had changed her responsibilities and mindset drastically. It wasn't possible to be the same after children. And yet she longed to return to those days, to have time when it was just Mairi, nothing more and nothing less, out walking for hours, sketching, exploring, understanding the land around her. Rosedale was changing, just as she had changed, and there was little ground left for them to meet.

More and more she retreated to the eastern side dale of Northdale, where the mining had not even a thought of carving up the land. The fields were still full of lambs in spring and the farmers still followed their old ways and calendars. Oh, they kept abreast of the local news and would be as quick as any to take in lodgers and earn a little extra, but once one got far enough into the dale, one could almost pretend that the rest of the world wasn't happening.

Mairi traced her old routes, walking up the dirt tracks past the little grey-stone farm buildings. They were sturdy structures set in the ground framed by lichen-encrusted trees. Up past the farmstead of Hanging Stone, wandering along tracks that weaved between high dry-stone-walled fields, and meandering upwards to the acres of heather, out onto the hill tops and across to the little spring of Job's Well where she had first been given that piece of petrified grass. Little tokens of the earth to line up on her dresser, and starting points with her husband. It all felt a lifetime ago.

She sat upon the rough sheep-grazed grass close to Job's Well, a half-finished sketch of the valley discarded to one side, and gazed upon the lay of the land. She felt the breeze move up over the fields and the heather, to brush up and over her body before disappearing across the open endless plains of moorland beyond. She was completely and blissfully alone. Tilda always tried to accompany her, even skipping school sometimes to Mairi's horror. She loved her girls dearly, and enjoyed their company, but sometimes she needed to be simply herself alone. Eliza must have felt the same, for she was spending so much time in Whitby these days that Rosedale was becoming the holiday destination. Mairi was losing her eldest, which she supposed was the way, and yet still she ached after her daughter. Thinking back to the two-year-old – wherever had that child disappeared to? – for whom one cuddle was never enough. The girls growing up meant she had more time for herself, and she was torn wanting her freedom but longing for the little girls again. Sometimes little William entered her mind, and she would smile sadly before remembering that it did not do to dwell on what could not be undone. Perhaps he was with her mother, being taken care of and most probably spoiled rotten given he was the only grandchild she would have access to.

Light humming drifted into her thoughts. Mairi twisted to see Atheleys crouched down by the well washing her hands. How was it that woman never aged? It was impossible that her grandmother had known this very creature in her youth, and yet given how many years had passed since Mairi had first met her, surely some change ought to have appeared. Yet there were always such people blessed with eternal youth.

Atheleys leant back, wiping her hands dry on the skirts of her dress before looking up and catching Mairi's eye.

"It's been a long time."

The woman merely shrugged. A long time was such an arbitrary concept.

"You've still been coming up here, all these years."

"Oh yes." Atheleys stood up and walked across to Mairi.

"I never made it to Commondale," Mairi continued. "That was remiss of me. I find I have more time, I really should make the effort."

Atheleys waved it off as a mere trifle. "You wouldn't find me." She knelt down beside Mairi and smiled sadly. Her hair, still loose, still unbrushed and still with half-tied ribbons dangling here and there, blew on the breeze. She raised her hands to Mairi's shoulders, then impulsively embraced her. "You'll never know," she whispered. "You'll never know it."

"Sorry?"

Atheleys pulled back and hopped nimbly to her feet. "I must be away."

"But I don't understand what you meant." Mairi started to get to her feet, eager to spend more time with the strange woman. By the time she was up Atheleys was a figure on the distance. It was a near-miracle how quickly she could shift across the moorland, the heather seemingly parting as easy as water when she waded through. Then her figure was gone and Mairi was alone at the top of Northdale wondering what it was she had missed.

She returned home to Tilda's furious, arms-folded, eyes-down sulk that she had left without her on another walk. It was almost as if Tilda was regressing, becoming a shadow of Adelaide in her need to cling to her mother. Tilda was missing Eliza, Mairi realised as she bundled her begrudging, yet delighted second daughter up on the settee next to her whilst opening a book with one hand.

"Now, let me read you this book I have just finished."

"Mamma, I'm not a baby," Tilda grumbled as she nestled in. "I can read."

"Of which I am very aware. But sometimes it is nice to be read to."

"As long as it isn't one of Pa's books about rocks and things."

Mairi smiled to herself, amused by Tilda's pretence of lacking both understanding and interest in what her father did. "Well, lucky you this isn't about rocks and such things. It's about a little town and some curious women who live there." Women who fear the coming of the trains and the modern age, she thought to herself, a pang as if she was wrong to feel despair when she saw the land, once wilderness, now carved up, and knowing there was more to come. She opened the book to the first chapter. "Now let me tell you a story about a lady called Miss Mattie."

Miss Mattie, Margaret Hale, Ruth, Mary Barton, all creations of Mrs Gaskell, would roam the pages, dancing in and out with older tales of Emma Woodhouse and Elizabeth Bennett in Eliza's mind. Little Dorrit was ever so good in poverty, Esther in Bleak House perservered. There was so much literature abound when her hands tired of drawing. It was a golden age for books.

Eliza put the completed copy of Jane Eyre to one side and gazed up at the sky from her bedroom window. Finally a moment of clear skies and sunshine to break the drudge. Today it had felt like a cloudy autumn of mist and twisted stagnant clouds. Her grandmother had pressed the works of the Brontes, well, the Bell Brothers according to the book covers, but everyone knew that West Yorkshire women by the name of Bronte were responsible. Were, for they were all dead now. Eleanor MacCaskill still lamented the death of the final girl, Charlotte, even though she'd been dead four years. It was strange, when reading Mrs Gaskell's Life of Charlotte Bronte, to think that her own great grandmother and aunt had been there in Haworth when the Bronte family had moved to the town. That she had seen the girls grow up before quitting the west side of the county to return to the east coast and Whitby. Muriel had spent more time in the west, working with some utopian ideal of a rich cousin, and then a period of keeping an eye on a more distant cousin, 'poor Jayne' as she was referred to. From what Eliza could ascertain, dear Jayne, who was these days in a far more stable situation, had never been poor in the monetary sense. Sometimes when Muriel and Eleanor were reminiscing, they would talk of poor Jayne's troublesome times and horrors, without ever explaining it beyond shared knowing looks. Then her great grandmother would pat her hand and assure her that a woman she had never met and did not understand was quite well now, after a time in York. After her time in York? What was that a euphemism for? No one would explain, much to Eliza's irritation. It was 1859, she was nineteen and surely adult enough to no longer need protecting from the cruelty of life. Goodness, there were women younger than her married with children. Mere girls already in their graves from the childbed.

She caught sight of the opened letter from Tilda, grumbling about her younger sisters and how she wasn't allowed to go live in Whitby. In a couple more weeks they'd all be reunited for the festive period. Eliza hadn't found the energy to write back to Tilda these last three days. She had enough grumbling of her own to do, but Tilda never seemed to listen, not properly. She probably didn't understand. Beside it lay another letter, from her trusted Whitby friend, Mary Linskill. When Eliza had first moved here, she and Mary had been able to meet up and talk about their dreams and aspirations – for Mary hoped to one day earn money from her art. Her family were not wealthy, and she had been apprenticed as a milliner in Whitby. The girls would meet up when they could, but even that had come to an end, as upon completing her apprenticeship Mary had moved to Manchester to work as a milliner. She was still excited in her letters, about the adventure and the travel and all the experiences she would have. So many things she could bring to her writing, for Mary saw future hopes in her poetry and stories.

Dear trusted Mary Linksill. For now she worked and read voraciously in the evenings. For such a slight, slender creature she burned with an intense energy. It was strange when one looked at her family still back in Whitby, and wondered where it came from. Eliza sometimes bumped into Mary's father, a great burly bulk of a human with a limp, who was well known as the town's constable, and likewise as a watchmaker. Mary's mother was pious, and a well enough liked woman; and the younger siblings seemed to be growing up well. But none of them had such a hunger for literature as Mary did.

Mary had probably read all the books Eliza was just making her way through. Ridiculous really, for Eliza was in a greater position financially and had not been forced to work to support herself or her family. She continued to work on her art and illustration, and was paid for a few commissions, but really the money she had earned to date was little more than pin money. But it was a start, and she was still becoming the artist she would be. Geographically they were a long way from the cultural centres of the country, but they were well placed in being an increasingly popular holiday resort for the wealthy. All kinds of great minds came to Whitby, why, they even said Charles Dickens had taken luncheon here once. And so Eliza had been able to secure short-term tutorledge from numerous artists and teachers, sometimes only for a couple of hours, occasionally for a few weeks, dependant on how long they stayed and how inclined they were. For some, the pay meant being able to extend their own holiday for another week. She knew she was spoiled, for with the support of her parents, and her great grandmother in Whitby, she simply did not need to worry about money. Her own life was indulgent ease compared to Mary's. It always made her feel a little guilty when Mary told her of all the books she had recently read, and Eliza couldn't simply comprehend where Mary was finding the time to read even half the books she managed. If Eliza had that kind of energy, why there wouldn't be a book left that she wouldn't have read by now.

But Eliza had her music, and still religiously played the fiddle most days, having devoured all the books of folk tunes, jigs and reels she could find. She had learned all that she could pick up from the people around her. She had learned most of what her great grandmother knew, although the old lady did not have the energy these days to play in duet with Eliza. And so to try and slake her thirst, Eliza would sometimes sneak off into the old town, to pass like a shadow by the old characters of Whitby, those of the sea and the fishing ships, those who had travelled and come here for work, not the genteel holidaymakers who helped Eliza with her drawing during the day. She heard music from the new land, from the Americas, from the settlers and those that had heard the music and brought it back across the waves to discuss over ale in the inns, or to play in the parlours of their relatives in the old whaling port on the Yorkshire coast. Sometimes she would be lucky and time it right down on the harbour when some of the foreign sailors from Norway landed, and brought with them the wild dark melodies of the Norse, played on a sharp, rustic sounding violin they called *hardanger*.

When Eliza was playing for hours into the evening, sometimes out in the garden, Eleanor would lay on her bed and listen, closing her eyes and returning to her youth. She recalled the dark, warm joviality within Chequers Inn near Black Hambleton where she had visited as a young girl, first discovering the fast reels and jigs of country music and moving away from the classical lines her tutor had been taking her down. She still had the book of folk music Angus had gifted her all those years ago. She would sometimes play one or two tunes with Eliza, but her stamina at ninety-seven was no match for a young woman. Some days Eleanor would grow frustrated with just how weak and frail her own body had become. Other days she didn't seem to mind so much and would lay on the bed, listening to bird song, or the sea wind, or Eliza, and retreat back into her memories.

Most of the time she found herself back in Whitby, but to a time long past when her children were still quite literally children. She'd look at the photographs of her growing family that had been taken in Whitby, of the sketches and miniatures of Stewart, Elizabeth, and Muriel as a young girl; childish attempts of siblings to draw one another, which was all she had left of Stewart now, long gone for decades. On bad days her memories of the moors of Commondale would flicker, of the sharp stench of iron in the blood, fistfuls of sphagnum moss, and Atheleys reassuring her that she had seen it with sheep before. But the baby had been stillborn and Atheleys had taken him. Eleanor had never dared look at him, and now she would cry, wishing she had dared to take a look at him, so he might have known that she did care and she did love, despite the fact that he had never once breathed true air.

Sometimes Eleanor would go out for short walks. She remained on her own side of the river estuary, for the steep paths down into Whitby were proving to be too much for her now. So out she would go, with her shawls and her walking stick, wondering at that she tired so easily when she thought back to how far she had walked in the past. Why, they would walk between Commondale and Whitby, and Eleanor had been all over the moors with her dear little donkey when she had been running a delivery service. She had travelled the length and breadth of these isles, and now she was down to doddering about on the east cliffs.

Doddering like an old woman. She felt like one as well today. Another tooth from her upper jaw had fallen out. She hadn't told anyone this time, and simply put it away in a cloth purse with the others. Muriel had told her, quite clinically, that at her age, what else could she expect? She was an old woman, and quite frankly, it was something that she had any teeth left at all. An old woman, as if Muriel herself was a spring chicken. Muriel had turned seventy, and her head of red hair was twisted with silver wires, great clumps of white hair. Skinny as she always had been, she had a distinctly bony, lithe appearance, filled out with those sharp, sparkling eyes.

The track from the house joined the lane and passed by a collection of small cottages. Old Horatio MacIntyre as he liked to be known, although Eleanor knew his real name was David Rose, lived in the furthest. He was about the same age as Muriel, missing the lower half of his right leg and if ever there was a physical cliché of an old seadog, he was it. His flesh hung a little slack about his grizzled face, his hair as wild and unruly as the clouds that would break across the stormy sea horizon. He'd been a fisherman and a smuggler in his younger days, with a canny knack of avoidance, both of the customs man, the prisons and even the pressgangs back in the day. He was frequently to be found on a little barrel outside his cottage, smoking a pipe, taking a nip of rum and regaling any passerby in conversation, tall tales about his days at sea, or belting out a sea shanty, accompanied by his scruffy little accordion. Sometimes he would hobble down to the harbour to talk with his younger compatriots and help mend fishing nets. When he was 'up top', he was intrigued by the house of fine women, that Mrs MacCaskill, her daughter Mrs Must (or Must-Hurry-Now as he called her) and the fine young great granddaughter Eliza, who had a naive curiosity he could imagine would get her into trouble in the not-too-distant future. He was teaching young Eliza all the songs he knew for her fiddle, and he delighted in telling her that his rum was smuggled, which it was, and seeing the look of horror that he might not have paid his taxes. Even better was it to tell her that some of her great grandmother's dealings hadn't always been brought to the attention of the customs officials. Some bits of amber always sneaked through from her Baltic traders and sailors she knew. He'd roar with laughter at her face and assure her that everyone in Whitby was at it to a greater or lesser extent. A poor man had to manage somehow, and besides, what was that money collected for? It was just sent down to London and never benefited the poor folks up here in the north.

It was a miserable November day, drizzling and with thick sea fret, and Horatio was not outside. Eleanor slowed as she passed the cottage, trying to ascertain if he was in the cottage by a bright fire, but the single window looked black and cold. He had probably headed down the hill into the old town and to one of the alehouses.

She wandered onwards towards St Mary's church with its churchyard crumbling into the sea. It had been a long time since that dreadful villain had presided over that church, she thought, remembering how he had blackmailed her over her husband. Dear Angus, hardly perfect, not at home for months on end. That had always been the life of a drover, but he had been quick to run away when the suggestion of arrest had come up, and he never set foot in Whitby again. Not that they became estranged. Eleanor had travelled the country with him. But being alone in Whitby facing the gossip and judgement of people who were no better than they had been hard. What a lucky thing Eleanor had been such an enterprising and independent woman.

She paused for a moment, her hands clasped together on top of the walking stick, wisps of white hair drifting in the sea mist. She was surprised to see that she had wandered into the abbey ruins, having veered off the path she had thought she was following. Through the eerie sea fret she could see a few people milling about. There always were these days. The tourists never stopped coming. They were fine gentrified folk from other parts of the country who all chattered excitedly to one another about taking the sea air and seeing the fine quaint sea port views of Whitby and Scarborough. Running about as though the locals were props put out for their entertainment. Not all of them were disrespectful and annoying of course, but Eleanor still couldn't adjust to this mass leisure and exploration. Mostly done because gossips at the card table were also doing it, rather than any real desire to visit. Muriel told her Haworth was even worse for giddy tourists since the last of the Bronte children had died, and Eleanor was thankful she no longer lived there.

As she walked, her foot caught on an unseen piece of masonry, and down she went into the deep wet grass, slick with mist dew. Eleanor let out a cry, her hands splayed out to try and break her fall. Her walking stick flew off. She lay on her side, grateful for all this deep grass that had cushioned her fall. A jolt of fire sparked up from her ankle and warned her she would not come out of this unscathed.

Two women, whom she had noticed in her periphery fussing over a sketchbook (in this weather!) came bounding across the hummocked grasslands to aid Eleanor.

"My goodness, my dear!" one of the women exclaimed as they reached the stricken lady. "You took quite a tumble there. Are you all right?"

"Yes, thank you," Eleanor murmured, feeling embarrassed. She took the woman's arm, whilst the other figure lingered awkwardly at the side before stepping off to retrieve the walking stick. "If you could just help me onto my feet..." She burst out in a flare of pain as rods shot up her leg. She took her weight back off that ankle and found herself leaning into the solid arm of her rescuer.

"Look, there is a fine tumble of masonry just there," the woman declared. "Let's go sit there whilst we think what to do. Come now." She and Eleanor started the awkward hobble towards the stones mentioned. "Meta dear, could you... Oh, I see you have found the lady's walking stick."

Eleanor let out a great huff of air as she sat down, grateful to feel herself steady again.

"My dear, are you holidaying with people here? Is there someone we could fetch?"

She looked up and regarded the women properly for the first time. The one who talked was the elder, perhaps in her forties, although age was a hard thing to guess, especially when life and work could take such a quick toll on undernourished faces. This lady was not undernourished, and judging from her dress and the fact she was on holiday, Eleanor doubted she was poor in any sense of the word. She was a handsome woman, a little rounded out from age, wifely duties and children, but still remarkable, and with twinkling eyes that shone with intelligence. The younger woman with her, who looked about Eliza's age, was slender and a little anxious in the way she held her body posture, but looking at the two, one could see a family resemblance. Perhaps mother and daughter.

"I live here," Eleanor answered as the daughter passed her walking stick across.

"Oh, a local; what lucky chance. I am so trying to talk to interesting locals. Our landlady has been gracious enough to tell me all her tales of Whitby, but I fear she must find me quite trying now and needs a rest. As do you," she quickly stopped herself. "I am forgetting that you are injured. Can we help you home?"

"It's not far..."

"Mamma, we did say we would be back soon," the daughter started.

"Oh, nonsense. Marianne is quite capable of looking after Julia for a few hours," she turned back to Eleanor with a conspiratorial look. "One of my younger daughters, Julia, has come down with a bowel complaint and quite refused to leave our lodgings. We're only here for two weeks. Now, if you'll take my arm, I think between that and your stick we should be able to get ourselves onto the track. Which direction must we take?"

Eleanor pointed off with her stick towards her home. "Five minutes, perhaps a little longer now I am incapacitated. You are very kind to help me."

"Not at all. We're all humans and kindness is a basic principal we should follow if nothing else." She offered her arm again then broke out into a wide smile that animated her face beautifully. "Why, I'm offering my arm to an unknown lady. I'm sure there's etiquette against this. We should be introduced."

"Mrs MacCaskill," Eleanor spoke. "But I feel that you should call me Eleanor."

"I know what you mean," the woman concurred. "I do believe I am going to like you. You must call me as my special friends do. Lily."

Special friend or not, by the time they reached the garden path, Eleanor was feeling intensely embarrassed and flustered hot despite the cold damp chill of the day. Not only had she been a terrible fool, lumbering about like an over-eager tourist who had never been to Whitby before, but from taking Lily's arm and being helped home, she could feel just how weak she had become in comparison to the two other women. Oh, Eleanor was not deluded about her age – the fact that so many people, and most of her peers were long dead made that very clear, but she had never considered herself old in the sense of decrepit. In the sense that she could be put on the shelf with the other toothless crones who took five minutes of creaking to get out of their chairs and barely had the strength to lift a teaspoon.

Muriel was at the door, alerted by the housekeeper before they reached the threshold. She looked horrified, as if a child she was responsible for had managed to sneak out undetected. "Mother, what's happened?"

"I just tripped, that's all," Eleanor said. "I must have twisted my ankle. These two kind ladies offered to help me home."

"Thank you, it's very much appreciated," Muriel said to Lily. Eleanor half expected her to make an additional half-whispered comment that her mother ought to know better at this time of life. "We must get you in and that ankle elevated."

With some huffing and awkwardness, they struggled in as a disorganised group, down the corridor and into the parlour, where a surprised Eliza, sketching at the far end in the bay window where the best light could be found, jumped up and hurried across.

"So much fussing," Eleanor grumbled as she was manhandled into her wingback chair. "Now, I must insist that you stay to tea, for you have done me a great service."

"I don't want to be any imposition..." Lily started.

"But Mamma," Meta hissed quietly, "What about Julia?"

"I do insist," Eleanor confirmed. "I must be allowed to thank you properly."

Meta looked exasperated as her mother needed no further encouragement and set herself down in the chair opposite the old lady. Her mother had been quizzing the old folks of Whitby since the moment they arrived in this damp, misty seaside town. Under that calm facade, she would have been desperately thinking of a reason to stay or come back soon. A lady as old as this, and a local: why, what stories they'd hear!

Eliza put her pencil behind her ear as she got up – it was a habit with her artistic implements as she worked. She already had a paintbrush speared through her hair from early watercolours. Picking up her great grandmother's shawl, she walked over to the epicentre and put it around the elderly lady's shoulders. "You've been running about in the mist not looking where you are going?"

Eleanor chuckled, "Something like that."

Muriel returned to the room with a footstool and a couple of cushions under one arm so that she could properly elevate her mother's leg.

"Perhaps we could send for a doctor?" Lily suggested.

"My daughter," Eleanor gestured to Muriel. "She is a doctor."

"A female doctor?" Lily exclaimed, sounding rather pleased with the notion. "Why I didn't believe we were allowed to enter such professions."

Muriel grimaced. "We're not. I'm not officially a doctor..."

"You are all but in title," Eleanor said, sounding very determined on the subject. No one would belittle Muriel's ability, even if much of it had to remain secret.

Muriel took off her mother's boot and stocking, setting her lips in a straight line as she considered the swollen ankle. Puffed out like a waterlogged corpse. Of course this was a problem for many old people, but she could tell even from a glance that her mother's other ankle was of far more sensible proportions. "Do say if any of this hurts," she said, as she moved her hands over the leg, pressing at certain points around the ankle and knee to gauge if any bones might have broken. "A bad sprain," she decided. "You need to keep the weight off it until the swelling goes down. Could be weeks I'm afraid."

Eleanor's face sagged and she leant back into her chair. It was as good as house arrest.

Muriel twisted in her crouched position to look over at Lily. "My husband, my late husband that is, was Dr Kaarel Must, the Edinburgh anatomist."

Lily's eyes widened. "I have heard of him. My husband studied in Scotland, so he's quite familiar with all the great minds from there, although I understood Dr Must was from the continent."

"Estonia."

"Yes, that was it."

"But he studied and qualified in Edinburgh. He wrote his books on anatomy in this country." Muriel looked away, feeling both intensely irritated and proud simultaneously of the great work of Kaarel Must. "Do excuse me, I'll go arrange the tea."

"You will have to excuse us," Eleanor added. "We don't entertain much and fail miserably at social formalities at times. We have missed all the necessary introductions."

"Nonsense," Lily laughed, "I am Lily, you are Eleanor and the rest has fallen prey to the accident of the day."

"Never the less. My doctor is residence is my daughter, Muriel Must. And the young lady hovering to my right is my grand..." Eleanor broke out into a smile. "I don't like to be reminded of how many generations have gone by, so I always say granddaughter, but in fact she is my great granddaughter, the eldest of four girls, Eliza Gaskin."

Eliza smiled. "Pleased to meet you."

"You must all call me Lily," Eleanor's rescuer beamed, illuminated by the crackling fire in the room, content in the cheerful warmth and ambience of the family room. She knew good people when she met them. "I am also a proud mother of four girls, although some are, shall we say incapacitated at our lodging house today. My second daughter, Meta is here with me just now." She peered curiously as Eliza turned her head to look at her grandmother. "Miss Gaskin, I have to ask, is that a paintbrush in your hair?"

"Oh!" Eliza blushed, reaching up to her pinned hair and feeling the brush. "It's a bad habit of mine when I'm working." She removed the brush and as she lowered her hand she felt the pencil as well. "It seems I'm always secreting art supplies about me."

"Another art lover. My Meta adores art; she's very accomplished..."

"Mamma!"

"Perhaps you'd like to..." Eliza gestured to the table beyond the cluster of women, over in the bay window. She had her sketching in progress there, backlit by drooping geraniums on the window sill, and curling rolling mist outside. The two young women sat down together at the table, and Meta let out a gasp when she saw Eliza's intricate, detailed drawings of a sprig of dried rowan leaves.

"This is exquisite."

"I'm still not quite happy. The standard for botanical illustration is so high...."

"I don't think I could ever manage something like this, so I don't even try," Meta sighed humbly. "I practice and I practice and maybe I should give it up, but it does give me great pleasure..."

"Great pleasure and yet you are always worrying over it," Lily called from the other side of the room.

"I like landscapes and architecture," Meta continued, ignoring her mother's comment. "And some portraiture. Although it is a talent to really capture the soul of a specific person on paper."

"And I don't know if I could do that." Eliza's eyes dropped to the bag Meta had with her. "Do you have your books with you now? Would it be possible to see?"

"Oh, they're not very good..." Meta started, clutching the satchel tighter.

"Here we are." Muriel returned to the room, bustling in with a tray of cakes, followed by the housekeeper carrying all of the tea paraphernalia. "Bread and butter, a fine lemon cake, and we were in extra luck as our dear housekeeper Mrs Argument had just taken a batch of scones out of the oven. And we have her very fine strawberry jam to go with them."

"I must make sure to rescue you again," Lily exclaimed.

There was a moment of revered silence as Muriel played mother, pouring out the tea and plating up the cakes and scones so that all would be well-fed, fortitude against the cold, damp November chill.

"I have to say," Lily started as she graciously accepted her plate. "You are lucky to live in such a beautiful place by the sea. Even in this dreadful weather one can see what a special place it is."

"Where are you from?" Muriel asked as she passed a cup of tea.

"Manchester."

"Manchester!"

"Well, not originally," Lily conceded. "Although we have lived there a great many years now, decades one should say. It was my husband's work that took me to the city. It has its flaws and its troubles, but there is a lot of heart there. We live on the outskirts, one could almost believe right out in the country, so we're not troubled by the smog as much. That anyone should be troubled by those living conditions..."

"I visited Manchester once," Muriel mused. "A lot of years ago."

"Oh really? Were you there with your husband? Did he come to speak? I never heard of Dr Must speaking there, but perhaps it was before my time."

Muriel shook her head. "It was a lot of years ago, before I was married. When Peterloo blew up."

"Goodness..."

"I'd gone with my cousin. She was married to a mill owner, not in Manchester, out in West Yorkshire, but..."

"Ah," Lily's smile dropped a few notches. "Of course there are some responsible mill owners..."

"Not Moses," Muriel snorted. "Don't worry, he passed away a great many years ago and I think it's safe to say Emmerline doesn't miss him, my cousin Emmerline. In fact, I think it's safe to say her life has blossomed since his departure. She's continued with the industry but become very focused on philanthropic works. She's built an entire village for the workers. I had a hand in helping with the healthcare."

"If only more of the owners followed your cousin's example," Lily sighed. "We've lived through some great times of want in Manchester and I fear there will be more such times on the horizon. We did what we could do to help, but there's so much poverty, you understand. It did feel all so hopeless some days." She broke off abruptly, looking a little embarrassed and thinking that these good people did not want to hear of the social woes of her adoptive city. Taking a gulp of tea, she veered the conversation in another direction. "As I was saying, Whitby is a beautiful coastal port. I know it's become a picturesque resort for the country to come and relax, but I do so love how the history is still present. You can imagine the old days. I've been talking to older residents since we came here, to get an idea of the town, and how it was back in the whaling days."

"Those days are long passed," Eleanor spoke. "I remember them from my girlhood. The great whaling ships heading out. And all the blubberhouses and factories that processed the carcasses on return. The shipyards, the herring fleets, even the trading ships coming over from the Baltic. Of course they mostly head into Hull now, bigger and easier to get to. I don't know that people today appreciate the size of those ships, or to imagine how many were packed into the harbour here."

"It certainly is something to see," Lily agreed. "When I was a young woman I briefly lived up north in Newcastle. The whaling was coming to an end even then I believe, but there were still some ships to see. Such a time of exploration and adventure. There is something rather proud about those ships when they are just setting sail out on a new season, all repaired and fully decked.!

Eleanor nodded slowly, sipping her tea, but made no comment.

"Of course, I don't over romanticise the sea," Lily continued. "There's a lot of sad stories connected to those ships. Why, my own dear brother..." she broke off, coughing on a crumb. "Oh, forgive me," she said, setting her plate down. "I don't often speak of him, I don't know why I brought him up. Perhaps the kindly surroundings here. He's been gone so long."

"He died at sea?"

"Yes, well, no, well..." she shook her head, more to herself than anyone else. "We don't definitively know for sure. My brother John, he disappeared at sea, and we never found out what happened. It's been, what, perhaps thirty years now. But a part of me still wishes someone could give me a definite answer. Not that I am the only person to have known sadness," she added with a tinkling laugh that held no humour but tried to cover her awkward embarrassment. Why did she feel the need to bare her very soul to this old lady? "A place like this by the sea will have more than its fair share of tragedies. It's the burden of fisherfolk. Some of the older residents I've spoken to have told me about the press gangs of the past. Of course we'd all heard about that time and were horrified, but in the great dramas of community suffering, I think we can sometimes forget that the individual tragedies are just as poignant. And there is a value to every lost life that we should not forget. Do you know, I feel I want to write about that time, but to focus on the individuals, somehow dig those lives back out of the past. Why, rather like a geologist after his rocks."

Eliza looked up. What curious women they were, and what a shame that more such people didn't live permanently here in Whitby. She'd never really thought too much about people long past, or that one might wish to unearth them again, so to speak. Was that what her father was fascinated by, unearthing the story of the earth.

"The press gangs," Muriel snorted. "Do you know we had a riot here?"

"Oh yes, Mrs Rose, where I'm lodging, has told me much about it."

"Did she tell you that my mother started it?"

"Muriel!" Eleanor scolded, glancing worriedly at Lily's shocked face. "That is an exaggeration, but you'll excuse my daughter, she was only a child at the time."

"I remember you marching off to the press gang tavern with the fire poker in your hand."

"I know, but...." Eleanor closed her eyes. She could still remember it so vividly. "The riots started after all that; I was back home by then. I know violence was not the answer, but what the navy did to us is unforgiveable. And they would not listen to people, that is the shame of the riots and that is the root of many problems. That people are not heard. I went to that tavern," she paused, looking over at Lily. "The navy had set up their headquarters there, you understand. They had taken my boy. He was only a young lad, but he was tall for his age. Not that I supposed that really mattered, they would have taken him even if he had been small. What was it they called those poor children? Powder monkeys? It's not right." Eleanor paused, looking wistfully into the middle distance. It had been so long since she had last seen her son, Stewart. He'd only been twenty years old when he'd died. "I admit I did hit a few things with the poker in that tavern, and I don't regret it. They needed to know what they were doing to us, but I don't think they took any heed. And it was too late they told me; my boy had been taken away to the ships. Later the riots really blew up and... and those poor men were sent off to York to be tried and hung. The press gangs had driven them to it, but no one would listen, and it turned into fury. And now I am old and people listen to me even less than when I was a young woman. But I see the same mistakes happening, leading to the same trouble. It's all cyclical. When the people are not listened to... one must acknowledge their tragedy and sorrows."

"But things are improving greatly, grandmamma," Eliza spoke up as Eleanor grew silent. "The advancements of this age..."

"I see it repeat. Every new generation thinks they will get it right this time, but as the years pass, those good intentions don't seem to get anyone where they would like to be."

There was a sombre silence as Eleanor seemed to drift between catching her breath and falling asleep. There was a gentle chink as Muriel set her teacup down.

"It was the navy," Eleanor started up again. "Wicked, heartless men. Remember that girls," she added looking across at Eliza and Meta.

"Don't let those uniforms turn your heads. I hear young women twittering over them. They tore families apart. And for what?"

Lily smiled awkwardly. "Some would say to keep the French out. But at what cost? I do think they, and many others grow so focused in the big narrative that they forget the individual lives."

Muriel shuffled awkwardly in her seat. "We have grown so very serious, and we did mean to be thanking you for rescuing my mother. If you are curious about Whitby, you ought to speak to some of the old fishermen. Tall tales a lot of them, but you'll hear of adventures on the ocean."

"Indeed I intend to," Lily bloomed. "And I also have note of a compendium of tales I will consult from the library when we get back to Manchester, or rather my husband will on my behalf for heavens above that a woman should want to look at books."

Muriel smiled wryly. "I've experienced the same problems."

"In fact, a few years ago I had the pleasure of meeting one of your countrymen, so to speak," Lily continued, "Indeed, it's his writings that I wish to consult. William Scoresby. I wonder if you've heard of him?"

Muriel snorted her distain. "I know him."

"Why, the vicar of Bradford? Don't you approve?"

Eleanor gave a tight smile. "William grew up in Whitby, he and Muriel played together as children."

"Really? What a playmate to have!"

"Indeed," Muriel scowled. "One that immediately disregarded one's intelligence and potential for the world based purely on their sex. Mother, did I tell you I had the misfortune to bump into him in Haworth a few years ago and he hadn't improved."

"I found him very pleasant company," Lily confessed, a little perturbed by Muriel's vehemence. "I met him up in Dunoon, Scotland of all places. I was visiting my sister at the time. Very pleasant, as I say, and what fascinating stories he told."

Eleanor smiled gently. "I think a lot of Muriel's fury is directed at society at large rather than Mr Scoresby specifically. You can imagine that it is not an easy road for a woman wishing to be involved in medical science."

"Indeed not."

"Mother!" Muriel huffed under her breath, feeling rising irritation flood her senses. "I'll go see if I can get some more hot water for tea."

The delightful conversations wore on through lunchtime and into up until supper, at which point Eleanor had fallen asleep and the young women had returned from an outdoor sketching expedition. Lily had clasped Muriel's hands in hers and begged her to assure her mother that as soon as her story of Whitby was written, she would be sure to send her mother a copy.

Eliza had looked to her great aunt questioningly as they returned to the parlour. "What do you think she meant? Is she writing all these in a journal she will send to grandmother?"

"I don't quite know," Muriel mused. "Perhaps her husband is collecting all these stories and will write a volume. You heard her mention that her husband works in the church? She didn't want to go into too much detail in the conversation. Those vicars are forever collecting and writing books. I don't know why she was so hesitant to speak too much on the subject."

"Unitarians," Eliza said. "Meta mentioned it whilst we were out walking. Some people can be a bit funny about it."

"I don't see why," Muriel muttered. "They're possibly the most sensible of all of them. Well, time will tell if anything comes of it. But a nicely worded journal might be a nice keepsake for Mamma."

In early December that year, Stephen stumbled out of the family home one morning to stare up at the hills in awe. The sun was starting to creep up over the high, dark horizon. It was like looking upon enlightenment from a dark pit. None of what he had read was new as such, and it all made perfect sense, yet to sit and compulsively read a book cover to cover that compiled everything the men of science had been discovering and witnessing, and in the amassing, to draw such a great revolutionary conclusion, was nothing short of mind blowing.

Already he was reading it two weeks after the London intellectuals, feeling provincial and behind the times. He reminded himself that he ought to be grateful he was reading it at all. In his letter old university colleague and now brother-in-law Jacob Mallinson, had recounted how the first edition had sold out within the first day. He'd felt duty bound out of ties of friendship and family to purchase two copies, and get one wrapped and straight into the post to the north. Of course there'd be another edition, demand was too great, but the slow would have to wait until next year now.

It had been a long time since he had last burned through candles, staying up until the text was finished. He had completed the text at five or so that morning, giddy through lack of sleep, euphoric at the immensity of this scientific leap forward. Such a great understanding of the world. He'd woken Mairi in an excitable state, telling her she must read this book immediately. Mairi had mumbled something, opening bleary eyes in the candlelight, and accepting Darwin's book, had drawn it into the layer of the bedclothes before succumbing to slumber once again.

He needed to talk to someone about this book, share in the wonder of the obvious order of nature, thus presented. Letters were not enough today. He thought of William Smith, long gone, and wondered what he would have made of all of this. He could imagine him sat at his table, roaring that he'd always known his uncle was a monkey.

Stephen wandered down the track towards the hub of the village in something of a daze. He would have to return home and breakfast, then get on with the business of the day, but now he wanted to see if anyone else was equally blown away. Miners were heading for the hills and work, breath frosting and steaming up in the icy air. The ground was slippery where puddles had formed. Folk said it was going to be a particularly rough winter. The hilltops were already white, and they'd had a little snow down in the valley bottom. The snow had mostly melted away to slush, which was now frozen in strange, harsh forms where it had been cast aside by cart wheels, animal tracks and the steady footsteps of men. Out of the gloom the naked tree branches cracked their way to the sky like ancient bones of ancestors past.

He wanted to stop the men he passed, and ask them, didn't the world seem like a new and wondrous place now that they'd read *Origins*... but of course they hadn't read it yet and perhaps they never would. Would any of this impact their imaginations, their lives or the way they viewed the world? He stopped outside the church. What would their reverend make of all this? Would he even read it, or merely listen to the opinions of others and spout that. He could understand what Mallison had written when he said that the church was taking a very defensive stance against the book.

Muriel Must, much to her frustration, did not acquire her own copy until January when the second edition was released. She might have borrowed it from the Gaskins when they had finished reading their copy, only that there was a dreadful snow storm which cut off the valley, and Stephen was not keen to trust the book to the postal services. Connections gradually opened up again, although travel over the hilltops of moors to Whitby was to be avoided due to the shocking deep drifts that swallowed up dips and hollows, turning the landscape into a heightened flat plain of treachery. Instead they would travel south, past Hartoft and Hutton-le-Hole to then cut across to Pickering and pick up the main route to Whitby there.

So it was that Eliza spent her Christmas separate to her family. Living at the coast with two older ladies meant that she felt her age a solitude. Muriel was still spritely and keen for conversation, but her great grandmother slept all the more. Even when Darwin's book had finally entered The Pines, and Muriel had sat by her mother's armchair excitedly reading out loud great long passages, Eleanor had drifted into gentle sleep, her frail skinny arms like bird bones resting in a nest of shawls upon her lap. The only comment she made by the end, suggesting she had heard more than they realised, was that her father had never been an ape. That man was a hob through and through, no doubt.

Eliza had looked questioningly at Muriel. "Was my great great grandfather a goblin?"

Muriel raised her eyes to the ceiling at her mother's nonsense. "Not in the sense you mean."

"He looked like one?"

"I have no idea, I never met him. He was dead by the time I was born. Well, they had to declare him dead."

"What do you mean?"

"He just disappeared. No one ever found out what had happened to him. He was probably swallowed up by a bog somewhere on the moors. It happens," Muriel paused, groaning at her knees as she got up from her chair. "When the ground is saturated those bogs can be treacherous, and it's easy to lose your way when the sea fret comes down."

Eliza thought back to that silly adventure up to the standing stone with her sister. Those initials carved into the rock in her amateur hand, written over by Daniel Iredale. How stupid that they had even gone up there in the first place, and in such dreadful weather. She and Tilda could have died. Good luck and nothing else that they had managed to find their way back to the road, and their father had been out looking for them. Sitting in this fine Whitby parlour, it felt like another world away.

Eleanor slept the days away more and more. It was one February morning of some date – she had no idea for she hardly gained consciousness most days now – that she awoke to find a visitor sitting on a chair by her beside. He smiled and took her hand, paper-thin now, and clasped it between his two youthful, strong palms like a treasure. Eleanor smiled, feeling a thrill inside that he had come back.

Angus patted her hand. "Time to be away now."

"Aye," she sighed. "I believe it is."

Muriel came into the room mid morning to discover that her mother must have passed away at some point in the night. She could sense that the room was empty when she entered, but she went through her duty as a doctor, and checked for breath and a heartbeat, of which there was neither. Her mother was quite cold. She sank down on the empty chair that had been shifted to the side of the bed, held her mother's hand and pushed her face into the mattress to try and stem the crying. She must have realised this had been coming, given how much her mother had been sleeping. Muriel knew the signs better than anyone. It ought not to be a shock, and yet here they were. Or rather here she was.

She suddenly felt incredibly alone in the world, which unusual for Muriel was very happy in her own company. It dawned on her that all her peers were dead. Well, there was still Emmerline of course, and her own dynasty of philanthropic little empire builders who kept her busy. Perhaps cousin Prudence was still alive, Derwa never spoke of her mother when she wrote, but Muriel's other two Longbottom cousins who had survived into adulthood were dead now. As were Muriel's parents and siblings. Once could say there were descendants, and where there were new generations there was hope, only that her descendants were one step removed and she could not acknowledge them completely, and neither them she.

She dried her eyes and composed herself, then went downstairs to her writing desk. She looked out on the snowy garden outside. There were letters to write and people to tell, but with the weather as it was, people wouldn't travel far. Eleanor had outlived most, there was hardly anyone left to mourn her. At least the Gaskins of Rosedale ought to manage it. She didn't know how to explain it so that the blow might not be so hard, so instead quickly wrote down the facts, urging Mairi and the girls to come soon. She heard the housekeeper enter at the back door, and hurried through to her before she had chance to take off her boots and cape.

"I need this to get to Rosedale as soon as possible."

Mrs Argument stared at her, eyebrows raised, mentally wondering if it could be put off till lunchtime at least. It was bitterly cold outside, with an unforgiving wind from the sea, and lazy sleet slapping down from the thick clouds.

"It's very urgent," Muriel held out the letter. "Ideally it needs to arrive today."

"Today?" Mrs Argument's voice rose an octave. "In this weather?"

"Yes."

"What on earth could have happened?"

"My mother passed away in the night."

"Oh good lord, bless me!" She put a hand to her mouth, "I wasn't expecting that, but she had been sleeping an awful lot. Going in your sleep is a blessing. You'll be wanting your family here." She took the letter from Muriel, opened her mouth to say something more, but her eyes were drawn to the staircase. "I'd best get into town and get this delivered."

"Thank you." A little bemused by the housekeeper's strange expression, Muriel turned and found Eliza on the staircase, half way down and nervous.

"Something has happened?"

"Oh, Eliza," Muriel's face dropped. "I've just sent word to your mother. I'm so sorry, my dear. My mother passed away in the night."

"Your mother," Eliza said the words almost as if she had never met the person. "You mean grandmother? But I only spoke to her last night.." she twisted to look back up the staircase. "She was awake for a little while and I went in to talk to her. I..." Her knees wobbled and she clutched onto the railings as if she was about to kneel. "Oh no, no. You're sending for Mamma? She's coming?"

"Yes, Mrs Argument has just gone out with the note." Muriel pushed down her own grief, switching across to her professional carer persona, the local doctor. She took Eliza by the arm and led her through to the parlour. "Sit down. I'll make some hot sweet tea."

Eliza sat and wiped at her eyes as Muriel departed for the kitchen. Oh dear, it was not supposed to happen like this. She wasn't ready for it. She just needed to talk to her grandmother one last time. She raised her eyes to the ceiling. But she wasn't there. She could talk all she liked, but she would not get an answer. How could it be that a person simply ceased to be? Eliza closed her eyes and wondered what it was to be dead. She couldn't comprehend it. There was too much in her head, so many memories and thoughts, and she only had a couple of decades' worth. Her grandmother had been in her nineties, how much had been packed into her mind?

Very quietly, she pushed herself back out of the parlour chair and crept back to the main passageway. The kitchen door was open and she could hear her Aunt Muriel sobbing over the tea. She didn't know what to say. She'd seen plenty of death, they'd had it in their own family when her brother William had died, although Eliza didn't really remember the time. From then they'd led something of a blessed life, seeing the childhood tragedies of their neighbours, and the death of adults, through accident, age or disease, but somehow the Gaskins thrived. Death was always someone else's companion.

Eliza crept up the staircase and went to her grandmother's door, her hand hovering up against the wood ready to knock. Her knuckles tapped ever so gently against the wood, lip service to manners, and she opened the door to the room.

The light reflecting off the snow made the room look brighter than it really was. An old, white-haired woman lay asleep in the bed. Grandmother looked so peaceful, and yet when Eliza approached the bedside she wasn't even sure that it was her grandmother. There was something wrong about the face, the expression or lack thereof. If she didn't know better she could almost, but not quite, believe a stranger had clambered in through the window and settled down in the bed. She sank down to the floor in bewilderment, her back to the bedframe. Whatever it was that made her grandmother the person she was, no, had been, it had already left. Had it flown away somewhere or did it simply cease to exist. Eliza pressed her hands to her eyes. She didn't know what to do with herself. She was paralysed by lack of suggestion.

When she took her hands away, Mrs Argument and another woman she didn't know stood over her with kindly expressions, their hair and shawls speckled with snow crystals.

"Oh, sorry, I..."

"Not to worry," Mrs Argument patted her hand as she helped her get up to her feet. "It's not an easy day. I think we'd all gotten to thinking she'd live forever, forgetting that we're all to return to our Good Lord one day."

"Indeed," the other woman murmured in agreement.

"My aunt..."

"She let you be for a while until we got back," Mrs Argument explained. "I've got the message sent to your mother, and your Aunt is downstairs writing letters. Mrs Harcourt has kindly returned to me to help."

"Help?"

"Wash the body, my dear," Mrs Harcourt explained in a manner as if she were addressing a three year old.

"We have to get her ready for her final journey. It's the way of things." Mrs Argument smoothed at the skin on the back of Eliza's hands. "Go down and see your Aunt, we'll take care of matters here."

Muriel was at her writing desk in the parlour, frustration rising as words failed her. She was always so proud of her eloquent letters, but what to say to people now? She had compiled a short list of friends and relatives who still survived and might have a passing interest. But would they? They hadn't heard from some of them for decades, and really, if no one attempted to keep in touch during life, where was the point of it at death? Of course she would write to Emmerline, who would pass on the news down the branches of her own family tree. Derwa would care. She came from the Longbottom branch, but as she was still estranged from her mother, she was her own little separate sapling. Muriel supposed she ought to write to cousin Prudence, Derwa's mother, out of duty. Her cousin William was long dead. There had been no children to that marriage and Muriel had an inkling she'd heard his wife, Magdalene, had succumbed to senile decay a couple of years ago. Jeremiah had also died, but he had a network of family in Canada. One of his girls had married a Yorkshireman and never emigrated. Who was she? Muriel would ask Derwa if she knew which of Jeremiah's children was still in the country. Then of course there was Jayne, Eleanor's ward of long ago, who would be devastated to hear.

There was a cough as Eliza entered the parlour. Muriel set down her pen. "Eliza," she said distractedly. "There's tea on the table. I'm just trying to compose these letters, but the more I think the less I remember the written English language. Thank goodness we already have a message away to your mother." She put her hands to her forehead and groaned. "The letter writing and administration," she grumbled. "I remember my mother talking about a man on the moors, back when she was a child. When this sort of thing happened, they just told him, and he went about telling everyone; in the right order as well, for he knew not to offend anyone. And he knew all that needed to know. What a blessing that system would be. But of course not everyone lives in walking distance. I even have a letter to Canada to write."

"We have family in Canada?"

"Distantly. A cousin of mine emigrated with most of his family. It is difficult with family abroad, unless they can afford to travel, you grow distant. One never knows how long letters will take or if they even arrive. I didn't always get any replies."

"It must have been difficult when your husband died."

Muriel looked at her curiously.

"Well," Eliza floundered. "Mamma told me he was from Estonia, Kaarel Must. There must have been family over there to write to."

Muriel returned her gaze to her pen. "Not that many. Well, at least that letter to your mother is gone. I will be glad to see Mairi, as quickly as possible."

It wasn't just the knowledge that her niece would be informed, or that there would be more support in Whitby that nagged at Muriel. She had seen her mother's will, and she needed to speak to Mairi, to make an agreement before that stupid solicitor started trotting about telling people too early of what they had inherited. Mairi and Muriel would need to decide the best way to arrange living arrangements, really, to think how it would all be done. Eleanor had left Muriel the property in Haworth and the old family home in Whitby. Jewellery and the other two properties in Whitby had been left to Mairi, on the understanding that she would spilt this between the three younger daughters when her own time came. Some money and items had been bequeathed to Jane. That left this house up on the cliffs of Whitby, The Pines, Eleanor's final home. This was the sticking point, and Muriel did not wish to see it cause trouble between Mairi's girls. Eleanor had been concerned as to how easy an independent career would realistically be for Eliza, and so she had planned to help out and provide the accommodation. Eliza now owned The Pines. It was done in goodness, but Muriel worried how the other girls would feel about this, or that it could risk Eliza at the hands of fortune hunters. Perhaps if they waited some years before telling the girls, and in the meantime Muriel could just live here with Eliza and no one would really explain the technicalities of what they were doing, then any heartache could be avoided? Perhaps.

Mairi would be here soon. They could decide the best way forward.

1860
Rosedale

The horses were exhausted. It was a lot for any being to clamber up what the locals increasingly referred to as the Chimney Bank Road these days, let alone beasts who also had a gig full of people to pull. But Mr Flintoft had been adamant he would conduct this tour in the correct manner. Whatever constituted a correct manner. Really, this had to be for the benefit of her aunt, for Mairi had no interest in the mining, and Stephen had been around all of the construction sites and mines that much, he ought to know it better than the leaseholders and engineers themselves. All Mairi saw was a loss of the quiet beauty of the valley from when she had first moved to Rosedale.

From the Western side, almost but not quite at the top of the long, steep bank, she could see across the top of the village nestled down below, and over to the opposing side of the valley, where the eastern mines had been erected, along with heavy duty industrial kilns. The entire area was buzzing with workers and industry. Dust plumed up into the atmosphere from the mining endeavours. Landscapes and nature felt lost as heaps of slag grew and holes widened. There were miners and engineers, many of whom had to walk into the area from neighbouring valleys on account of there simply not being enough accommodation close by. Navvies: rough, heavy-set men, even so as smartly dressed as they could afford, laboured heavily on the burgeoning railway lines that would loop like a closing jaw around the top head of the main valley, then shoot off across the moors to connect up to the mainline at Battersby. The railways were not in active use yet, still under construction, but the intention was that they would be up and running daily by next year. Mr Flintoft wanted to show them what had been done, what amazing things they were achieving. Mairi didn't want to be here, but Stephen was so fascinated by the entire process, she didn't feel she could bow out, and then of course Muriel was staying with them which meant anything to do with science and engineering had to be investigated. Mairi had hoped that perhaps Muriel would be at least a little distressed at the loss of wilderness. Muriel did not always blindly follow new innovation and industry as being right. Mairi had heard the stories of Muriel's horror at the child labour in the mills in Manchester on countless occasions. Not all industrialised production was for the greater good. But today Muriel was the obliging guest, and took in everything Mr Flintoft said with a smile on her face and no concern in her heart. The only questions were to better understand the processes, and not to query if anything had been sacrificed in the name of progress, and was that loss worth it?

The ironstone was in big demand and there was a lot of money to be made. One only had to consider that the industrialists were going to the expense of getting this railway in across remote high top moorland to appreciate how financially serious this entire venture was.

The horses were paying as much attention to the lecture as Mairi was. The passengers were out of the gig to examine the site, and in respite the horses were catching their breath. One was licking at a dirty lump of snow. Patches still clung on, even in July. It had been a bad winter and a bad year, in fact it was the first month that it hadn't snowed to some degree. Mairi had hopes she would finally get rid of her chilblains. There were gullies across the high moors that had effectively been filled in and flattened off with great drifts of relentless snow that were only melting now. Some revealed their macabre contents, frozen and preserved for months, and only as the air and the sun reached them, did the rot begin. Mostly sheep, and one deer, but a human corpse had been found in one gully, presumed to be a traveller who had lost his way over the moors in a snowstorm.

Mairi turned away from staring at the horses and tried to rejoin the lecture. Muriel had asked why the kilns were being built here in the first place. Mr Flintoft confessed he was an engineer first, and referred them to the geologist amongst them. Stephen explained why they had gone to the expense of building the kilns, so that they might roast the ironstone on site to remove the water and carbonic acid gas, therefore minimising the weight of what was to be transported out. It did leave a lot of calcinite dust about, he admitted, but it was good sense to cleanse the rock ore of these impurities before sending it so far by rail. Well, rail would be the future mode, at the moment they were still stuck with animal transportation on those dreadful roads heading south out of Rosedale Abbey. But not for much longer, Mr Flintoft added as an afterword, for mark his words, it would be a revolution.

The group stood at the bank top by a small, recently created reservoir. Close by a brick tower was under construction. Muriel, who was soaking up the information as if she were planning to write an article for one of the national periodicals, considered the position of the building and wondered what it was. "This isn't part of the kilns, is it, Mr Flintoft?" she asked, gesturing at the tower.

Stephen suppressed a smile. He had lived through the months of troubles and planning already.

"No," Mr Flintoft sighed. "This has caused me some headaches, but I assure you, it will be built in time, and to perfection. I have said, I will dance on top of it when it is complete," he paused momentarily for the delighted laughter of Stephen Gaskin's aunt-in-law. "Out of relief, or joy, I am not sure, but the dance will happen."

"Ah, Mr Flintoft," Muriel sighed. "I am sure this tower is more than a dancing platform for yourself, regardless of how well you may dance."

"It is the engine house chimney for my incline tramway."

Muriel's eyes sparkled. "Now this sound more intriguing than any dance I know."

"Indeed it is. And we have to get that rock up from Hollins' some better way than we are at the moment. The oxen do an admirable job of course, but this is the modern age, and steam and engineering can and will achieve wonders."

The plan was to calcinate the ironstone in great kilns high up on either side of the Rosedale valley. From there, two railways would begin, looping around the head of the valley at the top, to join on the west side, then head off across the high moors, past the Red Lion Inn of Blakey Ridge and over to the north-western edge of the moors where it would then be transported down a long steep incline to join the railway network of the lowlands.

"Of course, as well as all the railway lines, and necessary buildings for engineering, engines and wagons, there's also all the staff to think of," Mr Flintoft spoke as he helped Muriel back up into the cart. "A railway requires a number of men to man it, and to be on hand at the correct places. There's nowhere up here for a man and his family to live, so we're having to factor that in as well." He sat at the front and took up the reins. "They'll be at key points, so we're building something of a village up here at the junction. This is where the line that will run, roughly where my horses are taking us now. It will meet with the line coming from the other side of the valley. It will loop around the top of the valley head across there," he explained, pointing into the far distance, "and then come back along this side to join us up ahead. It will all be relatively high up and on the flat. A longer distance but far easier than going down into the valley to have to come up the other side. These valley sides are steep and the loads are heavy. That needs a great deal of power."

"Hence the engine house we have just seen," Muriel concluded.

Mairi leaned forward, looking ahead to the place where the junction would be. Ground had already been excavated and two cottages were already complete. She looked back to her husband. "I hadn't realised houses were being built up here."

He nodded solemnly. "The inn won't be quite so lonely anymore."

"They're already calling it Little Blakey," Mr Flintoft said with a grin. "I'm sure it'll be quite the community. One of the railway masters has already moved in, I believe. A man by the name of Amundsen."

"They're already in?" Muriel sounded surprised.

"You know them? Foreigners I understand."

"He's Norwegian," Muriel said," But Mrs Amundsen is a cousin of mine. Well, a cousin's daughter..."

"We have family living up here?" Mairi sounded shocked.

"Only just," Muriel grinned. "Derwa wrote to tell me they'd probably be coming up here later in the year. She told me September at the earliest. I've told you about Derwa. She lives with him, Tor Amundsen, and his daughter Agneta. A widower he was, well, they were both bereaved when they met, and helped raise one another's children. Decent fellow from the times I've met him. Mr Flintoft, might we stop by and see if they're at home?"

"Yes, of course," Mr Flintoft bought the horses to a stop at the cottages, equally curious about this revelation of connection to the Gaskins. Not that it was so strange for folk round here to have random relatives dotted about all over the place. The Gaskin-Amundsen link was another story to add to his repartee and folk were always after a new talking point. More things to tell the family when he headed back to Lastingham.

He was helping Muriel down from the gig when a slender young girl, almost of full adult height, appeared at the door with a blank look on her face. She stepped back into the shadow, a pale, blonde thing, then fled away into the house calling for mother. It was not long before a red-headed woman took her place, a woman only a few years older than Mairi, although more weather worn. The lines on her face spoke of a life of hard work, and a life that had not always been easy. Yet she was not too prematurely aged, and had a delightful spark about her. She paused for a moment, wiping her hands on her apron and stepping boldly outside, a questioning look on her face before she caught sight of Muriel.

"Why, Aunt Muriel," she broke out. "You're here! How on earth did you know? I haven't had a chance to write you yet."

"Pure coincidence. We are having a tour conducted by Mr Flintoft and he happened to mention the name Amundsen."

Derwa bobbed to him. "I wish I'd had a bit of warning. I was wanting to get settled in before letting you know, and then of course there's the fine niece of yours in the valley, I don't know if she'd..." she broke off looking at Mairi who had taken her husband's hand and was stepping down from the gig.

"We'll have a great family reunion here now," Muriel beamed. "My niece, Mrs Mairi Gaskin and her husband Mr Gaskin."

"The land agent. How do you do? I expect you've already met my husband, Tor. He's off up yonder today. The navvies are working round the head of the valley at the moment. He's not got so much to do yet so he goes worrying the railway engineers, them that lay the line like, making sure it'll be right for when he's dealing with the rolling stock on it."

"I have met Mr Amundsen a few times," Stephen said. "I hadn't realised the connection to my wife."

"I didn't know at all," Mairi spoke, feeling almost girlish, and suddenly a little more positive about all this change. "It's always felt so very isolated up here, and although people are very kind, you do feel a little of an outsider with no kin. You'll have to come down to the village."

"No kin?" Derwa laughed. "Now, you don't know your family history. There's nothing but kin up on this ridge. My cousin lives over at the Red Lion."

"One of Jeremiah's?" Muriel looked a little confused. "I lost track of all of his children. This must be the one who didn't make it to Canada."

"Ewat married the inn keeper's son," Derwa said. "She's my cousin, so I suppose she's as close to you as I am."

"Ewat? You mean Mrs Iredale?"

"That's the one."

"I'm related to Mrs Iredale?" Mairi sounded shocked. "I've been visiting her all these years and I had no idea."

"She probably doesn't realise. I am not in regular contact with her myself," Derwa said, breaking eye contact a little awkwardly and turning back towards the cottage. "Agneta, do come out and say hello. Some of these folks are family, some live just down in the valley. It would be nice to know who they are."

Agneta shyly exited the house, scuttling across to her mother to hold gently onto her arm as if one of them might blow away in the breeze. She'd seen the men about before, talking to Pa, but the women were unknown. Family of her mother perhaps, but not blood kin to her. Her own mother, she who birthed her, had died some fourteen years ago. Derwa had come into their lives when Agneta had only been a young child, and she'd been good to them, and made Pa smile again, so it was a happy situation of substitute mother, she supposed. She'd seen other girls almost pushed out of the family when the new woman came into the family. Even so, she wasn't so sure how interested these people would be in her.

"This is Mrs Gaskin and her husband, well, you've already met him on account of your Pa's work. And this fine lady is my Aunt Muriel who you've heard all about. And Mr Flintoft of course we've already met."

"The Rosedale workers and creators are a community in themselves," Mr Flintoft bowed.

"It's nice to meet you, Agneta," Mairi smiled. Something about the young girl, almost a woman, not really fitting in where she was, reminded her of her own youth. So long ago now it felt as though it could have been something she once read in a book. She smiled wryly to herself, as if she were a great age at thirty-nine. Still, some women her age were starting to be grandmothers. "I have four daughters, they're all at home at the moment. If you'd like to come and visit us sometime, you'd be most welcome."

Agneta looked terrified at the prospect, a blush flooding up her neck at the attention. She'd heard about the daughters from the letters her mother read out to her. They were probably all very sophisticated and well refined, educated girls who wouldn't have much use for the daughter of a steam engine engineer.

"We will visit the village, once we've settled in," Derwa said when she realised her daughter was struck dumb. She suspected she felt the same, but age and experience had lent her confidence Agneta had yet to acquire. "You'll have to excuse us but we are only just unpacking and not ready for guests inside yet..."

"This was an unexpected visit, nothing to apologise for," Muriel waved off her worries casually. "We ought to all head up to the inn and terrorise poor Mrs Iredale. Given most of the family is off in Canada she won't have had so many relatives descend on her all at once."

"Regretfully, another time," Derwa said. She still wasn't sure whether her sister had been meddling and Ewat would not wish to consort with her. Rosen had a nasty tongue in her head and precious few, if any, scruples about the version of the facts she told. In front of an audience was not the arena to find out.

Muriel nodded, guessing what was worrying Derwa. "We'll let you continue with your chores. Moving in and unpacking does feel relentless for the first week or so, and it will be very different here from where you were living before."

"Yes."

Mairi smiled gently. "It was lovely to finally meet you."

"You too."

The usual pleasantries were conducted by all parties, and the tour of the Rosedale Mining railways under production continued, the gig and horses trotting off in the direction of the Red Lion Inn. Mr Flintoft talked of Ingleby Incline and pointed vaguely in the direction with his whip.

Derwa put an arm around Agneta's shoulders and the two of them turned slowly back to the house. "Let's get that mangling finished," Derwa said. "Then we can get the sheets hung out to dry. Enjoy it whilst we can. When there's all those trains coming back, I don't know whether dry and clean will go together anymore."

"That fine lady is your family?"

Derwa smiled. "Indeed she is, although I never met her before. She's the Mairi from my Aunt Muriels' letters."

"So strange," Agneta mused. "They're not how I pictured them."

"Folk rarely are. Come on, away inside with you. Sometime when we're settled we'll go down and visit them. Hopefully they're good folk, and one of her younger girls ought to be about your age. It'd be nice for you to make a friend or two around here. You don't want to be stuck with just your mother for company."

"Oh, I don't mind you at all," Agneta said earnestly.

Derwa broke out into laughter. "I know, I didn't mean it like that. But we'll get settled in this place. From what your Pa's been saying, there's going to be a boom in mining here. We're going to be living here for a good few years to come."

July may have served a break in the poor weather, but it was hardly the blazing summer that the farmers hoped for. When the last days of July chimed through, the locals were horrified to be met with the occasional lazy snow shower. Nothing remained on the ground, melting away as soon as it touched the earth, but even to see snowflakes in August was ridiculous. The snowfalls did more than set heads shaking for it damaged harvests, and folk worried how they would feed themselves that winter. Thank goodness for the mines and the railways – there were so many employment opportunities if the worst happened. Hopefully there'd be enough money about that local folk wouldn't starve.

Despite the poor working conditions, the mining corporations were desperate to get profits boosted, production up and things moving. The profit factor was very dependent on transportation out of the valley, for there was only so much that could be done whilst the pack ponies were the only way of getting the processed ironstone out of the valley. The navies put their backs into the coming railways and powered through the work, cutting out flat roadways for iron railings to be laid down. The speed and volume of earth moved felt as if hill and bog simply had not existed. Over at Ingleby, a miracle was worked of engineering and elbow grease. The project was an immense amount of work, some said too much for humans to overcome, and yet it was completed within fifteen months. Mr Flintoft had raved about the problems and the solutions, for it was both an engineering nightmare and inspiring challenge. This was the great industrial age and nothing would stop them.

The problem at Ingleby was not a long distance, nor was it particularly boggy. They needed to get from the top of the moors down to the plains of the spreading Vale of Mowbray. It was a mere 1430 yards, which made it sound like a casual stroll. But it was steep, at some points a one in five incline. That was a big ask for an engine drawing itself up, but with heavy wagons from the mines going down the slope without losing control? Impossible. It could not be done. And yet they needed the rock down there, to be sent on to the industrial north towards the River Tees. So simply physics would be employed, Mr Flintoft explained gleefully. Not that he was working on that project, he had enough with getting the produce of Hollins Mine up out of Rosedale, but he kept abreast of proceedings, as did Stephen. It was a frantic, energetic time, booming with innovation and industry. And at Ingleby, they would employ gravity, with carefully controlled rope pulleys in a large drum house at the top conducting empty wagons from the bottom, which would be pulled up the hill by the weight of the rolling full wagons heading downwards. It would be a marvel when completed.

Agneta Amundsen had heard much discussion of the railways and the mines. When she wasn't at home listening to her dear Pa, she was spending increasing amounts of time down in Rosedale Abbey with the Gaskin girls. Sometimes she would stay overnight, because the bad year of 1860 had rolled over into January and still the snow fell. Even down in the valley, which was a noticeably different climate to the moorland tops at Little Blakey where her own family lived, there was a permanent covering of snow and great drifts adding undulations to the landscape. Up on the tops there were corridors in the snow to get from door to door, and entrances along the roads and tracks. Her mother, Derwa, spent a lot of time helping the other families get set up in Little Blakey. Some of them came with little children, and neither the children nor the parents were used to such remote living. From the stories Derwa had told, Agneta understood that Derwa had been raised in these parts, so she appreciated how life could be and how one needed to be prepared. Since leaving her home tract in her youth, Derwa had lived in the towns and the lowlands. Experiencing the contrast helped her to understand how much of a shock moorland life could be for folk who were not used to it. Agneta had vague memories of the intense cold of Norwegian winters, but she had been so young when they had left and come to England that the memories were as real and relevant to her as the pictures in her childhood story book.

Derwa did her best to keep the cottage warm, and bizarrely to Agneta's understanding, the great drifts of snow against the walls actually helped to keep the wind out and the heat in. But truth be told, it was more comfortable at the Gaskin's, and it always felt like a special treat when it was decided that the snow was coming down too heavily again, and she would have to stay overnight. She'd share the bed with Adelaide and little Charlotte, and two toasty bed warmers at the bottom of the bed. A great pile of quilted blankets, and a woollen hat on each head. They were positively cosy.

Out of the four Gaskin girls, and all four were in residence over that winter, it was the third daughter, Adelaide, who matched her in age and temperament. It was also Adelaide whom Agneta found she got along best with. She was a quiet, home-loving girl who enjoyed her knitting and her baking, and did not wish to leave her mother or the home fires. Charlotte was like a young pet for them to fuss over. Tilda, only a year older, seemed like a foreign being, desperate to be out and tramping, doing, and fighting silently against what seemed to be expected of her sex and her position in the family. She was kind, pleasant company, but Agneta found that she had nothing to say to her that would hold her attention for more than a minute. The eldest daughter, Eliza, was much older, and a young woman at that, already twenty. She was accomplished, stunningly beautiful – Agneta had heard all the local lads speak of her – and yet awkward and disinterested. There had been vague mention of her studying art in Whitby, to the point that they had hardly ever seen her in the valley, but a grandmother had died and something had happened about the house and Eliza wasn't comfortable going to the coast at the moment. Agneta didn't really follow the younger girls' chatter and she didn't ask them to explain it better.

Charlotte had gone to bed that evening with a cold. Adelaide had gone with her in nursemaid role, assuring Agneta that she should stay up yet and enjoy the company of the older girls. Agneta had been terrified, but didn't dare say so, and besides, Tilda wanted a malleable audience to talk at, and had virtually dragged her to the fireside snuggery for reading. Someone was going to see this book the way she did. Eliza was hunched over her drawing boards in the corner of the room, fingerless gloves on her hands, smudged with charcoal as she sketched the winter scenes of the room. Usually she worked on the most delicate and detailed drawing of plants and flowers – Agneta couldn't believe such things were possible with just a sheet of paper and a pencil – but in the winter nights she said the light wasn't good enough to work in such detail and so she decided to work on bigger, bolder sketches. Even then, they seemed very fine and delicate to Agneta's eyes.

Agneta and Tilda were curled up together under blankets by the fire. Tilda had gotten hold of a copy of *Wuthering Heights* – her Aunt had known the writer before she died, didn't Agneta know? Agneta hadn't known that, but nothing about this family seemed impossible. They huddled together and read chapter after chapter together, Tilda huffing down her frustration that Agneta read far more slowly than she did.

"It's amazing, isn't it?" Tilda breathed. "All that freedom going out onto the moors. Don't you think Heathcliff is awfully dashing?"

Agneta wasn't sure, and fumbled over her words.

"He's a monster," Eliza muttered. "I don't know why any woman would want to give up any freedom or advantage for a beast like that."

Tilda rolled her eyes. "My sister doesn't want to get married to anyone ever. She's an artist and she makes her own living." She gave out a little snort. "Eliza doesn't understand romance."

Eliza pulled a face. "No one should let their head get so filled with romance that they would accept someone like Heathcliff."

"I'd make him a better person."

Eliza laughed.

"I would," Tilda retorted. "Besides, you wouldn't understand. You're not interested in other people." She turned to Agneta. "You know she's had three proposals and she turned them all down?"

Agneta was surprised it was only three.

Eliza's fingers tightened around the charcoal until it snapped in two. "You don't have to spread all my history to any old person..."

"It's only Agneta!" Tilda protested.

"And don't make me out to be some heartless monster. I am interested in other people."

"Not in the way a good woman should be," Tilda responded, mimicking Mrs Drying the younger. "She'd make a dreadful wife, why, I don't know why anyone would propose to such a creature."

It brought a smile to Eliza's lips. Tilda could be an entertaining mimic when inclined. "I hardly think the Dryings are to be taken as law on anyone's personality."

"But she's right. Your worst nightmare would be if Mamma ever left us, because then you'd be expected to look after all of us and yet you wouldn't, would you? I bet you'd run off and abandon us all."

"Tilda," Eliza admonished, a look of horror on her face. She thought of Agneta, her own mother dead many years and being raised by a woman they had recently learned was part of their own family tree, albeit distantly. They were privileged in that they had both their parents, food to eat every day, an education and no demands on them to go out and work. Tilda didn't realise how hard life was out there for other people. Not that Eliza truly appreciated it either, but she'd spent enough time in Whitby, listening to her Aunt talk, and seeing how the poor lived, squeezed into those dirty yards, hoards of scraggy children pouring out of each doorway. "You mustn't talk of such awful things."

Tilda tutted back and sulkily returned to the book, thankful to note that Agneta had come to the end of the page. "It's just an imagined case. You needn't worry, Mamma will always be here."

There was a loud bang as the front door was opened, ripped from a hand by the wind and thrown wide with gales and snow. Two or three men – it was hard to gauge by noise alone – entered the building, voices raised and concerned. Their father was one of them. Someone said loudly to shut the door, and with some effort the door was slammed shut again. With the bang, the howling from outside reduced. Eliza picked up her lamp and went to the window, drawing aside the curtain to look outside. There were a couple of inches of snow piled up at the bottom of the window. It was a surprisingly bright night, but the snow always did this. A blizzard had blown up again, a particularly bad one. They'd be digging trenches to get their own front doors open down in the bottom of Rosedale tomorrow morning. Agneta would be lucky if she got back home tomorrow. She'd probably be better off staying here for the next few days. Some of those moorland roads would be impassable for weeks, even for those farmers who had sleigh-carts to deal with wintry weather. There was only so much a horse could cope with.

"I think it's brandy's all round," a voice said as the parlour door was opened. Eliza recognised it as Mr King, one of the railway board's masterminds and all round leader of the great mining project. As they had bought the mining rights from Pappa's employers, and at the end of the day it still was the ancestral land, the railway men worked closely with their father the land agent.

"Ah, ladies." Mr King looked surprised to find them in the sitting room, as if they ought to be outside playing. He, their father, and the village constable – one of the farmers who had taken on the post for a year, and was looking rather out of his depth, hanging meekly behind – wore an encrusted cape of snow each, aged weathered eyebrows of white puffed out frostily.

"Girls, do you know where your mother is?" their father asked.

"Good heavens, get out of that parlour!" the housekeeper shrieked as she caught sight of the small drift that had blown in the entrance with their arrival. The effect was added to by shakings of snow jolted from bodies as they walked down the corridor. The piles of snow were now turning to slush, but hardly melting. There was no fire in the entrance hall and it was decidedly cold. The household was focussing its energies on keeping specific rooms warm, and that was taking effort enough.

Mairi descended the stairs as the bedlam of disrobing outwear began at the front of the house. Boots, capes and heavy coats were removed. The housekeeper found herself with armloads of wet, chilled clothing to take down to the kitchen to try and thaw out and dry.

The constable nodded awkwardly to Stephen. "I'd best be off."

"There's nothing we can do tonight. We just have to hope they can hold out."

"Aye, but I reckon I'll get a bunch of men together, shovels, carts, tools. Soon as the snow calms and the light rises, we want to be setting off."

"Very good; good man," Mr King said. "Make sure you come by here. I want to go up there as well."

"I as well," Stephen concurred.

"Couldn't trouble you for a bed tonight?" Mr King added as the constable was shown back out in the terrible night, another blizzard ripping into the house and sending Mairi back up a few steps to keep out of the worst of it. "I don't feel inclined to venture out again."

"No trouble at all," Stephen assured him, having no idea if they could accommodate the man. He looked to his wife for help, who was descending the stairs for the second time.

"That's not a problem. I've been with Charlotte," she added. "She's got a chill."

"Should we send for the doctor?"

"I don't think it will be all that serious, but I've put her to bed early to try and ward it off before it becomes anything. Adelaide is up there with her." Send for the doctor, she mused. And even in this blizzard, it was a possibility now that the mines had come and the population was booming. Rosedale had acquired its own surgeon apothecary. Not as sophisticated as her Aunt's own medical knowledge, but Muriel was over in the west of the county with her cousin Emmerline, and besides, it reassured folk to know there was someone to hand. Business provided enough work for him, for there were always accidents and injuries, mostly easily fixed with no long-lasting damage to the men, although there had been some amputations, crippling injuries that saw an end to working life. Between that and the domestic woes of farming folk, there was enough of an income to be made for now for the man to stay.

"Shall we go through to the sitting room?" Mairi suggested. "It's much warmer there, comfortable. I'll get hot tea and toast brought through."

Tilda crunched herself deeper into the blankets, a scowl on her face as the men entered. Even if it had only been Pappa, this brought an end to the book discussion. They looked like there were serious matters to speak of, and even if they were short of discussion topics, they wouldn't want to listen to her thoughts on Heathcliff and his wild, dark soul. "Come on, Agneta," she said, standing up and making the decision for both of them. "You can sleep with us tonight."

"I hope you're not leaving on my account," Mr King said, quietly glad the young girls were leaving. They'd either become too distressed to hear what was happening, or start up with that melodramatic twittering that young women were so fond of. He noted that the eldest remained at the table, but then Miss Gaskin was a rather calm, composed young woman. From what he had overheard, talk was that she was saving herself for a better match than what the local masons, miners and farmers had to offer. No one was sure who the lucky fellow might be, and no one dared to question her father too greatly either. Age be damned, if he wasn't currently married he might have thrown his own cap into the ring.

"It's the warmest place to be now," Mairi said, giving Tilda a stern look for her shortness of manners as she marched out of the room, a meeker Agneta following in her tred. How curious that Tilda had suddenly decided to adopt Agneta away from Adelaide. It was probably because Adelaide was currently absorbed by nursing duties. "I don't suppose there will be much to do for a week or two now, with the snow falling so heavily," she commented as she closed the door to keep the heat in. "Work on the rails will be impossible."

"We weren't expecting such a sudden blizzard," Mr King spoke. "There's been work going on the moors up until recently."

"Really?"

"And there'll be a great many man hour put in tomorrow. There's a group of navvies working up on the high moor north of the Red Lion."

"Around the Eskletts area," Stephen added.

"God forgive me, those men are working for me," Mr King said. "And they've not been seen. They've not come down for shelter, neither in the valley nor to the Red Lion. We're mounting a rescue party for tomorrow."

Mairi looked stricken. She knew the area Stephen had mentioned. It was endless open moorland, certainly now lost to many feet of snow, freezing temperatures and gales. Why had they not come off the tops earlier? Hardened, fuelled by a mentality to get the work done and finished. No man stops for a little bad weather. "Will they have been able to shelter up there?"

"There's a few huts, temporary things put up for them whilst they're working aross the moors," Stephen looked grave. "They're not really up to giving enough protection against this type of weather, although we must pray they got to them and will hold up till morning."

"Otherwise..."

"Otherwise we will be digging corpses out, Mrs Gaskin," Mr King spoke, too worried to think of pleasantries and saving a lady's nerves from the harsh realities of life. His own wife would not have stood to think on the possibilities, but Mrs Gaskin had a quiet reserve about her. She seemed at times unshockable.

Eliza looked up at this comment. A farmer wouldn't leave his beasts out in weather like this. A gang working across the moor was left to get on with things. Thinking it over, she was sure one of the Iredales was working on the railways now. Daniel's younger brother, Seth, that was it. He ought to know what best to do; ought to have known better than to have stayed out there, but he was young and would have gone with what the older men would have told him. She hadn't seen Daniel in a long time, wished him well enough and hoped for the best for his brother. She hoped it would be all right.

She went to bed not that much later, finding Tilda and Agneta already asleep with a copy of Wuthering Heights open, spine up on top of the quilts. She mercilessly shoved the girls across, for they were sprawled right across the bed, and clambered in, shivering despite the layers of clothes, socks and hats she was wearing. She was sure she could see her breath in the air. I'll never be able to sleep, Eliza thought as she pulled the quilts up to her chin. I'll be sleepless throughout the night, shivering, listening to the snow pattering against the window and wondering what will happen to those navies out on the high moor.

She must have fallen asleep, for when she woke it was daylight, accentuated by the brightness of the snow. Tilda and Agneta were gone, and Eliza lay for some time, luxuriating in the ownership of a bed all to herself, before she got up and swiftly washed and dressed. Pulling a couple of shawls around her shoulders, she hurried downstairs to the kitchen where it would be much warmer.

The housekeeper was kneeding bread on the table, with Tilda close by hunched over a newspaper that was a few days old – nothing had come through to the valley in the last couple of days. She'd seen her mother in the parlour with Agneta and Adelaide. Apparently Charlotte was over the worst now, and was sleeping it off in bed. Nothing to have worried about, her mother assured her, but Eliza could see the worry lines around her eyes. It was easy to say when the thing was done. How did a woman stand to be a mother, to do all that worrying? To have so little control over what fate intended to plunge her child through. It must be relentless, submerging to the point one would never have chance to think of anything else.

Tilda looked up as Eliza poured the last of the tea from the teapot. It was over stewed, but warm so she didn't care. "You're up late," she said. "It'll be all that snoring you were doing last night."

"I do not snore!" Eliza said, banging her teacup down.

"Careful, Miss!" the housekeeper said as she thumped the bread dough. "I'll not have any more crockery breaking this week, thank you very much."

Tilda tittered at her sister.

"Not reading *Wuthering Heights* with Agneta anymore?"

"She's gone to *play* with Adelaide again," Tilda rolled her eyes. "I don't think she understands it."

"Miss Amundsen is a girl with a straight head on her shoulders," their housekeeper huffed in time with her kneeding. "And you two would find better things to do than mock her."

Tilda sniggered but took heed and looked back to the newspaper.

"What are you doing reading Pa's newspaper?"

"He's finished with it. Besides, I ought to keep up on recent events. Business of the world and all that. Have you been reading about all this squabbling going on in the Americas?" Tilda asked. "Can you imagine what Aunt Muriel would have to say about it all? I bet she's got an opinion on it."

"She's always got an opinion on everything," Eliza sighed.

"All because some old man called Abraham got elected. And now all the people in the south are worrying that the people in the north are going to boss them about. I don't see why we need to worry about any of their nonsense. They left our empire a long time ago so it's not really our problem. But the papers write so much about it. Have you seen the pages and pages...?"

"Everything has a knock on effect," Eliza said, thinking on all the rants she had listened to from Aunt Muriel. "The south will be worried the north will stop them having slaves."

"That can only be the kind thing to do. No one should have slaves."

"Oh, I wonder about that myself," the housekeeper muttered good-naturedly. "And yet here I am."

"No, they shouldn't. But our industry is connected to it. They grow a lot of cotton in the south, and our British mills use it..."

"Oh, we'll just use something else." Tilda declared in a grand way. "That's Aunt Muriel talking now. She's always ranting about the mills of Manchester. If I hear anything more about manufacturing in Manchester, I'll scream. We should treat people with kindness and everyone should be paid for a day's work."

Eliza turned her attention to the housekeeper. "Has Pa already gone?"

"Oh yes," the old woman nodded. "Him and Mr King set off hours ago. Off with a party of local men. Heaven preserve them, I hope they find them all alive and quickly."

Eliza thought back to her mother's expression this morning. Worry. She'd be worrying about Pa now. She got up and looked out of the window. The snow storm had calmed, and there were only soft flakes drifting down like tiny downy feathers. But the snow looked deep, drifting up and over the garden wall. Someone had shovelled a substantial path through to the wood shed. "I hope they'll be all right," she said quietly to no one in particular.

"Don't you be worrying, lass," the housekeeper patted her with a floury hand. "They'll be back before you know it."

They did return much later in the afternoon, as it was growing dark again, much to the relief of the entire village. News had crept round, despite the weather, and all had looked to the hills during the day, wondering what had happened to the railway workers, and if their own men would safely get up there and back before nightfall.

Their menfolk returned cold and ice-bitten, but in high spirits, for they had managed to rescue the railway workers from the deep drifts. They had indeed found themselves snowed in, having only survived the blizzard by sheltering in the huts at Eskeletts. The huts weren't really up to protecting against the winter winds and chills, but the snow drifts had provided insulation and kept them safe. Food supplies had been very low, and the doors caught fast by the masses of snow piled up outside. There had been great relief and joy when the rescue party, well kitted out with sleds and shovels, had arrived to dig them out. No one had perished, although some had caught chills and would need to rest up. Not that there would be any more work on the line for the next couple of weeks whilst the moors were lost to the wintery landscape. A few, including the Iredale lad had chosen to stay up at the Red Lion Inn, a couple at Little Blakey, led by Tor Amundsen, who had aided the rescue party, then the rest had come down to the relative barmy sanctuary that was Rosedale Abbey. Lodgings had been secured for all, then the residents themselves had headed home with plans of shedding sodden, ice-cracked clothing and snow-laced boots, to enjoy a warm fire and hot food. Mairi must have been more worried than she wanted anyone in the household to know, for when Stephen came in through the door, she seemed to bodily throw herself at the man, customs and behaviour be hanged, regardless of the fact that Mr King was just behind him.

The rescue, the survival of the navvies and the fact that they were back to work on those remote moors three weeks later was hailed as the mightiest of successes. Nothing would stop progress, the relentlessness of the railways or the industrial improvement of this country. By the end of the year it would all be up and running and the country would step back in amazement at what could be achieved by human endeavour.

By November that year the entire line and production process had been running for months: the railways, the incline descent at Ingleby, the mines, the kilns, the community hell-bent on pillaging the earth. Rosedale was a different world to the one Mairi had first come to as a young bride. Most folk saw the changes as positive, bringing jobs, money and prosperity to the remote communities. These were people who lived hard, subsistence lives, and was it really for her to criticise when she did not need to worry over finances, and lived in one of the far better properties in the village? Yet she missed the open countryside, and the feeling of being completely alone. To walk, to stride out for hours with the wind blowing through her hair, feeling the sun on the top of her head as she did away with conventions and removed her hat. She still longed for it all.

She spent a lot of time pouring over years' worth of sketches from her wanderings, collected feathers, pebbles and rocks, dried out gnarled sticks of heather where the flowers had long since dried and fallen from their perches. She spent more time at the piano, sometimes idly playing slow, lazy tunes that had no specific route or goal or time limit for that matter. Some days she'd amble into her own compositions, beautiful waltzes she had written, sweeping piano pieces inspired by the landscape, but she would never reach the end, just drift off and find herself staring out of the window with a sigh in her throat.

One morning, when there was just herself and Stephen at the breakfast table, she looked directly at him, waiting until he would feel the intensity of her stare and look to her. "Do you know," she began when she finally had his attention. "I have lived in this place over twenty years and I have never been to Commondale."

"Commondale?" He looked surprised for a moment. "It's just a little village."

"I know. It's the place where my grandmother came from. I should like to see it."

Stephen closed the periodical he was reading and set it down by the toast. "I don't have much to do today. Why don't we take the gig out and take a ride over there. We'll go all over."

She looked out of the window. "It does look cold outside."

"That's never stopped you before."

Mairi broke out into a smile. "Let's. Just you and me."

So after years of family, work and social engagements, where they had always found themselves separated or with company, Mairi and Stephen, and no one else, hopped up into the gig pulled by their trusted family horse, and set off from Rosedale Abbey on that crisp November morning. Heading north out of the village, they went up Knott Road, taking them up the east peak of the valley side, swiftly moving above the railways, the kilns and the mines, but not the noise and the clouds of industry. The gig moved steadily and swung around beyond the head of the Rosedale valley to join the high road from Hutton-le-Hole to Castleton. The track joined the major road as it was, north of the Red Lion Inn. Twisting in her seat, Mairi looked back to that familiar, remote and yet now hemmed in building, with the railway lines passing by at some distance on either side. A train with fully loaded wagons was passing by, heading off in the direction of the incline, where the wagons would be pulled down by gravity, tempered by the empty wagons drawn back up to the top.

They entered Commondale from the south, following the road up along the side of Commondale Beck, and the new railway which went as far as the village of Danby behind them. As they approached the central junction in the village, Stephen pointed at the steep slopes back up to moorland. "There's talk of a brick works going in here."

"Brickworks?" Mairi looked perplexed. "Out here?"

"No stranger than all that has happened at Rosedale. The plans are being formed, I'm sure there'll be a brickworks here in the next few years."

"More chimneys?"

"I'm afraid so," he smiled gently, pulling her across to him. "People here need the work. The hope. You've seen how tough life is for some of the locals."

They parked up the gig at the inn in the middle of the village, paying the stable lad to make sure the horse was fed and watered. Stephen went into the inn to enquire after the site of Pines Lodge, the farm where Eleanor MacCaskill had spent her childhood with her brother and sisters. They knew it had been destroyed in a fire almost twenty years ago, but Mairi still wanted to see it. She regretted not having made this trip a long time ago.

Whilst she was waiting for Stephen, she asked the boy if he'd heard of Atheleys, but he shook his head saying there was no family by such a name. He scampered off to find some oats for the horse. She was probably dead, if she had really known Eleanor. Besides, there was something odd about Atheleys, like a gipsy or a vagrant. Mairi sensed that no one would know where she ever was, even those who knew of her existence.

They walked up the steep road out of the village, as directed, to the site of Pines Lodge. The innkeeper had warned them that there wasn't much to see these days, what with the stone having long been taken by other farmers to repair their own buildings and walls. They reached a point where a rough track went off from the main road to the right, and there was a crumbling of stone that had clearly been treated by a mason at some point. It was a ramshackle ruin that served no purpose. Not much was left. Nettles and bracken grew upon the land, and a line of three young Scots Pines grew, reaching for the sun. There were some scatterings of broken, charred timber – mere scraps, although it was little more than romantic fancy to say they had been there for twenty years since the fire that had been the talk of the valleys at the time. These scraps could just as easily be the leftovers of bonfires and campfires of travellers since.

The sun was bright, but the air was of a distinct chill. Mairi stepped up onto a pile of stonework and gazed back down into the dale. So this was where her family had all begun. It was another country to the world her own mother had brought her up in – all that finery and courtly backstabbing. Thousands of faces, cities and travel. Back here most people would have been born, lived and died within the same village. Going somewhere like Whitby might have felt like an exotic excursion.

Stephen offered her his hand as she stepped back down. "It's the nature of everything."

Mairi raised her eyebrows questioningly.

"Change. Nothing is static. Not even the earth we walk upon. The speed of change varies, I'll grant you that, but things are being created, decaying, changing... nothing is permanent."

"So even the mining will end?"

"It won't go on forever. The ironstone will come to an end." He paused, noting the hopeful look in her eyes. "It'll be decades before they reach that point."

The couple walked back into the village and took a late lunch at the inn. They returned to the gig and rode up the road and past the remnants of a farmstead that had once contributed so much to Mairi's own heritage. The road began to descend away from the moorlands. Stephen drove the gig down towards Kildale, then swung off on the road to Baysdale. Neglecting to drop down into the little farm hamlet, they continued on the moorland ridge, following it around until they reached the top of the infamous Ingleby Incline.

"It is something to be seen," Stephen assured her. "And Flintoft never managed to get us this far on his tour."

As Stephen spoke to one of the men at the railway workers' cottages at the top, to secure the horse and gig, Mairi stood at the top of the incline and stared down in awe and a touch of horrified nausea. She'd listened to so many discussions about the steep nature of the incline, and just what a descent had to be made in a relatively short distance. Walking up it would have been hard work, but getting wagons heavy with ironstone down it without them running out of control? It seemed like insanity.

Up at the top they were on open moorland, and to the side of the straight line there was forest going down the hill. Beyond that, in the hazy distance, looking like a child's playroom set out upon the floor, were forests and fields, dots of farmhouses and specks of livestock. Steam whistled up from the toy trains at the bottom which would continue with the transportation once the precious load was at the bottom. To look at that steep drop made her knees feel weak.

Before her there were three railway lines plunging downwards. Set over the middle line there was a tall, bulky shaped heavy stone house, panelled at each end with wooden panels. It stood awkwardly as if on thick legs, it stood akimbo the line. This was the drumhouse, which controlled the ropes pulling or dropping the wagons down, powered by gravity, controlled to some point by the counterweight of the empties coming back up. The ropes were there to try and make sure nothing got out of control. Guide ropes lay waiting down the middle of the railway lines. Nothing was moving at the moment, as a batch of wagons had been successfully sent down, and the next were being prepared. They were hefty, open topped, wooden sided wagons, with great cast iron wheels with the look of oversized cart wheels. They were lined up at the top, as if at the edge of the world, at a great precipice, with nothing before or below it.

Stephen appeared by her side. "I've just been talking to the foreman," he told her. "There's another incline just across the way that they decided not to use when initially starting work here. It goes up to another ironstone mine, although from what I understand it is not producing anything anywhere near as good as what Rosedale has. They don't think it will last that much longer."

They wandered away from the Incline Top, and down the steep bank in a somewhat hazy diagonal towards the other mine. Its own incline route was much smaller and modest in comparison to the great drum houses and engineering they had just seen. Progress moved so fast. Mairi felt distracted, not really listening to anything Stephen was talking about. He was still the animated boy when going into subjects of science and discovery. Even at fifty-five. She wandered onwards, away from the mine and through the landscape of these steep banks, somehow transfixed by the spread of the lowlands before them. Yorkshire seemed to going on forever. The air was cold and clear and they could see for miles.

Setting down on a rock, she took a deep breath of clear air. Her mind was an unanchored loss. Stephen approached, a little wary of how his wife was, how she had been for months. He was aware that something was changing. It was upsetting but did not know how to fix it, how to make her better.

He sat beside her, pulling her into him to warm her, and they watched as the sun began to wane in the late autumn, as early nights pulled close, and long shadows marked the shortened days. Life had been so busy with the girls, visiting family at Whitby, and his own agent work and geological surveys. Years had rushed by and they had been intensely focused on such a small geographical space. It was rather bizarre to consider they had never come here before today.

"We've been here a long time," he commented.

"Could you ever imagine leaving?"

"Not without you."

Mairi looked at him and smiled. "It's funny, to think where we are now and yet to think of how this marriage started."

"Nothing is stranger than life itself. I certainly didn't know it at the time, but you were what I needed. I wouldn't have wished to live any of this without you."

She smiled gently, kissing him before standing up and offering her hand. "Come, I want to go walk down in those woods," she said, gesturing below them. "I've never been here before."

"It is growing dark now..."

Mairi waved off the concern. "It'll be a clear moon tonight, I'm sure of it. And the forests aren't so dense in these parts. We'll soon come out onto open ground again."

They wandered like children, Mairi leading the way, feeling a spark of the old joy, traversing over new land and old paths, seeing new trees and plants, natural arrangements of rocks she had never seen before. Stephen felt as though years had been taken off both of them, watching his wife brighten again, a moonlit youthful woman full of curiosity and joy, leading the way across this land. They came out into an opening, the lines for the major Ingleby Incline ahead, just discernible in the dusk. Mairi came to a standstill a few metres ahead of him, out in the clearing, whereas he had just stopped at the tree line. She was beautiful, joyful, the person who had brought meaning to his life. He'd never felt so content or full of love as at that moment.

In the distance somewhere there was a deep groaning sound, unearthly and sickly. It went on for a moment or two, then ceased with a bang. Curious, but hardly concerned, they looked at one another, then in the direction up the hill. They couldn't make out the hill itself, only the horizon at the top, where a silver shimmer of light gave the clouds and sky a navy hue against all the black. Stephen wasn't sure how they were going to find their way back up to the cottages where the horse was waiting. Mairi, stood further out, creased her brow as she saw lines of fire spark up in the darkness, as if someone had drawn on a black sheet. Thunder was booming and growing louder. She turned back to Stephen to say something to him, that something was wrong. Stephen lifted a hand, as if that simple action could possibly draw her to him across such a distance.

Then the thunder was upon them and a flurry of runaway wagons hurtled down the incline, the control chain broken. Like wild cattle, almost bouncing and jostling, sparks kicking up from the iron railways. Mairi almost spoke to him and then she was gone. The wagons rushed past. Stephen blinked back his shock. All that was left was a red mist hanging in the air.

Stephen Gaskin never spoke another word for the rest of his life.

The foreman tumbled into a swift panic when he realised the gig was still waiting for its occupants. The incline had just had a bad case of runaways. He had set everyone out on a search mission, to check the entire incline, both sides, to assess the damage, and all the while praying to God that no one had been caught up in it all. Carrying his lantern, for it was very dark now, he had come upon Stephen Gaskin, crumpled to his knees at the edge of woodland, staring in horrified silence at the railway. They couldn't get him to say anything, or react to their own words, and assumed it was simple shock. One of the brake drivers from the drum house who had come down with him, stood to the side, his own lantern illuminating the iron girder Gaskin stared at. The man's face crumpled into a distraught frown, realising the droplets on the iron, on the stones, on the blades of grass, were blood. As if a living being had been evaporated. No one dared to ask where Mrs Gaskin was, the lady who had arrived in the gig with Gaskin earlier in the day.

One of the engine drivers, a man who had suffered his own grief with three of his children succumbing before the age of five, gently took Stephen's arm, and guided him onto his feet before leading him back up the incline to the cottages. His wife prepared some hot sweet tea, which they got down him, but he appeared to see and hear nothing. Like a mute, well trained child, they got him into the gig, and the engine driver drove him over the moors in the night back to Rosedale Abbey. It would have been better to wait until morning, but he couldn't let the man stay there. The bank was alight with lanterns, with the talk of search parties and workers. There was a crumple of destroyed wagons at the bottom. Lots of repairs and work to do.

When the railway men got to their colleagues down at the foot of the incline, they were congratulating one another to hear than no one had been caught up in the accident. There had been no fatalities. Then news filtered down that the Rosedale land agent had been found near the railway lines and his wife was missing. The man had lost the power of speech. Blood smears were found. Rags. Bits of flesh. One of the younger lads threw up into the bracken. Folk sat round in numbed groups, passing a bottle of rum between them, unable to think of anything to say. Lost. As the first hints of dawn appeared, the more hardened men took a few wooden boxes and sacking, and made a line to go up the incline, gathering up the pieces as they went. It was horrific, distressing. They were all human, and with their careers in the railways and heavy industry, they'd all witnessed bloody accidents and maimings before now. People had been pulverised, for when those wagons went out of control, some reckoned they could reach towards a hundred miles an hour down that incline. Many men had died. And yet it was worse to think this was, or rather had been a woman. A few of them knew Mrs Gaskin by sight, a pretty woman with four fine daughters.

When Stephen and the engine driver reached Rosedale Abbey, the village was lost in darkness and deep sleep. The engine driver, feeling as though he was intruding into a level of society to which he did not belong, awkwardly lead the land agent into his own house and set him down in the parlour. He didn't know what to say to the man. It was clear that the rest of the household was sleeping, and somehow it seemed wrong to go and wake the children from their slumber to deliver the worst of news, yet was it right to allow them to go on a few more hours in ignorance? He set himself to practical matters, crouching and lighting the fire, and getting some water on to boil in the kitchen so that they might have some more hot, sweet tea. He didn't even try to suggest sleep, for he knew from personal experience it would be days before that came. Even then, they may have to buy something from the apothecary. He sat and watched this tall, dignified man numbly take the cup and drink as he was told, his face blank and emotionless, almost dumb to the facts of his own life.

The engine driver almost screamed for joy when there was a knock at the front door. He put down his own cup with an embarrassed clatter and hurried through to the door, praying to God there'd be a relative or a woman or someone who would know better what to do. On the threshold stood the Amundsen family, Tor, his daughter Agneta who had already known the sadness of losing a mother, and Derwa, a strong, steady and quiet woman with melancholy about her. He had always suspected she'd known far greater tragedy and heartache than anyone, her own husband included. There was something in the woman's step that suggested she understood from personal experience just how dreadful and unjust life could be, and that there was no recompense, and quite often no empathy either.

Tor cleared his throat awkwardly. "We are here to help. How is he?"

The engine driver looked across the grave faces. Thank God, he thought. He'd heard that Mrs Gaskin was distantly related to Derwa Amundsen. Family. This was what they needed. "Shock, I think. I am not certain he understands yet. Not really." He paused, glancing back into the house. "He hasn't said anything yet."

"About Mairi...?" Derwa said, squeezing her daughter's frail hand as tears silently poured.

"About anything."

"What about the daughters?"

"All asleep. You should come in," he added, remembering his manners even though this was not his house to be offering. It was crisp and cold out, a frost hardening for the morning. The family entered and the door was softly closed.

Derwa, followed by Agneta, went straight to the parlour. Derwa went to take Stephen's hands to ask how he was, a little taken aback by how he didn't seem to notice her. It was as if his soul had already gone. She realised in that awful moment that she was going to have to break the news to the rest of the family. Tor and the engine driver lingered in the front entrance. The driver shuffled awkwardly.

"You did good, bringing him home."

"It's nothing though, is it? I don't think he even knows I did it. And I think they'll need help for the clear up. I should..."

"You want to head back now, in the dark?" Tor sounded a little surprised, but supposed it was natural. Now that there were other people to hand the torch over to, the atmosphere of grief would become too much.

"Yes. I'm of no use here. I won't rest."

They opened the door and Tor pointed to the track heading up out of the village. "Follow this road, it'll take you up to the mine, and from there you can find your way along the railway to Little Blakey. The quickest way back will just be to walk the lines. But be careful. We don't want..." he left the thought unspoken. No more tragedies on the lines today please.

As light started to appear along the top edges of the hills, movement was heard upstairs. Agneta started to cry again, so Derwa sent her into the kitchen to attend to chores. She could help the housekeeper, who had already arrived but had been asked to stay in the kitchen until requested as there were family issues to attend to. She'd been put out that Mrs Amundsen had appeared just as you like, and had assumed the right to boss her about, but had huffily agreed to wait. She'd complain to the mistress later on when she came down. Tell her she wouldn't be standing for anymore of this nonsense.

Derwa didn't want any more people to know before the girls, and she didn't want Agneta's tears to set off any anger – she'd seen people lash out in grief – as if Agneta was presuming a right to greater grief. She certainly wasn't and Agneta was a shy girl, lacking in confidence. Derwa didn't want her to have to carry anyone's initial fury.

Tilda was the first to appear, skipping into the parlour and glancing at her father without noticing his strange demeanour. "Morning Pa, you're up early." She jumped as Derwa Amundsen, whom she'd not noticed, stood up from one of the armchairs. "Mrs Armundsen, what are you doing here?"

"Could you please bring your sisters down to the parlour now?"

"Eliza's just getting dressed. And I don't think Charlotte's even awake..."

"Now please."

Tilda's smile dropped, and she looked to her father who merely stared at the wall. She wanted to ask where Mamma was, but the question died in her mouth. She felt ill, hoped it was just early morning hunger, and nodded silently, hurrying back upstairs to get her sisters. Whatever this was, she felt she wanted it over as soon as possible, and yet as she ran in to Charlotte and Adelaide, shaking her youngest sister awake, she wanted to stay in this warm, happy sanctuary and not have to deal with whatever it was downstairs.

Soon the girls were in the parlour, Charlotte still in her nightdress and rubbing her eyes, Adelaide looking terrified, Eliza seemingly put out that she was being treated like the other little children. What did Mrs Amundsen think she was doing here?

Out of formality Derwa looked to Stephen, in the vain hope he may start speaking and wish to break the news to his daughters himself, or at least offer some consolation or something. "Mr Gaskin, would you like...?" He didn't appear to hear her. Now that she was on the moment, she wasn't sure herself how to say the words. She looked at the girls, thankfully growing up swiftly, but even so this was not a good time to lose a mother. She had lost her own mother at a young age, younger than Tilda now, although not by death but through shame and heartlessness. It was still loss.

Tor entered the room and stood gravely by Derwa's side. "Ladies," he spoke, in his beautiful voice, almost perfectly Yorkshire now, but with a melody of Norwegian in the intonation. "There has been a very bad accident at Ingleby Incline."

"I don't see why we need to know." Tilda huffed.

Eliza felt her stomach tighten. This was bad. This was very bad.

"There were a number of runaway wagons. I'm afraid your mother was struck..."

Adelaide started crying. Charlotte didn't appear to understand, looking from one face to the other, before back to Mrs Amundsen. "Is Mamma in the hospital? Can I go look after her?"

Derwa shook her head. "No, my dears. Mairi... your mother, she was killed. She's with the angels now."

Adelaide's tears turned to full wailing, panicked terror. She looked about desperately for something to cling to, a step or two towards her father, but he did not respond. It was if they had a mannequin and nothing more upon the settee. Eliza watched her younger sister, those desperate, insecure, needy little hands reaching out for Mamma who had gone. Always it had been Adelaide clinging to Mamma. Abruptly she pushed past the others, ignoring Derwa as she started to say something, and fled out of the house. She ran down the lane, skidding here and there on ice, oblivious to the cold and the steaming of her own breath. Reaching a grassy verge by a hedge, away from the houses, she collapsed onto her knees and threw up violently, feeling her whole body burning with fury. As she wiped at her mouth, she was surprised to find her face slick with tears. She hadn't realised she was crying. She screamed hoarsely at the winter light. "No!"

Tilda had gone a few steps after her sister, furious that she was running away. She was the eldest, she was supposed to mother Adelaide now, but instead she was running away, worried that she wouldn't be able to go off painting her pictures. When she turned back she saw Adelaide had buried her face into Mrs Armundsen's skirts and was sobbing uncontrollably. Tilda ran across to her and pulled her away. "Eliza should be doing this!" She shouted. "She's the eldest. Make her come back."

"Your sister needs some time," Tor spoke.

"NO!" Tilda shrieked, swinging Adelaide around into a hug like a rag doll.

Charlotte stood to the side, her bottom lip trembling. "My Mamma?"

"I'm so sorry," Derwa went to the girl, already thirteen and quite tall, but clearly the baby of the group, and embraced her. "She's gone from us." She looked over to Tilda and Adelaide, who had collapsed together in a sobbing mass. From there to Stephen, who had seemingly woken up, distressed at what he was seeing. Still mute. He went down on his knees to Tilda and Adelaide and embraced the two slender shaking girls, pawing them up into a great hug.

Derwa stroked the back of Charlotte's head and looked to her husband. He had gone through this himself, although not in such violent circumstances. She gave him a silent look, to ask if he was all right and he nodded brusquely. Squeezed her forearm. Derwa repressed her own tragedies, having dealt with her ghosts a long time ago. She couldn't let them come back. Not for anything.

And so the Gaskin household went into mourning. The mirrors were covered, the piano shut up and moved to the corner, covered over with a black sheet to take up a new post as a table top. The girls lingered listlessly in the house, no one knew what to do or say. Pa stayed in his study. He never spoke but he was there if anyone needed time to sit or be embraced. Eliza buried herself in duty, writing the letters that had to go out, although there didn't seem to be too many. She wrote to their Aunt and Uncle on the Gaskin side, and Anna Mallinson and family were soon travelling to Rosedale and installed in rooms at the inn. Awful letters had to be sent to Aunt Muriel, who was staying with her cousin, and to their dear friend in Sowerby, Mrs Jennifer Burton-Waugh. Jennifer was in Rosedale shortly after their Aunt Anna, a stately grey haired woman in her fifties, distressed at the news and desperate to do something for the girls. From Mairi's side of the family a letter arrived from Emmerline Whitfield, Aunt Muriel's cousin. Muriel had broken down completely at the news of Mairi's death and it was impossible to move her at this time. Emmerline did not wish to further add to their distress, but Muriel was not of sound mind at the moment and Emmerline was very concerned for her. She felt dreadful as she knew the girls would need as much support as could be given, and grieved that she could not make the journey at this time, although Eliza and her sisters were to understand that they could write to her at any time about anything. She would ask one of her children to go to Rosedale as representation, to do what they could.

They heard no more from that side of the family before the funeral and although Eliza wondered what it all meant, she was too numbed from the loss of her mother to worry long over it. The Gaskins were in the village, in fact the entire village was out in mourning and the volume of sympathy and concerned looks was beyond overwhelming.

She was suffocating in good thoughts and well intentioned actions and yet none of it would bring her mother back. None of it would give her chance to say goodbye, or embrace her mother and assure her that she loved her. That it had never been about her when she had run away to Whitby. At night, when it was quiet and she was alone, there would be moments when the realisation that her mother did not exist would hit her again, with a fresh, gut wrenching horror that such a thing could even be possible. How could she have existed, with her thoughts, her caring words, her knowledge, her history of so much travel, and all that music running through her veins. And with the slam of a wagon, it never was.

Charlotte and Adelaide went away with Aunt Anna after the funeral for a break. Tilda and Eliza remained, although it was not companionable, for Tilda seethed at Eliza with unspoken accusations and fury. Eliza was blind to it, which only made Tilda's anger worse.

One morning in December there was a knock on the door. The housekeeper was out buying eggs, and Eliza went to answer the door. A well dressed, in fact expensively dressed slender woman of middle age, forty or so, with sandy blonde hair and a sprinkle of freckles across her nose, stood waiting. She had a particularly stylish hat pinned to her hair, so that when she looked in certain directions, it wasn't possible to see her face. She looked up and smiled at Eliza, then turned to gaze out on the street as a couple of farm labourers leading a horse and cart ambled past. The two looked at the fine lady out of brazen curiosity, one man taking on a look of shock. He turned to his companion as they got away from the Gaskin house.

"What the hell is that woman doing there?"

"Looked right fine. You don't know a woman like that."

"I did."

"Knew her?" he waggled his eyebrows.

"Not like that..."

"So what's her name?"

"Be buggered if I can remember, but I never forget a face. I saw her when I was living over Commondale way. She was there when they had all that trouble over at Pines Lodge, you know, that farmstead that burned down."

"Oh Aye, I remember. Don't they say a witch grew up there?"

"Kid's stories I reckon that. She didn't grow up there, but she was there. I saw her about the place a lot."

Eliza stared at the woman. She had a certain poise, or quiet confidence about her that she'd never seen in a woman before. "Can I help you?"

"Miss Eliza Gaskin?" the woman asked. "No, please, don't be shocked," she quickly added. "It was just a guess. From what I've been told of the Gaskin daughters. My mother has sent me in person to send condolences from all the family. I'm sorry it's taken me so long to get here." She paused, putting down her bag so that she might shake the young woman's hand. "I haven't introduced myself. I'm Miss Mowbray, Miss Charity Mowbray."

Eliza looked non the wiser.

"I'm Mrs Emmerline Whitfield's daughter," she explained. "I suppose in a distant way you and I are sort of cousins. I should give you my card."

"Oh no, that's not..." Eliza started although found a card in her hand, an expensive cream card with fine printing, and Miss Charity Mowbray's name and address upon it. "Would you come in?" Eliza offered, opening the door wide. "My father is here, although he doesn't..."

"Talk. I understand. Grief is a hard one to deal with." She smiled kindly and touched Eliza's arm as they entered the parlour. "You must allow yourself to indulge at some point, really indulge."

Eliza backed off as if she had been bitten. "Do you have news of Aunt Muriel? We're all very worried about her."

"No better, no worse. I haven't seen her yet, but my mother tells me she's essentially catatonic. I will travel onwards after I'm finished here in Rosedale. Try not to worry. These things need time."

"Would you sit down," Eliza gestured vaguely at the armchairs. "I'll go fetch Pa and Tilda, and get some tea."

"That's very kind." Charity set her bag on the armchair but did not settle herself. Left alone in the parlour, she wandered a little, examining the family portraits in frames, of the girls when younger, of a grouping that included Muriel, and an old woman who must be her mother's Aunt Eleanor. She ambled to the window, looking out at the snow, then looked to the scatterings of sketches and drawings laid out on an odd, high table top that was obviously a piano covered over with a great sheet. There were a couple of pencils scattered, and a cushion in the windowsill. Eliza had been perched there sketching before Charity had arrived.

Charity settled herself on the still-warm cushion, and gazed across the piano top to the woman sitting silently on the piano stool. She looked sick with worry, great dark circles under her pretty eyes, and dishevelled blonde hair hanging long about her face. Their eyes met and Charity smiled.

The woman looked shocked. "You can...?"

Charity nodded.

They remained in silence, as if there was nothing more to say on this revelation. Charity looked about the room before returning her attention to the woman. "They will be well with time, please don't worry on that account."

"There'll be no sadness, or tragedy..."

"This is life, I'm afraid, there's always plenty of both," Charity spoke honestly. "But there is going to be happiness as well. I can promise you that. Even Eliza will come to find her niche."

"And Stephen?"

"He'll be looked after."

The woman looked away to the floor. "I'm going to miss so much. It was the same with my own mother."

"I do understand." Charity reached across the top of the piano and squeezed the woman's hand.

"I can't stand to see them so sad."

"There's nothing anyone can do about that. This is life. But please, I ask you try to find some peace, some rest. Don't linger too long like this. I've seen the alternative."

The woman nodded although didn't yet look wholly convinced. Charity let go of her hand, and stood up, returning to the armchair in readiness to meet the family.

Historical Note

This is a work of fiction. All the characters in this book are fictional. Indeed, there are some characters in here who were well known historical figures, if the sharp-eyed reader can spot them. But even they appear as highly fictionalised versions of themselves. I have tried to keep the story in keeping with the history of the era, but I have no doubt there will be countless errors. I hope these don't detract from the telling of the tale.

Primarily this is a tale of the history of Rosedale, of the communities that lived there and the industry that came and changed everyone's lives. Rather like that of the French glass blowers who came centuries earlier, today the population and community has settled back as if it never was. Remains of Victorian industrial architecture do still remain around the valley, ruins of an industry long since gone.

I am a great reader, and two particularly famous writers do appear in the story, although not referred to with their more well-known names – one for he did not have his pseudonym at the time of his appearance in this story; the other as she chose to use her more familiar name reserved for special friends. Both these writers did holiday in Whitby at the times and circumstance as described. Once lesser known Victorian writer also appears in the story.

There is so much historical detail and reference to local features and legend that I try to stick to in my stories, that there's simply too much to account for in a historical note at the end of the book. To replace this there is a blog on the internet where I am gradually working through all the historical aspects of the series. This can be found at: https://yorkshiresaga.wordpress.com/

Having said this, I would like to reference some books that have been invaluable during this book. Rev J C Atkinson's *Forty Years In a Moorland Parish* was useful in describing some of the winters experienced on these moorlands. *A History of Rosedale* by Raymond H. Hayes, and *Rosedale Mines and Railway* by R. H. Hayes and J. G. Rutter were invaluable for the histories of the village Rosedale Abbey and the surrounding communities, as well as a more focused history on the industrial history and complexity of the iron ore mining at Rosedale.

I like to see the books as standalones, but as everything else, they are interconnected and the stories of previous books do play into the characters' own personal histories and mindsets. The next book will skip across the family tree branches to follow Miss Charity Mowbray in more detail.